OPEN YOUR EYES

Elisabeth Oweson

OPEN YOUR EYES

A NOVEL

GRAND PAS

Cover design: Carl Johan Hane/Cjhdesign

www.grandpas.ch
www.elisabethoweson.com

—Hey, sorry, there's something wrong with one of the tires. I called a colleague, but it will probably take a little while. Do you need anything from the gas station?

The taxi driver opens the passenger door, and the icy, damp, December wind spins around Linda's legs. It's snowing large wet flakes, and the suburb is dark and uninviting, despite the Christmas tree in the middle of the roundabout. It's only eleven o'clock at night, but she should be home by now, since Karin needs to go back to Skåne early tomorrow morning.

—Could you buy me a Lotto ticket? Two panels, ten weeks? she says.

For the last five minutes she's been thinking that it would be fun to give Tobias a Lotto ticket as a Christmas present because it would upset her parents, Anita and Gustav, on Christmas Eve: Lotto tickets aren't gifts. You don't play that way. But it probably wouldn't create a big polemic, not in the Adeus family. Everyone would smile politely, biting their tongues, as they have always done with the gifts they don't like.

Her budget for Christmas presents shrunk drastically when she insisted on paying for Karin's flight, but without her help, Linda wouldn't have been able to go to the office Christmas party. She always stands back, especially at this time of the year when Tobias's company has its annual conference, and he is gone for several days. Linda had hoped that Anita and Gustav or her brother Håkan would babysit, but everyone was busy. And the school girls she and Tobias occasionally use as babysitters all have final exams, so no one has been interested in working on a Tuesday evening in December.

But Tobias will laugh at the Lotto ticket. Linda leans her head against the headrest and lets the warm feeling of belonging to something and someone spread through her body. They're a team—she and Tobias against the world—and even more so since her parents still feel guilty about Håkan taking over the family business. Linda and Tobias know they get along, and they don't have to be grateful forever for something they received from her parents. What happened with the firm was for the best.

—Here, says the taxi driver when she opens the door again. Bought one for myself, too.

She waves a second Lotto ticket in the air before she puts it in her wallet.

—As a Christmas present to myself. We'll share the lot, if one of us wins, right? she continues and laughs. Oops, sorry. It's cold. I'll close the door…No, no, you can pay when my colleague arrives.

Linda nods, but she's unsure why. Was she nodding to the idea of sharing the profits if they win or to paying later? The chance, or risk if you will, of winning is so small. How many times has she been told so, not only from her mother but also from Håkan? As if she hadn't taken all those statistics classes. You don't buy the ticket primarily to win; you buy it because it's fun, it's a thrill. The hope of winning is always present, but not what you expect.

Christmas party. It sounds more fun than it is, and now Linda regrets that she accepted the invitation. She's happy she can blame having to leave early on their young children; a four-year-old Fia and soon-to-be-six-year-old Lotta are the best excuses in the world, although they have been sound asleep for many hours.

Linda texts Karin to make sure that she stays so they can have a glass of wine and some time to talk, more time than what they had before Linda had to leave for the party. In Skåne, Karin had been busy getting the second and last Christmas market in line for the weekend, but she would never say no to Linda. They have been best friends since university in Lund, and Karin is also Lotta's godmother. Since she has no children of her own, it isn't difficult to persuade her to come.

Linda checks her e-mails as well, making sure she answers two job-related things that her hung-over colleagues can deal with tomorrow. Is it smart to show she's working at this time? The others will resent her. She shivers; the heat of the car is all gone. What is taking the taxi service so long?

Linda's phone lights up with a text from Karin: "Where are you?"

She peeks out at the taxi driver, who's trying to keep warm, stepping up and down on the wet ramp where the snow has already melted.

"I'll be right there," Linda writes, without really knowing.

A black Mercedes limousine without a taxi sign drives up and parks behind them. The driver jumps out and hugs Linda's taxi driver. Linda looks away. Colleagues? Seems more like they are old friends. And she isn't sure that she wants to take a car with no taxi sign.

—It's cool, the taxi driver says when she opens the door, as if she had read Linda's thoughts. This is Nikos. He usually drives private customers only. He'll take you home.

She gives him Linda's address, but Linda hesitates. Her cell phone beeps—Karin seems stressed.

—I have to hurry home, Linda says to the taxi driver.

—I'm so sorry for the delay, Nikos will take you home safely.

"Is this how you get kidnapped?" Linda thinks when she gets in the black limousine. It smells of brand-new leather, and the whole back seat shines, like the rest of the interior.

—Have something to drink if you want, Nikos says. There's water. Or Coke.

Linda shakes her head. That fun, light, bubbly party feeling is all gone, and she feels how little energy she has left after working all day. And Karin—maybe she's just as tired?

Nikos drives quietly and smoothly, as if he were her private chauffeur, and Linda can't help smiling at the thought. If only for a day, what a luxury! It doesn't take more than ten minutes to get to her street. It lies quiet and dark. Everyone has gone to bed, but there's a light in their kitchen window, and Linda has apparently not been kidnapped.

She pays, unsure if it's the right price because she doesn't remember what the meter was on when they stopped at the gas station.

—Do you need a receipt?

No, she doesn't. Her job won't pay her expenses anyway.

—I'll wait until I see you get in.

—Thank you, that's not necessary. These neighborhoods are calm.

—You never know. All customers are equally important.

After she puts the key in the lock and opens the door, she looks back; the limousine is still there. Linda waves, but he still doesn't move. She hears him leave when she closes the door behind her.

—Hey, Karin says.

She tugs her thick sweater and yawns. Her frizzy bright-red hair looks like a microphone around her head though the hair is long and massive, so different from Linda's shoulder-length thin, straight blonde hair.

—I must have dozed off, right after I texted you. Thought you'd be home earlier.

Karin makes a quick braid of her hair. There's no need for a rubber band to hold it in place.

—There was something wrong with the taxi, so we had to stop, and—no, I'm so stupid!—I forgot to pay!

—The taxi?

—No, the Lotto ticket!

Karin looks incredulously at her.

—Did you buy a Lotto ticket?

—For Tobias, for Christmas. I know, it seemed like a good idea—

—But not anymore, no, that's for sure. Keep your Lotto ticket. What if he wins? Horrible thought.

—Stop. I know what you think of him. But, you know, if he were to win, we would share it. That's how we play. Would you want a glass of wine?

—The plane leaves at seven tomorrow morning, so no thanks. I should have taken that taxi—

—I'll call a new one. They're usually by the square.

Karin doesn't stay at their place like she used to. Not even when Tobias is away. But Kerstin, one of their mutual friends from what they call the Culture Club, always has a guest bed made up, and she also lives a stone's throw from the city center.

"When I come to the big city, I want to see as many of you guys as possible" has been Karin's excuse for not staying with Linda, and Linda understands, even if she gets a little hurt. She rarely sees the other Culture Club girls herself—three or four times a year at best.

—Hug the kids from me, will you? I put their Christmas presents on your bed. They are amazing, your girls. A little obsessed with Santa Claus maybe but, otherwise, the cutest in the world.

Linda smiles. The girls haven't talked about anything but Santa Claus for weeks. When he will come? How does he manage to visit all the kids? Will he have time to meet them? Linda has answered that he most certainly won't have time to meet them, but if they continue to be good this year, at least they will get their gifts.

—Say hi to Tobias, too. If he comes back.

—When he comes back, Linda says.

—You know what I said.

—And I don't believe you. You've said that since I met Tobias, and it's eleven years ago. We're a team, Karin. And that means the world to me.

Linda looks out the window.

—Thanks for coming, she continues. You are awesome, and I wouldn't make it without you. Good luck with the Christmas market.

—In a few years, I will call you for help. Or maybe I'll call your daughters.

—Get ready. The taxi should be here any minute…There it is.

They hug. Linda must, as always, stand on her toes to keep from putting her nose in Karin's armpit. She follows Karin into the hall and watches her wind a big scarf several times around her neck. Her coat is raspberry red. It doesn't match her hair at all, but it somehow doesn't matter. Anything goes for Karin.

—Take care, Karin says. Be strong, okay?

She closes the door gently behind her. From the kitchen window, Linda can see the taxi sign disappear.

Her fatigue is gone, and the discussion about Tobias has made her more upset than she wants to admit, even to herself. She wants Karin and Tobias to be friends, but it never clicked. How can her best friends not love each other? She pours herself a glass of white wine from the bag-in-box in the refrigerator door; it's not what she wants, but maybe it will calm her down. Tobias will be home tomorrow evening. This year, his company has combined the conference with a Christmas party and extended the stay by one day. They had to sacrifice a Sunday to make it work, and Linda finds it incomprehensible. How can they keep asking for more days away from their families at this time of the year? It's insane, but there's no use whining about it. Their jobs are important, for both of them.

The main road, still visible behind the useless noise barrier, is quiet, as good as deserted. The wet snowflakes have turned into real snow, making the ground white. It's half past twelve, not even late, and Linda is sad that Karin couldn't stay for a while—they haven't seen each other much, hardly talked, and Linda has that stubborn feeling she's abusing rather than nurturing their friendship. Perhaps Karin prefers talking to Kerstin, who, just like Karin, has no children. Maybe she fits better into Karin's life, right now. And Linda can't understand why Karin has to mention that she doesn't trust Tobias every time they meet. Tobias usually laughs about it and says it's because she didn't take a chance on him and now she still has no man in her life. He says she's just angry and jealous. Linda smiles at the thought. To see Tobias and Karin together is confusing, since they resemble each other, although Tobias's hair is more of a sand color. They have a striking physical resemblance otherwise, both tall and broad shouldered. They fill up a room with their presence, which might be why they don't really get along—or why Karin doesn't get along with Tobias.

Linda is the one who could have been angry and jealous, but she's not. Sometimes when she thinks of Karin's life, it stands out as much more fun, creative and free, everything they dreamed of and all they wished for when they met, after having quit their nearly finished studies. Karin lives the life Linda put in a box and forgot. She retreated after the years with cultural sciences, chose a safe bet. But it had probably been stupid not to put the business studies in use, and now she's still close to the cultural world she loves, working as a middle manager in the accounting department at a publishing house—it's not that bad. And Karin actually does the same thing when she uses what she learned in law school while working as a mediator in family conflicts during the cultural low season in Österlen. So there's nothing to be jealous of.

Linda finishes the glass of wine and puts it in the dishwasher.

What's that sound?

Something is tapping at the front door. Maybe a dog or a fox? There are foxes in the neighborhood. She has never seen them herself but has heard they can be almost tame, happily prowling around the villas looking for food.

Then she hears a key in the lock, and a chilly gust of wind pushes into the kitchen. Linda freezes. Tobias shouldn't be home

11

until tomorrow, and the extra keys are with her parents, and with her mother-in-law, but she lives in Denmark. She tiptoes out into the hall.

A woman stands with her back toward Linda. She closes the door gently and puts a black weekend bag on the floor before she turns around and recoils when she sees Linda.

The woman is remarkably tall, taller than Linda, with shoulder-length blonde hair. She's wearing a slim-cut light-gray wool coat and a big pink floral scarf. They look at each other with surprise.

—Hello, says the woman hesitatingly. What are you doing here?

—I...live here.

The woman measures her top to bottom with a faint but confident smile.

—No, you don't live here, she says convincingly. Not anymore.

Linda doesn't recognize her. Have they met before? Why does she hold a key to their house? What is she doing here, in the middle of the night?

Her mouth is dry, and she can't speak. She tries and tries to remember the woman's face, but nothing springs to her mind. The woman, however, seems to know who Linda is. The discomfort spreads in Linda's body, and she knows she should tell her to leave, to just go away, that there must have been a mistake, that she doesn't belong here.

—Not anymore, the woman repeats. You've moved, to those new apartments, she continues.

—Oh, Linda says and leans against the wall. Who says?

—Tobias, of course.

Linda doesn't know what to say. She draws a strand of hair from her face and crosses her arms over her chest. She should feel better than she does; she should be confident.

—I'm very sorry, Linda says, and clears her throat, but I don't know you. I have no clue who you are, but I don't think you've come to the right house. Now, excuse me, but I'm getting up early tomorrow, so I don't have time for you and your games. I think you should leave. Now. Or I'll call the police.

—I chose the tiles in the guest bathroom. I know you don't live here anymore, the woman says decidedly.

Linda freezes again. She feels the heat on her cheeks, shakes her head slightly—is it a hallucination? Has she had too much wine?

But the woman doesn't disappear. She's still there, with that confident smile on her face.

—Excuse me, what did you just say?

—I said, I chose the tiles, in there.

She points at the shattered door to the guest toilet.

—The white mosaic, the blue border. You must know you have had nothing to do with that.

Her voice is calm and deep, not in the same pitch as Linda's.

—No, I didn't, and it sounds weird because I live here and you don't, right?

—Yes, I think so. But since Tobias said you moved, I must believe him. There's not much evidence of you living here, is there? What do you say?

As if Linda would be invisible. How ridiculous. The whole house is full of her stuff, her and the children's. And Tobias's, of course.

Her heart pounds. It pounds so hard she can hear it in her ears, on top of her whizzing blood flow. She twists her ice-cold fingers.

—Why would you care? Linda says. I don't know who you are. If you want me to believe that you have had anything to do with how this house looks, you'd have some work to do. It's the stupidest thing I've heard. I must go to bed now. I think you should leave. Go. Now.

Her head is buzzing, and she has a headache that is pulsing at her temples. There should be aspirin in the bathroom cabinet, but she can't walk that far; her legs are too heavy.

—Hey, stop it, the woman sputters. This is insane. Why would Tobias pretend you moved if it wasn't true? I have evidence that would surely satisfy you. I painted the inside of the shed, for example, the one Tobias built last summer. I am the one who labeled all the tools hanging on the walls in there. And you didn't, right?

Although the woman is upset, she speaks clearly, as if Linda were a child, emphasizing each word. Maybe she realizes Linda has had a drink or two.

Linda stares at her. Painted the walls of the shed? They aren't even painted as far as she knows. There are no tool labels either. Her slight tipsiness makes her confident enough to respond.

—So what color is it? she asks defiantly.

—Heather green.

They watch each other, like two dogs wondering whether they should attack or just keep sniffing.

—You don't believe me, do you? Have you seen it? If you're not here that often, I guess your priority isn't to check the shed. Tobias told me you're not that fond of gardening, so I guess you don't care too much about it.

Linda is nauseous and keeps thinking of the kids sleeping upstairs. This must be a dream. It pulls and tugs at her mind, and she wants to push the woman out the door, close it tightly, and call the police. Instead, she takes a deep breath. She must answer. Take control.

—Maybe we should discuss this some more, Linda says.

—Yes, the woman says. Why not? We could start with the shed since I'm still wearing my coat and boots.

Linda doesn't want to leave the house, and least of all to see the shed. "Psycho" is the only word that comes to her mind. They do exist. What if she is murdered, dismembered, buried in the garden shed? No one would notice. It would take days, maybe weeks, before anyone would come here.

—I don't know, Linda mumbles.

—Get a grip. Put on those boots, the woman says, pointing to a pair of green boots next to the shoe shelf.

Linda doesn't recognize them. It's as if her brain no longer can distinguish between fact and fiction—it would be better to go with the flow and see what happens. She just wants it to be over. She

15

wants to wake up. But when she sees the woman, she looks quite real, and when the woman takes the key to the shed from the hook at the left of the front door, Linda shudders.

The woman is right though: Linda never uses the shed. There are no more tulip bulbs to be planted, which she did when they moved in. After having tried with snowdrops, crocuses, and daffodils to turn the tiny garden into a colorful plot of land, she also experimented with various other flowers and shrubs. During the year of maternity leave with Fia, she devoted more time to the garden than to the house, but other than the daffodils, nothing remains since the deer and rabbits nibble on most everything that grows. The black currant bush still hasn't started to grow berries, which is perhaps just as well since she doesn't know when she would have time to make jam. The green thumb she had hoped for is simply not her asset.

Still, she insisted on a garden shed to hold all the gear they inherited from the previous owners when buying the house and the garden stuff she got for her birthday, before she realized she didn't have a talent for growing anything. The tiny shed also holds the children's outdoor play equipment, winter gear, and bikes, along with the plastic pool they used when the children were smaller. The area under the balcony where they used to keep it all is now occupied by the birch wood they received from Tobias's colleague.

She glances at the Chinese urn in the hall window. Tobias brought it from his home, and Linda has never liked it, but it might come in handy now: she could crash it on the woman's head. Before she has a chance to think further, they are out of the door, slipping over the small stones.

They slow down. The visitor doesn't hesitate as she walks toward the shed, which isn't too surprising since it's possible to catch a glimpse of it from the house. But it's pitch black, and someone who had never been there would at least have stopped to figure out the direction.

Under the exterior lamp that automatically switches on when you get close enough, the woman opens the padlock and reaches for the interior-light button. She steps aside to let Linda in.

Linda gasps. The shed is painted light green, and all the tools she put into the farthest corner are now hanging neatly on the walls and shelves with labels above each hook. She swallows, swallows again. When could this have happened? The shed leaves no clue to if it was in late summer, early autumn, or before Christmas, and it doesn't smell of fresh paint.

Linda's heads spin from the wine, and her heart is pounding harder, all the way up her neck. Lightheaded, she needs to sit down.

—I think we had better get back to the house, Linda says, her voice trembling.

Linda doesn't know how she gets back to the house. It's as if she were a ghost, floating through the winter night. Arriving at the front door, she turns to the woman and looks her straight in the eyes.

—I think you should come in for a moment.

Linda trembles, afraid of the silence that could say more than all the words they exchanged so far, and which would also mean this evil dream becomes reality. She can't help staring at the woman, and a wave of hatred flares up—she's like a cat without claws. She could throw her down the stairs, but that wouldn't change anything.

The woman nods.

—Yes, that's probably just as well, she says, pulling off the gloves. My name is Maja, by the way.

—Linda, Linda says automatically and shakes Maja's warm hand.

*

—I've stayed here, now and then, Maja says quietly as she leans back against the kitchen chair. Her eyes wander over the cabinet row, as if she is already planning the next renovation.

Linda envisions Maja and Tobias choosing doors and floors that match. But the tiles in the guest toilet that she and Tobias chose, Linda had come up with the blue border herself. It wasn't Tobias in any case. She suddenly can't remember if she actually went to a tile store or if they just decided from something they saw in a magazine from a house that resembled theirs, with the same floor plan. Had Tobias bought the tiles without her?

—Forgive me for asking, but why do you think you chose the tiles? Linda says.

—Do you think I'm making it up? When you moved out last year, that was one of the first things I told Tobias we must do if I were to stay here. The bathroom upstairs is okay, but the guest toilet, which is what you see as a guest, was shabby and worn. So we went directly to the tile store. I have some clothes here, too, in the closet in the bedroom, she continues, and a pink glow spreads across her cheeks.

Maja looks luminous, but what she says is so absurd that Linda has to laugh. Tobias's mother, Anne, has left a few things, makeup and a scarf, but that was last year—and perhaps the last time—she visited. It isn't very surprising since her eye vision is so bad. It has been a wonder she has even come to see them and been able to climb the stairs.

—No, I haven't seen any clothes, Linda says. I live here. Permanently. Not like you, who just think you live here and that you should stay here. I would have noticed if there was another woman's stuff in my closets.

—But since you're not here that often, it wouldn't be too surprising, right? I mean, now that you've moved.

Maja's eyes are calm and understanding.

—I can show you if you don't believe me, Maja continues.

She is so convincing that Linda guesses she must do as Maja says, and then she'll ask her to leave. She regrets she didn't push her out the door when she first heard her in the hallway. But if she just gets Maja out of here, she can call a locksmith and get the locks replaced tonight.

Linda nods, while the nausea combined with some kind of horror spreads through her body. She lets Maja lead the way up the stairs. Maja moves with such ease: she fills up the space and doesn't hesitate; her steps are exact, every movement fits into the house.

There is something improbable in the situation—that someone else knows almost every millimeter of the house. As if Linda hasn't made an imprint, but Maja has.

The children turn restlessly in their beds, but Maja navigates silently past their door, into Linda and Tobias's bedroom and turns on the lights. The bed, where the Christmas presents Karin left for the children are, is temporarily illuminated before the bulb goes out with a pouf.

Maja turns on one of the bedside lamps.

—Where's the poster? I told Tobias to have it framed. I love Monet. We have planned to go to Paris and see the water lilies for real. Has he already told you? Maja says.

Linda sees a shadow of a nailhead on the wall opposite the bed; it hasn't been there before. And she doesn't know what poster Maja is talking about because there has never been one. Tobias knows nothing about art, and he has never wanted to go to Paris. It has been Linda's wish for far too long. He hates Frenchmen, he says, though as far as Linda knows, he has met none, at least not in France. Linda was in Paris on an Interrail trip after high school and has wanted to go back ever since. She wanted to go there on their honeymoon, too, but Tobias proposed they go somewhere warm, and on their limited budget, they got two weeks on the Canary Islands instead of four days in Paris.

That Tobias would have bought a poster of Monet's water lilies sounds even more amazing, bordering on ridiculous. But if Maja is crazy, a psycho, it's probably best to either keep or discard the allegations.

She tramples across the soft carpet, toward the closets, and when she turns the key, the door pops open. A colorful collection of dresses is exposed, and Linda blushes. These are her secondhand finds: all the dresses and gowns, the short wool sweaters and fine cotton blouses she had been bargain hunting, first in secret in Stockholm and then in Lund. In secret, since her mother hated these "rags," as she called them.

"We can afford to buy clothes, Linda."

But Linda had loved the transformation, thrown out her jeans, and found her true self in the feminine '50s dresses. It had been her mother's, Anita's, own fault since she had shown Linda one of her own old dresses with a stiff petticoat and suggested that Linda could wear it to one of the prom parties. And when Linda reluctantly tried it on, she couldn't stop staring at herself in the mirror, at the transformation. It wasn't until she left home, when she quit business school and took the train down to Lund, that she adopted the style fully. And even though more than ten years have passed since she abandoned the style right after meeting Tobias, who, incidentally, didn't care about what she was wearing, she kept almost all the dresses, together with the curly Persian coat that once belonged to her grandmother.

—Here, Maja says, pointing. Do you recognize this stuff?

The colors dance in front of Linda's eyes, and the clothes hangers dangle. She sits down with a thud on the bed, shakes her head. Right next to her dresses, taking up half the closet, there are garments that are not her own. The shawl Tobias said was his mother's dangles on a hanger.

—Who are you? Linda asks quietly, and the tears make her throat swell.

She swallows, but it burns. Sweat breaks out, and she shivers and rubs her wet hands against each other.

—What do you want? What are you doing here? Why do you pretend you know everything about Tobias and me when you know nothing at all?

Maja looks down at her but doesn't answer, and Linda knows why she doesn't. Because it's not possible to say "I'm your husband's mistress" in a way that sounds convincing, or friendly, or even—real.

Linda has never heard of someone named Maja, never seen a note, no text messages, no letters. Nothing that would tell about her existence. Is the makeup in the bathroom cabinet, which Tobias said was his mother's, also Maja's? Should Linda have understood? But she had found these lost items when Anne had been visiting; there was nothing suspicious about that. Or rather, Tobias had found them, when he had cleaned out the room in the basement when his mother had left. It was just an eye pencil, a powder compact, a blush.

Linda takes the fewest steps she can to get down the stairs, leaving Maja behind, hoping she will stay for a while on the second floor. Linda hesitates between the living room and the kitchen, and then chooses the living room. She walks up to the window, chewing on her lower lip, trying to collect herself a brief second before she sits on the sofa and stares out into the darkness. A lone streetlamp blinks helplessly, and she caresses the sofa's worn blue cotton fabric.

—Okay, Linda says when Maja enters.

Maja stops, as if Linda shot her.

—Now tell me everything, everything I don't seem to know about you and me and Tobias.

—Can I have a drink? Maja says.

The folly. Do what you want. Make yourself at home.

—Help yourself.

Maja goes into the kitchen and comes back with a bottle of whiskey and two glasses. She pours a little in one glass and looks

21

questioningly at Linda, who nods. Maja sits on the armchair's edge, with both hands around the glass. Linda takes a big swig of whiskey, even though she hates all kinds of hard liquor. It burns all the way down to her stomach.

Maja explains that she met Tobias four years ago, at a conference, actually. She was his client, one of the more important, when he became responsible for a few of the bigger customers.

As Tobias's situation was quite complicated with small children and everything, they've let it take its time. They have not been in a hurry with a new relationship, but they feel comfortable in each other's company and have still seen each other now and then and traveled when he hasn't had the children or when he needs to leave for work. They have, of course, been mostly in Sweden, which has been fine with her. They have been to Oslo once. And now that the kids are older, it will get easier and easier to leave, when Linda will have the kids every other week.

Linda's head spins even more. Have they traveled in Sweden together? Have they gone abroad? When?

—And since we both enjoy the Swedish mountains, I joined Tobias and the children and went skiing for a few days. We didn't stay at the same place. Tobias takes the children's reactions seriously and doesn't want them to feel that I somehow take your role. I'm not their mother. So I mostly met Tobias when the kids were in ski school, and some days we had lunch together and then dinner one evening.

Linda doesn't like the cold. She hates skiing, and when Tobias suggested that they go to a mountain hotel for five days, she had protested wildly. He had once promised that the money saved by not going on ski holidays would be earmarked for a trip to Paris, but last year he had changed his mind, insisting that it was about time to teach the children to ski. Linda remembers the discussion and remembers that she refused to go along, how she said that her part of the cost would be saved so she could go to Paris.

She listens to Maja's story. Is this really about her husband? And then the anger hits her, pumping in her chest, against her temples. Doesn't she know Tobias after all these years together? Memories of summers whiz in her head, but she can't keep them separated.

—I have stayed here, off and on—not that much when the kids have been here, because we want to make time for ourselves, but sometimes during the holidays and such. But now that you have moved out, which I believe is such a great arrangement, for the kids and all, it will be easier. I don't quite understand why Tobias didn't move. I mean, a new apartment would probably have been a lot better for us—for me. But he keeps saying that he loves this house and doesn't want to leave it, that it has some kind of soul. He feels that someone has built this on his own, from scratch. Which I guess is true.

Linda's hands are like icy dead birds in her lap. When would she have moved? She and the children had gone down to her parents' summer house in Falsterbo last Easter. With five days of torrential rain and biting cold wind, they sat in the little drafty guest house freezing. Anita had not wanted to open the big house since Easter was early, and Anita and Gustav themselves wouldn't arrive until late April. Tobias had stayed at home to help the guys who would redo the guest bathroom. Linda and the kids were just to keep out of the way. Was that when Maja had moved in, convinced that Linda had left for good?

—And it was a good thing that you and the kids could go to Thailand, when we went to New York…

Wait, wait. Stop the time. Prevent this woman from killing it all, ripping the love from her body. Linda and the children had celebrated New Year's in Thailand last year, and Tobias had been forced to cancel because of his work. But New York—she had never been there, and neither had he. Where did Tobias get the time—and the money?

—…incredible, in Times Square. Magical.

—Hey, Linda says and takes a deep breath. Hey. Stop it. Listen to me.

Her voice is strangely clear. The carousel ride her thoughts have been on stops for a brief second.

—Tobias and I are married. I live in this house, and it's the only place I have lived, always together with Tobias, besides the apartment we had before we moved here. I live nowhere else but here, certainly not in an apartment farther away. I never have.

Maja looks at her in disbelief as she takes a sip of whiskey. Linda stares at the bottle. She could drink all of it. Her own glass is already empty.

—I am the one who planned what the guest toilet would look like. I chose those faucets and the toilet and the sink and the tiles. I am the one who makes decisions about everything in this house since Tobias doesn't have time. And you, you seem to think you have been sharing your life, part time, with a divorced man. I can assure you that you haven't. Tobias is married. To me. And this is my home. Our home.

Maja's narrow eyes search Linda, as if she spoke a foreign language and Maja could grasp only a few fragments.

—You didn't decide on the inside of the shed.

—Look, I don't care about the color of the walls, Linda hisses. And now I want you to leave because I have to work tomorrow. Please write down your name and phone number so I can call you.

Maja puts the glass on the coffee table and rubs her hands against her thighs.

—I don't understand. We've looked at houses, me and Tobias. We would move for real, Maja says, more to herself and to the whiskey glass than to Linda.

Suddenly, she seems less insolent.

—Why haven't you moved?

It's Linda's turn to talk very clearly.

24

—I haven't moved, because I didn't know that my husband, as it now seems, was having an affair with another woman. Do you understand?

A double life. While she had her head full of preschool and food shopping, sausages and fish fingers to save time, her job and swimming school, and packed lunches for excursions, and ear infections and the tummy flu…Her eyes fill with tears.

—And now, would you please leave us in peace? Because I will not go any further into this right now. It's almost Christmas, and we have children…Don't bother us, any of us. Do you understand?

It's suddenly the only thing she can think of: to not destroy Christmas. Christmas must be absolutely normal, the way it should be. The girls have nothing to do with this.

—And where have you been looking at houses? she says with a smile, as if she wants to continue to be tormented, as if this demented woman's stories need to hug her like a boa constrictor until she chokes.

Linda has the upper hand now, when it must have dawned on Maja that Tobias has sort of cheated on her and not on Linda.

—We've been around this area, a little farther down toward the water. Tobias thinks it's nice down there, and I love the water, so it would probably be a good solution.

Maja looks at Linda before she continues:

—We were there several Sundays, in November. It's a great area. Have you been there? Tobias would be happy living around here somewhere for the sake of the children when you would take turns having them. But then again, he loves this house.

She looks around, trying to comprehend what it might be about the house that Tobias is fond of, and Linda follows her eyes, sees the bulging IKEA Billy shelves, and thinks she should move the heavy art books. A brown leaf falls from the ficus in the corner. On the carpet, two pink ponies with golden manes seem to play along with some dolls and a heart-shaped bag in shiny plastic.

Linda swallows and swallows, as if her mouth were full of thick, cold porridge. In November...those Sundays when she cleared out the boxes at her parents' house, the boxes that Håkan said he didn't care about. Old glass, lots of linen towels from the respective grandmothers, children's books, games...Anita wanted to get rid of it all as if she was mentally preparing for a move. Tobias had said that he trusted Linda. She had to take what she wanted. It wasn't his stuff.

If it's true that Tobias had been out those Sundays and searched for houses in the area, then he probably also met their mutual acquaintances: preschool parents, Håkan's friends, her old classmates. But no one has told her anything. No one has asked her who her husband's company is. Has he enjoyed these potential encounters, triggered by the thrill of living the lie to see how far he could push it? Or has he been presenting Maja as his sister, a cousin?

Linda begins to fear that it isn't Maja but Tobias who is the psychopath. How will she manage to tackle this when he comes home? What if he becomes violent? Though he has never ever been. Even so, it doesn't sound like an impossible scenario.

—I think I should leave, Maja says. I—I will to talk to Tobias. After Christmas.

Maja writes her name and telephone number on a piece of paper. She shakes Linda's hand politely, but now her hand is as cold as Linda's.

Linda closes her eyes and leans against the door as Maja leaves. Then she goes into the kitchen, sits down on a chair, and puts her forehead against the table's surface, which is covered in breadcrumbs. Her head explodes, she can't think properly. She ought to cry, but her headache somehow stops the tears from coming.

She gets up, turns off the light, and goes up the stairs, up to the bedroom, though she doesn't want to lie in bed. It isn't hers any longer, but a place Tobias shared with Maja. It's disgusting.

Distasteful. But she must sleep. She goes into the bathroom, sees the gray face in the mirror. Her eye sockets are almost black, carved out of her skull. She opens the bathroom cabinet and searches the shelf filled with square packs and little plastic bottles, but she can't find anything for a headache. She takes out one of the packages.

—How much can you take of these? she says to herself as she tries to read the small text. "One tablet as needed."

She takes two pills and swallows them down with water. She brushes her teeth and washes her face, like she does every night. She pulls off her clothes and lets them fall to the floor and puts on her nightgown. She wraps herself in the bedcover and lies down on the bed. Her eyelids are already heavy.

*

The room spins. The clock radio shouts out that it has been snowing overnight. She stares into the darkness, and her stomach turns as she remembers last evening. Or was it a dream? The headache is still there, and she remembers taking some pills. She also had whiskey, and the combination might not have been the best. She stumbles out into the bathroom and looks at the pill packaging again, holding it against the angry lights.

She reads the following: "Maja Örnklou. For back pain."

Linda leans her head against the mirror but then turns toward the toilet and vomits.

—Are you okay, Mom? Lotta asks anxiously behind her back.

—It's okay, honey, it's okay. A little nauseous, that's all. I probably had something bad to eat. Come on. Mom must take a shower—

—I need to pee.

There's, of course, no reason to call in sick the day after the Christmas party. It's business as usual. And tonight, Tobias will be back home.

The snowfall continues over Stockholm. The wind comes from the southeast, and it's no longer possible to distinguish the individual flakes; it's a white mist that blurs the outlines of the houses along the quays. Linda gazes through the window in the small kitchenette in her department, imagining that if she doesn't think about Tobias, he doesn't exist. He should have called, but he hasn't. She forgot to ask Karin yesterday if he had, but it would have been strange—he never calls only to talk to the kids. What would he have said to them? And if he calls now, will she answer?

Linda is ashamed that she never believed Karin when she said she couldn't trust Tobias. She should call her, but now it's like a thorn in the heart, and she can't remove it. It's as poisonous as the spindle that put Sleeping Beauty to sleep. And Linda wishes she was the one to sleep for a hundred years and wake up as if nothing happened, nothing of what Karin predicted since they'd met Tobias that first evening.

She could call Karin right away. She should have landed and is certainly home by now. But what would she say? That Karin has been right all along, or at least for the last four years? As if admitting that Linda herself doesn't have a clue about what's happening. That she doesn't get or grasp what others see or experience. She's so busy getting everyday life, work, the children, and preschool to flow that she hasn't understood the obvious—that her husband is seeing another woman. He's not even trying to hide it but does it overtly. How many of their preschool acquaintances have known about this? How many are laughing behind her back?

—Did you get the e-mail with the pictures from the Christmas party?

Linda wakes abruptly when one of her colleagues enters the kitchenette.

—There was one of the entire department. You look so tired in the photo, Linda, though you didn't in real life. We all look tired today, however. You left early, huh? You should have seen what happened later in the evening. I have some gossip about a few of our colleagues—how about a lunch?

Her colleague laughs to herself as she dips a tea bag in hot water.

—Yeah, I had to leave early. The sitter couldn't stay, and Tobias is at the annual conference—

Linda puts her hand to her mouth. The nausea is so sudden that she is afraid of throwing up. Conferences, people cheating on their wives and husbands, blurred images from the night's meeting with Maja—has all this happened?

She takes her cup of coffee and flies out into the corridor and back to her desk. She looks right at the e-mail about yesterday's Christmas party. She isn't the only one who looks tired. Her colleague's face is flushing, and she wears a too-tight sweater in leopard print. In the picture, Linda presses her handbag under her arm, and since it's as black as her jacket, it looks like an abscess has grown out of her armpit. The flash seemed to have stuck on her face, which glows bright white, and her smile is so weak that it's barely visible. She gets the notion she isn't really at the party at all, as if she is about to disappear, to fade away. Yet she felt so happy when she left, happy and excited. Was it the hard liquor that had given her the power or the weak lighting in the bathroom? In the picture, her shoulder-length straight hair is dull, neither blonde nor mousy, or maybe both. Compared to her colleague's short bleached hairstyle, Linda doesn't stand out. It doesn't matter, but she regrets having chosen the black jacket. What would she have chosen otherwise? The only things even a little festive she owns are the secondhand dresses that hang next to Maja's clothes, and a few summer dresses.

She deletes the e-mail and stares straight at the wall and then down at the paper stacks in front of her, where the numbers jump around. She flips through the papers as if she were looking for something, frowning and letting tears drip onto the invoices. Now and then she looks at the phone or takes a sip of the cold, bitter coffee. Half an hour. Almost an hour too early for lunch.

—Did you see the e-mail…

Another of her colleagues is standing at her table's edge.

—Mmm.

—Great fun, huh? You left early?

—You know, I have a lot to do.

Linda can't be bothered to talk more about this nonsense. As if it was the only fun in the lives of these people, a stupid Christmas party. As if they didn't understand that there were other things happening in life—you could come home at night and get a visit from your husband's mistress. She stiffens as the cold spreads through her body. What did Maja do in their home, in the middle of the night? What if Linda hadn't been there? Imagine if Maja had gone up to bed, or met Karin? Or kidnapped the children?

The children. The sweat trickles in her armpits. Maja could have asked for money. Did Linda even ask about the reason she came?

—Yeah. All right. But if you had stayed—

"I would have seen my colleagues behave like monkeys. Yes, I missed that. But, hey, I don't care about their primitive behavior."

That's what Linda would like to answer, or scream. Either would do.

—Could we discuss it at lunch? she says instead.

Her colleague, smiling jerkily, looms away. Linda can't lift her arms to the computer keyboard. The last words have taken all her strength, and she lowers her head against her chest. No one here can understand what she's going through, and none of them are close enough friends. She can't tell them. She doesn't even know where to start such a story.

"I came home yesterday, and suddenly the door opened and a woman said she lived in my house?"

30

Or:

"My husband's mistress for four years came to the door, so I asked her to come in. I had no idea she existed! Go figure!"

The person she would like to call, now that she can't call Karin, is Bibbi, her best friend of the mothers at preschool. Bibbi will understand. Or Bibbi will listen and draw the right conclusions. She will be as pissed off as Linda is but can't express because her brain is like a spongy jellyfish.

It's Wednesday, soon lunchtime, and it isn't possible to call Bibbi. She's at work and has no time for an incomprehensible story of a nocturnal visit from an unknown woman who claims she is Tobias's new love. In addition, Linda can't speak more than two words before she starts to cry, and the thought of lifting the handset makes her hiccup.

—Ready for lunch?

The two colleagues, who are excited to tell what happened after Linda left the Christmas party, stand ready at her table. Linda nods, logs out of the computer, and reaches for her purse. They take the elevator down to the canteen in the basement. Linda isn't hungry. Today's dish is breaded plaice with some brown-rice salad, and then there are all sorts of options for those who are on any of the popular dieting methods. The publisher handles a huge number of best-selling diet cookbooks and there's no way of escaping them down here. There's an entire shelf if you want to learn more, but Linda has never had a weight problem, and at this point, the thought of food is enough to make her queasy. She chooses a carrot soup, while her colleagues take the plaice. The smell of fish is overwhelming, and she wonders how any sane person could even imagine eating mass-cooked fish at all. It smells like school, fish fingers all the way, no matter what you write on the menu.

—I wonder what his wife says; do you think she knows? one of the colleagues says between mouthfuls after telling them how she saw one manager leave with one of the younger girls from the marketing department and how they jumped into a taxi.

—They may live in the same direction, Linda suggests.

—No, they don't, the other colleague says. I know that he lives on Lidingö, which is to the east, and I see her on the subway going south in the evenings. I always get off before her, so in any case, she lives farther south than Enskede.

—But she might have a new boyfriend, or she stayed at some friend's house? Linda says.

—Are you defending him? Think about his wife. But maybe she's used to it. Or doesn't know what's going on. Imagine yourself; you surely wouldn't have thought something was going on, would you? I mean, a Christmas party could be long, right? And, it's evidently not the first time, according to the rumors.

Linda puts away the spoon and looks down into the bleak orange soup.

—When I worked in the marketing department, he was running after everyone, but that was before he married. When he got married, we immediately felt sorry for his wife, the first colleague says.

—And don't you feel sorry for her now? Linda mumbles.

—Honestly, the first colleague says, I don't care. If she's so stupid that she stays with him, then she should probably blame herself. She must have realized it by now. And she stays with him. That said, I don't care at all, but he's a dick.

—Or his wife is, her colleague says.

—She may not know, Linda says.

—Then she's either blind or she has her things going on as well. What do you know?

—Nothing, Linda says. I have to go, anyway.

She gets up and takes her tray, half running out of the canteen, hoping to avoid everyone she knows in the elevator. She's such a fool. A complete idiot in fact, but she prefers not to hear it from someone else. Especially not from her colleagues, who know

32

nothing at all about what happened last night, nothing about what happened to anyone. She knows that she's fooling herself. She tries to protect herself from everyone's talking, everyone's opinion—but it will never work. She's a fool. But the biggest idiot must surely be Tobias.

The preschool Solstrålen lies on the ground floor of a block of flats, in what, when the house was built, among other things has been a cheese shop and a bakery. Allegedly, the part where the kitchen is located has even been a bicycle-repair shop, and surely this must have been a friendly small-town neighborhood, but no trace of that remains. Especially not in wintertime when the slush covers the sidewalks and the houses' grayish yellow badly plastered facades are no longer hidden by bushes and trees.

Linda tries to open the heavy front door before she discovers that the "We're outside" sign is dangling behind the glass. She walks around the corner, following the rough concrete patches, laid out to avoid slipping in the slush.

The back of the preschool opens onto a grove of trees, which is nice in the spring but gloomy in December. There's a fence around it, an absolute necessity for the staff at this time of the year, to make sure that the kids can't get out. A small hill separates the area from the next row of identical houses maybe seventy meters away.

The staff is standing at the corner, stamping their boot-clad feet and dressed in layers of down jackets and ski pants. Next to them, with shining eyes and hair, stands Gabriella, the mother of two of the children who go to the preschool.

Linda slows down, takes an unconscious hold of her own hair and smoothens it out. Their conversation ends when they see her, and Linda doesn't want to talk to anyone. She just wants to pick up the kids and walk away, though not necessarily go home and wait for the door to open so she can try to play "happy wife"—if she even remembers how to do that.

—Are you okay? Gabriella asks. You look a little—tired.

—Christmas party yesterday, Linda says. So yes, I'm tired.

She turns to the staff and asks about the day, if the kids are all right. It comes automatically, and she hardly listens to the answer, although she captures that even if it snows tomorrow, there will be an excursion as usual. She hears her own voice echoing across the field, which will soon lie in inky darkness. Two small figures emerge from the shadows and waddle toward her, not yet accustomed to the baggy overalls and heavy boots.

—Linda, it's great to see you here! someone shouts behind her.

Linda cringes, closes her eyes, and tries to disappear from the preschool yard using the power of thought, but when she opens her eyes, there's no way of avoiding Marita's shimmering pink face.

Neither Linda nor Tobias has been involved in the meetings. They don't sit on the board. They only read the information they receive. They try to read it, at least. They had, of course, asserted during the interview, when they got the spot for Lotta, that they were willing to work, and they had understood that the preschool was a parent cooperative. Everyone must do their part, and Linda and Tobias do as they are told: take their Friday afternoons of work when they are scheduled and manage the tasks they have been appointed. But at the bottom line, the only thing they need is good day care.

—It will be great fun with a flea market, don't you think? Marita says.

—But that's after Christmas, right? Linda says, wondering if they need to talk about this here and now.

Responsible for the cooperative's parties, Marita's most important task is to create cohesion. When she proposed to the board that they could raise funds through a flea market, the idea was wildly acclaimed. Flea markets have worked splendidly in several other preschools, but that has, without doubt, been due to the event being held not in January, but either in late spring, when you can be outdoors in the preschool yard barbecuing, or at the beginning of December, when cheap, odd-looking Christmas gifts and the traditional hot toddy, glögg, are the attractions.

—You are responsible for the chocolate tombola, Marita continues. There's this large wheel that Oliver's dad made, great fun for the kids.

Linda did not even know Oliver's father, Peter, who happens to be Bibbi's husband, is a crafter of any sorts.

—Who else will be there?

—Tobias, I hope, Marita smiles.

—We'll see, I'm not sure he'll be home.

Linda knows he won't be home. He has planned to go to Copenhagen with the children to visit his mother, and Linda wants nothing more but for him to leave and never come back. She doesn't even want to hear his name.

—It doesn't matter who's there, as long as there's someone from your family. Every family has a task, Marita says.

—But there must be another family as well. Weren't we supposed to be in pairs?

—Oh, yes, it's you, Tobias, and the Mårtenssons.

Linda closes her eyes. "The Mårtenssons"? It must be a joke.

"A hundred bucks that I will be left alone with Bo, in a stupid chocolate tombola," is what passes through Linda's brain.

Bo works from home. Someone has said that he is writing a children's book and that his publisher told him he must devote more time to it. But mostly he is the person responsible for the family, comprising five children: his, Stina's, and the one they have together.

—Could you please call them? I can't do everything.

—I won't have time, Linda says. You know, accounting, and January, there's a lot of work, and I would really appreciate if you could do it.

—If you tell me right now that you won't forget the bake sale, Marita says with her face so close to Linda's that Linda gets a puff of stale coffee. And I won't remind you. We need gluten- or lactose-free choices, she continues. Many of the children are allergic. And no buns or cakes or bread should be brushed with egg. We already have people who voluntarily signed up for cinnamon buns and stuff like that.

When she pronounces "voluntarily," it sounds like an incantation. Marita says she has a recipe she has seen on a TV show, some spelt muffins with fruit, super healthy.

—Fruit is nature's candy, she adds. And if you can't bake, you ask someone else. Maybe Tobias?

—I told you he won't be here! Linda says, tired of hearing his name, tired of being perceived as a unit with him.

No way that she will bake. Showing up to this activity is more than enough.

Marita turns around, and Gabriella pats Linda on the shoulder.

—I understand from Bibbi that you're having a tough time at home. Just tell me if you need help.

A tough time? What would Bibbi have said? And when? They haven't spoken in ages—and why has Bibbi talked to Gabriella? Linda makes an effort to look happy.

—That Tobias travels a lot? Gabriella says.

—Right. He does. But—yes, you know. Nothing to do about that. It will be all right.

Her voice is shattered, and she's so close to crying she must turn her head. She thinks of Christmas and of the children and of herself and the nonsense life she must have lived.

—Oh—Gabriella smiles—I understand how lucky I am. Mats comes home every night. No traveling unless we travel together. We went to New York for Christmas shopping—

Linda takes a deep breath and shouts again to Lotta and Fia, who slowly retreated with their playmates when Linda continued to talk. Together they move toward the gates, and when they are halfway, she sees Bo's minibus stop and his tall figure unfold. He

37

looks as tired as Linda feels. His hair is unbrushed, and he's wearing an old fleece jacket over his wrinkled shirt. He carries a shapeless canvas bag in his right hand.

—Linda? We will…if I understood Marita right. The flea market. But I…

He stops and looks at her from top to bottom.

—You look tired, he says, and sounds worried.

—Hey, Bo, I really should be going, Linda answers.

—Well, yes, no, of course, especially this time of year. Tell me if you need help with anything, he says mildly.

Did she get that right—he has five children he basically takes care of on his own, and he wonders if she needs help? Linda shudders at the thought of living with him and shakes her head.

—Our families are supposed to arrange the chocolate tombola, after Christmas. But Tobias will be away, so it will be just me.

—Stina is also out of town that weekend, Bo says. And I can already say that I probably can't be there when it starts. There's basketball training, and I have to pick up and drop off—

—Don't forget to be there.

Bo shakes his head warily. Maybe she should offer him help instead.

The silence between them gets awkward. Linda clears her throat and weighs on her heels.

—Yeah. Yes, that's right, I won't forget it. No, I'll surely be there. And I won't forget the kids either. I forget most of their stuff though, or some of it, each day.

He rattles his car keys nervously.

—Okay, Linda says. But if you won't be there in time, what if you did the baking? Because I can't.

She has no desire to explain that she doesn't want to do it either. Bo's face lights up.

—Yes! Of course. I'd be happy to.

—Marita said it should preferably be gluten- and lactose-free. Not brushed with egg. She had seen a recipe for spelt muffins with fruit on a website or on television.

—Good, good, Bo says, nodding. I'll check that out. So that's a great way to split responsibilities. You'll be here early, and I'll come later, with freshly baked muffins. Great. Thank you, Linda. If we don't see each other before Christmas, I hope you'll have a nice and restful time with your family so you'll be more at peace when we meet the next time.

He stretches out his arm and puts his large hand on her shoulder, pats her gently, and then hurries up to the preschool, disappearing around the corner with the canvas bag dangling over his arm.

Before Linda has had time to move, Bibbi comes running, crouched, with her eyes on the phone screen.

Bibbi and Linda have known each other since Lotta and Oliver were babies. They met at the public nursery school when they both moved to the suburbs with their families and their first-born babies. They had both bought their first houses and felt like— adults. Living the family life suddenly. It's with Bibbi that Linda has spent the most time, and perhaps she took the place Karin once had as Linda's best friend; it's so much easier to discuss children, teething, baby food, and pregnancies with someone who has the exact same interests.

And although Bibbi is the contrary to Linda in most ways— she is happier, crazier, more intense and spontaneous, and laughs easier—she gets Linda in a good mood, probably because she doesn't spend hours planning her time, their family, and their days or nights. They are also different in appearances: Linda is taller and thin, while Bibbi is short and dark. Her stout figure chugs against Linda at full speed, like a freight train, and it's only when they nearly collide, and Linda is about to open her mouth, that she looks up.

—Darling, don't have time to talk, I'm so late. Is everything okay?

—No, not at all, Linda says. Can I—can I call you when I get home?

—Tennis with Oliver, it's the grand finale. Got to love December. Can we talk tomorrow?

Linda nods, swallowing the salty tears that run down her throat.

—Sure, she says. Or after Christmas. I'll call.

—Don't cry for me. I'm not worthy of those tears, Bibbi says and laughs.

Linda laughs, too, involuntarily. And Bibbi doesn't see how Linda's face twists into a silent scream as she gets the children into the car, because Bibbi's already gone.

*

The girls run to the door as soon as they hear the key in the lock. Linda shudders. Not even twenty-four hours ago another key was in the same lock and Maja stood in the hallway. She still sees Maja's eyes, catlike, luminous. As if she were a vampire, a bloodsucker.

Linda's tummy turns, and she struggles to breathe calmly, staring down at the sausage frying in the pan and pouring the macaroni into the boiling water. The sausage was all she could find in the freezer; she hasn't been able to think about food, she isn't hungry. Three minutes and the macaroni will be ready; in three minutes he won't have time to come near her. He will only have time to hug the children and wash his hands. She doesn't want to smell him or feel his hands against her body. She only wants him to go away. Five days until Christmas Eve. On Christmas day, she will tell him she knows. And destroy—everything?

She stops her thoughts. It's not her fault—none of this is. It's all his. And she protects him in the same way that she wants to protect the girls. But she can't understand how they would celebrate Christmas if she told him now, and then to not say anything to her parents, nothing to Håkan or the kids. It's better if she lies only to herself. If they are both acting innocent.

The children are laughing in the hallway, and she hears Tobias's excited voice. It sounds exactly the same as when they said good-bye on Sunday morning, and he has barely had time to be away. Yet it's as if he has already moved out, as if he were visiting.

—Hello, honey, he says and peeks into the kitchen. How was the Christmas party?

—Good. We're ready to eat. Children, come and eat!

—Sausage? Tobias says.

—Yes, Linda says without looking up.

She knows he notices that she isn't herself, that something is wrong, and that he can't quite put his finger on what it is. He isn't going to ask right now because sometimes she's both hungry and angry at this time of day. Tobias has, over time, learned to wait if he needs to tell her things, like about new jobs trips, or ask how her day was.

Linda hears his heavy steps on the stairs and into the bathroom. Meanwhile, Lotta takes her seat on the kitchen sofa and Fia in her Tripp Trapp chair, and as Tobias sits down opposite Linda, she's incredibly happy that she doesn't have to sit next to him. She pours ketchup over the macaroni and mixes it in, again and again, until the macaroni is a light-pink color. She has no appetite whatsoever. The mountain of macaroni and the sausage rounds, burned in the middle but almost pink at the edges, make her nauseous.

—The conference was great, Tobias says with his mouth full of macaroni. However, when it comes to the food, this sausage is a thousand times better. There's no way in hell that white fish and rice is meant for a grown man.

—You sweared, Lotta says.

—Swore, Linda says and nails one macaroni with her fork.

—And how was the Christmas party? he asks again.

—I already told you. It was good.

—People behaving badly?

—The usual way. You should know.

41

Linda's voice is tender and cracks because she sees Maja before her, her blonde hair and broad shoulders, her shimmering pink complexion, so fresh and—good looking. Everything that Linda isn't, like in the picture from the Christmas party, where she appeared translucent, close to invisible. And Maja could come out of an ad for shampoo or skin cream, vacations, toothpaste, flower-scented perfume, or maybe vitamins for women. Linda is the same person, only before the transformation. If it were as simple.

—So what have you girls done while I was away?

Lotta and Fia begin to talk about their time at Moderna Museet last Sunday, and Linda lets them do the talking. An art museum is the least possible resistance for her, and there are always activities for children. She keeps poking around in the pink macaroni, which has turned cold and sticky.

—We had pancakes for lunch, Dad! Fia says happily and climbs down from the chair to sit on Tobias's lap, but he gets up and fetches a beer from the fridge.

—Do you want one?

He swings the bottle in front of Linda's face, and she shakes her head. It's an unnecessary question since she never drinks beer on a weekday. He opens the cap and sits down, lifts Fia onto his lap, and drinks the beer directly from the bottle, though he knows Linda doesn't like it.

"That's the way we do it in Denmark," is his usual excuse, which he normally says with a laugh to explain both his behavior and the drinking. You can always have a beer in Denmark, even for breakfast. They call it *morgenmad*, "morning food." The Swedish word for breakfast, *frukost,* resembles the Danish word for lunch, and when Tobias is in that mood, they can have lengthy discussions about what actually is the right word.

Linda dumps the remaining macaroni in the trash can and puts the plate in the dishwasher.

—Karin came, too, Lotta says.

—Yes, that's right. Great, Tobias says. I haven't seen her in a long time. How was she?

He's not the least bit interested. Linda finds it hard to breathe when she reflects on what Karin said—in that she doesn't trust Tobias. And Linda hasn't called her and told her she was right, nor has she asked her the burning question: what do I do now?

She can't let go of that question. What happens when you have found out? She didn't find it out; someone happened to tell her. A story that's completely improbable but, nonetheless, contains too many correct details, leaving no doubt it's true. And instead of screaming, she must now hold back the anger and the knowledge for six days. It's like standing at the bottom of a glacial lake and holding your breath, with heavy stones around your feet. You just can't scream. You can't move either. And to top it all off, her hands are tied. Is she a Houdini? Will she get through this and resurface?

—She was fine, she says. Good. She has her Christmas markets now, the last one this weekend.

—So she's busy, like the rest of us. I need to go to town on Saturday—

—We have to buy the Christmas tree, Linda says.

—I have to shop for Christmas gifts.

—But first the Christmas tree.

They look at each other for the first time since he came home.

—What's going on with you? Tobias says. Don't be so bloody angry.

—You sweared! Fia says.

—Swore, Linda says.

—Stop correcting them all the time, god damnit.

The children watch him but don't dare say "sweared" again, or "swore" for that matter. The air is suddenly thick, and the kids slip out of the kitchen and into the living room, where they turn on the television.

—If I say I need to go to town, that's all. I can get the Christmas tree, too.

—We don't need to buy more presents. We have discussed this a thousand times. The kids don't need more gifts.

—But I need a Christmas gift for my mother, a gift I can take to her when I see her after New Year's. And I want to get it now and not think about it anymore.

He's lying. Linda knows he is, and she's even more certain that he understands she knows, but he doesn't give in.

—And what would you buy her? I mean, it must be an important gift since it can't wait until January?

—I don't know. Do you have any good ideas?

—Why not a new shawl, instead of the one she left here?

—Yes, that's a good idea. And I could take her the old one as well.

—No, why? It could stay here, until she comes back, Linda says.

—She won't come here anymore. You know that.

—But that's what you say if you forget something. It means that you will return. She might not have forgotten to take it; she might have hung it here because she felt at home, as if she lived here.

She stares at him, trying to make him uneasy, wanting him to confess. Now. Linda's cheeks itch of heat.

—How could my mother possibly believe that she lives here?

His voice is full of question marks, and Linda thinks he looks stupid. A stupid Dane who can't connect the dots. He brings the bottle to his mouth and gulps the last of the beer.

—She's not crazy, he says.

Crazy. Maja seems psychopathic enough. What if she and Tobias don't really know each other? Or have only met once and Maja only imagines a life with Tobias?

She walks up to the kitchen counter and pulls out the drawer where they collect all loose bits and bobs: rubber bands, tape, small notepads, matches, paper clips, and extra keys.

—If your mom won't come here anymore, then maybe you could get her spare key, she says with her back turned to Tobias.

He doesn't answer.

—Did you hear?

—Well, what does it matter if she has a key? You don't have to be so darn insensitive.

—She won't need it anymore.

He shrugs.

—And your parents, do they need one?

—They live ten minutes away, Tobias. If we lose ours, surely that's convenient, don't you think? I can't exactly go to Copenhagen if I am locked out, can I?

—I'll check, he says. There's no hurry.

"Well, it is," Linda thinks. "But you just don't understand, yet."

The days until Christmas are the slowest ever. Linda wakes up each morning with a desperation in her body, a heavy sadness. Her work is the only consolation since she doesn't have to think when she's there. And every night, Tobias asks her how she's doing, but she avoids him and everything he says, looking mostly at the floor. He works late. She stands in the basement and washes, irons, folds. She disappears down there because she knows he wants to watch TV when the kids have gone to sleep, and she sneaks upstairs and goes to bed. Even if she isn't asleep when he comes in an hour later and asks, "Are you asleep?" she doesn't answer. He doesn't listen when she tells him she has a lot to do at work, that they are preparing the financial statements already.

She finds herself wondering if it matters—she doesn't notice any difference anyway—even if he is seeing someone else. She doesn't understand when he has had time to meet Maja if he didn't do it during working hours. She sniffs his clothes, but they don't smell of perfume, and he has no marks on his collar. It's not like affairs in the movies. It could have been a bad dream.

*

Tobias puts the Christmas tree in the hallway, where it takes up all the cramped space even though constricted by a net.

—I'm off to town, he shouts and slams the door.

Linda wouldn't say thank you. She has brought up the tree stand and puts the net-clad Christmas tree on the hall floor to get it in place before she lifts the package into the living room and gently places it on the carpet. When she cuts the plastic net, the Christmas tree slowly untangles as if it hesitates over the possibility of surviving in here.

—We must have lots of glitter, Fia says decidedly.

—Pink, Lotta says.

The girls agree that the glitter should be pink and explain there's pink glitter in "nujaak". It takes a little while before Linda understands that they're talking about New York, and the only one she knows who has been there lately is Gabriella. Surely, she has bought tons of decorations that the children have talked about at preschool, and it wouldn't surprise Linda if the perfect woman's perfect Christmas tree is sprinkled with pink glitter. Their supermarket only carries plain glitter, and that will have to do. She tries to forget about New York, where she has never been, but where Tobias went with Maja. It sounds insane.

Lotta and Fia are so excited they don't even notice that Tobias isn't around. It's as if sprucing up the Christmas tree is an all-female chore. Linda attaches the lights, and the girls hang every shiny Christmas ornament with great care, no higher than one meter above the floor. Linda moves a few of them, but the tree still has a strange shape. After ten minutes the girls get tired because there's no more glitter and shiny stuff to hang.

Three hours later, Tobias is back from town. He opens the door, carrying two large paper bags from a home-electronics store. He doesn't comment on the Christmas tree, trying to look as if he is busy.

—You were going to get a shawl, Linda says, and wipes the crumbs from the hot dog buns off the kitchen table.

—Have you already had lunch? Tobias says, surprised.

—It's a quarter past one, Linda says.

—Is there anything left?

—There's sausages in the freezer.

He takes off his sheepskin coat, leaving the bags in the hall.

—What did you buy? Linda asks.

His face lights up. He loves buying all kinds of appliances.

—A juice extractor. There was a sale, and if it isn't this year's Christmas gift, it will be next year's, he says proudly.

—What's she going to do with a juice extractor?

47

—Healthy drinks. Isn't that great?

Anne doesn't care about healthy food and drinks; Linda knows no one with less knowledge of what you should or shouldn't eat. She eats what she likes, which is food she has had since she was a girl: open sandwiches, herring, pork chops, meatballs, brown sauce, cooked potatoes. A juice extractor will be as interesting to her as a football.

—And the shawl?

—It would be strange to take her a new one and then the one she forgot. What would she do with two shawls?

Linda is near the point of saying that an extra shawl is probably more useful than a juice extractor, but she decides not to.

—Have you seen the Christmas tree, Dad? Doesn't it look good?

Lotta and Fia show him around proudly, but he doesn't comment other than a "fine" and a "great." Which is enough, apparently, since the girls are shining with pride.

Linda watches them from the kitchen, thinking of Bibbi, who doesn't get along at all with her mother-in-law. She avoids her. At least Linda doesn't have that problem. To tell the truth, she has more issues with her own mother. Linda wishes she had talked to Bibbi, to anyone. Her body aches with the hatred, the not knowing, and the inability to question anything Maja told her—she knows it's true. It's not just about a few secret messages or strange phone calls. This is for real. But no one has time to listen to her, not now. It will have to wait until after Christmas, as Linda said. Linda needs to know if everyone else has known about it. All the parents at the preschool. Everyone in the area.

—That's it, he says and sits down opposite her, with a beer from the refrigerator. Next weekend we are free. And together. At home.

He can't know that the coming weekend he talks about will be anything but a cozy family moment. If she can keep it until Tuesday, and if she can play this sick game all the way through Christmas Eve.

She walks back into the living room, moving the decorations, hanging up a few angels. For each piece she hangs on the Christmas tree's sprawling branches, she realizes it's the last Christmas they'll celebrate together, and Tobias hasn't even been taking part in decorating the tree. Not even that.

—Merry Christmas!

The girls and Tobias stand in the doorway. They are holding a tray table she has never seen, and because she hates to have breakfast in bed, it's the one thing she never would have bought. On the tray sits a large cup of coffee, two sandwiches with cheese, and a large glass of what looks like green juice.

Tobias leans forward to give her a kiss, but she turns around to arrange the pillows behind her back.

—I couldn't resist it, so I bought a juice extractor for you, too. And there are accessories, so you can make lots of other things. Try it!

Tobias is shining with joy in his black robe, and the children look curiously at Linda when she lifts the glass and sniffs the contents.

—What is it?

—Spinach, among others. And ginger. Supposed to be super healthy.

She tries it. It tastes weird, and above all, it has nothing to do with Christmas. The children also try it but grimace when they swallow.

—It's strong, Lotta says politely.

—It's disgusting, Fia says.

—You must try it with your grandmother, Linda says, putting the tray table aside. She gets up and grabs the tray again.

—Don't you want to eat here? Tobias says. It could be cozy, couldn't it?

The tears are clogging her throat. Has he forgotten that she hates crumbs in the bed, or is he thinking of Maja? Or of himself? Has she somehow asked for a juice extractor?

—We can watch the Christmas program, Lotta suggests, and Linda nods.

—Right, that's what we'll do on Christmas morning, she says. We'll sit in the living room instead. That's much cozier.

Tobias sighs but says nothing. He takes the tray from her hands and carries it down the stairs.

*

It's still Christmas. And it's a quarter past three.

—Merry Christmas, Mother-in-law! We should stay here— Södertunet, the brightest shining star in the suburban sky! Tobias shouts and stretches his arms toward Anita.

In one-tenth of a second, Linda thinks her mother will push them all down the stairs in dismay because they have neglected the ever-important Christmas TV highlights, but no words come over her lips before she is surrounded by Tobias's worn sheepskin coat.

—Merry Christmas, Tobias! Anita squeaks from the coat while she detaches herself with an embarrassed laugh and blushing cheeks. She presses forward a faint smile, while Tobias encouragingly pats her on the arm a few times, as if to reassure her that she can still breathe.

Linda looks down so Anita cannot see that she's laughing. It's the first time she's laughed in almost a week, and it's not even particularly funny that Tobias is making fun of her mother, but she needs to laugh. She stomps off the worst wet snow from her boots, onto which salty stripes from last year flow out like a failed watercolor painting.

Linda, Tobias, Lotta, and Fia are just a few kilometers from the small houses on Norrtunet where they live themselves. Yet, Södertunet is like another world, polished and cherished, where even the snow looks whiter and fluffier than at their house, on the other side of the main road. The children have been jumping back and forth between the street and the sidewalk all the way, happy over the snow and blissfully unaware that they are somewhat overdue for the Donald Duck show, which is exactly what Anita said they shouldn't be.

51

—Girls! Welcome and Merry Christmas! Anita says and bends slightly at the knees to pretend to be aligned with her grandchildren. The TV program is already on in there. Please put your boots here in the hallway.

The kids sneak past her and throw themselves around their grandfather's neck. Jackets and boots fall on the hallway floor like autumn leaves, and Linda wonders if the patent-leather shoes they have received from Anita will ever be used.

—Look at this Christmas! Tobias says. This is such a lovely house, made for festivities—that's what I've always said.

Linda stares at the big fir wreath with silvery Christmas ornaments surrounding the entire gilt-edged mirror above the hall table. She and Tobias will forever have to bring their children to her parents' house for Christmas because Anita and Gustav would never deal with the traditions in any other way, and because they will stay in this house, where Gustav was raised, until they die. Linda neither can nor wants to understand, or indeed re-create, the traditions and values her mom follows. And she can't say she's in love, either with this house, where she certainly grew up, or with the house she and Tobias live in. They're just houses. They bought a house just big enough for their needs. It was pure accident that they ended up there, so close to her parents' home. And yet so far away. That Tobias even spends time being the perfect guest is more than she understands.

—Merry Christmas, Mom, she says and Anita startles, as if she hasn't seen her until now.

—Merry Christmas, darling. You look tired.

Linda leans forward, trying to unzip her boots. Her newly washed hair clings to her face.

—I am so glad to see you here. We have already started, you see. Håkan came at half past two, and he would, of course, watch Donald Duck, Anita continues, showing her son-in-law into the living room.

She makes it sound as if Håkan were a very small child when he's actually thirty-five years old, and certainly he's not very happy to watch cartoons or celebrate Christmas with his parents, sister, brother-in-law, and nieces. Last year, Linda had suggested that he should go somewhere, but Håkan's response—"With whom? And be completely alone on Christmas Eve?"—still echoes in her head. It had never occurred to her that it could be more enjoyable with the company, regardless of which company it was.

Linda takes off her coat, being left alone in the hall. She runs her hand over the hall table's cool marble top, sweeping down two pine needles that have come loose from the wreath and shying away from the realization that the gesture could have belonged to her mother. She looks in the mirror. Below her eyes dark circles seem to press down her cheeks, and her hair crackles when she pulls it from her face. Her cheeks are unnaturally orange after an attempt to put blush on top of the pale skin.

"The brightest shining star in the suburban sky"—where did Tobias get that from? Linda knows all the streets by heart, every curve, every single plot of land. She knows where it's slippery during wintertime and where to steal apples in fall, where to see the first crocuses, and what garden has the most magnificent lilac by graduation time in the beginning of June. The only thing that has happened over the last twenty years is that the trees are bigger, and several of the houses changed hands. Some of her old classmates have taken their childhood homes in possession and let the parents move into apartments in the city, where they can go to the theater, cinema, and opera or hang out after work with twenty-five year olds in trendy costumes, pretending to be young again.

Here, in the suburbs, lies a faded memory of hopes, glances, and must-dos—all that Linda never even tried to live up to but, implicitly, is considered to be obliged to care about, as if she had never grown older than she was in that uptight graduation picture hanging on the wall in her parents' bedroom.

In the living room, she finds Håkan, now surrounded by Lotta and Fia. Linda's father, Gustav, is installed in his favorite armchair. Donald Duck flickers past on the TV, and Gustav chuckles at the elves with the checkered chess color. Håkan stops staring at the TV, detaches himself from the girls, and gets up.

—Merry Christmas, sis, he says and gives her a big hug.

—Merry Christmas, Linda responds and hears how her voice trembles.

—Is everything okay?

She nods, wriggles out of his grip, and looks down at the floor.

—Just a little tired.

—Going somewhere over New Year's?

—Nope.

She is on the verge of saying "thank goodness" but stops herself.

—We'll go somewhere later on, Tobias says. We're going skiing, right?

—I don't know if I can come along. We'll see, Linda says.

They don't have much in common, her brother and her soon not-to-be husband. Håkan seems to be taken right out of a Christmas ad, in his white shirt, a soft sweater, and a nicely pressed pair of pants. His black suede loafers have no traces of dust. He has always had an interest in clothes, and that he now has a chance to go to Italy on business suits him. Next to him, Tobias is a wrinkled copy, but for the first time, Linda sees that his shirt has been half-heartedly ironed and that his jacket is pilling.

She sits down on an orange-colored pouf, assuming they must have bought it to calm Anita's eagerness to renew the home. Gustav puts a porcelain mug of steaming mulled wine in front of her, and a silver plate of gingerbread immediately gets the children's attention.

Linda doesn't like mulled wine. And she's tired of gingerbread.

—Merry Christmas, everyone! Anita shouts. Håkan made the

mulled wine. It's delicious, isn't it? she says before she has even brought the drink to her mouth.

Håkan doesn't budge; perhaps he has already had too much of it. The smell of liquor protrudes, itching in Linda's nose and throat. She has never liked mulled wine. It's messy, sticky, and leaves a sugary liquor coating in your mouth, which numbs the taste buds. Tobias winks at her with a wry smile, and she closes her eyes. She hates him.

—Great, this mulled wine. Though it's not the same as the Danish, he says, just like every year.

—We have never had the chance to try the Danish version of which you speak so fondly, Håkan says.

—It's a secret recipe, not like here in Sweden where everything is for everyone. I can't just steal it from my mother. With a little luck, I might inherit it. Who knows, Tobias chuckles.

Anita and Gustav laugh politely.

—And how's the printing industry? he asks Håkan. Earned any money lately?

Håkan shoots him a stiff smile.

—Great, actually. Maybe not as good as the computer business, but...

Tobias laughs and rubs his hands.

—No, you know, it's better business than ever. We're breaking all sales records for December. There isn't much that can stop the progress...I have other stuff going on as well, so next year will be amazing I think. For me, that is. For us, I mean, he says, giving Linda another wink.

His gestures are always a bit too wide and somehow fit in well with the claim that he has "some other stuff going on," which he has always claimed to have. It's his way of being, and she has lived in the belief that it's quite natural, knowing that this some-times incomprehensible "stuff" creates a certain dynamic. All of his projects involve more money, but so far no attempt has been particularly successful. He has imported folding scooters, phone cases, and some kind of tummy trainers similar to those you can buy at the TV shop. There have been different, more or less popular, toys and computer stuff he had spotted somewhere during a trade show. Mostly buy-and-sell since that is what he thinks he's good at.

Since September he's also been doing a distance-learning class in the United States. Linda doesn't understand how that happened, but he said the company pays half the fee. Maybe that's not even true; perhaps it's another thing he made up.

She finishes the last of her mulled wine, and Gustav fills her mug before she has a chance to protest.

—I'll just go check the food, Anita says and rises.

—I will be happy to help, Tobias says. You shouldn't be on your own on Christmas Eve...

Anita giggles like a teenager as he wraps his arm around her waist and leads her to the kitchen.

*

Anita is happy everyone has finally arrived. This is a journey into Christmas Eve, and she'll play her role as hostess, mother, wife, mother-in-law, and grandmother to perfection, just because she is forced to do so. She cares as little about Christmas as her adult guests—the exception possibly being Tobias, who is as jovial as always and rarely shows signs of dislike of anything. And Gustav, of course, but he isn't a guest although he behaves as one. But her children are not very enthusiastic, and it's probably her fault they don't like Christmas, but what can she do about it now? That's just the way it is. They are all part of this play, once a year.

Everything is meticulously planned. She has only to bring out a few dishes that are not to be on the smorgasbord and get the drinks for everyone.

—It's great to have your help, she says to Tobias. If you could get the beer for us and the soft drinks for the children, I'll just give a last hand to the food. Or just bring the beer, will you.

—Have you been looking for apartments? Tobias says while he rummages around in the refrigerator.

Anita shakes the pan of meatballs and sausages vigorously.

—Do you have a timetable? he asks.

—What for?

—The house. To move.

—Oh. No. There's no hurry. We can talk about that later.

She smiles stiffly and bends down to find a nice plate for the food.

*

The others are finishing the mulled wine. Their eyes are on the television screen and the short cartoons that flicker past. The sounds from the TV are accompanied by the tinkling of the silver spoons against the porcelain when the booze-soaked raisins are being dug up. The plate of gingerbreads is empty, except for a few brown crumbs.

—Are we ready to eat? Anita says, tapping the soda bottles she has in her hands. I figured the kids could sit over here.

She nods toward the chairs at the far end of the table.

Linda knows it's just because Anita wants to make sure she doesn't have to be responsible for Fia and Lotta.

—Now the girls will finally have their meatballs, Gustav says. You know how much I like them, too. Grandma's in particular.

Fia and Lotta nod shyly.

—If you could please bring some water, Gustav, and maybe Linda could light the candles? Anita says. Do you like our Christmas tree by the way? Isn't it a success? The seller had to open dozens of those nets; how could you possibly see what a tree looks like if it's packaged? And as expensive as they are. Who wants to buy a pig in a poke?

—A spruce, rather, Gustav nods. He wasn't very happy, the vendor—

—But it all ended well. It's better than all the others. The back's a bit scanty, but it doesn't show.

Nobody says anything.

—I think it's nice, Lotta says. But I would like more glitter.

—And glitter isn't my thing, Anita chirps. So that would have to stay on your Christmas tree at home.

—Mom likes glitter, Fia says. Dad, too. And me, too.

—Well, isn't that just great. Aren't you lucky, Anita says. So you can have it at home then. In this house, the glitter won't come over the threshold. I want the red Christmas ornaments and those old straw decorations, which is tradition for me. Christmas is all about tradition, not novelties.

—I believe Christmas is all about family, Tobias says. And how lucky we are, who may all be together!

Linda is so tired of him. Tired of how he pretends to care about these people. Why does he go on like that about the family—he who has had another woman for four years? She wants to shout at him to stop it, but she doesn't. Of course she doesn't. She smiles at the children and helps them sit comfortably in the chairs that are too low for the dining table, at least if you are a child.

*

—And this one's for Linda! Tobias shouts as he pulls out a large flat package from behind the sofa. Merry Christmas, sweetheart!

Linda looks at the brown wrapping paper, around which sits a crumpled red silk ribbon she recognizes from the gift box they have in the workroom. The ribbon is only tied once around the package. It's too short to make a real gift wrapping. The paper is creased and gaping at one corner.

—Oh, how exciting, Anita says without empathy.

Linda unwraps the package and turns it around. She sees the green and blue spots on the surface, interspersed with white splashes. And the famous bridge. It's Monet. All of it.

She nods thoughtfully.

—Thanks, she says. Great.

—Yeah, isn't it? I've tried it in the bedroom, and it looks beautiful.

—Yes, I understood that you'd tried something. Saw the nail.

—Oh, did I forget it?

Tobias smiles sheepishly.

—Darn, he says.

—You sweared! Fia says.

—Swore, Linda says.

—But it's beautiful, Anita says. And such a great Christmas present for Linda, who likes art. Very thoughtful.

—Yes, Linda says.

She already gave Tobias a new shirt and a tie. She will not give him the Lotto ticket; it's folded among the receipts in her purse, and that's where it will stay.

Her mother gets a glass bowl and her father a book about World War II. Håkan gets a restaurant discount booklet. Linda knows of no one who frequents restaurants as much as he, which isn't strange at all since he is single. He doesn't need a discount booklet; he can afford to eat out every night. Both he and Linda are well aware of this, but she couldn't protest when Tobias came home with the booklet and said they wouldn't use it anyway so they might as well give it away. She will never visit a restaurant with Tobias again.

Linda balances on the sofa's outer edge as if she were at a cocktail party full of people unknown to her. She knows where every single towel is held, on which shelf the applesauce has its place in the food cellar, and in which bowl the potato peeler stands on the kitchen counter. Yet everything feels strange, unfamiliar and soulless. When did this house go from being her home to being just any house? Not the moment she left home or when she started studying in Lund. It must have come later. Maybe when they had children, or when they bought their own house. Somewhere along the way, the familiar scents and the chirping wood floors became another world with barely perceptible shifts in the interior. She hugs the heavy, soon-empty water glass in her hand, pulls her skirt, and tries to sit comfortably on the sofa. Her whole body is itching.

She thinks of the bloody poster. She had wished to get the book on Cypriot icons, a large and heavy work she has longed to buy for years but never thought she should spend money on. Just before Christmas she had seen it again, at the book sale, and she had hinted about it to Tobias, hoping he would get the message. He could have purchased the book on the German avant-gardes, too, but he understands nothing about art and barely understands her interest. Her mother understands, and somewhat shares, her interest, but because art, in a way, caused the family conflict when Linda moved, it remains an abscess that may burst if poked at, and, therefore, she does everything to pretend that the poster is a great Christmas gift.

With what Linda knows about Maja, the entire poster is an even larger abscess and it will crack, just not tonight. But tomorrow. Should she just let the framed poster fall to the floor? The protection is probably made from Plexiglas, and the effect won't be as grand as if there were broken glass everywhere. Tobias most certainly doesn't know who the artist is, but it's written in big letters over the water lilies so that even he won't feel stupid.

Linda shudders while following her father's movements over the bottles in the shiny brown cocktail cabinet, a dance reflected in the windows overlooking the terrace and the garden. From the kitchen she can hear Anita rattling coffee cups while chatting merrily with Tobias. Fia and Lotta are playing with their presents on the carpet in the library; Tobias has, together with Håkan, taken the TV back into the upper hall, its annual appearance in the living room having come to an end. They shall not watch television; they shall socialize. Anita has already, almost imperceptibly, cleaned the coffee table with cleaning spray to remove the sticky traces of children's hands. A whiff of synthetic lemon lingers and sends the Christmas scents back to the bottom of the cardboard boxes where they can rest until next year. The dry birchwood logs crackle in the fireplace. When everyone eventually has gone, Anita will panic over the smell of smoke, as always. Which is why they almost never light a fire, except for at Christmas.

Linda knows her dad's dance is only the prelude to what he appreciates the most—the discussions around the coffee table. For Christmas isn't over yet, although both the dinner and the gift distribution are completed. Now awaits coffee and liqueurs, conversation, and gratitude. This is what Gustav enjoys; it's his part of the feast.

The sofa cushions only look fluffy when Anita has pounded them into shape, which she must have done when spraying the table. The gold pendulum clock ticks rhythmically and then hums and begins chiming—eight times. They have started early; Christmas is after all for the children. Tobias and Anita come out of the kitchen, and Håkan strolls down the stairs. They all gather around the coffee table. Gustav monitors drinks, and they are all merry and cheerful.

Anita pours coffee, and Linda stares with disgust into her cup after the first hot gulp; it's too bitter. Anita must have brewed it in advance and let it sit for a while, like the coffee in a dull roadside restaurant. Or has she been distracted by Tobias's presence and put too much ground coffee into the filter?

—And how about you, Håkan, Tobias says. Still no ladies in your life?

The room becomes quiet.

—No one who has the opportunity to come over on Christmas Eve anyway, Håkan says, swirling his glass of cognac.

—So there is someone, Tobias says.

—I didn't say so, did I?

—In for a penny, in for a pound.

61

—I said that there were no ladies who had the opportunity to come over on Christmas Eve.

—Håkan travels too much, Anita says. He has no time for a family, not yet. And the firm is doing better than ever, right?

It is. The printing firm, which Gustav once started and Håkan has taken over, has more than quadrupled its operations in just a few years, since Håkan was appointed the CEO and Gustav retired. The company now belongs largely to Håkan, while Anita and Gustav have only a small number of shares, just for the sake of it. Linda wasn't considered competent enough since she didn't finish business school. And they threatened her in every way possible so that she would realize she was missing out on something. Linda knew she was. But she never wanted to run or own the firm.

—What about those printers in Italy, are they any good? Gustav says.

—The best in Europe, Håkan says quietly and flattens his short and rather thin blond hair. Owning the majority of them is our biggest stroke of luck. The quality they deliver isn't to be seen anywhere else: photographers, artists…basically, all quality books are printed there. And the market for coffee-table books, like the one you received, is growing. Books like that.

He points at a thick book with a bird on the cover. Anita and Gustav both lean forward, and Anita pats the book.

—How exciting, Anita says.

—What's it about, really? Gustav says.

—Birds, Anita says.

—He's a nature photographer. He documents the special conservation areas. Beautiful pictures, Håkan says.

—Yes, very beautiful, Anita says. Is he Swedish? There might be images from Falsterbo?

—He's Italian, Håkan says. But it's possible he has been in Sweden.

—Otherwise you should invite him. He would appreciate it if he likes birds?

—Mom, there are perhaps other places on the earth's surface that are more fun, Linda says.

Anita lifts her liqueur glass filled with chocolate-colored Bailey's, the contents threatening to spill on her lap.

—The good news is that the company is doing well, Anita says encouragingly. But now I would like to hear some news from you, Linda. How's work?

—As usual, Linda says and stirs her coffee, scraping the bottom. She knows Anita dislikes it since it will damage the delicate porcelain in her grandmother's old mocha cups, but considering they are only used at Christmas, the wear is probably minimal. Linda takes out the tiny silver spoon and puts it on the tray.

—How nice, Anita says. It's fortunate that you both have work. I don't think you would have come as far in the art world. Sorry.

What Anita wants to say is that finance is a better and safer option than cultural studies. Linda being a middle manager in the accounting department at a publishing house is something that makes Anita more proud than if Linda had been a curator at a museum, a role Linda still dreams about. But the museum world is a tight circle, and Linda has no contacts. Most of those she studied with in Lund are based in Stockholm, the few working in the cultural sector that is. Many, like Linda, have some other education as well and keep themselves in the borderland between culture and commerce.

—And Tobias has a lot to do—that we know already, Anita says and looks at Gustav. Don't we, Gustav?

—Yes, we do. And we hope it will bear fruit. Education has never been a bad choice.

Linda smiles. It didn't sound like that when she gave up business school to focus on cultural sciences. Both her parents had considered it "a hobby." And they both had a field day when Linda told them about her job in the accounting department. They believed cultural sciences had been an unnecessarily long and expensive detour and that she had lost three, almost four, years. Meanwhile, they had also shoved her out of the family business. She had to face the consequences. And she did. Linda has never whined, never commented on their decision. But she knows they have a bad conscience because they always want to ensure that she and Tobias survive.

Gustav clears his throat.

—We have been thinking, me and Anita, that you are struggling, you and Tobias, he says, facing Linda. And you never whine. It's been many years now since Håkan took over the firm, and it's his business, so we can't do anything for you there.

Linda squirms on the couch. She hates this talk about money, and she knows it's the same for Håkan. There is nothing to discuss.

—Therefore, we have a little extra Christmas present for you. Actually, it's basically all set, and we had to leak this to Tobias to get the documents ready, so now we are only waiting for your signature.

He takes out a plastic folder and pulls two papers out of it.

—It's the house. Our house, that is. This—

He stretches out his arm and makes a semicircular motion, looks around as if everything were new to him.

—The house was once given to your mother, he explains. It was my mother who showed foresight, your grandmother. She herself had received the house as a gift from your grandfather so that if something were to happen, no one could claim the property. Back then, a lot could happen if the husband died. The relatives could argue that they were entitled to things that didn't belong to them, and among your grandfather's relatives there were one or two he wanted to keep at a distance. So when we got married, Anita and I, my mother saw to it that Anita became the owner. Now it doesn't matter, but it was a nice gesture. At least that was what we thought.

Linda is petrified. What is he saying? Her mother is giving her the house? Or them? And Tobias—has known?

Her eyes could pop from their sockets as she stares at the papers on the coffee table. Her father wags his pen expectantly and smiles, just like her mother, who leans toward her and pats her on the cheek.

Linda jerks from the touch of the damp hand that smells of—onions?

—It's time to forget the past and look forward.

What she is trying to say is that Linda hasn't been part of the now-successful company, and this is a way to relieve her aching conscience since she understands that Håkan lives a good life, while Linda and Tobias are struggling in the suburbs.

—But, no...And what about Håkan?

Linda can't think of anything else to say. She swallows, swallows again, gasping for air.

—You can't..., Linda says.

But Anita answers that of course they can, and it's not that they expected any gratitude, it's just a gesture to make things equal.

—And Håkan has been informed and given his approval—haven't you, Håkan?

—It's your house, Håkan says. You do as you wish. I don't need it.

—Håkan, it's not fair, Linda says and rolls her eyes, to make him understand that he must protest.

She needs to postpone this decision.

—What's going on? Tobias says. Can't you be happy? It's amazingly generous, he says facing first Anita and then Gustav. I'm sorry. Linda's just shocked.

—I don't understand why, Linda says. I don't understand at all. We haven't asked for this, Mom.

—You may not get everything you ask for and you may not ask for everything you get.

Linda gets up from the sofa.

—And we just want to help you, financially.

—We don't need money, Mom. We'll be fine. Right, Tobias? We have enough money, don't we?

She stares at a point above his head because she can't meet his eyes, doesn't want to see his sweaty, ruddy face and his happy countenance. He must have been delighted when he signed these papers giving him a new house at no cost, pretending, on one hand, to live with Linda and on the other, secretly, with another woman.

—No, it's not as if we need to borrow any money, Tobias says and reaches for the whiskey bottle standing on the table. He pours too much of the orange-brown liquid and sets the bottle back with a bang on the glass surface. Anita moves it to a coaster.

—It isn't about borrowing money, Anita says impatiently. We want to make sure you have a capital.

In Linda's mind, it's not a capital. It's a millstone around her neck, for how can they afford to live in this big, drafty house? They can't just sell it. And she doesn't want to stay here, not on any terms.

—But how did you plan around this? Linda says with despair in her voice. Will you keep living here? And pay the rent, right? Because we can't pay for two houses. We can't bear all the costs—it's impossible!

—Calm down, Gustav says. Nothing happens right now. Everything is as before. It's above all a technical agreement.

—But why? You could have written it in your will!

Linda's voice rises in falsetto, and she looks around, but everyone just seems to think she's embarrassing herself.

—Excuse me, she says. I have to…I'll be back.

*

Linda tries to focus on her own reflection in the uneven surface of the toilet mirror, but she can't. It's as if she were heavily drunk, which she isn't. Her hair sticks to her sweaty face.

—Bloody stupid Christmas, she says as she pulls down her panty hose.

She sits down with a thud on the toilet, hitting her elbow on the wall. She must think clearly. What's going on? Why does she have to be grateful, and why hasn't Tobias stopped everything, told them to rewrite their will with a mention that the house should be theirs? Håkan could even sign it, saying he accepted it. Or—why not just say it was her house? Why should Tobias have a part in it anyway? And now they are waiting out there for her to sign the papers and let this end as an altogether super-successful Christmas.

Because they don't know what an idiot their son-in-law is. They don't have a clue how he has deceived their daughter for four years, that he pretends to live with another woman, and that he even goes house hunting with her, while Linda empties boxes of their old crap in their basement—in case they move, eventually.

The pieces fall into place. They must have been thinking about it for a while, that the house should become her and Tobias's. Which is why they insisted on opening those old moving boxes in the basement, in order to know what to take and what to leave. And Tobias has played the game, making sure Linda takes care of her part of the contract, even before it's signed. While he takes his mistress on house hunts. For he must know that if he and Linda were to divorce, he would get a considerable amount of money when this house is sold. Did he tell Maja to pay Linda a visit, to speed up things? In that case, she wouldn't have come before Christmas. Or does he think it's possible to force Linda to sign?

She takes the white terry-cloth towel and wipes her sweaty face. The towel is smeared with brownish orange from foundation and blush that won't stick to her shiny face. Does she tell them now that they will divorce? It's impossible. She can't ruin everything for the children.

She sees Håkan in front of her, how he just shakes his head at her behavior. Håkan is calm, serene. As calm as their dad. They are also very much alike in appearance with broad shoulders and the same downy blond hair that won't lie still. Sturdy. Tobias is, too, but more—Danish. Loutish. And his hair isn't blond; it's almost yellow. She laughs, but her face contorts into a grimace, and she closes her eyes and breathes deeply to keep from crying. His hair is yellow, as if there had been an error while dyeing it. She never saw it like that before, but it's an unnatural color. And then her mother, with her sprayed helmet of hair. Linda knows she resembles her mother, her long, narrow, and pointed pale face. Bland.

She pulls irritably at her hose, which she now realizes are twisted, before she opens the door and tries to focus on walking straight. Don't cry.

*

They are still where they were when she left the room, and everyone looks up at her, even the children, who apparently know what has happened, or will happen.

—Are we moving? Lotta says, jumping up and down. Are we staying with Grandma and Grandpa?

Linda laughs a little and explains that probably isn't the idea. Anita looks embarrassed.

—A big happy extended family, that would be something! No, dearest, although that would be much fun, we won't live together, Anita says.

—Generation accommodation, huh? Gustav says.

—Now, just sign below so we can open the champagne, Tobias says.

There are now five champagne glasses and a magnum bottle of champagne on the table; to celebrate this the happiest of all the Christmases, the one when Linda and Tobias got a house. A Christmas they will never forget. A Christmas no one will forget, perhaps not even the children.

Håkan nods toward her. They are all in this together, aren't they? The whole thing is a puzzle, and she's the last piece. So what should she say or add?

—Isn't it enough if Tobias has signed? she says. I mean, we're married.

—We want both of you to be the owners.

—I thought the house was passed on to the women in the family, she says. As private property.

She's pulling it too far, but she wants to delay it all and make them understand that they can't do it.

—It has never been a private property in that way, only technically owned by your mother and your grandmother, so the outside world would know it was theirs. But that doesn't matter now, right?

Her mother's voice is hard, and she looks straight through Linda, as if she wants to tell her something. To stop being so childish, maybe. Her mother has decided, and she will not see her plans fail.

Gustav waves the pen again. He looks dejected, and Linda understands that they all expected a happier outcome of this offer, this amazing generosity. Linda is, as usual, the one who makes things very complicated.

—If it's money you need—, Anita says.

—We have money, Mother, Linda says.

Anita's facial features are tense, and she glances toward Gustav nodding in his armchair.

—Then please calm down, Anita says. You know I get upset by that tone. And your father and I have no reason to be guilty, right, Gustav? You had a chance. You had two chances, and Håkan took it. And now we would like to give you the house, which must be enough.

Håkan raises his glass of cognac and spins it in his hand.

—Yes, we know that story, Tobias says. And no shame on either of you, right? Linda hasn't said that she wants anything from you or from Håkan, has she?

69

—No, I certainly hope not, Anita says, shaking her head so that her helmet of hair swings.

Gustav clears his throat and holds out the fountain pen again.

—Will you sign so that we can celebrate?

Linda takes the pen, and although she hesitates, she signs the papers. It must be possible to change it if she needs to.

—There, there! Gustav says and pops the champagne. Cheers, everyone! Cheers to you, Linda and Tobias, and to your new home!

Linda lifts her glass and toasts her parents, avoiding Tobias's glance, and takes a big gulp of the golden liquid while sweat trickles down her back.

*

—Tobias, she says in a low voice. Tobias? Shall we leave?

He doesn't answer. His fingers fly over his mobile phone's keypad, and something that looks like a smile spreads across his rosy cheeks. A yellow lock of hair dangles from his forehead, and his broad shoulders move in a suppressed giggle. He finishes his champagne.

Linda rises.

—We need to go. Thank you for tonight, she says loudly and firmly, but inside, her body is shaking of sadness and despair.

—We've hardly had time to talk. The girls don't seem too tired? Anita says.

She challenges Linda in a way she wouldn't Tobias.

—What? Tobias says, looking up from the screen. Shall we leave? Linda? We've had a good time, Anita. Don't worry.

The girls are super-tired. Fia has tried to fall asleep on Linda's lap for the last half hour, and Linda has barely managed to keep her awake. She knows that they have a twenty-minute walk home, and at least one of the children must walk on her own.

Tobias gets up, thanks Anita, and hugs her as hard as he did when they arrived and then hugs her again, as if to emphasize how great this night has been.

Linda walks past him, letting her worn, now rubberized indoor shoes squeak against the parquet, hoping that the black soles will leave ugly marks that will never go away. Behind her, Tobias's weight makes the floor creak.

—See you all again soon, Tobias says to Anita, and Linda wonders if he understands how little they will see each other in the future.

—Thank you for tonight, and for all the presents, Linda says. The food was delicious as usual, Mom. And thanks for—the house.

Gustav gets up, comes over to Linda, and gives her a hug while he mumbles something in Linda's ear, but she's too upset to hear what he says. Merry Christmas, perhaps, but who cares about that now?

*

There's something soft and quiet over the Christmas shimmering suburb when Linda, Tobias, and the girls slowly walk next to each other through the desolate streets. That's to say, Tobias carries Fia on one arm, holding a paper bag with Christmas gifts in the other hand, while Linda tries to get Lotta to walk just a few more steps. She has left the poster at her parents'; she will pick it up later on. Her mother wrinkled her nose when she understood there would be things left standing in the corners, which she doesn't like. Linda doesn't even want to bring it home, ever.

From the windows of the houses glow warm yellow lights; Christmas trees and candlelights cast long shadows in the white gardens. There's a light snowfall. Linda doesn't recognize herself anymore. The soothing atmosphere has changed to contempt for everyone and everything that doesn't fit in, all those who cannot afford to live here.

—Who were you texting? she asks.

—The job. You know, there's a lot this time of the year, with new computers and systems. Must do some work over the weekend—

—Yeah.

—But tomorrow I'm free. Tomorrow it's just you and me and the children. It will be great. I can pick up the poster so we can get it up on the wall.

—It can wait.

—Don't you like it?

For a moment she has the urge to tell everything, so he can stop playing theater, but then she hesitates. It's still Christmas. But that poster will never end up on the nail in the bedroom, where it apparently has already hung.

—Sure. We ought to see those water lilies for real sometime. Where they are, outside Paris.

—Water lilies? They're the same as in the pond in the woods, aren't they? We don't even have to go there. You can watch them every day when you wake up.

His laughter irritates her more than ever as she knows he promised Maja a trip to Paris. If he only knew that she knows. If he only knew that she met his mistress.

—We're a good team, you and I, he says. It's just too good.

He doesn't say "too good." He says *"fortraeffligt"* with the Danish intonation Linda always loved, but right now she doesn't want to hear him express how good they are together.

She's suddenly convinced that he thinks she should have access to the family business. Why else wouldn't he even so much as protest or say "it's just too much" when they offered them, gave them, the house?

—And now we have a big house, too! As soon as your parents move out, we are moving in. It will be amazing.

—They will ask us to pay for their accommodation, if you didn't get that, Linda says. Which is blackmail. It will be blackmail.

—Oh, they could ask Håkan for money in that case. They can sell their part of the company to him. They can't come to us, and if they do, we'll get back at them. You shouldn't worry. They haven't thought it through—that's my take on it—but now it's done. Let's go home and get a good night's sleep. Perhaps not just sleep, huh? he chuckles.

—I will sleep anyway, she says.

She shudders at the thought of him even putting a hand on her, or still worse, his heavy body wallowing over her. Never. Never again.

—I will sleep, she repeats.

When Linda wakes up to a soft child's hand patting her on the cheek, she doesn't know where she is. There's a metallic taste on her tongue, reminding her they drank champagne, a lot of champagne, last night at her parents' house, and when she remembers why, she opens her eyes and faces Fia's bright smile.

—Mom. I'm hungry, she says in what is meant to be a whisper but which wakes Tobias.

—Get out of here, he says, and pushes Fia out of the bed. We will be down shortly.

When Fia disappears and Linda leans back against the pillow to collect her thoughts, he presses himself against her and fondles her breasts. She sits up, gets out of bed, and goes into the bathroom with nausea stinging in her throat. She takes her bathrobe from the hook and walks down the stairs.

—Aren't you coming back? Tobias shouts.

She doesn't answer. She puts together the pieces of what happened yesterday and why she signed something she doesn't want, something she now regrets. She was forced. That's how it is. They forced her—everyone forced her. Why? Why would her parents get rid of the house? Why do they want to punish her and Tobias with owning something they can't afford to live in?

—Ah, the smell of coffee, Tobias says as he enters the kitchen. Linda tries to remember if they ever had any tradition on Christmas Day. Probably not. Same old cheese, spreads, and strawberry jam and a rather boring loaf of bread. Fia has already had her breakfast. Lotta is poking a finger in the butter under the slice of cheese.

—Don't play with the food, Linda says. Eat the sandwich now, please.

—Are we moving? Lotta asks.

74

—We'll see. Not now anyway. Grandma and Grandpa still live in their house until they find something else, so I have no idea.

—Will we get our own rooms?

—We'll see, I said. Now, finish your sandwich. I'm sure you'll find some Christmas-morning programs on TV.

It feels like it takes forever for Lotta to finish eating, and then finally, Linda and Tobias are on their own. He slurps his coffee, and she shudders. Can't he just stop being such a slob?

—We must get out today, he says.

—Your mistress, Maja, came here the other day, she says.

He slurps again, as if he didn't hear what she said, but instead of swallowing, he looks at her and she sees how he struggles, as if the truth is hard to swallow, as if there were pebbles and then mountains in that coffee.

—What?

—You heard me. She was here last week.

—She would have told me.

Linda takes a breath she doesn't even feel, one breath without oxygen. Her head spins.

—You little shit. You fucking piece of shit. You can go to hell. Or just move to one of those houses you've been checking out with her. Or perhaps to that apartment where I live?

Tobias moves his weight from one leg to the other before he gets up, takes the coffee cup, and turns his back on her.

Between them grows a wall of barbed wire.

He raises his hands against his head, rubs his temples, and rests with all his weight against the sink. It looks as if he is stretching one calf.

—I…I'm sorry, Linda. I thought…I didn't mean to…*Faen.* I don't get it. It's not…Sorry.

Linda listens to the sounds of the TV and then the bright voices of the girls, the delight. She lifts her cup, but her hand is trembling so badly that she has to support it with the other. She freezes and

75

sweats at the same time, and her head pounds. Now, there's no way back, no pretending. Her thoughts flutter like a collapsing house of cards, helter-skelter. There is no right or wrong.

"This is for real," she thinks. "I have no life."

Tobias turns to face her.

—I hope you can forgive me.

He pulls his hand through his hair, and that blond lock of hair falls onto his forehead. He looks like a small child who has been caught with his hand in the cookie jar, and there is a faint smile on his lips that Linda can't interpret. Is he sad or embarrassed? Does he think it's embarrassing that he failed to keep it a secret, that his mistress screwed up what was a watertight arrangement?

—It won't be repeated, he says. Really—really it's over.

—Oh, yeah?

Over? How can it be "over" when he was house hunting with Maja a month ago?

He approaches her with his hands outstretched, as if he wants to hug her. Linda moves farther into the kitchen sofa, not wanting to be caught in his sticky familiarity.

—It's nothing, not anymore. I'm—sorry. What more can I say? She, Maja, doesn't want to hear or believe that it's over. But I have you. And the children. I want to be with you. Today and every day.

Linda nods frantically. He's right. He has got her and the kids and a house and, since yesterday, yet another house.

—You had, you mean. Because after what she told me, you can forget about me. Once and for all, please forget about me because I will forget about you. And when Christmas is over, you can move out. Why not to her place?

His big hands hang along the sides of his heavy body, and his bare arms, with reddish hair, glow white against his robe.

—I won't move, he says. Why would I? We're good together.

She closes her eyes. Are they good together? She wonders what he's comparing them to because if you're good together, you don't

76

need someone else—you don't need to seek comfort elsewhere. Good together. She can't explain it herself. She has never compared their relationship to anything. But now that she knows what Tobias has done, she can't, in any way, share his point of view.

He clears his throat and pulls out the chair opposite her, and she opens her eyes.

—We need to talk about this, he says.

Linda feels queasy. The tension, the past week's continual inhalation, is being released, and now, when she gets oxygen into her lungs and into her head, she wants to spew it all out, everything she has withheld. She stands up and leans backward to avoid getting close to him, and he lifts one hand to grab her arm, but she shrugs and screams like a scared mouse.

—It's Christmas. We can't do anything about it today. You could have waited. Did you have to bring it up now? he says as if he believes it will pass, as if it were a headache, an upset stomach, or perhaps a children's disease—some unknown rash that will be healed over in a few days.

—I have to…I have to get out, she says, and almost stumbles over Fia standing in the doorway.

—What are you doing? she says with wide eyes.

There's something about children that makes it impossible to hide feelings from them. They suck in the moods and words like sponges and ask questions that can't be answered.

What are they doing? Linda would like to understand that, too. They talk as adults do; they don't even argue. There's nothing to argue about. It's over. It doesn't exist anymore, what they were discussing, what Tobias thinks they should talk about. Linda has no words, nothing to say, nothing to add.

—We're—discussing a thing, Tobias says when Linda doesn't answer. But we can do that some other time. Let's plan the day!

He pats his knees to make Fia approach and sit down, but she stops in the doorway, and Linda walks past her and up the stairs.

—Where are you going? Fia says.

The stubborn child wants answers. Clear answers.

—I need to shower. Go to your father.

She stands in the shower and turns on the hot water so that it steams and almost scalds her breasts. But it doesn't matter if she burns up. With her back against the white tiles, she slides down until she sits huddled, with water splashing over her head, and lets the tears flow, gush, flood. There's no one to notice. She sobs so much that she can't breathe, pressing her hands to her eyes, to her mouth.

It's Christmas Day, and she has just ruined it for everyone, including herself. And now she must get up, get dressed, and spend time with her family as if nothing has happened. Because it's Christmas. And because she has nowhere to go and no one to tell. This is the family she has and what she thought was all she needed.

Linda's jaw clenches so hard that her head creaks. She shouldn't be the one who is punished because of Tobias being unfaithful, but now, suddenly, it's all her fault. What had she expected? She waited for a week, concerned about everyone else's feelings. She's been a good girl.

She gets out of the shower and looks at her red eyes in the bathroom mirror. Tobias is waiting for her in the bedroom.

—Get out.

—We have to—

—Get out.

—We should go pick up the poster.

Linda wraps the towel tighter around her body.

—Is there anything you want to tell my parents? Maybe say "Excuse me for stealing your house"? And, perhaps, ask them to tear up those papers?

He twitches, opens his eyes, blinks, a little confused.

—Why? he says.

—Because we're getting divorced, Tobias. And the house shouldn't be yours. Not a single square meter will be yours.

—But it is already, he says. I signed a month ago. What you signed yesterday doesn't matter. We have to share it, Linda. The house is already mine.

The days are filled with silence. Linda and Tobias only talk to the children, not to each other. Linda has downloaded the forms for divorce and filled them out, and even though Tobias refuses to sign, she posted them when he left for work on the second day of Christmas. Did he go to his job? Or did he go to Maja to celebrate Christmas with her, trying to tell her that he needs to be with the children and his ex-family, because that's easier, but that he's free, now?

He picks up the poster, too, and hangs it on the hook in the bedroom. Linda immediately removes it.

—What's wrong with the poster? You said you liked it. I think it's fine.

He might think it'll pass and that Linda will change her mind. She eats so little that she almost faints when the weekend comes, and she asks him to take the children somewhere so that she can sleep. She lies in bed and stares at the ceiling and lets the tears run down her cheeks until the pillow is cold and wet.

*

They will celebrate New Year's at the Hamklints'.

All of them, of course. At Bibbi and Peter's everything's cool. The kids go to the same preschool, and they know each other well. Easy as pie.

This is the third time they will celebrate together, which means it's now a tradition. They had a good time when they started two years ago, and now it's more about knowing they have somewhere to go so they aren't alone on New Year's Eve. Though that's just what Linda wants, to be completely alone. To dwell on the emptiness that penetrates her body.

Two years ago, it had started off a bit weirdly with a few board games that no one understood. Moreover, Peter and Tobias weren't very close, and Linda had barely made it through midnight, but then Peter announced that they should go to Thailand the following year, which in the middle of the night and with a glass of champagne in one hand sounded like the greatest idea.

Last year, when they were in Thailand together, it was much easier just because it was warm. Linda wishes she could remember what it's like to stand in a thin summer dress in the tropical night, not freezing, but the only thing that comes to mind is her disappointment that Tobias wasn't there. He had been forced to change his plans just before Christmas; a major customer needed help around the New Year, and it would have been impossible for him to leave. A major customer. It sounded important, so—obvious. How could she have guessed that he wasn't telling the truth? And he had not insisted on them canceling the trip because he realized that Linda had been looking forward to the trip and to the summer heat that she loves.

Linda holds the phone in one hand, ready to call Bibbi and say they won't make it this year.

She and Bibbi still haven't talked, and she's not sure she wants to. It's as if Tobias's infidelity and Linda having Maja in their kitchen is no longer something to discuss. At least not with her voice trembling with tears, wanting to hear that she has done nothing wrong. She might want to dwell on it, and she does, but she can't decide what response she's expecting. She's afraid someone will say that she's stupid not to have noticed.

Fia has had a fever all morning, she began complaining about a headache and then watched TV with her eyes half-closed but didn't want anything for lunch, her head hanging. Now, at half past four, she has vomited three times. Between the outbursts, she's been dozing, burning with fever.

—I think you should go, and take Lotta, Tobias says. I'll stay and take care of Fia.

He sounds almost relieved. They will avoid having to play "happy couple" in front of Bibbi and Peter.

—I'm not sure Lotta will make it through the night, Linda says.

—Who cares? Go. You needn't stay until midnight.

Lotta gets to decide, and she decides she wants to go and she wants to see the fireworks and stay up until midnight.

—Please come, those of you who are still standing. You shouldn't stay at home! Bibbi laughs on the phone, and so the matter is settled.

It's strange to prepare to go to a party without Tobias. To put on a dress, have her hair done, put on makeup—things she has only done for his sake, for him to see that she makes an effort to look her best, even though she's a tired mother of two small children. She stares inside the worn, pink makeup bag: a tube of foundation in a too-light-beige color, black mascara, a terra-cotta blush that looked orange already on Christmas Eve, and a pale-pink lipstick. She has unconsciously forgotten that they were going to a party; it happens that she buys something she doesn't need but wants for special occasions—a glittery powder, an eye pencil in gold, or a darker lipstick. And each year, she wonders why it was so important, something that will only be used one evening and that Tobias doesn't even care about—he hasn't looked at her in four years. The pale-pink lipstick doesn't match the orange-brown blush, but there's nothing to do about that now. There's nothing to do about anything. It's too late.

It takes ten minutes to walk to the Hamklints', and the streets are well-known to both Linda and Lotta. Yet the darkness is penetrating, and Linda has to make an effort to not walk too fast and transmit her discomfort to Lotta, who is holding her hand tightly. The lights of the taxis speeding past search their bodies, creeping under their skin. Lotta's tiny face is glowing with anticipation.

Many of the streetlamps are broken along the path that leads to the townhouse area, and what is usually just a bunch of trees is now, in the darkness, a forest, growing larger and deeper with every step. The wind increases, and Lotta stumbles beside her. Linda's fear fades as the path opens up in a well-lit roundabout, just as safe and welcoming as a marina where boats come sailing in from the darker waters. There are pops and whistles everywhere as the sky lights up with flashes of fireworks that have gone off too early.

Lappängen, where the Hamklints live, is set on a slope down toward the water, nestled in the forest that forms a natural noise wall facing the passing highway and geographically sandwiched between Södertunet and Norrtunet like a shard of confusion: the square boxes don't fit into the rosy wooden villa idyll. When you enter the area, the scene is deceiving: only two of the houses in the front row have a view over the water and they are also freestanding and not townhouses. The townhouses are obscured by the grove surrounding the entire area, which also turned out to be a common, with an interdiction to remove any trees.

The row of houses where Bibbi and Peter live aspires only to geniality and coziness, which is now reflected in the adults and children dressed up for New Year's parties who laughingly dart into the warmth of the homes from their cars parked on the street. Linda gets the feeling that she doesn't belong here, where she comes through the forest, sneaking in from behind the houses, like a gnome. She slows down her steps and pulls a little at Lotta's hand. They should have taken the car, but she doesn't like to drive even the shortest distances when she has been drinking, and after all, it is New Year's Eve. She has shown up at the party, and she wouldn't want to miss out on a glass of champagne. She stamps her feet to get the heat back in her toes.

The doorbell is broken, and has been since the Hamklints moved in. Linda knows that it rarely pays to use the knocker either; it's better to just step right into the noise and shout, "Hello!"

The second they step over the threshold, Bibbi calls out that there's food for the kids. The kitchen table is almost knocked over when four children throw themselves over the meatballs and sausages. Bibbi hugs Linda and rushes to the cellar to fetch champagne, and Linda has a perception of a knock on the door, but it might as well be at the neighbor's. She looks for Peter, who has somehow passed by without greeting her, and now he comes out from the living room and heads for the door.

He leans forward and hugs somebody, probably a woman as short as Bibbi; she's undetectable behind his broad back. When Peter moves aside and stretches out his hand to who must be the woman's companion, Linda sees a woman's glossy dark hair.

—Did you invite Gabriella? she whispers to Bibbi, who puts a champagne bottle on the counter and stretches for glasses from a cabinet.

Bibbi shrugs and grimaces.

—It was Peter's idea, I guess…I'm not sure. I know them as well as you do.

—But on New Year's Eve? Linda says.

—Bibbi, the guests are here! Peter shouts from the hall.

Linda stands still and looks at the sausage- and meatball-eating children while Bibbi gives her upper arm a squeeze, grimaces again, and disappears behind her into the hallway.

To invite Gabriella and Mats is almost equivalent to treason in her eyes. And why hasn't Bibbi said anything? Linda doesn't know Gabriella's husband Mats, but since she doesn't like Gabriella, it somehow feels impossible she would have a nice husband. As far as Linda knows, Bibbi isn't close to them either, so they must be Peter's friends since it was his idea to invite them.

Gabriella has become the one person she and Bibbi gossip about in the many hours spent giggling over a cup of coffee after preschool. Gabriella, with her perfect hairstyle, her perfect calm, her perfect children, her exquisite, perfect clothes. Her and Mats's children are never at preschool if they have the slightest cold. Their overalls are never dirty, and their clothes are never crinkled or worn. Gabriella is a stay-at-home mom, a housewife. The perfect housewife. Now she glides down the hallway's worn rug and into the kitchen in her ten-centimeter high heels, wearing a tight, black, sequined dress. Linda looks down at her own shiny flat ballerina shoes and tries to even out the imaginary crinkles of the flowery nylon dress she, an hour ago, thought was rather festive.

—Linda, how great to see you! Where's Tobias? Gabriella says as she hugs Linda like they were old friends.

—Fia isn't doing well. Tobias is at home with her, Linda says.

—Oh, I'm so sad to hear, Gabriella says mildly, looking around the small kitchen. This is so cute, she says, and turns to Bibbi.

Linda wonders what she, the perfect woman, sees as cute—is it the strange bright lights or the Santas and angels the children made last month at the preschool and that are invading the kitchen counter? Or is it perhaps the Christmas cards on the refrigerator door, the same kind of Christmas cards that Linda and Tobias have in their kitchen, showing pale kids in Santa hats? It couldn't look anything like this at Gabriella and Mats's home. They live three hundred meters away, in one of the two houses with a sea view.

—I've never been inside these houses, Gabriella says. They're really cozy. I understand why you like it so much.

Bibbi nods and says they will renovate the kitchen this summer, that Peter and his brother will do it themselves. Linda looks at her in surprise, but Bibbi avoids her gaze.

—Where are your children? Linda asks.

—Oh, they're at home with the babysitter. It just complicates things if they're up late. We prefer having the same routines as usual. Children are most comfortable with that—no surprises.

No surprises. As usual. Linda nods and squeezes her left hand so that the nails cut into her thumb's thick skin.

—No, why are we standing in the kitchen! Peter says and claps his hands before he grabs the champagne bottle and leaves for the living room. Bibbi sails along, and Mats, who still hasn't said hello to Linda, slips by. Linda is alone in the kitchen, where Lotta just stretched out her hand and whispered that she doesn't like the meatballs.

Linda takes one meatballs and puts it quickly in her mouth, nodding toward Lotta. It tastes of allspice. She puts a napkin over the leftovers on the plate and throws it in the trash can before she follows the others into the living room. In the doorway Peter stops her.

—Is it the winter vomiting disease? he asks.

—Look, it's only Fia who's ill. Not us. Could just as well be food poisoning. And she often vomits when she gets a high fever, like now.

—You need to be cautious this time of the year. The winter vomiting disease is very contagious. You basically only have to breathe in the same room to get it.

Linda smiles, wondering if he knows he hasn't even said "welcome."

—Well, yes, I know. If you want us to go leave, we will.

—No, no, that's not what I meant, but we're going to my mother's tomorrow—

Peter is interrupted by Bibbi coming into the kitchen, trying to find an ice bucket and more glasses.

—Let's toast! she cries. Cheers to Christmas being over and to a new year!

—Well, that was unnecessary, Peter says.

—It can only get better, Bibbi says and shakes the curls from her face.

—There's nothing wrong with Christmas. Please think of the children...You don't have to destroy everything for them.

—Seriously, it's nice that it's over, even if Christmas is cozy, Linda says.

Bibbi puts her champagne glass on the counter and turns to the stove. Peter breathes heavily, his nostrils pumping and the bald spot on his head, that he tries to cover with strands of hair, shining.

—Right, it's cozy for everybody, for kids, for adults, isn't it? That's why we celebrate Christmas and insist on skiing with your parents, Peter says.

—Where else would we be? In your mother's apartment in a housing program in one of the less charming suburbs of Stockholm?

They both leave for the living room.

Linda picks up after the kids, putting the dishes and cutlery in the dishwasher. The children's eager hands are reaching for the bowl of popcorn, and she hands it to Oliver, telling him they shouldn't eat it all at once.

—Hi Mats, Linda says when she enters the living room.

—Oh, hi, he says shaking her hand. Nice to see you. And where's the hubby?

He pats his straight blond hair. His light-blue shirt is open at the neck, and from the breast pocket of his marine-blue jacket, a patterned silk handkerchief folds over the rim, like a wilted tulip.

—He's taking care of a sick kid, Linda says.

Mats laughs mechanically as if he doesn't know what those words mean. There's a chance he doesn't.

Linda tries to talk to Bibbi instead, but her back is turned to Linda in a way that makes it impossible to engage naturally in the discussion she and Gabriella are having. She takes a sip of champagne, remembering New Year's Eve in Thailand, how she and Tobias tried to call each other, but the time zones had played a prank on them, and Tobias had blamed it on that he was working all the time. So there she stood on the restaurant's terrace, on her own, with a glass of champagne in one hand, feeling more alone than ever. The warmth had been of little comfort. She had thought of tsunamis and how she would save two children if it was to happen again. After half a glass of champagne, she had picked up Fia and Lotta, who were with a babysitter in Bibbi and Peter's apartment and had gone to bed.

—Yeah, but Linda forgot to pick up the kids the day before Christmas last year, remember?

Bibbi laughs beside her, giving way to Linda, opening the closed conversation.

Linda blushes and tries to laugh. She and Tobias had forgotten that the preschool closed early the day before Christmas, and Bibbi had to step in and pick up Fia and Lotta. Gabriella looks at her with big eyes.

—But that's awful for the kids! she says.

Bibbi laughs with Linda; they agree that these things happen— in their world.

—I don't think so, Bibbi says. My children love to be the last ones. That's when they get all the attention. Now, the teachers aren't super excited when I finally arrive, but they never show that to the kids.

—Educators, Gabriella corrects.

—It will be harder later on, Linda says.

Bibbi and Gabriella watch her and Linda looks away.

—After the holidays, I mean. You get used to being on holiday.

Gabriella tilts her head to one side.

—But you have family here, right? Your parents? And a brother, isn't it?

—Yes…I do. But my parents don't help us much. They have… other things to do. And my brother, well, he doesn't have the time, with his work.

—You know, I forgot that the preschool was closed just the other day, Bibbi adds quickly.

Bibbi tells how they had been standing outside the preschool pulling at the door. She had to bring the kids with her to work instead.

—But then in the afternoon I bumped into Gabriella in the store, she concludes. For the umpteenth time, you were stuck with your heel in that entrance grille.

It's Gabriella's turn to blush, and Linda has to look down to not laugh. That's a never-ending story between Linda and Bibbi.

—The heel broke, Gabriella says in a serious voice. So there I was, on tiptoe. It was so sweet of you to help me.

Bibbi smiles. Linda wonders what she did to help. Got some glue? Put Gabriella in a shopping cart?

—And so we came to the conclusion that you had nothing planned for the New Year, which was more easily fixed, Bibbi says to Gabriella.

A mistake is what this is. Gabriella and Mats must have forced themselves on Bibbi and Peter, who couldn't say no. But didn't Bibbi say it was Peter's idea? They are, nevertheless, almost neighbors.

—That's nothing to make fun of. They should change that entrance grille right away, Peter says.

Linda looks at him in surprise. Why does he care about Gabriella being stuck in her sky-high boots in a supermarket?

—We are so excited to be here, Gabriella says. Aren't we, Mats? Mats toasts and nods. Peter fills his glass.

—I'll just go check the last things in the kitchen, Bibbi says. Linda follows her and shuts the door behind them.

—Is Tobias also sick? Bibbi asks.

Linda shakes her head.

—But it's better that he isn't here.

She swallows, swallows again. She must say something.

—We're getting divorced.

Words she has never uttered, never thought she'd say. They sound strange and unpleasant, itchy. And both unreal and real. Her tears start flowing, these useless tears.

—What? Stop it. Now? I mean—why?

—He's had a mistress. For four years. Since Fia was born. She, the mistress, came to our home before Christmas, though only I was at home, me and the kids, but they were asleep. She told me everything, and she had clothes in the closet—

—What? You must—you've got to be joking! Haven't you noticed? Oh my God...

Bibbi takes a step back and throws her arms around Linda. She becomes entwined, like a package, not sure what to do. "Just keep it together," she says to herself.

She knows that it's the most distasteful part, that she hasn't even noticed Maja's clothes hanging next to hers. Or the makeup. Or that Maja has renovated the guest toilet, although that's not true.

—It's not a closet I use everyday...

The explanation falls flat on the floor.

—And she left other stuff, makeup..., she says over Bibbi's shoulder, as if it would sound more credible.

Bibbi lets go.

—But, my God, Linda, it can't be true. But are you sure, I mean are you—are you getting divorced? Serious? Have you told the kids?

—I have told no one. You're the only one who knows. Promise you won't tell. Promise.

Bibbi nods, and while she checks the potato gratin in the oven and arranges the salmon on the plates for the first course, Linda tells her the details in such a hurry she hardly remembers what she says.

—And what about Christmas? Must have been awful if you didn't tell the children. Do your parents know?

Linda shakes her head.

—You're the only one who knows.

—Wow. No, but...oh, my God. I never thought...I mean, you didn't either, I presume. How do you feel?

Linda finishes the last of the champagne. It's lukewarm, and there are no bubbles left.

—Awful.

—Come on, let's sit down. I'm totally shaky; you must be, too. You need more champagne. Can you bring two of the plates?

—You won't say anything?

*

Back with the others, Linda finds it difficult to converse. She glances at Bibbi to try to gain recognition, or a hint of understanding, but—nothing happens. And maybe it's for the better since she has asked Bibbi not to tell the others. Bibbi talks to Mats, and Peter talks to Gabriella. The dinner is too small for one comment to not be heard by everyone. Yet Linda hoped Bibbi would just put a hand on her shoulder or serve her a little more wine or simply toast. Instead, Bibbi ignores her.

Her mobile phone's ring tone is unwelcome, and the cutlery clattering against the plates is distinguishable when the conversations stop. Linda hesitates—maybe it's just her mother wanting to wish her happy new year. In that case, she doesn't want to wish it back.

—Shouldn't you take that call? Peter says.

Linda picks up the phone. The display says "home" in large letters. Peter leans toward her.

—Problems?

—Peter, stop it, Bibbi says.

Linda rises and walks out into the hallway while Bibbi disappears to the kitchen and Peter, Gabriella, and Mats tentatively try to start a new topic related to the three of them. Their small talk and Bibbi's noisy kitchen work create a wall between them, but Linda has a feeling that everyone's ears grow as large as saucepan lids toward her own increasingly rhythmic murmur. She turns off the phone and stares at the mess of children's jackets, overalls, and winter boots lying on the floor.

—Look, I think I should take Lotta and go home. Fia's fever is heading in the wrong direction. And it doesn't feel right to stay here with you. I'm really sorry.

—But can't Tobias fix that, give her something to bring the fever down? Bibbi says, entering with meat and potatoes. Can't you stay just for this? Or at least have some more champagne…Peter, could you open another bottle? Next year can only get better!

Bibbi toasts with a wobbly movement in the air and lifts the empty bottle toward Linda, who puts her hand over her glass.

—We were supposed to have the other bottle of champagne at midnight, Peter says.

—Thanks, I don't want more anyway. Fia isn't doing well. I'm so sorry. I'm a bit worried.

In reality, Tobias has also been sick for the last half hour. She doesn't want or dare to think about it, but she looks for the dessert she brought; the chocolate mousse is perhaps chock-full of bacteria. Then she would destroy the Hamklints' visit to Peter's mother's.

—Yes, then I think you should leave, Peter says hastily. No worries. It's a new year every year! And next year you will all be healthy, right? And Tobias will be back. It can't become a habit that he's off doing other things when we have decided to meet!

Linda smiles tensely but doesn't dare to look at Bibbi.

—No, no, of course not. He'll be back. He likes celebrations.

Half an hour later, Lotta finally understands that they must leave. Linda is sweaty and her dress is too tight and clings itself against her hose as she struggles to get Lotta into her overall. She wonders if Tobias will be awake when she comes home and if he has taken care of Fia or if she has been vomiting all over the house, left on her own.

The happy voices you associate with a party rise from the table; Gabriella, Mats, and Peter seem to have found each other and Bibbi's sparkling laughter spreads all the way out into the hallway.

Bibbi comes out and hugs Linda, long and hard.

—Darling, I'll talk to you soon. Take care. And take care of the children. You should stay here, you know.

—Another time, Linda says. Have fun...Bye! she cries out to the living room, but the others don't seem to hear.

—See you next week, Bibbi says. Call me if there's anything I can do for you. If you need to talk.

—Yeah. Sure.

Linda would have preferred to shout, "Why did you invite Gabriella?" so loud it echoes out to the driveway, but it's a lot easier this way. She doesn't destroy their New Year's celebration. They have each other.

*

Linda drags Lotta behind her on the slippery winter streets, watching all the happy people dancing and listening to the laughter seeping out through the open windows. She belongs nowhere, and now she's on her way back to a home where she doesn't want to be.

She tries to remember if she ever had a pleasant New Year's Eve, but all that comes to her mind are memories of drinks in plastic glasses, drunk men running around lighting fireworks, freezing cold summer cottages not intended for winter use and wet mist creeping flush with the ground, student parties where she couldn't find anyone she knew at midnight, and parties where her friends emptied her champagne bottle and locked themselves in a dressing room.

Then, she tries to convince herself that all the people she sees through the windows will wake up tomorrow and find their party wasn't a success.

Norrtunet lies quiet. There are no whistling fireworks, and the tiny houses seem to have decided not to celebrate. Linda puts the key in the door and draws a deep breath of fresh air before she opens it to the acrid smell of vomit. Tobias staggers toward her, his face a strange gray-green color. If she hadn't known better, she would have thought he was drunk.

93

—You could have stayed.

—They have new friends.

The New Year's must-do has disappeared, and they have turned over the reins to Mats and Gabriella. She will never again have to wait for the clock to strike twelve with any of them and remember that Tobias fooled her.

—Damn it, there were others? That could have been fun. It's so stupid that I caught this—

Tobias suddenly throws himself past her and into the guest bathroom.

Linda follows Lotta up the stairs and into the kids' room, making sure she goes to bed. Right next to Fia's bed is a yellow plastic bucket, but she sees, to her relief, that it's unused and Fia is asleep. She tucks Lotta in and then walks into the bedroom and sits on the edge of the bed. Bibbi's right. The new year can only get better.

When Tobias comes in, she doesn't even turn her head.

—I think you should move to the basement. First of all, you're sick. Second, I don't want to share the bedroom with you.

—Have you told Bibbi?

—What if? She's my friend.

—She has got nothing to do with us. What did you tell her?

—That we're getting divorced.

Tobias stops, presses the blanket to his chest and looks like a small child who wants comfort, or to perhaps get into her bed. Linda shudders at the thought.

—I don't want a divorce.

His voice is hoarse, and when he leans toward her, she feels his stinging breath.

—Do you hear me? I don't want it. There is no reason for it. I love you.

She hears herself whisper words she never thought she would say:

—But I don't love you.

94

"I hate you," she thinks, but she can't form the words and get them over her lips until the clock has passed midnight.

She hears Tobias vomit again in the guest toilet, and no one wishes her Happy New Year.

—Please have a seat.

The cured salmon and the potatoes with dill, all soft enough to be divided into small pieces even with a fork, is already on the table. The silver cutlery gleams as brightly as the silver candelabras, while the linen napkins lie like dead white doves over the plates. Anita lights the candles while Gustav puts the wine bottle in an ice bucket. They sit down at the dinner table, Linda on the short end with her back to the window, where she has always sat, and Anita and Gustav opposite each other, so they surround and enclose her. They are choking her without realizing it.

She's being cranked back in the time machine to the familiar and uncomfortable: Linda is eighteen again and should be doing something on a Friday night other than having dinner with her parents. The setting itches, like an old woolen pullover. She squirms in her seat.

Anita has already asked, "Did you see that the chairs are newly upholstered?" to which Linda politely answered yes, but she sees no difference from Christmas, just three weeks ago. It's the same cover as before, but Anita says they were so worn they had to do something—and that it was better to wait until after Christmas so the children wouldn't spill on the new covers. The winds of change don't always sweep over Södertunet.

Anita and Gustav give their take on how the opera was last week, but Linda only listens with one ear: not grand, a little too pointy, there's too much focus on the theater nowadays. You go for the music, so if you close your eyes, you can still enjoy that, but Gustav fell asleep. Anita tells her about the supper they had afterward, a true success, simple but tasty. It's a fun group of people, their opera gang, which is sometimes more of a movie bunch, sometimes a bridge team. Linda stares right in front of her. Hums a little.

—Well, how sad that you didn't go to Copenhagen, Anita continues. You don't see Anne that often, do you?

The salmon grows in Linda's mouth. She chews frantically, but she can't swallow the lump. She takes a gulp of wine, realizes that it's too big; it's like swallowing a tennis ball. When the acid rises into her nose, she sneezes straight out over the table. Anita and Gustav look at her with disgust.

—No, Linda says.

—What do you mean? Anita says. That you don't see Anne too often?

—It isn't sad that I couldn't go to Copenhagen.

—But you like Anne, don't you? She's so sweet. You could need a break, get a minivacation, and since you can always stay at Anne's place, you don't even have to spend any money on a hotel room. You looked tired at Christmas. And Anne is great with the girls.

—She was. Her eyes are failing her. Besides, we are getting divorced.

Anita's face loses all color. She puts down the cutlery and glances at Gustav before she turns to Linda. Gustav lowers his wineglass so slowly that Linda wonders if she's in a slow-motion movie.

—Divorce? What happened? What have you done? Anita says, her voice pitched so high it could crack glass.

—Nothing. Nothing at all. Tobias, on the other hand, has had a relationship for four years with a woman who came to see me some time ago.

Anita's pupils dilate, the color returning to her cheeks as if she was the one who'd been caught in the act. She puffs her rigid golden helmet of hair nervously, glancing again at Gustav before she wipes her mouth with her linen napkin.

—Isn't that a bit farfetched, to get a divorce? I mean, would that make anything better?

Linda reaches for her wineglass. This time, the wine burns all the way down to her stomach and soothes her temporarily. Farfetched? If her mother only knew.

—No, Mom, I don't believe there is another solution. How would you feel if someone had been cheating on you for four years? I've thought about it, wondered if I could pretend as if nothing had happened. But—that would be dishonest to myself. I didn't get it, but now I do. It's my turn to respond.

Red spots appear on Anita's throat while she sweeps the napkin over the table. Linda knows that her mother thinks she is a disappointment, the daughter who never shapes up or gets her act together, even though she appeared to be on track. A kind husband, not supertalented, but pleasant, cheerful, hardworking. Father of their two children. And now Linda falls back into financial insecurity, zero status, and with all the prerequisites for a normal suburban life flushed away. It's like in Monopoly, when you have to go back to "Go." Or "go directly to jail."

—But Linda dearest, you can't say that, there must be things you agree on. You still have children together. Think of the children, of the girls, please! And Tobias is…both pleasant and…well, you've enjoyed your life together. You haven't noticed anything strange in him—neither have we. I mean, you're as happy as ever, aren't you?

Gustav looks at his wife and then at his daughter and back again, his head lowered, a troubled look on his face. There's no sound from him, even though his mouth opens and closes like a goldfish's. He clears his throat.

—Yes, this is not good news, he says with a sigh. But please tell us if you need help. We had no idea…I mean…At Christmas, you seemed very good together. As your mother says, happy. You seemed to be a great couple—that's what we thought, wasn't it, Anita?

Linda looks down at the soft pink salmon on her plate. The smell of dill is overwhelming.

—You can't possibly believe it will get better if you divorce? Isn't there marriage counseling? So you can try, anyway. One shouldn't give up without a fight, Anita says.

—What are we going to try? Mom, Tobias has had another woman for four years! Four years! It sure seems as if he gave up a long time ago, don't you think?

—But then he would already have left you. And look at him— he's still around. There's a big difference, Linda. He didn't say anything because he wants to be with you. Time, yes. What is time, anyway? Four years. Could be long—or short.

Anita wiggles a little on her chair, and Linda takes a bite of the mushy potatoes. They're cold and the stew tastes of flour.

—My dearest, now, don't let a few days blur the picture. It must still be better, safer, for the kids if you stay together. Divorces are, in a way, a mild form of child abuse, Linda. It might not be easy for you and Tobias, but involving the girls in it...because you want things to be different. Perhaps you will change your mind? And where will you live?

—Stop, Mom. You don't understand what happened. Don't poke your nose into it. This isn't a point of discussion if that's what you thought. It was information.

Linda again reaches for her wineglass, her hand now shaking. Anita's mouth twitches in discontent when Linda gulps down what is left in the glass.

—Why do you complicate things? Anita says. Why hasn't Tobias been happy? Haven't you been kind to him? He must be missing out on something, which you should surely be able to discuss.

—Anita, it's probably not about being kind, Gustav hums between mouthfuls of salmon.

—Have I been kind to him? What do you mean by that? Has he been kind, cheating on me for four years? We've been a family,

Mom, a family with small children. It's based on that you trust each other, that you do what you have to do, taking care of each other, the children, the house, of the life you share.

—But that's what I mean, dearest. He has done well, hasn't he? I mean, you have had no suspicions against him. He has been a good father and a great support for you, too. Look at it from other perspectives, all perspectives, Linda.

Anita scrapes her cutlery against her plate and moves a piece of salmon around in the white sauce, as if to clean everything up, a sign of how upset she is.

—He must surely have missed something. Now don't make a big deal of this. He might very well have a good explanation from which you could also learn something.

—Anita, enough is enough, Gustav says and looks up from his plate. Now let Linda be. This is hard on her. Don't make her feel guilty.

Linda stares at her mother, boiling inside with held-back anger that pushes upward, as if she were a chimney. She wants to scream, but—they don't. This family doesn't scream.

—What the hell do you mean, Mom? she blurts out between lips that are so rigid her skin is nearly bursting.

She bashes the napkin on the table.

—What is it you want me to learn from my husband? That it's okay to fuck around with others when you have a wife and kids at home? That it's okay to let other people move into your house because you can make space in the closets or because your wife doesn't care about makeup? What? Is that what you want me to learn?

She leans a little closer to her mother and the candlelights flicker when she continues in a low voice:

—Then I can tell you that I don't want to learn and that I never will. I can't even believe this is how you want life to be—a stylish facade that hides a world where you pretend and lie to each other.

You're my mother, and you can't even support me or show some compassion instead of throwing all that crap on me. I am the one who suffers most from all this. You go on about the children when they don't even know what happened, and if a divorce is difficult for them—how do you think it is for me? Can you even understand what I'm going through?

Anita looks straight ahead. She purses her lips into a narrow dark-red streak, but Linda can't stop herself anymore.

—I'll try to be a happy and good mother anyway, let the days pass and do what needs to be done, and have this idiot I happen to be married to at home every day because I don't know what else to do. And you, you think I should ignore that Tobias has been having an affair for several years and that it's perfectly acceptable. Well, then sit here and lie to yourself in your nice house, in your stupid, bourgeois world where you all play by your own rules. Behind the four walls, you can do as you want. That's great. Good luck, Mom. Live the lie because I won't.

Linda fumes with anger as she barges through the hall. The mirror, which is no longer surrounded by ball ornaments, shakes on the wall. She grabs her coat from the hanger and snatches her purse from the chair at the entrance, slamming the door so hard the small pane of glass rattles.

She runs with tiny steps, trying to get away from the house, but long shadows seem to pull her into the past, into the family that doesn't speak of inconveniences, doesn't complain. "Solve the problem" has always been the motto. And, now, Linda tries not to solve the problem, but to sneak around it, to get out. Leaving everything behind in a tangle of relationships—and property. Because that's the real issue. If Linda divorces Tobias, the house will no longer be a family belonging.

The sharp evening air scrapes against her face, and she gets flashbacks from the past; how she tiptoes up to her room in the attic, trying to dismiss that feeling of inadequacy, that she can't behave and is unable to find a solution. Being left to her own destiny and thoughts indefinitely. Days. Weeks. Until she is taken into favor again, until her mother explains how this will be sorted out. But Linda is no longer a child, not a teenager either. She has her own life. She should be able to smile at her mother's mendacity, to ignore it.

The street is slippery, and she slows down at a street corner, suddenly not knowing where to go. She breathes heavily, almost panting, with her eyes closed. The freezing rain is like needles against her skin, and an angry heat pushes its way up her collar while her hair lies tight around her cheeks. She shivers, pulls her heavy, shaggy coat around her body.

A door opens in the dark facade on the other side of the street; bubbling laughter from people holding wineglasses seeps out of the door. A black dog silhouette gallops over the plot of land, frozen snow crunching under the animal's paws, and enters. Christmas lights are still hanging in the bushes along the road as if to melt the ice on the sidewalk.

The icy rain drips over her head and mixes with sweat, turning into a cold film closest to her body. She sees her mother before her, in her cashmere jumper set, smelling of camphor—how she pulls her cardigan around her when she sits down, asks Linda's dad to serve the wine, chirps about her life but doesn't ask a question. She's luminous in her own world, as if she was playing theater and the dining room was her setting. All the scenes are carefully rehearsed. And then the knife flying out of her mouth, stabbing the air. No, not a knife—it's a snake, a snake's nest: "He must surely have missed something" and "Maybe you can learn something?"

The shadow scene from the lighted house where the dog disappeared through the terrace door drags her eyes back. That's the way she would want it: happy, nice, easy, in sequined evening wear. She can't remember a single occasion when someone moved laughingly around in her kitchen with a glass of wine in one hand. Yes, she

102

can. They have had fun evenings with Bibbi and Peter, with her old high-school buddies, with Tobias's colleagues. But not in that way.

Heavy footsteps are approaching her from behind. The black and white, just passably shoveled sidewalk has frozen again and is a dangerous field both for her and for the man whose contours she now discerns. He stops in front of her. Linda turns her head away, her lips almost disappearing when she bites them tightly. Don't cry—don't appear weak.

—You must forgive your mother.

Her father is looking for words, breathless. His scarf is untied, maybe he didn't have time to tie it before he left. He keeps his beret in hand and spins it while he's seeking a way to express himself.

—Neither of us mean that what has happened is your fault. She cares for the girls, Linda, and she's worried for you. We both are. We are on your side. But you can sort things out. You can discuss this as adults do. It's never black or white in life. And you have so much together. Don't forget that.

Linda doesn't respond. Tears cover her cheeks like a wet carpet.

—Linda, Mom doesn't wish you any harm.

This time, it's different. They have reached an invisible limit to what she can take, and there are no words left, nothing to answer to.

—Dad, I don't care what she wants. But maybe she could learn something if she listened to any of Tobias's fantastic explanations and tried to see how easy it is to understand and forgive. I have fought like an animal to get our life together. It doesn't matter that I haven't known or seen any of this, but it is what it is. He has let me down. I can't trust him anymore.

Her voice crackles.

—I didn't think it would end like this, she says.

They stand in silence for a while, Linda looking quickly at her father, his tired, troubled face, his arms hanging down his sides.

103

He is unable to find more words and puts a trembling hand to her wet cheek.

—You'll call, won't you? he asks gently. We love you, my dearest child, he adds in a low voice and sighs and then grabs the fence with both hands to gain speed, enough to get back up the hill.

—Be careful, Dad, Linda whispers.

He doesn't hear her, and she wishes he had given her a hug. There's a sign hanging over his shadowy figure when he disappears.

"Solve the problem," it says.

Linda looks at the clock.

Who would rise, voluntarily, at half past seven on a Sunday morning in January? It's a brilliant idea, the one Marita has had. Linda's irritation rises with every second she looks at the thermometer which refuses to move above minus twelve degrees Celsius. All the other houses on the street are pitch dark, and the streetlights are concentrating on showing the white blanket of snow that now covers the treacherous ice from yesterday evening. At least they won't have to stand with sleet covering their feet when selling hot dogs. If anyone comes, that is.

She remains in bed for a while, staring at the ceiling, thinking about last night. A wave of loneliness washes over her—not even her parents can understand what she is going through. They believe that it's she who is wrong, not Tobias. What if it is? What if it's her behavior that has caused all this? She tries to remember any bigger discussions, times she has been cranky, times when they haven't agreed or when she has picked a fight. But that's not how it has been. They have been united and worked next to each other, like everyone else. And wasn't that what her parents had seen as well?

Tobias wants to talk; Linda doesn't. So far, she has continued to stay late at work. She hasn't been able to meet with Tobias because he can't seem to understand why Linda is so upset and why she thinks their relationship is over. Linda can't forget that Maja has a key to their house and can come back any time. And Linda would like Tobias to explain how he has had time to talk to Maja and break up with her when he hasn't even explained to Linda what Maja was doing at their house that night.

She has kept a straight face at work, where everyone is focused on getting the figures in place. There isn't a single department or manager who doesn't ask for a report or an indication of how the year has been, how they are doing. But how will she manage today? The only good thing about Tobias and the kids being away is that she won't have to act in front of the children; she will somehow cope with the preschool parents. She must get out of bed. Tonight Tobias will be home again, but if it wasn't for the fact that he will be bringing back the kids, she would have called and said he needn't show up anymore, ever.

Linda puts on a pair of long johns, her baggiest jeans, and her old yellow ski pants she, to her delight, found in the basement. She adds double layers of fleece jackets. After a moment's hesitation, she opens the closet and takes out the Persian fur coat. It isn't pretty, but it will keep the cold at bay.

*

The sun has barely found its way over the rooftops when she stops outside Solstrålen. The cold stings her cheeks, and the sidewalk outside the preschool is covered with a layer of fresh snow. She stands for a moment and watches how the parents and children move inside, as if they all lived together in the preschool, as if some sort of cohousing. Linda shudders.

The heat floods over her when she opens the door, but nobody seems to see her. They are all busy sorting out what could be sold at the flea market, choking with laughter at the stuff they have found in closets and garages. Linda tries to open her heavy and incredibly warm fur coat, but the buttons are stiff. She can feel the sweat trickling down her back.

—What are you wearing? one mother says, laughing. My grand-mother used to have a coat like that.

—Mine too, Linda says. It's hers.

—You might want to sell it at the flea market? the mother sug-gests.

Linda laughs politely, noticing that the other mother's jacket is the same as everyone else's, with fur around the collar and a small belt.

Marita shows her the lottery rings, one purple and one green, and then all the chocolate one family got from their employers, including four boxes of Aladdin and two boxes of Paradise, which she gigglingly says must have been left-overs from someone's Christmas—who would even think of eating milk chocolate these days? Linda thinks about the red box of chocolates Tobias got from work. They have opened it and eaten it all, except the cherry cordials.

Someone is brewing coffee in the kitchen, and there's a large pan of hot dogs on the stove. In the backyard, four dads are setting up tables and arranging the things that will be sold. The flea market takes shape, and the parents all seem so uncannily at ease.

—Here we go! Marita shouts, and her cheeks flare with enthusiasm. Sell everything you can!

Fact is, the yard is already full of seniors from the surrounding tenement houses. They are rooting around in the boxes and checking out stuff that's presented on the tables. Linda waits a while in the heat before she pulls down her hat and takes her place behind the chocolate wheel.

—You have baked, I hope? Marita, who sneaked up behind her, says.

—Bo should have done that. He will be here a little later.

—He'd better have. We're counting on everyone. Did you remind him?

—That's not my job. He'll be here.

Marita's smile is stiff. Linda can tell that she doesn't believe Bo will bring anything—how would he have remembered that?

*

—Yes, now...here I am, Bo says. What can I do?

He rocks back and forth and raises his hands. It's just after ten o'clock.

"What can I do?" Could he not just stand next to her and sell the remaining lottery tickets?

—Hello, Linda says, crouching in the heavy coat. You're late.

—Yes, yes, sorry. But I had time to bake yesterday, several bags of those spelt muffins. I found the recipe online. They are good. How has this been up till now? You must be freezing. You should warm up, or—perhaps I can get you a cup of coffee?

He continues to move jerkily back and forth as if he's looking for something or as if he can't decide what to do first—pick up the muffins, fetch coffee, or just stand beside her behind the table.

—No, that isn't necessary. Or, yes. Maybe. I'll go in for a while.

—Where did you say Tobias was?

—At his mother's.

—And are you okay at home? You don't need help? I could swing by if there's anything—

—No, thanks. He took the kids, so I'm home alone.

And Bo's help is the last thing she needs.

—And where is Stina? she asks perfunctorily.

—In France. Or somewhere...skiing, for her job. I don't remember where.

He clears his throat.

—There are so many places to go.

—Don't you ski?

—Yeah, but the kids...Well, I like cross-country skiing. Stina does downhill. And the children, they need to start somewhere, but there are so many...skis and boots, you know...But with the oldest, that would work. But then someone needs to take care of the youngest. Do you ski?

108

—Nah...I don't. I mean, I did, but I don't like it. But the kids have been skiing a few times with Tobias. We should...we will go in a few weeks. I don't like the winter much, she says, looking out over the preschool yard. I guess I should have gone with them..., she says, her voice fading when she thinks about how he walked around with Maja and the girls last winter. Because Linda wasn't there.

—A lottery ticket, perhaps? Bo says to an elderly lady with a knitted cap on her head.

The lady says she wants the dark chocolate if she wins, and Bo pulls the box of expensive dark chocolate aside and says it could be arranged.

—Now go warm up, he says to Linda.

As she walks toward the door, she sees more ladies gather around the table, and Bo seems to like to spin the wheel and wave with the lottery-ticket rings. Bibbi and Gabriella stand in the entrance with their heads close together, and their shiny black down jackets glimmer. Through the glass door, Linda can see how Bibbi's eyes open wide and Gabriella's mouth moves quickly, her nape twitches, and she waves her hands. Bibbi takes her arm, and Gabriella's lips close. They both look at Linda when she tries to get past them.

—Linda, Bibbi says. How are you? Is everyone okay?

—Hello. Thanks for New Year's. Well. Tobias and the kids are in Copenhagen. At his mother's.

Bibbi nods, biting her lip.

—And otherwise?

—Okay.

Gabriella smiles at her.

—Too bad you couldn't stay. It was great fun on New Year's Eve.

Linda apologizes and goes to the kitchen, takes a plastic cup, and pours coffee from a glass pumpkin. Gabriella follows in her trail.

—Hey, is it true…I mean, Bibbi says Tobias had…I mean, he…
Are you getting a divorce?

It's as if someone has shot an arrow straight into the mind of
Linda, and when she turns around, she sees stars spread across the
room. Maybe this is for the best, so she doesn't have to conceal
the truth. Because it's true. "Are you getting a divorce?" The question echoes between the buildings, and she grabs the countertop to
keep from falling. The coffee flows over her hand.

She stares at Gabriella, trying to come to her senses while she
reaches for the paper towels in the holder on the wall. She swipes
the gray sheets over the spilled coffee on the bench and her hand.
Her mouth is dry. Her eyes follow the fence to the grove in the
backyard and the little playhouse farther away.

—I don't know what you have heard. I told Bibbi not to mention it.

—Oh, I thought that was why you left, on New Year's Eve. Because you didn't feel well, I mean, because of the infidelity.

Her look is kind of stupid, eager as a puppy's, and her face
craves more information. No: more gossip!

—So it's true? Bibbi said she had clothes at your place, in your
closet? But you must have guessed? I mean, Tobias is incredibly
charming and all. I've seen that at the preschool parties if not elsewhere…

Linda smiles. Why is she smiling? This woman claims her husband is charming as if there's something obvious in him being unfaithful? And that Linda must have realized that he isn't the faithful
kind but ignored it?

—No. I haven't guessed. But then I didn't know you considered
him charming either.

Gabriella stops smiling.

—That wasn't what I meant. But he hasn't exactly hidden his
interest in women.

Linda wipes the sweat from her upper lip. The fur coat lies like the dead animal it is around her shoulders, heavy and limp. Now that she reflects on it, she can remember seeing Tobias surrounded by other moms from the preschool, standing on a patch of grass outside a house at an end-of-year preschool party. She doesn't remember whose house they were at, but she has a feeling that her and Tobias's eyes met for a moment, and she nodded because she believed he saw her and he showed that she was the one he cared about, not those women in skimpy summer dresses with colorful sweaters over their shoulders.

—The kids don't know yet, Linda says. It's...complicated. Maybe you can keep it to yourself for a while.

—Why haven't you told the kids?

—They're better off in case nothing changes, right?

Bibbi knocks on the doorframe. Her smile is stiff, and when Linda eyes her, she looks out the window.

—Well, I was probably a little drunk on New Year's Eve, Bibbi says.

—I begged you not to tell.

—I know. Look, I'm sorry. But—it will seep out eventually anyway. And I haven't told anyone else. Promise.

Gabriella's eyes, lit by hunger, devour her, waiting for more. But Linda doesn't want to, nor can she, give either of them anything. All she has is a conversation with Maja and Tobias's explanation. A marriage in dissolution. Her own will to let it all disappear, vanish in fire and smoke. The hopelessness. There's nothing more to tell.

She shrugs.

—What are you doing, girls? Marita says, rushing into the kitchen. Aren't you going to work? You know, all the garbage out there is selling like hot cakes. The pensioners in this area are on the ball! And the lottery tickets, they buy them like crazy. I'm completely fascinated. You should go help Bo sell them, Linda. He can't keep up.

—He got here ten minutes ago.

—Come on, Marita. She has other things to think about, Bibbi says.

—What's so important? Make sure this flea market moves. We don't want to end up with a lot of unsold things.

—It's nothing. My stuff, that is. Come on, let's get out of here.

Linda takes Bibbi's forearm and pushes Gabriella in front of her.

—So what do you do now? Have you moved out of the house? Bibbi says in a low voice.

—We're figuring things out.

Though Linda hasn't figured anything out. It's not until now, when Bibbi asks, that she realizes she must move out. Or make sure Tobias moves out.

—Do you have a period of reflection? You do, when you have kids, right? Gabriella says.

Linda nods. Though there's nothing to reflect on.

—It's so sad, Gabriella says. Super sad. Tell me if you need any help, or if you want to talk. We're right here.

There's nothing Linda would talk to Gabriella about. They don't even know each other. Linda doubts Gabriella even knows the names of her daughters.

—Sure, Linda answers. Sure, I know. Thank you.

Bibbi doesn't say anything. They go in different directions in the yard, and she sees Gabriella leaning her head against Peter's arm. Seconds later, their eyes meet Linda's, but they look away.

They are probably buddies now. Just as well that Bibbi and Peter and Gabriella and Mats have each other, a new preschool community, new trips, and New Year's, and Walpurgis—and perhaps even Midsummer evenings to plan.

But now Linda and Tobias must tell the kids, tonight. Tomorrow the news might have already spread to the other kids, and they'll ask if it's true. Do kids talk that way? Do they care?

She walks back to the chocolate tombola and Bo, who now stands alone, waving a single lottery-ticket ring from which hangs ten tickets. She shouldn't have left him there. The table shows large gaps from the chosen chocolate boxes.

—It seems to be going well, she says.

Bo says the lottery tickets have been sold with great success and that he handed over the muffins to Marita.

—I think it's soon a wrap, he says. If she doesn't put us to work somewhere else. In which case it's better to stay here and look busy.

Linda guesses he's trying to be funny, and she smiles politely. She wonders if maybe she should call Håkan. She could stay with him temporarily; he travels a lot. And she would only need to stay with him until she finds something of her own. Until then, she and Tobias could live every other week at the house. Is that workable?

—What's up? Is anything wrong? Bo says.

—No. No. Or, we're getting divorced. Me and Tobias. But it wasn't supposed to leak, and now it has and I'm a bit confused and startled, as you might imagine. I'm not used to getting divorced. I don't know how it works. I don't understand why either, to be honest. It's all…very—

She starts to cry. Her shoulders are shaking, and she puts her hands over her face but can't stop the tears. It's like a waterfall. It's only now she realizes that it's true. That she told something in confidence, that Tobias has been unfaithful, that her parents are completely uncomprehending, that she has no one to share this with. She's alone.

—And we haven't told the kids, she sobs, and now everyone knows…and I can't do this on my own, and I need somewhere to stay—

Bo hugs her. He holds her tightly and leans her head against his shoulder and makes sure she doesn't fall, although it feels like she does. He strokes her hair like no one has before. Then he lets go of her and clears his throat.

—I'm sorry to hear. Really. I mean—I'm awfully sorry for you. It happens, you know.

He smiles a brief smile, which is immediately erased as if he remembers something he doesn't want to remember.

—But it has to be told. I know it's hard. That's all I can say. It's better to put it in motion. Now you don't need to pretend anymore. You couldn't have prevented it. That's the way it is.

He leans across the table as he sweeps away some dirt before he continues, now more like a mumble:

—When it's in motion, there's nothing that can stop it. I can't say life gets better right away, but eventually it does. I can promise you that.

Linda wipes her cheeks clumsily, holding one hand under her dripping nose.

—Is it definite? I mean, there could be a way to…well, you know, sometimes you still stay together, because of—

—No, we can't stay together because of the kids. It's not enough.

She lifts her head, realizing they are in the spotlight, she with her eyes red from crying and he with his head tilted and his thumb and index finger on his chin, as if he were an art connoisseur. She straightens her back.

One of the down-jacket-clad women sails past together with her husband, who's also dressed in a shiny down jacket. Linda knows she's completely out of place in her ugly fur coat and yellow ski pants, just as out of place as Bo in his worn, pilling fleece jacket and his knitted red woolen cap.

—I heard…, the woman begins and tilts her head to one side.

Linda guesses she now connects the divorce with Bo and is about to protest, but she closes her eyes instead.

—We need to get going, the woman says. That's enough for today. We've done our thing, and the hot dogs are not really a lunch, are they? We're not interested in what's left here anyway. Bye for now!

When Linda opens her eyes, they have disappeared around the corner.

—If you also want to leave, then do. I can manage this on my own, Bo says.

—I have nowhere to go.

—Then I'll take care of you here.

*

The chocolate wheel sits on the empty table in front of them. It's only half past one, the hot dogs are sold out, and the interest in the gadgets left on the tables will fade as the sun disappears behind the apartment buildings. Bo dismantles the table. The ground is trampled, and where the table once stood lies a white rectangle of untouched snow as an empty memory.

They have been acting before a thrilled audience, she and Bo. Heads have been close together, and there have been whispers and nods sent in their direction, as if the audience can't wait for the next scene to begin. But no one has come up to them, and Linda has felt an odd safety in Bo's company. He has taken care of her, made her laugh, made her think about something else for a few hours.

Perhaps it's a necessity, just like Bo said. It couldn't have been kept secret; gossip is a law of nature, and everything has to come out of the box sooner or later. She has nothing to apologize for, nothing to be ashamed of. The only thing that offends Linda is that Bibbi didn't respect her wish. It's as if her life was sold to the highest bidder, without respect, without consideration. And the children. Her throat tightens. The girls.

Marita is standing on a chair by the entrance, crying out that they have made around a thousand dollars, and the other families roar with joy. This is followed by backslaps and handshakes.

"A thousand dollars," Linda thinks as she stands at the back, watching the down jackets' conspiracy. There are twenty children at the preschool. Once they have cleaned and brought everything back to order, some of them will have spent more than eight hours of their Sunday here, in the freezing cold—to bring in a thousand dollars. That's fifty bucks per child, and she can't imagine a single family here who couldn't and wouldn't rather pay that amount in a year. But she doesn't says anything. She claps her sheepskin mittens, which gives off a muffled puffing sound.

—Thank you all for today. Well done! Marita shouts. See you at the preschool party in mid-March!

The families cheer again. Few things can make parents of young children more peppy than a party without children, where they also can devote all their time to talking about their offspring. Linda pulls up her shoulders and slides her hands into her pockets. She doesn't want to attend anymore preschool parties and especially not with Tobias. Is there any way to get out of it?

Gabriella finds her way to Linda.

—Just so you know, I didn't ask to be told. I haven't had any premonitions or whatever. It's not like we talked trash about you when you left.

Linda doesn't respond.

—Bibbi only wants to help you, and so do I. She was really— sad. I mean, you're good friends since way back. So she couldn't keep that secret, on New Year's Eve and all. Please don't be mad at her. Please. I didn't…I don't want to ruin your friendship.

—No, I sure hope not.

—I hope everything will be all right. And that you're not mad at me. It's not my fault.

She smiles, as if they, too, should be friends.

—I have some spelt muffins left at home. Would you join me? Bo says.

Linda nods.

—Then, follow me.

Gabriella looks, still smiling, at Bo, but he doesn't smile back. Linda knows that if Gabriella had dared, she would have asked, but she doesn't. It's as if a firework goes off in Gabriella's head, or just a sparkler that in the last second gives off that warm, explanatory glow. Linda feels how Gabriella watches her and Bo when she follows him down to the cars.

Linda turns around. Bibbi waves, but Linda doesn't wave back. If she wants something, she can call.

Tobias looks around the hotel room. He is convinced he has overslept, but there's no one calling; only the phone beeps from his wake-up call, and he tilts his head into the fluffy pillow. Was it a dream, or did he follow Maja, one of the major customers, to her room?

The moment the thought passes through his head, he knows it's not a dream. He remembers telling her he's in the middle of a divorce. He closes his eyes again, thinking this workshop wasn't meant to be this way. He thinks of the kids: Lotta, who's almost two years old, and three-month-old Fia. He sees Fia's little body under the adrenaline mask the other night when she got false croup and they went to the emergency room. Linda said it was okay that he left for the conference and that she realized how much it meant to him. He loves her because she seems to cope so well with everything.

Since he met Linda, Tobias has never even thought of being with someone else, and he knows he should tell Maja it was a one-off. He puts his arms behind his head and decides it's something that can happen when you go to a business conference but that it has no significance since only he and Maja know about it. They're responsible adults who don't make a big deal over the fact that they shared a bed, one night.

He picks up the phone, presses "Linda," and counts the signals going through.

—The Jacobsens'.

Tobias grimaces. It's Karin, Linda's friend, who answers.

—Hi, Karin, it's Tobias. Is Linda there?

—Hello. No.

—Where is she?

—Drove Lotta to preschool, of course.

—Didn't she take her mobile?

—Obviously not.

—Tell her I called.

—And that you love her?

—Eh, yes.

He hangs up. Tobias has no problem with Karin. She's the one with the problem. Perhaps with herself, he thinks. Why is she still single? She's square and rigid, at least with him. Her charisma is different; there's an energy field around her one can almost see, and it was precisely what attracted him more to her than to Linda when they first met. It was at a bar in Malmö. The big, tousled red hair makes everyone turn around, and she is tall and rather heavily built but without being overweight. She takes up space and moves into a room in a convincing manner—it sparkles around her. But as soon as Tobias approached her that evening, it was as if she pushed him away. When he instead turned to Linda, Karin had become even weirder. As if it was her job to make sure that Linda ended up in the right hands, as if she had ownership. And with each step closer he took to Linda, Karin's eyes narrowed, which had challenged Tobias even more.

Tobias must admit that Karin is very good with children, naturally trustworthy and—cool. Linda hadn't hesitated to call her when it became clear Anita and Gustav couldn't lend a hand on the days Tobias is gone.

—That's impossible, Anita had answered, without even trying to sound regretful. We have been invited for a weekend with good friends, which we need before Christmas.

Linda is used to it; her parents haven't helped out much, though Lotta was their first—and for a while, only—grandchild. Now that they have two, they still seem pretty disinterested. Given that her brother, Håkan, has no children and not even a relationship, one would think that Anita and Gustav would devote all their time to Lotta and Fia, but despite the short physical distance, the contact is neither particularly intense nor overly cordial. But Linda would never complain. In the family Adeus, you bite your tongue, you don't discuss, and you keep your head up, stoically. You don't crouch for eventual wallops awarded; you pretend you're not disappointed, sad, or destroyed.

In the name of truth, Tobias's mother isn't the one to dart off to Stockholm either if help is needed, but that is for a different reason: she is losing her eyesight. Anne would have liked to lend a hand, but if you can't see properly, it's difficult to take care of young children. There may not be many Christmases *left where she can and dares to travel by herself. Tobias has already realized he will have to go to Copenhagen in the future for the children to see their grandmother, but this year she'll be there at least.*

Tobias wonders if he should wait and call Linda again—if she has just gone to Solstrålen, she should be back home in twenty minutes. He glances at the clock. A quarter past eight. The conference should start at nine. He can shower and have breakfast and then call again. On the other hand, it's not very important to call right now. What more will he say than what Karin suggested—that he loves her? There isn't much to tell. And he's only been gone for twenty-four hours. If something important had happened at home, Karin would surely have mentioned it.

He wonders if Karin understands that he must be at this conference concerning a new job and new responsibilities that he, so far, has only touched, and in a much smaller scale. Taking care of large customers requires time and care, instincts, agility, and responsiveness. They believe in him, which is a huge step forward, in his eyes. And in Linda's, he assumes. He should have thanked Karin for helping out though, but it doesn't come naturally to him, to say thank you. He assumes she enjoys seeing the kids, too.

The phone vibrates in his hand, and he is so absorbed in his thoughts of his family, he's convinced it's Linda who's texting.

"Thank you for yesterday. Will we meet for breakfast?"

He stares at the screen and responds:

"Soon."

Then he erases the message. It doesn't come naturally to him to say thank you.

*

The hotel corridor is long, and it's covered with a patterned carpet in light-green tones. Behind the heavy doors you can hear muffled voices, which amuses him. The doors look and feel sturdy, but instead they are made of thin plasterboard. Even their house, the "do-it-yourself" of the '30s or '40s, is better insulated and more solid than this complex from the late '90s. He walks past Maja's room, the corners of his eyes burning and his forehead getting sweaty as he remembers last night.

—*Tobias!*

One of his colleagues opens a door and joins Tobias as they head toward the breakfast room. The sun still isn't out, and the darkness seeps through the large windows facing the lake.

Tobias gets yogurt and fiber flakes, juice, eggs, and coffee. Hotel breakfasts are among Tobias's favorite things, and after putting the first round on the table, he goes back and gets breakfast rolls, cheese, and marmalade. He and his colleague sit down by the window, and another one joins them.

—*Can I sit here?*

It's Maja. She's wearing a soft white blouse that clings to her body, with a V neck so revealing that Tobias has to look down into the yogurt to not blush. Her pants are black and tight, and her knee-high boots are shiny. Despite it being November, her cheeks are as pink and smooth as yesterday, and even though he wishes he would feel remorse or disgust, he doesn't.

—*Of course, he says, smiling at her.*

She puts a jacket on the back of a chair and goes to get breakfast.

—*Is she your customer? the colleague says.*

Tobias nods with his mouth full of cereal.

—*Some guys have all the luck.*

His colleague grins, and Tobias lifts an eyebrow.

—*Depends on how you look at it.*

—*Thanks for yesterday, Maja says when she sits down. An interesting and intense day.*

Tobias clears his throat and wipes his mouth with the napkin, well aware of the sweat on his upper lip.

—*Yes, it will probably be even more interesting today, he says hastily and smiles at her.*

She puts her hand on his thigh and strokes his leg gently beneath the table.

—*I hope so, she says.*

—*Tobias?*

Tobias looks around, startled. Standing next to the table is his mother-in-law, Anita. Her skinny frame reminds him of Linda's, but her hair is puffed and sprayed, like a helmet around her head, and it makes her look much older

121

than she is. She wears a pair of plaid pants she supposedly finds sporty and, therefore, appropriate in the countryside, but around her neck a pearl necklace dangles against a gray turtleneck sweater.

—So this is where you are! That's incredible!

His colleagues and Maja greet her politely.

—And you? Where's Gustav? When did you get here?

—Gustav will be here soon. We drove up yesterday afternoon. But you weren't in the dining room last night?

—We had a separate room. There's quite a few of us, Tobias says.

He's now standing up, holding the napkin in his hand and then wiping his mouth, though he should be wiping his forehead.

—And these are your colleagues?

Anita looks at Maja and his colleague with the X-ray eyes he knows so well. Maja smiles back, but Anita doesn't.

—These are my colleagues, and this is Maja Örnklou, one of my new clients.

—I understand, Anita says.

—Maja, my mother-in-law.

When he introduces her, he isn't sure of how she will react since he told her he was in the middle of a divorce. He can't do anything else but let those words sink in and hope she doesn't care much about his family business—and why would she? Tobias is sure that his lie doesn't matter to Maja, and he isn't lying now: she is his mother-in-law. He's not getting divorced though. That it isn't even his intention is a different matter.

The two women don't shake hands, but they nod politely at each other.

—I guess you'll be back tomorrow? Anita says.

—Exactly. Tomorrow after lunch. Going straight home.

He is on the verge of saying "to the family," but he stops himself.

—That's great. Yes, there's a lot on Linda's shoulders with the children. We would have gladly helped her, but it didn't work for us this time. Luckily, she has her friends. Well then, have a good time, and we'll see you for Christmas.

—Say hi to Gustav if I don't see him.

Anita nods, looking again at Maja and then straight into Tobias's eyes.

He swallows and tries to smile, but it's as if he can't move his face muscles. He knows that she knows. But how can she?

Outside Bo's Pippi Longstocking house, the darkness is already compact. The house's pinnacles and towers are stretching toward the sky along with spruce and birch trees. On the creaking porch, a wilted broom leans against a low bench, and the door is decorated with a large wreath of willow clad with white feathers, as an explanation to why the song says "Christmas lasts until Easter."

Bo opens the door and shouts, "I'm home," but laconically shrugs his shoulders when there's no noticeable reaction.

—We have a nanny who helps us. She's very popular among the kids, he says. Coffee or tea? Need help with those pants? Sit down, and I'll pull.

Linda protests, but Bo has already started to pull down her thick yellow ski pants. He folds them and puts them on the bench, and she covers them with the fur coat.

He tells her to sit by the window and make herself at home before he puts on the kettle and opens the cupboards to find teacups. Linda sits down and leans gently against the wall. What is she doing here, with Bo Mårtensson? She involuntarily raises her eyebrows to the question that pops up in her head, thinking about how stupid she was to have cried and let herself be comforted by him. They don't know each other. Linda isn't even sure she wants to get to know him, even if he seems—sweet. Caring.

—I don't want to intrude, she says to Bo, who puts a teapot and a plate of muffins in front of her. I won't stay that long. Tobias and the kids will be home tonight, and I guess I must—

—Have you moved out?

Linda shakes her head. She must move out of the house. It's so obvious and yet so difficult. Bo nods.

—It seems the best is to break up, anyway.

There's something rough about it, but Linda understands what he means. The option to "just go on as if nothing has happened" doesn't exist.

—When will Stina be back?

—Tomorrow, well, yes, probably.

—Is it like this all the time?

—That she travels? Well, yes. Every week. But not much over the weekends. It isn't for pleasure; it's work.

They fall silent again, and Linda blows the tea to cool it down and takes a bite of a spelt muffin. It tastes surprisingly good.

—I had no clue you were a baker.

—No, of course you didn't. We don't know one another.

Linda blushes.

—No, you're right…Thank you for inviting me. Thank you for taking care of me today. I'm sorry I wasn't much companionship or help.

—I've always thought you seemed pretty—uncommunicative, reserved. But you're not. It was great to get to know you a little. We are rarely there for the preschool activities. We don't have time.

Linda's cheeks are still hot, and she wonders if she should say what she thinks—what she thought—about him, too, but decides not to.

—We know fairly little about each other, she says.

—Do you socialize with many of the other families?

—I really only see Bibbi, Linda says.

Bo nods.

—I've only caught a glimpse of her husband. And the other woman, Gabriella? Yes, they seem to meet quite a lot, those two families.

Linda squints at him.

—What? Gabriella and Peter? They barely know each other. It's mostly Tobias and I who see Bibbi and Peter.

Bo takes a bite of his muffin.

—I work from home, but I have noticed him, Hamklint, Peter you said? And the woman you talked to today. They seem to have a lot to discuss.

—Do they have lunch here? But Bibbi works in Kista, which isn't next door—

—No, no, the other one. Gabriella? And Bibbi's husband, Hamklint.

Linda takes a sip of tea and glances out onto the street. She sees her own reflection in the dark window, and Bo's thin face, where he munches the last crumbles. Gabriella and Peter, would they do lunch? Hardly. Peter works in the city.

—What happened between you and Tobias? I don't want to be nosy, I just wonder if I can help you.

She stiffens and must push back the feeling of abandonment and despair that rolls over her.

—His mistress came to visit and told me. One evening, when he wasn't home. I don't know why she came, but she had her own key. And she thought I didn't live in our house any longer, that I'd moved. That we had divorced.

Bo doesn't twitch, just nods and swallows another bite of muffin with a sip of tea.

—Tobias doesn't want a divorce. He thinks it's fine as it is. I had a picture of me being a woman who forgave, but this has been going on for four years, and I can't get over the betrayal. I can't. It probably sounds bizarre. We have children, and I haven't suffered from it either...I just haven't been aware of it. I don't know what I'm doing.

Bo rests his chin in his hand and moves his spoon with a gentle clinking sound in his tea. He smiles a little awry.

—No. I understand that. Four years...And you haven't—
She shakes her head.

—No, really. I haven't seen a thing. I couldn't imagine. He's skillful, perhaps. Or maybe I am just blind.

126

He takes a pinch of the muffin.

—Sounds more like he wanted to live a double life. That he thought it a good compromise.

Linda gets a vision of how Tobias waved good-bye to her and the children and then went to the airport to meet Maja, to go somewhere else on vacation. And to think he could do this without a second thought.

Bo points at the teapot, but Linda declines the offer. Her children will soon be home. And Tobias.

—I should probably go. Thanks for the tea, and thanks for today.

—Hey, I just thought of one thing…, Bo says slowly. If you can't find anything else, I might have a temporary solution for your accommodation. We have an annex to the house that's empty. My father lived there, but he moved to a home for dementia some six months ago.

His gaze is empty, and he hastily wipes his eyes with his hand.

—But you can rent it for a while if you want, he continues in a rushed voice. You shouldn't be living at home. I say this from personal experience. Give me a week, and I will get the house cleaned out. You can come tomorrow and check it out if you like.

Linda panics. What's he looking for? She's not moving to—his house. She has a family to take care of, two children, two girls who will soon be home and she has not seen them for several days.

All Bo's questions suddenly fall into place. There's a nanny who takes care of the children, and Stina who travels all the time, and he barely even knows where she is. Linda feels sick.

—Thanks, but I'm sure I'll manage. I will probably stay with my brother. My parents also live in the neighborhood.

—Yes, I understand. It was just a suggestion. But the house is empty, so…feel free.

Linda smiles because she has to.

—I must go. Thanks for today. For the tea and all.

Bo nods and follows her to the door, holding out her yellow pants as if they were a gift.

— Just call if there's anything I can do. I know what it's like, what you're going through and it—it isn't fun. But it gets better once you're on the other side.

It sounds as if he describes a childhood disease, or how to remove the appendix. As a minor surgery which will hurt a little. It will pass, and you'll be back on your feet, as keen as a lark.

Linda thanks him again, but she just wants out of the house, away from it all. It's as if he stands in her way on purpose, just wanting to hug her. He wraps his long arms around her, and he smells like a wardrobe, just like her old clothes in the attic.

—Thanks, she mumbles into his plaid shirt.

—Thanks. I mean, it was fun. To meet you. Hope to see you soon, then. And give the house a thought. I would gladly show it to you. I work from home, so you can come over any time.

She hurries out of the house and onto the narrow garden path, the light from the open door following her. She knows that he's still there because his shadow remains in the box of light.

—Careful, it can be slippery, Bo cries. And good luck.

Good luck? With what? Separating, moving, divorcing? Good luck. What an idiot.

Anita writes. Not physically, not on paper. The diaries she kept have been thrown away, and she doesn't want anything to remain, no evidence, nothing for others to decipher. It would maybe be better to forget it completely, but for Anita that would be too simple. There are things that deserve to be remembered because they are part of who you are and what you have become. You can't close your eyes to reality, but you don't have to risk others peeping in to your past.

She writes in the windings of her brain, dictating the same text over and over again to be sure only she knows it and that she will always remember the words. At random intervals she adds text, but so far she hasn't removed anything; everything that exists is too important to cut. The text isn't long. "Things the Children Don't Need to Know"—that's what she calls it, and some parts also include Gustav, but not all. A few of the memories they keep so tightly between them that she is sure he will never divulge the secrets because they are just as painful for him.

The miscarriage for example. Gustav would never tell anyone about it. His grief had almost been bigger than hers, perhaps because it meant the end of their abilities to reproduce. When the doctors told them that a new pregnancy would put Anita's life in danger, he had cried, something she had never seen him do before nor since. She had, strangely enough, felt a relief, as if their family had to be considered complete and that the decision could not be appealed and, therefore, didn't need to be discussed.

Other things are none of his business. Neither Gustav nor the children know how much Anita hated her mother-in-law. Wished the life out of her, with which she almost succeeded. At least she died, and Anita pretended to cry at the funeral. Gustav didn't shed a tear, but that's something she finds completely normal. And when Gustav speaks in high praise of his mother, Anita is always on his side, while she rehearses in her brain that the kids will never know how the lady really was, at least to her. She'd called Anita a peasant because she didn't grow up in a town but in the southern suburbs. In a suburb other than the one she herself had let Gustav grow up in. Anita's was farther from the center and not considered as good and promising. She also claimed that Anita walked like a cow, with those slender legs—thighs should have flesh. How had Gustav found such a wretchedly skinny girl? Anita cried on her pillow, but no one bothered to comfort her, not even Gustav who had heard his mother's harsh words. This was when Anita learned that the family Adeus doesn't whine. You clench your jaws, or show who you are and what you can do. But you don't whine.

But then, when the lady realized that Anita had fun on her own and that Gustav might be left behind, she regretted it. In any case, she didn't imagine Gustav finding someone else. Afterward, the harsh words continued, and she pointed out to Anita that she should learn to cook instead of dreaming of becoming an actress, that her meatballs were inedible. Anita put her acting dreams on the shelf and took a cooking class. Yet the bitch was never satisfied with anything she'd done. More than that, she took pity on Gustav.

There are more lines in the book "Things the Children Don't Need to Know," events that might not change their lives much but don't concern them. Then there are things that do directly concern them and would change their relationship to her, which is unnecessary. She's Linda's and Håkan's mother, and she doesn't intend to destroy their relationship by allowing them to accuse her or contest her doings. All that's needed is that she knows what she tells them and what she doesn't.

When she adds a new chapter to the book she, therefore, devotes a few days to rehearse her role to perfection, as if she were both on stage and in the audience simultaneously. She's her own biggest critic, always alert, but anxious to be at her best. "Repetition is the mother of knowledge" is something a teacher once told her, and Anita has made it her life mantra.

When Gustav and she have had coffee in the kitchen, which they have most mornings because rituals are a haven now that Gustav doesn't work any longer and he prefers to do errands or meet their friends over lunch, Anita takes a few deep breaths, goes through both the text that needs to be saved in the archives of "Things the Children Don't Need to Know" and the one she intends to present and sits down comfortably in the armchair by the window. She's ready.

*

—What happened is, of course, incredibly unfortunate, Anita says to Tobias, and smoothens the beige woolen fabric of her skirt. She locks her hands in her lap and clears her throat, twitching her head like a little squirrel who has forgotten where she hid the nuts and, therefore, prepares to run in an entirely different direction from the one she originally planned.

—Yet, she continues, now with her head raised, I can't understand why it would be so difficult to fix. Linda is obviously very sad and disappointed. And surely you realize that, too. She would never be able to inflict the same thing to you, or anyone else, she adds quickly. In that, Linda and I are very much alike.

Anita smiles to herself and plays with the shiny earring on her left earlobe. It hurts, always a little more on the left side than on the right, but it's something you have to endure. Clips are always a little heavier, but she likes the weight; it's as if they improve her posture. That's also why she sits with her back straight, on the edge of her chair. If she leans back against the hard upholstered back, she would find it difficult to rise and also difficult to stay in control and take command. And in this situation, you must take command.

—You can see things from different angles, of course, she says, and puffs her hair. One can see it as you drifted apart. Or your feelings for each other are gone. But that's not the case, is it? You

131

haven't stopped…loving—she clears her throat because that word isn't one she usually takes in her mouth, and it has a greater significance than she wants to discuss—caring for Linda? I've rarely seen you so tight as on Christmas Eve, and it's a good sign, at least from my point of view. One could call it some sort of crisis. It's not that unusual.

Anita lets her eyes scan the living room, the orange pouf that screams for attention, and which should probably be reupholstered; the dining table with the dark chairs; and the winter light playing on the chandelier. Harmony—if you forget the orange. This room has had its fair share of crises, too, but that isn't anything she intends to talk to Tobias about. She meets his gaze and smiles.

—So, she continues, crises come and go. That Linda takes offense is nothing you or I can do anything about. But we can help each other to minimize the damage, don't you think? There are two ways to look at it; one is yours and the other Linda's, but you belong together, don't you? You have a future. And you have kids. It would be very sad if you couldn't get this to work, just because you—well, you know what you have done.

Tobias opens his mouth as if to answer, but Anita holds up her hand.

—I know what I know and what I have seen. It doesn't concern me. Your conscience is your conscience. Now—

She clears her throat again and clasps her hands. What happened to the carpet fringes? She frowns and bends down to shake the rug. When the fringes land in straight rows, she sees the dust swirling up in the bright winter light.

—What do you want, Anita? Tobias says with his drawling Danish intonation. Do you think we should refrain from divorcing? Then you should probably talk to Linda and not to me. I have no problem with staying with her and the girls. I know what I have done, as you say. It has happened. But Linda has filed for divorce, and now she claims we should take turns living at the house, every other week. It's easy for her to say; she has family here. I have no idea where I'll stay if I don't live in our house.

He shrugs, but smiles at her, disarmingly.

—Tobias. We have an issue as you understand. As our house is now your property.

He raises his hands as if to say that these are the rules of the game.

—You have to fight, Tobias.

Tobias leans forward, elbows on knees.

—Anita, he says.

It sounds like "Anide," and she doesn't like it.

—It's not that I don't want to fight. Look, I'm still here. I'm going nowhere. I might not be the best husband on earth, but I want to continue living with Linda. She's your child. And your child wants to give up. I don't see how I can fight someone who has already left the boxing ring?

This is exactly what she expected. He is, deep down, a kind and understanding man, and he's sorry for what he did. Everyone can err. Linda is the narrow-minded, the one who has no margins. Everything should obviously stay within the standards; there are rules she wants to follow.

—Yes, that's a dilemma. But what if you aren't fighting hard enough? You have to believe you can win, right? And divorcing, isn't that giving in a little too easily? Who wins? None of you, Tobias. You lose, the whole family will lose. Gustav and I, too. Have you thought about that?

His gray eyes are barely visible behind his thick eyelids, and the sun shines straight on his ruddy face.

—I thought—maybe it's all about money, Anita says with a certain planned hesitance.

There's a twitch in the corner of Tobias's mouth, almost invisible. He pulls at his jacket and puts his arms behind his neck.

—Money?

—I mean, this house is a house. Only a property, so to speak, an asset. And I understand that you're not at ease, financially. Not that you can't manage, she hurries to add. I know you can. We discussed it at Christmas, and I don't want to interfere, not at all. But perhaps a buffer would be good. Money that could put a little flavor to life. And you might need…to find a way back to each other?

Tobias clasps his hands and leans forward. He smiles.

—You would give us money, is that what you mean? Isn't that a little late, now that we're divorcing, which is what Linda wants? I'll get money, Anita, when the house is sold.

—Thank you, Tobias, I am very well aware of that. We don't need to discuss it. What I am talking about is your relationship.

Anita won't let him get to her. She has been counting on him not understanding immediately; you have to take it step by step. Quietly and gently as with a child.

—I don't see it that way, that you will divorce. These are ideas that may pop up, the simplest, most common solutions to marital problems. The easy way out. In my opinion, you have a disagreement. Or a discussion. Something you can—and should—talk through, not only once. You must try to understand her, care about her feelings. And show her in action you are the person she picked out, whom she decided upon. Not true? If you play your cards right, you get a bonus. That is to say—if you actively work on not getting divorced. This will be your job in the coming months. Since you have children, you have a reflection period of half a year, am I right?

Tobias nods.

—Why do you ask? What are the odds that Linda will change her mind and wish to continue the marriage?

Anita takes a deep breath.

—I don't know. I can only conclude she's upset. The rest is for you to find out. And above all, fix.

Tobias shakes his head.

—Thanks for your concern, Anita. But it isn't about money; it's about something else that Linda's gotten into her head—that I'm lying. I don't, of course, I don't. You know me, don't you? But I can't fight against a confused brain. I'm sorry.

He gets up, but Anita continues:

—Twenty thousand dollars, Tobias. You get twenty thousand dollars if there's no divorce.

He sits down again, the chair creaks, and Anita wonders if it will hold his weight.

—Does Linda know?

—She doesn't care about money.

He smiles faintly.

—And when would we get the money?

—As soon as you can tell me there won't be a divorce.

—But why? I don't understand why, Anita?

—Because this house will do you good. It has before. Now, maybe we can discuss the details? And by the way: the weeks when you don't stay at home, you can stay here. So we can keep ourselves updated on what's happening.

—Thanks. It reminds me—it's actually my house.

—Yours and Linda's.

Håkan takes the paper bags from Linda and puts them in the trunk of the car.

—Do you think you could help me with two moving boxes? That will be all.

He doesn't want to go into the house and see Tobias. It has nothing to do with him, but he nods. It's for Linda's sake. Has she thought it through? Probably. Linda may not have the strongest of emotional repertoires, at least not outwardly. None of them do really; they're all pretty—indifferent. That's what he's been told. Coming from a family like the Adeuses, where external conflict isn't regarded as either constructive or desirable, one learns to hide aggression. This may, therefore, be easily taken as if nothing sticks to them and that conflicts just pass them by.

Håkan reflected upon it at Christmas, when he didn't understand why Linda couldn't sign the papers. What was there to discuss? And now, in retrospect, he knows he should have understood. Anita and Gustav too, for that matter. They all know Linda, and yet none of them understood, or wanted to understand. As if the most important thing was the Christmas present—no, the distribution of the Christmas present. The gift has never been important, only the handover. The recipient can think what he or she wants about the gift as long as it doesn't show. He had to admit that he'd had his thoughts elsewhere on Christmas Eve, but it feels wrong to bring it up with Linda now. There will be another time. There's a time for everything. When she called and told him about her and Tobias, Håkan knew that it would take even longer, but it doesn't worry him too much.

The house looks so tiny and sad now that he knows what has happened and what Linda has decided. Why do some houses become cheerful, welcoming, and others only gray? Håkan has always liked this area because the houses somehow exude pride on a small scale. Every single house was actually built with the thought "I can do this," and the first proud owners could see the product of their labor. Of that joy, nothing is left, at least not when it comes to Tobias and Linda's house. They have resigned, and the possibilities of the settlers have turned into suburban gloominess.

He stays in the hallway while Linda takes off her shoes and enters. From up above he hears her short muffled orders to Tobias. Håkan looks around. On a hook hangs her yellow ski pants. He remembers them from his childhood. Why has Linda kept them? They must be a thousand years old, and she can't possibly use them. He can see her in front of him on the ski slopes in Sälen in yellow pants and a blue jacket because he looked the same, as if they were a team. Team Adeus from Södertunet, Sweden. Anita or Gustav must have found the clothes on sale. Håkan has no memory of them ever complaining as kids; why would they? They said thank you, put the clothes on, suffered. That's why it's even more amazing that Linda has kept them. He remembers how she hissed at him, saying they at least didn't have to go on the same ski lift. It was enough that he was her younger brother and was dressed just like her.

The lid of the blue urn in the hall window hasn't been put on properly and it bothers his sense of regularity. He tries to arrange it, but something inside pushes the lid back up. He lifts the lid, only to see some Polaroid pictures popping out. Håkan can't help taking them out of the urn and checking them, frowning. He's interrupted by Tobias's heavy steps down the stairs and puts the lid back on the urn and the photos in his pocket.

—Hi, I can take that one, he says.

Tobias puts the moving box in front of him.

—Great, he says.

Linda is already behind him, with the other box in her hands.

—Let's go, she says.

Håkan nods toward Tobias, who closes the door behind them.

—Thanks for helping me, Linda says as she sits down behind the wheel.

—Are you sure this is what you want? Not that I have a problem with you staying in the guest room for a while, not at all. I am hardly at home. But—I was thinking about the girls.

—We have to start somewhere.

Linda's voice cracks from the five short words, and Håkan understands. It can't be an easy decision. He doesn't have to take anyone else into account, but it's perhaps precisely for that reason: it seems so complicated. To invest not only your time but all of you, and then some, to make things work. He only has his own family as a reference point and can't tell whether Anita or Gustav ever made that investment, not as he himself would do. But he knows that Linda, just as he would have done, has thought this through, calculated, analyzed. And after staking everything on one card, which happened to be Tobias, she concluded that it was wrong.

In this way, Håkan and Linda are very similar. That he asks her again only means he already knows the answer. And he's sure it also means it's a decision that will not be subject to appeal, so there's not much more to discuss. He won't interfere in their relationship; he doesn't want to snoop around. What he has seen and heard is enough to assure him that Linda knows what she's doing.

—So it's official now? he says.

Linda sighs and says she had to tell her boss because she has to change her hours. And that most of the preschool parents also know, by accident.

—People talk. And then I will meet my old friends, from Lund, you know, today.

—The Culture Club, Håkan nods.

He knows because he has been introduced to two of the five other members, besides Karin, whom he sees more like a friend.

And Karin is the only one in the group whom he really appreciates. The other two, whom he has dated, or maybe they have dated him, are not his type, but it isn't Linda's fault. She wasn't the one who thought they should meet. Now, both girls are married, and one of them has children. He's happy that he isn't the father and, overall, very happy not to have been selected. Håkan can't see how Linda fits in the group, but it might have to do with the fact that they hardly saw each other during the years when Linda was studying in Lund. He and two friends came down to the carnival, and they put their backpacks at Linda's, but that was about it. He has spent time with Karin, both then and later, and he likes her, her directness, her poise. Well, she has poise, not that she is unfeminine, but she is—tough. Believes in herself. And doesn't let someone else decide what she should do. She runs her race.

—Anneli still talks about you, Linda says.

—Well, tell her I say hi, Håkan says. But please don't say I talk about her. So, where's Tobias going to stay?

—I don't know. He will have to solve that somehow. It's none of my business. He doesn't want to move, and I have started to look for something else, but it's too expensive for me to pay for both the house and a rented apartment. And I won't get money until we sell the house.

Håkan can't help thinking that he insisted on Linda signing the transfer papers for their parents' house.

—I just wonder…Mom's and Dad's house—

—I know. Or I don't. I guess it also has to be sold when we divorce.

—That was probably not what Mom and Dad had planned.

—I don't know what they had planned at all.

But Håkan is certain they have a bad conscience, a constantly bad conscience, because they excluded Linda from the firm he has now managed to get in shape. And they are ashamed, for they believe that she has no money, or not as much money as he and they have. He and Linda have left all that behind. There's no discord; Håkan is certain of that.

—You're still not angry—

—Stop. I know that it's their, mom's, guilty conscience. But you're the one who has made the firm profitable. It's your merit.

They drive over the bridge and continue toward the city. It's nine o'clock on this Saturday morning, and Håkan usually isn't up this early on the weekend. But, now, he will borrow Linda's car for a few hours to shop for some stuff at IKEA. Linda laughed, both at the thought of him going to IKEA and borrowing her car, but his own is too small for bigger things, and doesn't everyone load up at that big furniture store? Meanwhile, Linda will meet her friends, and because she still needs to bring her clothes and some other stuff over to the guest room, this is the best solution.

—Drive up to Valhallavägen. It's easier, he says.

After a moment he adds:

—And if you could work at the firm, would you?

—Why would I?

—I need someone, long-term. I would like to work abroad for a while, with the two Italian printer companies we purchased. And regular business at home is actually quite simple, more of financial control. The customers aren't difficult to deal with, and most have been around for ages.

—Sounds fun, Linda says dryly.

They giggle, the way they only do when they're alone, as they did when they were little.

—Oh, you know what I mean. You could have done this as well as I do.

—Please don't say you have a bad conscience, too!

—Not particularly. But I would like for you to take over, rather than someone else. And somehow I think the staff would like it, too.

—I don't know, right now...

Håkan realizes it's the wrong timing, but it will never be the right timing, and the thought has been lingering in his mind for a while. It would have been wrong to talk about it at Christmas, and since he and Linda rarely see each other, it would have been just as bad to call her and ask.

—You don't have to decide anything now. It will probably take a while, but keep it in mind. A lot could happen.

Linda stops in front of his house. It's actually a loading zone, but there is no one unloading anything on a Saturday, and the short time it takes to carry up her stuff there won't be a problem. They take two IKEA bags each, filled with clothes, into the rickety elevator and manage to get the moving boxes in, too. Håkan gives her a key from the key safe.

—Here. You can come and go as you please.

—Thanks. I'll be here tomorrow night, and we'll see how it goes, I have to say good-bye to the kids…

Håkan hugs her, knowing she will cry.

—You can do it. You're not alone. And you are stronger than most.

They walk together down the stairs and out to the car. He decides that he'll call when he's done so they can figure out a good time for him to return her car. He lingers a while on if he should mention the photos but shakes it out of his head. He has got nothing to do with Linda and Tobias's private life.

*

The wind is freezing cold over Djurgården, and the water is as gray as the sky. Linda doesn't understand why she decided to walk out to Liljevalchs. Perhaps because she couldn't find the right bus. The inner-city buses are unknown to her, not like the subway, but she knows the streets well. When the cold wind bites her neck, the decision doesn't make sense, and when the snow begins to fall, it's still worse.

Anneli, Kerstin, and Emelie are waiting for her outside the museum. She sees them from afar and runs to meet them, with the snow whipping her face. Maria can't make it, and Karin is not around.

—One should have followed Karin's example and gone to the Canary Islands! Emelie says and hugs Linda.

Karin leaves for the Canary Islands every year. It's just her and the pensioners in January and February. Though Karin rarely indulges in sunbathing, she looks for inspiration in the colors, shapes, and nature. And thaws, for the south of Sweden is cold and windy until spring. When she has reasonable sales figures before Christmas, this is her way to treat herself.

The Culture Club usually goes to the Spring Salon, mostly because it's how it all started, with the women thinking that they were either creative and innovative or that they, with their critical eye and references to art and literature, were superior commentators. None of the women who created something has ever been accepted, and now everyone except Karin is more involved in administrative cultural work. Their own art manifestations have become more hobbies than the dreams that they used to have of living off their creativity. Karin has never bothered to come to Stockholm for these exhibitions, and this year Linda certainly understands why. Either it's totally uninteresting, or it's her inability to focus. Where the others stop and seem to ponder on the art, she walks straight past. There's nothing in the video installations and sculptures that attract her. Her thoughts are spinning around Håkan's offer to work at the firm and around the fact that she will leave home tomorrow. Leave the kids and Tobias, leave the house. Their house. She holds her wet coat over one arm, and it gets heavier and heavier the farther she walks into the exhibition and the more she thinks about this being the last weekend they have as a family. She should be with the kids.

She hears the others murmur but keeps them at distance. She has nothing to add, either about art or something that may interest them, and she has no desire to talk about the girls because she doesn't believe she will make it without crying. What was she thinking? That she would simply pat them on the head and say, "See you on Sunday"? Is this how it will be from now on?

They decide on an early lunch. It's only a quarter to noon, but the café is known for its delicious cuisine and desserts, so it's more by chance that they get a table where they can all fit in. Linda orders soup, but it's the freshly baked, warm bread that tastes the best. She spreads it thoroughly with butter.

—I must tell you something, Kerstin says between her mouthfuls of salad.

Kerstin is tall and slender and has her short thin blonde hair cut so close to her head you almost can't see that she has any hair. But it looks good, especially since she almost always is dressed in black and has her very own style. Linda likes that she is consistent. And with her job at Moderna Museet, it certainly is an excellent fit.

Linda can't understand how Kerstin could choose salad when it's so cold outside. Isn't she freezing?

—We had a visit from an event consultant, for the opening of the new exhibition, in April. It's tight time wise, as usual, but, yeah, that's the way it is. And we're on a tight budget. I don't even know if it's possible to do anything with that sum; just to rent a tent costs a couple thousand. In any case—this may be something you already know about, Linda. I think she lives somewhere near you. She told me about an acquaintance who had had a visit one night by a woman who asked why she was there, at her own house. The visitor argued that she—the woman who lived in the house, that is—had moved out. That she—the woman who came to visit— had redone the bathroom. And repainted the shed and somehow lived in their house, even had clothes in the closet! Do you get it?

What a shock! And how could it even happen? Have you heard about that, Linda?

The piece of bread in Linda's mouth is suddenly like rubber, sliding around with the butter, and she doesn't know what to do with it. Swallow? Spit everything out? Throw up, in the soup?

She hears the ooohhhs and aaaahhhs and noooo waayyyys but can't really take them in, can't understand that Kerstin is waiting for a response.

—How are you? Are you okay? Emilie says and puts her soft hand on Linda's shoulder. Her fingers are short and stubby, her eyes peering behind the dark frames that are too round for her equally round face.

—That's me. It's me, the one you are talking about, Linda says. You're talking about my life.

Kerstin laughs, a little too loudly, as if it were the funniest thing she'd ever heard, and Anneli laughs almost as high, but Emelie doesn't.

—Stop it, Emilie says.

Emelie pulls her colorful Peruvian shawl closer around her shoulders. She has worked as a volunteer for several years on an archeological site outside Lima and longs to go back, but now that her husband has a permanent job, it's no longer as easy to move the whole family. Linda recognizes Emelie's "stop it" for they have laughed at her, too, when she has told them how she tries to organize those trips, which are actually financially detrimental to her and her family, but she still manages to make it sound like they are important for humanity. But now the laughter isn't about the entire humanity, but about Linda and Tobias.

When the laughter stops, everyone stares at Linda. She knows that the color has faded from her face, not that she had much before Kerstin started, but she definitely doesn't have any now. She thinks that it's probably unusual to faint when you sit down.

—But…it can't be true, Kerstin stutters. I mean…why should it be you? It's just a story I've heard…From that consultant.

Linda knows it's Marita. Marita, the preschool party planner. Who does nothing but arranges parties, everywhere—at preschool and in museums, or wherever they may be needed.

—Because it's an ordinary story that could happen to anyone? Linda says. Believe me, I know it's about me. And I know who your consultant is: she is the mother of a child at the preschool.

The others stare down at their lunches, but no one eats.

—I'm so sorry. I didn't know—and I usually don't gossip like this. I thought it sounded so absurd, bizarre, that's all. And I didn't know what to say when she told me either. I guess she felt the same. Like…what do I do with this information?

Linda wants her to stop talking. This information? Is this something you need to tell everyone, a public interest? Would this be a story in the local paper, like those articles on recent callouts by the local police?

—But how are you? Emelie asks. Are you divorced?

—We're in the process. I'm moving out tomorrow, staying every other week with my brother.

—At Håkan's? Anneli says. Say hi from me.

Her cheeks flush, and Linda knows she hoped Håkan would be interested in her, but they never got that far. Now, Anneli is married and has children with a man she met on a dating site.

—Sorry, she says. How are the kids?

—I don't know. We haven't talked much about it, only mentioned that we will alternate weeks at home—

—But will you really? Kerstin says. Isn't that tough on you?

—Tobias doesn't want a divorce.

The others look at her. Linda can't decide if it's disgust or dismay that shows on their faces for the traits are confusingly similar.

—Are you joking? So he had a mistress whom he told that you had moved out—

—That we were divorced, Linda says. Yes—

—That you are divorced, okay, and now he doesn't want a divorce? I'm sorry for saying this, but it sounds completely crazy. Especially since he has been interested in a lot of the other moms at your kids' preschool. That's what the consultant said, anyway.

Linda presses her lips as hard as she can and hopes she won't start crying. Because the last thing isn't true. It's clearly something Marita has invented to make herself interesting, to spice up the story, as if it wasn't already enough.

—I don't think she has all the information. It's true that there's a lot I haven't noticed, but I would have noticed if he had hit on the other moms. The kids' preschool is small, and we have always attended the parties together—and left them together, too.

—I'm just saying what she said.

—But you're wrong. She's wrong. Can you stop now? You make it sound like I knew nothing about Tobias at all! And it wasn't the bathroom she had renovated; it was the guest toilet. But that isn't true either!

Kerstin raises her eyebrows and looks at the others as if to say she knows what she knows.

—I assume you've talked to Karin, Emelie says and grabs Linda's arm. I'm happy that you are such good friends. They are the ones that save you when things like this happen. Tell us if you need any help. It might be difficult to get Karin back from the Canary Islands.

—Exactly, Linda says.

If only it was about getting her home from the Canary Islands. If only it wasn't about Linda having not yet called Karin.

—Bring the kids over for dinner. We need to get together.

It wasn't a question; it was an order. And since February some-how seems longer than the twenty-eight days indicated on the cal-endar and is as equally tough work-wise as January is, and since Linda can't work long hours the weeks she has the girls, she might as well let herself be pampered. Although it's by Anita. It might ease the children's anxiety if they feel they are being cared for, that there's a family, that it's not weird that their parents no longer want to live under the same roof.

Neither Anita nor Linda has apologized. But Linda knows that the news that she now lives with Håkan every other week has reached Anita and Gustav, though she isn't clear about who has leaked the information: Håkan or Tobias. She hadn't meant to say anything, and she has no intention of apologizing for her decision. They are getting a divorce. In a little over four months.

—We're having dinner at Grandma and Grandpa's. That will be great, won't it?

Lotta and Fia nod. There are no protests, and Linda realizes that they are unsure if there's even a margin for protests anymore. She struggles not to cry when the girls' eyes follow her features, asking no questions, trying to understand what she has said.

Anita asked them to come right after preschool, and Linda picks up the kids unusually late because she has to. But the girls don't protest about that either, even though it's only the two of them and one boy left at preschool at half past four. The staff has grown tired of waiting outside in the cold and dark, and the teacher wants nothing more but to close the preschool up and go home. When Lotta and Fia say good-bye, the boy is left alone. His parents always come at five o'clock, and Linda can't remember how many times she has felt sorry for him. Now she thinks that he's lucky; he has somewhere to stay.

There are lights in the windows of the beautiful wooden house, but Linda can't lift her head properly. She sees only the beam of light on the ground. Had she looked up, she would have seen her mother's shadow and how it dissolves and disappears when Linda and the children approach the stairs.

The bag from the supermarket that Linda carries in one hand is crammed with sausage, macaroni, milk, bread, breakfast cereals, bananas, and cheese since Tobias managed to empty the refrigerator and the pantry last week without filling it up again. It's probably a part of his strategy, a warfare he intends to pursue. Fia pulls on Linda's other arm, and Lotta drags her feet in the sleet.

—Why can't we eat at home? Lotta whines. I don't want to eat here.

—It might be fun to see Grandma and Grandpa, Linda says cheerfully, though she knows it doesn't sound honest.

—I don't want to. I don't, I don't—

—Please, Lotta, stop it. It's only for tonight, I promise. All the other nights, we will have dinner at home.

—I want Daddy to be home. When will he be there?

—Dad's coming on Sunday. You'll see him on Sunday.

They ought to have the weekdays with one or the other parent and then every other weekend, to make the weeks shorter. Or, they won't be shorter at all. She doesn't want to have any weekends off; she wants to see the kids every day. But it seems like Tobias wants that, too.

The children shouldn't be a part of this agreement. She doesn't want them to sense the conflict, which they obviously do. This is only the second week, and it isn't normal that they aren't all at home at the same time. It's everything but normal, just as abnormal as it is to have dinner with her parents midweek. They never did. They never even received an invitation. She stops at the first step and wishes she had told her mother that it's impossible, that it's tough for the children.

—I want to go home!

Fia's shrill voice echoes over the empty, dark street.

Linda opens the door to her parents' house.

—How good to see you here, Linda, her mother says. Great, the food is almost ready.

Linda sets the grocery bag on the floor with a thud. The girls clutch her leg and don't want to take off their overalls. They look at their grandmother with suspicion, as if they know intuitively that there's something fishy about the whole arrangement.

—Won't it be great to sit down? Being a single parent isn't ideal. There's so much work, and you're on your own. How are you doing?

Linda takes off her coat. She knows that Anita also knows that it's the first day of her first week with the kids, so there's not much to discuss.

—It will be fine. We'll make it, won't we girls? Why don't we start by getting out of those overalls?

The children do nothing to help her. They whine and push each other, and Anita eyes the dirty garments that land on the floor. Tobias hasn't taken the trouble to wash them either.

—You may have to wash those. Well, not here, of course, since then they'd have nothing to go home in, I guess. They look disgusting. Do you have any change of overalls?

—Do you know what an overall costs?

—I'll check on the potatoes. Please, go into the living room.

Fia lies down on the cold marble floor and screams at her highest voice, just as she did on the doorstep, but there's possibly a smaller audience here. She spins around in her pantyhose and static electricity charges her hair, making her look like a troll.

—My dearest little one, there will soon be meatballs, Anita says in falsetto.

—Because Grandpa likes them, Lotta says.

Anita looks questioningly at her but then nods and walks away.

The thought of Grandpa liking Grandma's meatballs as much as she does makes Fia stop spinning on the floor. Linda picks her up and carries her into the living room. The table is set in the dining room with silver candelabras and white linen napkins, too festive for a family dinner. It's as if there's never an ordinary day here, as if every day were a feast.

It only takes about a half second, but Linda has time to perceive that the table is set for six people and not five when Lotta shouts "Daddy!" Anita comes out from the kitchen triumphantly, holding the meatball platter as if it were something she should sacrifice to a house god. She fends off the kids, who throw themselves into the arms of Tobias, and she pats the back of the chair to make Linda sit down. Linda could kill her.

—Daddy's here, Mom. Dad's here! Fia shouts.

Linda doesn't want to ruin her joy but just wants to fall dead on the ground herself when she sees Fia's and Lotta's undisguised delight and relief that they all are gathered.

The girls hug Tobias, and he smiles apologetically, as if to say it isn't his fault that he is loved, loved by all—by his in-laws, by their children. Perhaps by Linda, too?

—I can see that, Linda says.

Lotta slides out of Tobias's grip, walks over to Linda, searching to hold Linda's icy-cold hand.

—Hello, Tobias says. This wasn't my idea. But I'm staying here, so it might not be a surprise that I would be at dinner.

Linda stares at him, then at Anita, and then at Tobias again. What's going on? He stays here with her parents? And why hasn't anyone told her?

—Where's Father? Linda says. Mom, where's Dad? Where is he?

—Oh, he's playing bridge with his friends. He will come eventually. I thought it was best if we had dinner early because of the children.

Linda can't breathe. It should happen automatically, something the body takes care of by itself without her having to make the effort, but it no longer does. Perhaps her heart has stopped beating. She glances at her mother, but Anita turns her back to her with an "oh dear, I forgot the lingonberry jam" and leaves for the kitchen. Gustav would never have let this happen. He may not even be aware of what is happening, right now, at his home. He said that Anita only wanted well, but this, he would have stopped. Dad's on her side.

—Wine or beer? Anita shouts from the kitchen.

Linda wants something stronger—a whiskey would do. Or why not a whole bottle of whiskey?

—Beer, thanks, Tobias shouts back.

Anita's eyes don't meet Linda's until she asks them to help themselves. Anita's steely gaze penetrates her as if to say that it isn't easy to do away with either one's parents or one's husband. And that Linda isn't the boss around here.

—Wasn't this a good start to the week, Lotta, Anita says and serves her some potatoes. Isn't your Grandma clever?

Lotta nods.

—Dad, will you come home with us, too? Fia asks.

—No, I won't, not unless your mother wants me to. I stay with your grandparents because I have nowhere else to stay the weeks when your mother wants to be alone with you. And Grandma had the idea to shorten those periods to start with, the times when we aren't together.

—It's no secret that the girls yearn for you all to be at home, Linda, Anita says. And you know what, you should have dinner, just the four of you. You need that, she continues with her gentlest smile, tilting her head to one side. Grandpa and I can have the leftovers if there are any, but please don't think of us.

151

—I can save a few meatballs for Grandpa, says Fia as Anita leaves them.

Linda sits quietly, her back straight, hands in her lap. She's no longer hungry. She looks at Tobias, who eats with a great appetite, and at the children, who press themselves against him, wanting to be close.

—I think that Dad can come home with us, Fia says.

There's something challenging in her words, which she surely doesn't understand, that hits Linda with more energy and more power than she wants to acknowledge. A four-year-old's obvious insubordination. How do you handle that?

She doesn't want to fight, not in front of the children. They can't understand. They may be sad, but it is what it is.

—Dad's all right here, I can assure you. At Grandma and Grandpa's? He has meatballs every day.

—Come on, Linda. It was your mother's suggestion.

—And you're not independent enough to say you can make it on your own.

—I have no other family here, you know that. If it bothers you, talk to your parents. I find it an excellent solution right now, yes. And in this way, we can meet more often.

He means no harm—Linda gets that too—only that the children are the most important thing they have. Anita's the one to blame. In her desire to patch up their marriage, she's choosing the wrong side, Tobias's side, which makes Linda angry. No, furious. How can Anita presume that infidelity will just pass? What reference points does she have? Anita knows nothing about their life, nothing more than what she's inventing—that Tobias is the best man Linda has ever met and that their marriage, therefore, must be saved. And even worse is that Anita would have a part in piecing it back together.

—Can't we try to get together and talk about this?

—Yes, I think that's a great idea, Anita says coming out of the kitchen again, leaving the door wide open. And I'll take care of the girls so you can go to a nice restaurant, just the two of you. That's an excellent idea. Decide on a day. I'm flexible.

Lotta and Fia stare at Linda as if she were a meatball to stick a fork in or a fish to hook. An easy target.

—Friday? Tobias says.

—Yes, that's perfect, Anita says. We're free. Should we say Friday, Linda?

—Next Thursday, Linda says. I can't make it before that. And I can't that Friday. Or on the weekend.

She won't give in, and she sees that Anita is about to say something. Maybe they have theater tickets, but she takes a deep breath.

—Very well, then. Would that work for you too, Tobias?

He answers that it will be great and that he looks forward to it.

—Hey, it wasn't yesterday we went to a restaurant together, Tobias says cheerily. And now we don't even have to pay a babysitter! Are there any meatballs left, by the way?

The candles flicker, and there are enough people in the restaurant to create a faint background of murmurs mixing with the soft music. It should be perfect, and it should be romantic. It's the first dinner at a restaurant that Linda and Tobias have had together, just the two of them, since the kids were born.

Linda sits down on a sofa that threatens to devour her, and Tobias immediately offers to take her place.

—You can't eat with your chin on the table.

The waitress looks concerned, and Linda tries to rise from the soft cushions.

—And it's better if you look at me and not at all the others, Tobias says with a laugh and winks at the waitress who giggles before she presents the menus and pours the water.

Linda doesn't answer. The restaurant suddenly seems filled with girls in low-cut, tight dresses and high-heeled boots.

She pulls on her short pale-blue woolen cardigan.

—You look nice, Tobias says and strikes his annoying hair strand from his forehead. Very stylish. Have I seen that one before?

—I don't know. Probably. It existed when we met.

—You had some funny clothes back then.

Funny? Eleven years ago he had said that she looked nice, old-fashioned, but in a good way. Linda feels more good-looking than she has in a long time, in the clothes she removed from the closet and took to Håkan's, so that only Maja's stuff was left. Tobias hasn't moved anything. And, obviously, neither has Maja. Did they, this week, when Linda hasn't been at home? Maybe Maja lives with them now, repaints, tiles the bathrooms, replaces the flooring.

Linda scratches her neck and straightens her hair.

—Well, this is cozy, isn't it? I have never been here before, have you? he says.

—No. I don't go out that often.

He laughs loudly. Too high.

—Forgot that, he says. But you have had a full week to do so.

—Three days.

—But this is a place they talk about.

Linda doesn't read restaurant reviews; she doesn't care. Tobias perhaps needs to take customers out but not frequently, and it doesn't require him to keep updated with the newest restaurants. Obviously he does anyway. What more has he done that she hasn't known about?

They glance at the menu in silence. Meat or fish, maybe chicken? Linda decides on the chicken, which she immediately regrets. She could have chicken at home. She should have ordered fish, which is good for your body, too. The only fish they eat at home is fish fingers, though she knows that the children get salmon patties at the preschool. She should cook that someday. Tobias orders steak, and they agree on some red wine.

Once they have toasted, he extends his hands toward her across the table. Linda recoils.

—What is it?

—Nothing. I...I'll just go wash my hands.

Linda gets up and looks around.

—It's down the stairs, over there, to the right, Tobias says.

She nods and pulls at her twisted cardigan.

The food still hasn't arrived when she returns. Tobias is leaning back on the soft couch, wine glass in hand. She sees he has already filled it up.

—The kids don't seem too happy about this, he says. I mean, it's not a good solution. It's all very artificial—you staying with your brother and I with your parents. And the weeks are too long for the children. And for us.

On that Linda agrees, and she's happy that she isn't the only one who's squeamish about it.

155

—Should we split the weeks in some other way, now in the beginning? she says. Three days, two days, and then every other weekend? That way, it might feel shorter, for the kids, too.

—And for your parents. I'm not so sure they like having me around.

Tobias grins and Linda laughs politely. She would actually like for Anita and Gustav to grow tired of Tobias.

—You'd only have to start looking for some other place to stay. That's the easiest way to make it less artificial.

—I intend to keep the house, whatever happens. I believe it's invaluable for the girls, knowing that there's a "home."

—So you'll bail me out? Linda says.

—I don't even want you to move. I want us to try again. Hey…I know that what I did was wrong, but I don't want us to separate. We belong together. You and the kids—you're everything I want, all I ever wanted.

His eyes are shiny, and Linda is certain he wants to talk about his father, the father who wasn't there when he grew up. He has told her so many times how important family is to him. That they mean everything to him.

—You make it sound like it's my fault.

He swishes the wine in his mouth. It looks as if he'll spit it out again, but after a few rounds, he swallows loudly and takes another sip. Then he clears his throat and takes a deep breath.

—There's this other dilemma, he says, leaning back on the soft cushions. Which is your parents' house. Which is now, officially, ours. And it's clear that your mom's a little worried about it, the way you act, that is.

—The way I act?

His eyebrows twitch, enough to explain that this, at least, is not his fault. Not the way he sees it. Linda nods.

—In that case, it's probably better that you make yourself at home. If you think you can afford to bail me out of that house too. Seems like you have plenty of money. Excuse me for asking, but where does that money come from?

—Let's see, there's a chicken with fennel and mashed potatoes and one entrecôte, the waitress interrupts at just the right moment, when Linda has almost decided to get up and leave. Tobias changes tactics.

—We should do this more often. Just you and me. Nice to get out of the house. Good thinking there, by your mother.

Is it good thinking by Anita? Is this the best solution to it all, them spending a Thursday evening at a restaurant in town—when it's as if Maja is sitting next to them?

—When is Maja collecting her things?

—Why are you talking about her? I told you it's over. I can throw away her stuff if that's what you want.

—It's up to you.

—Will you move back if I do?

They eat in silence, only the cutlery scraping the plates reveals their movements. But the food is good, better than Linda had imagined. It's been a while since she's had something else other than food that the kids like, and at Håkan's she hardly dares to touch the seemingly unused pots and pans and has mostly had soup and crisp bread.

—Sorry, he says, when he takes the last bite. I owe you an explanation. But I have broken up with Maja. You and the kids—seriously, it was super awkward, stupid, unforgivable. I hope it isn't unforgivable. It's the stupidest thing I've done in my life, and if I could have it undone…if we could get back together again… Because I really don't want a divorce. It's not that I want us to stay together for the kids' sake; it's not about that. I also understand that there are families that divorce and that some have to. But that's not what I want. I never wanted it, you know that. And I hope and believe that deep down you don't want it either. That what we have is more important.

He stretches his hands toward her again, and this time Linda doesn't hold back. She lets him take them, lets her cold hands be embraced by his big and warm hands, though she knows she shouldn't.

—Stop.

She tries to pull them from him, but his grip is too strong, almost like a cramp. Her eyes are overflowing, and she closes them. It's all wrong. She chose the wrong person, and now he sits opposite her and is more wrong than ever. Still, she lets him take her hands and comfort her, or whatever he does. She's like an alcoholic who can't keep from drinking, because it's so simple, the simplest thing in the world. Just to start over, or not even that. She only has to continue where they were before the visit from Maja.

—Linda, don't cry. I want us to be friends, for the sake of the children, and to be able to continue our marriage. I understand that it isn't easy to get over, but…for our sake. Because we are a family. I miss you. These weeks have been…too long. Too heavy. I can't…I know I've done everything wrong. I want to repair it. Tell me what I should do to make things right. If it means I have to burn those clothes, I will.

He must think that it sounds charming and fun because he laughs. Linda keeps her eyes shut and smiles so he will believe that they are in sync in this story, that the protagonists agree that things like this can happen and that what they have together is the best they can get.

And she nods. It's supposed to mean, yes, please burn the clothes. Sometimes she misses him, too, but when she does, she thinks of what he has done and is filled with such rage that she gets out of breath.

The last piece of chicken is tough and stringy, and she clears the wine glass to get it down.

—Want more?

He lifts the wine bottle, but she declines the offer, and he empties the rest in his own glass.

—This is the way it should be, you and me, together, Tobias laughs. For the rest of our lives! Do you want dessert?

He winks and glances through the menu.

Linda doesn't like desserts.

—No, I don't think so, she says.

—They have a walnut pie that is good, he says. I've heard. And a toast to us!

Linda raises her empty glass. It sounds so simple when he says it out loud. Simple and obvious. And completely crazy.

—Can I have this weekend with the kids? she asks.

—If that's what you want.

She nods.

—Since you are leaving with them soon, on that ski trip. I would love to see the girls more. I will miss them.

—Won't you miss me?

The last two years, Tobias has booked the ski trip during the winter break because everybody else where he works is gone that week, too. For Linda, it's the opposite—if they had waited for two weeks, she would have been able to go because the financial statements would have been done. Tobias had booked during the winter break again.

Lotta and Fia were so excited to get to take the night train up north and back. All the way up to Åre. Why they had to go there Linda hadn't understood, since Åre seems to be mostly for families with older children. But it was Tobias who decided, and back then, when he had booked, she had just sighed. She can't stand the cold anyway.

Linda survives only through pretending everything is normal, although nothing is. But when she comes home to the deserted house, she believes the pressure over her lungs will crush her chest. She staggers into the hallway, sits down on the floor with her arms around her legs, and rocks back and forth.

"I'm going insane," she says to herself.

Wandering around the empty house is so painful that she only goes home to sleep; the rest of her time she spends at work. She comes to her senses while nibbling an old bulging slice of crisp bread in the kitchenette at work at eight o'clock one night, and she's not even hungry.

"They'll be back home soon," she thinks. "They'll be back home on Sunday. It's only a few days and they're having fun. I have to finish the financial statements."

After two days, she wishes she had gone along because it suddenly seems so silly and childish to not be able to give the girls those few days of parental interaction.

At a quarter to nine on Sunday morning, she finally pushes open the door to Håkan's house, after pressing the wrong code four times. The door opens, and then closes very slowly, though Linda wants it to slam and looks around. The street is empty. Not even the corner bakery is open, although there's a smell of freshly baked bread. Östermalm residents have no early habits, but in about two hours, the café will be full and the line will fill the street.

The elevator door is the old, rattling kind, and Linda doesn't want to be heard, doesn't want to wake the house. She takes the stairs, even though every step echoes in the stairwell however softly she tries to move. Breathless, she reaches the third floor and presses the key into the lock. She is absolutely sure that Håkan's asleep. He was probably out and about yesterday, or at some friend's house. His shiny kitchen looks completely unused, and during the two weeks she has spent here, she's the only one who has had breakfast—the days he's home, he buys a sandwich and a cup of coffee at the corner and eats in the car on the way to work. She hasn't seen him cook any food because he has been away for almost the entire time.

Linda stands perplexed among all the shininess. She feels like an intruder, which she is objectively, but Håkan has said that she can come and go as she pleases, that it doesn't disturb him. And now Linda needs someone to talk to. It seemed like the most natural thing in the world to talk to Håkan, although they haven't had much contact over the years and they have barely seen each other during the weeks she stays at his place. But he's still her brother. And they have never been enemies, even if they have never socialized with particular intensity.

What should she say to him? What could he do? It's suddenly not at all natural to come barging into his apartment, especially not if he's still asleep.

She had only intended to surprise them. When she stood on the bleak platform this morning, she again regretted not having gone on that trip. And she only just wanted to pick up the girls, go do something together, bring back that family feeling. For every day she is alone, like those days when she has stayed at their house, she wonders if she's the one who has gone crazy. Suspicious, envious and crazy. Does it really matter if Tobias had an affair, when she hasn't noticed anything? Nothing at all. And he has not been mean or unpleasant or less present. Their life has been as usual, exactly as it has always been.

She shudders at the thought. As usual.

When she saw him step out of the railway carriage and then Fia and Lotta, her eyes had filled with tears, and she had stopped for a while, letting the heat fill her body; there they were, her family! And then Maja had peeked out of the carriage and come down the stairs. The family picture had frozen, as if the cold had coated her eyes with ice. Everything had become crystal clear and then completely blurred, and when she dried her eyes with the glove, it had been as if the four people melted into one. She had blinked and seen Maja turn around and wave. She'd seen how the children stretched their arms and waved back before they took each other's hands and walked in front of Tobias to the underground passage. Linda had hid behind a pole.

Hadn't he said that they had broken up, that they didn't see each other anymore? Maja's clothes are no longer in the closet. Linda has checked, and it's empty since her clothes are also gone. The makeup in the bathroom cabinet has also disappeared. But they go on holiday together.

*

Linda hears a door open and turns around to apologize to Håkan. But it isn't Håkan. It's a young man, maybe ten years younger than she, wearing only underpants, and he has a body, because it's impossible to ignore that body, that makes her blush and stare down at the floor. His curly blond hair makes him resemble an angel that just landed. She doesn't dare to look up at him, and he doesn't move.

—Excuse me, she says. Pardon.

—Sorry?

A second later, she hears Håkan open the bedroom door. His hair is disheveled, and he ties his dark-blue robe around his body.

—Linda? What are you doing here?

Linda looks at him and then back at the young man, and it strikes her that she doesn't know anything about her brother and that she doesn't have any business being here. That he has a personal life, things she didn't know and that she currently can't grasp.

—Sorry, I must go. I didn't mean…I'm sorry, Håkan. I didn't know. I'll…I'll take my things. Or I'll get them…call me when I can get them. It's probably best that I move back home.

The words stumble out of her mouth, and she's ashamed of everything she says, but she can't take it anymore. It's like walking in quicksand, as if her whole world has suddenly started to move out of sync. Nothing is as it has been; nothing is as it appears to be.

The young man stands perfectly still in the corridor, seemingly unmoved by the commotion and apparently not aware of his charisma. Håkan holds out his arm and approaches her.

—Linda, I'm sorry, it's not—

He stops. Starts over.

—You can't move back home, he says.

It's not a wish; it's an order.

—Do you hear what I say, Linda. You can't move back home. You must drop the idea of Tobias.

—He's my husband, and this is my life, my family. You know nothing about it, and I know nothing about you, and we have had a good life…We've actually had a good life together. Stay out of it.

Linda's tears are overflowing, and she can't talk anymore. There's only a pitiful whimpering coming over her lips, and there's no ending to it—she can't stop the sound, a sound from an abyss.

Håkan hugs her tightly, letting her tears and snot wet all his sleeve, but he doesn't let go even when Linda tries to get out of his hold. She softens and feels her body relax.

—I want everything to be as usual. Just as usual. I want to go home. I want to see the children.

He holds both her upper arms, looking seriously at her.

—Don't do anything you'll regret. By the way. There's one thing I haven't told you.

Linda shakes her head. It doesn't matter. His life doesn't concern her, just as her life doesn't concern him.

—I don't care, she says.

—Wait a second.

Håkan walks past her, stops by the entrance, and starts searching the clothes. He comes back with a few pieces of paper and hands them over to her.

—You can check them out later. I don't know what it's about. You might already know about it, and if you do, I don't care. But if you haven't seen them…well, that's up to you. That's up to you and Tobias.

Linda puts the papers in her pocket. The young man in underwear has vanished, and she walks to the front door, wishing that she had never seen him, that she hadn't come here. What you don't see or know is better. Secrets are supposed to be kept. She already knows she won't be going back to Håkan's; he deserves a private life.

Her footsteps echo in the stairwell. If people wake up early this Sunday morning, it's not her fault; it's the fault of the planets, the world, life. She has nothing to do with it. It's not under her control.

She gets into the car and takes a deep breath. Leave or bite the bullet? Confront or resist the urge and swallow the disappointment? Believe and hope that everything will be fine? It can only get better, if she stops getting in the way. Maybe they happened to meet on the train, Tobias and Maja. She could have been in Åre skiing, couldn't she? Everyone goes there, right? Those who have abandoned Orsa and Lindvallen, who have bigger kids, they ski in Åre. Tobias said that they had broken up and that they haven't seen each other since. It could have been a coincidence, or maybe they had already planned this trip and didn't want to cancel. So why should she make too much of that—that she waved on the platform? It's so bloody stupid.

When she starts the engine, she remembers the papers Håkan handed over. Sometimes this family is completely hopeless in their insinuations. Why can't they just spell things out? She stops the car and searches her pocket for the papers.

They are Polaroid pictures. Seven, eight. She holds them like a fan in front of her, pulls out one and inspects it, then another, and another…Tobias is on all of them. Together with girls she has never seen, and that are not Maja. Some were taken at beaches she has never been to. The swimming trunks he's wearing tells her that some of the photos must have been taken a while back, more than three years ago, but some are probably from last year.

The roar leaving her throat is something she has never heard, and she's so afraid of herself that she can't help but yell again. She wonders if this is how it feels when you go crazy, really crazy.

*

Linda drives aimlessly around town. Aimlessly, but not as recklessly as she would like, because on Sunday morning the streets are still deserted. She would like to accelerate, slam on the brakes, and change lanes while shouting and swearing at everyone around her. It's not at all her way of driving, but the rage and the urge to scream are still there. She turns up the radio to the highest level, hoping for rock or heavy metal, but it's only sweet pop melodies on all channels, things to wake up to after a night out, perhaps in an unknown bedroom or with the love of your life. Where's the music for those who are betrayed, those who are angry, disappointed, devastated? Linda hits her hand on the steering wheel though she wishes she could use the horn.

What is Tobias doing? What has he been doing? And how has all this escaped her? Linda is blinded. She sees the photos in her head, and they flash in her subconscious. Colorful holiday pictures, places where she has probably never been. Were there two or three women? She doesn't want to hear how many women Tobias has been involved with. Her whole body itches. She's sweating and freezing at the same time and hopes, suddenly believes, it's only one woman, but in many pictures. But she has to know. Now. She slows down, stops the car, and turns off the engine. She picks up the pictures and looks at the images again, from beginning to end.

Who took the photos? Who even owns a Polaroid camera? Did he buy the camera and ask someone, anyone, to take pictures? What was he thinking? Or did he go with someone who wanted to immortalize those days? Had they been digital, he would have been able to save them in a secret file on his computer. But here they are, made into silly Polaroid prints.

She stares out the car window. It's gray and dreary, and sleet covers the ground in the still-deserted city. Two buses drive past. They're almost empty, and the few people riding them are staring out the windows, headphones in their ears.

Linda has no memory of Tobias returning home with a tan, which means the trips must have been short, probably just a weekend. When could it have been? She searches in her memory for opportunities and can only remember that Tobias, except for last New Year's Eve, has always had last-minute problems around Midsummer, when Linda and the kids have left for Anita and Gustav's summer house in Falsterbo. Each year, the same thing. He has always been enthusiastic when the Midsummer celebration has been brought up, and then, only days before, always excused himself directly to her parents, saying that work must come first and that "this year" he has an exceptional amount of work to do before vacation. Always exceptional, before Christmas, around New Year's, at Midsummer. Sometimes at Easter, too, it strikes her. She and the girls have spent several cold and wet Easter holidays in Skåne, helping Anita spring-clean, as an installment on the summer days to come.

As far as Linda can tell, there are at least three different women in the photos. Three different times and three different pairs of swimming trunks. But how? She can't digest it. He doesn't seem to have hesitated to lie either. Lies, straight to her and her parents' faces. And perhaps Maja's?

Linda wants to rip the photos to pieces and burn them. She doesn't want to accept that it's this easy to fool her. How many times in the last weeks has Tobias told her he loves her and that he wants to stay with her and the children, putting the pieces back together? That they are the ones who matter to him, that it's over with Maja? Maybe it is. But how could she trust him now? What if he keeps in contact with the women in the photos, too?

Linda presses her hands hard against her eyes, seeing flashes in red and yellow that hurt in her head. How can she be so gullible? The tears, the cursed tears, flow in rivers, and it doesn't matter how much she blinks because she can't see anything anyway. Snot is running down her nose and onto her coat, leaving traces as if a whole family of snails has wandered back and forth over her. She might as well be dead. She means nothing to Tobias, and the way things are now, he means nothing to her. Nothing at all. And everything. Indeed—everything.

When the tears stop falling and she breathes normally again, it's as if life has disappeared from her. She looks out the car window again, and although the gray looks much brighter now and there's a chance of a beautiful winter day, it's only a statement of fact. The only things left to do now are practicalities. She needs to make sure she picks up all her belongings from Håkan's since it's impossible to stay at his place any longer. No matter who the man in underpants is, the meeting has already made her realize that it's not fair that she encroaches on Håkan's privacy. She's not mad at him, it is what it is, but he could have told her; that would have been the easiest thing. She asked him to set up house rules so they wouldn't get in each other's way. And there haven't been any problems whatsoever. It's her own fault, what happened this morning. She had said she wouldn't be there this weekend and then she was. Linda swallows. She made a huge mistake, not Håkan.

But she's angry with everyone else. Angry and sad and desperate. The longer she sits in the car, staring out, the more her reaction amazes her. She's filled with something she never cared about, always backed away from—anger. Something you don't show in the Adeus family, and why is that? Wouldn't it be about time that someone got furious and talked about their wants and needs? Though if nobody reacts, what should one do with all that anger? That's how her mother has planted it in the family consciousness, that the anger is misguided and hurtful; it's a lot of noise that does no good. If you can master it and consider the outcome, the anger will subside. And you will be calmer, more relaxed.

Linda rubs her temples. She has tried to apply her mom's thoughts, a "non violence" for families, but when she thought she could reboot—swallow her disappointment as she has always done, put the lid on her feelings and stoically explain to the outside world that on infidelity, no one else is to judge, that you have to decide yourself—then everything collapsed. The decision felt so easy, this morning. For the sake of the children.

But who is she, Linda, to let all this happen? Who gets caught in these people's games and whims—why hasn't she noticed? Doesn't she see the signs?

Her phone rings in her purse. Tobias probably wonders why she isn't at home. She had promised to be there, and she has missed the children so desperately, but she can't let go of the picture, of them waving at Maja. She picks up the phone and sees who it is. There's a third and a fourth signal before she responds.

—Linda, what's going on? And why haven't you called? Why on earth haven't you called? Please, tell me. You know that I'll listen.

—I can't.

Linda's voice is shrill and afraid, and she tries to fend off the anger with frustration and sadness, everything she has accumulated and pressed down her throat, like an overfed goose.

It becomes quiet. Linda hears breathing, both her own and Karin's.

Then she yells into the phone:

—Because you were right! Don't you understand! You were right all along, and I didn't want to listen. And because I don't want you say, "What did I tell you; he's an idiot!" Because I have two children with him, and because I had just decided to not give a shit about the fact that he had, or has, another woman and move back home—where else should I go? And then you would never have needed to know.

There's another pause of silence, this time probably for a minute or more, and Linda listens to it and her breathing and thinks about how it feels to be this angry. It felt tremendously good to scream. To use her voice, being allowed to express what she wants and ignore what the other person is feeling or thinking. But it's wrong to yell at Karin, who has done nothing but call her. Who only wanted well.

—Sorry, she says. Are you still there? Sorry, I didn't mean—

—It's okay, Karin says. You know, it's great, that you're shouting. Though I'm not sure I have heard you raise your voice for the last eleven years.

Linda doesn't understand what she means. Hasn't she raised her voice? Doesn't she? Of course she does. She must have been angry, but—maybe not particularly upset, not that many times. Because she felt confident in what she had and that she and Tobias had a kind of agreement, something that resembled what Anita and Gustav always had. You can resolve conflicts in other ways. If there are any conflicts. Which there haven't been. Outwardly. The thought confuses Linda. What's happening?

—I shouldn't yell at you, Linda says weakly. It's not your fault. I…I don't know what I'm doing anymore. I don't know who I am and why this is happening to me. What's wrong with me? What should I do? I'm here in the car, and I don't want to go home.

—No, I should apologize. I haven't called, at all. Emelie called me.

Linda sighs. Emelie, who always must ensure that everyone is informed about everything. And that the message reaches everyone. And find out as much as possible to make sure there are no misunderstandings. She truly is an archeologist to her fingertips; she digs and digs to expose every detail that may be hidden or that no one has had an idea to check.

—She thought I had more information, but I knew nothing.

—I understand.

The shame makes her stomach wrench, and she swallows the acid reflux.

—You know me better than anyone, Linda says. And I…feel so ashamed. I didn't see it, I didn't understand. And you read Tobias better than I did.

—You're still in love, Karin says. You can't see through the one you love. It's impossible. But there's nothing wrong with you. Please, don't think that of yourself. I thought that your love would fade, but apparently it hasn't. I have compared you to a lot of other people I know, other relationships.

—It would have been better if the love had faded, I can tell you that much.

They laugh, and Linda is infinitely happy that they do, that she can laugh with tears falling instead of crying. And she tells her everything about Anita and Gustav's house, and how difficult it is to handle and that she doesn't want it, that she doesn't want to live her parents' lives.

—So what's the next step? Karin says.

And Linda continues, talking about the move to Håkan's and this morning's two encounters and how Håkan gave her the photos, and Karin listens. It's now that Linda's anger returns, pushing against her sternum as if she were pumping up a huge balloon within her.

—But who was that guy you met at Håkan's? Karin says.

—I don't know, Linda sputters. I don't care who he was, and I don't want to know unless Håkan tells me. I don't want to delve into his private life. Maybe he isn't ready for it. What do I know?

—Do you think he's gay?

Linda doesn't think anymore. She doesn't understand why no one can be honest and say what they want.

—I don't think about what he is or what he isn't. Right now I have to get a roof over my head. On my own.

—Yeah, I'm sorry. You can always come here.

—It's a little far to commute, Linda says. But I might have another solution, temporarily.

—You have to take care of yourself. And the girls.

—We do. We take care of them. I think they're okay. Or, I don't know, but I really try—

—Calm down, Karin says. Calm down. I am sure they aren't mistreated. But you are. And it's not your fault, remember that. I can always help, to mediate, I mean—

—I don't think that's a good idea. You know us too well. And there's probably nothing to mediate on. I know what I want.

Karin's response is short and harsh.

—But it's probably not what he wants. And that's where things get complicated. But there's nothing wrong with you. You're the strong one, Linda. You have done nothing wrong. You're the kind of person everybody respects because you go your own way.

—And what if I don't want to?

—But you do.

When they hang up, Linda is both calmer, since she has told Karin what has happened, and angrier, because she's the one to suffer while everyone else seems untouched, safe in their conviction that everything will work out and return to normal. Tobias may not want what she wants—what does it matter, really? They're only getting a divorce. They will sell the houses. And Linda's life will go back to normal. However normal it can be when you've lost faith in the man you thought you would share your future with.

She starts the car. The windshield is white with fog, and she puts the fan at the highest level. She searches until she finds a radio channel with classical music and hears the "Moonlight Sonata" being played, slow, sad, and full of the same melancholy as she while she drives back to the suburbs.

It's already ten o'clock when she's on the street where Bo's house is located, the only house that doesn't follow the pattern of either adhering to the Functionalism or the traditional wooden houses, and there's something appealing in how it stands out. Plus, the house somehow matches Bo, who doesn't fit into the picture of how the people in this suburb look or what they do for a living.

Is it okay to call on someone's house on a Sunday morning at ten o'clock? It's too late to change now since she has already put her hand to the knocker and hit it three times against the door.

—Linda! How good to see you! Come on in!

Bo is, as usual, wearing a checkered shirt, now paired with some worn dark-brown corduroys. On his feet are gray woolen socks. His hair is a wild mess, and it doesn't look as if he has bothered to shower.

—I won't stay—

—Oh, no worries. Stina's not here anyway. Two of the children are at a basketball camp, and the younger ones are playing upstairs. A cup of tea?

Linda nods, gets out of her boots, and follows him into the kitchen. He pours the tea before she has had time to sit down on the wooden bench. It smells of cinnamon and sugar in the kitchen, spicy and sweet, warm and cozy. She runs her hands over her cold thighs.

—Up early? Have you been out for a walk?

Linda shakes her head. She has no desire to talk about what happened, to poke around in the wounds that are still bleeding. She can taste the blood in her mouth as if she licked it from her own internal lacerations.

—No, I'm waiting for the children and Tobias to come home from their skiing holiday. They should be home shortly.

—Lovely. Yes, well if you like skiing. How was the weather?

She has no clue, hasn't bothered to look, but guesses it was cold and dark; that's her memory of skiing in Sweden. When they were kids they'd gone over New Year's, which was cheaper than in February but also much colder and darker.

—Were you going somewhere? You said maybe during the Easter holidays? she asks politely.

—No, well, I'm not sure. Perhaps. We'll see.

His laugh is dry, and he pulls his hand through his hair. In the backlight, a small cloud of dust shows around his head.

They slurp their tea, and Linda gets sweaty in her heavy sweater but leaves it on since she won't be staying. She sets down the teacup and counts to ten, not to seem too desperate.

—I have a problem, and that's why I came. I am sorry to bother you. That house…or apartment, that you talked about—

—Yes, would you need the house? Want to see what it looks like?

He smiles, as if it were the best he'd heard in a long time.

Linda shakes her head, not caring how it looks.

—It might just be a month, a few days a week. I'll try to find something of my own, but I've had too much to do at work lately…I'll pay a monthly rent, but I won't be here that often.

—Sure, you do as you want. That's up to you. But it's great if you want to rent it. It has been empty for a while. Stina's not too keen on subletting it, but I'm not even sure she'll notice.

—Oh, well, I don't want to get between you…Did you say it's empty?

Linda hears the panic in her voice. She doesn't mean that empty is bad; it has to be furnished. She has neither the time nor the money to engage in interior decoration right now.

—Nobody lives there. But it's furnished, so you don't need to buy anything unless you want to. Bring sheets and towels though. And don't worry about Stina. She's hardly at home.

174

Linda nods and takes another sip of the tea, which is now cooler. The taste of cinnamon lingers on her tongue. Has Bo got a habit of adding cinnamon and cardamom to everything he makes? Aren't those spices that hide all other tastes, like if the food is rancid or old? What has it got to do with tea?

—Good for your blood circulation, Bo says. Cinnamon, that is. Did you know that? The Indians use it a lot. I found a Yogi Tea for Christmas; isn't that the flavor you miss now?

Those teas, Linda has seen them at the supermarket, but never bought them. It sounds like mumbo jumbo: Yogi Tea. Sometimes she wonders why the supermarket even tries to sell them. Those who are interested in that kind of specialty products would rather go to a health-food store. But apparently not. Does Stina also like Yogi Tea? Do they meditate together? Or do they do yoga? Is that how they get their strange relationship to work, by having a higher mental level together?

—So where's Stina?

—Oh, at a conference. I'm not sure where. But she'll be back tonight. New work week waiting. Those important Monday morning meetings.

He laughs, but when Linda looks up, he covers his eyes with his hand. He clears his throat.

—And how about you and Tobias? Or, I guess it's going in one direction; I mean toward divorce. Because you will divorce, won't you? Otherwise, you probably wouldn't want to stay here, I mean.

—Yes, that period of reflection sort of makes it take more time, but otherwise, yeah, it's going forward.

Linda looks out the window. She should go. They must wonder where she is since she promised to be home when they arrived. But Tobias hasn't called. She takes some big gulps of tea. They have nothing to talk about.

—And the kids, Bo says. Are they okay?

—It hasn't been that long, so it's hard to say. And now they have been on vacation. They almost get more attention now.

It sounds absurd. Lotta and Fia are more in the center of attention than ever before, almost more than when they were newborns. The days with the girls are the most important, and it seems to be the same for Tobias because the kids can't stop talking about everything they do with their father: what he made for dinner, the bedtime stories he reads—he who almost never read to them before, let alone cooked anything.

—Yes, initially, Bo says. And the older they get, the better they become at using it. In a way, it's probably better that they are small when this happens. They're not as manipulative.

—Do you mean they test you?

—Oh yes. But with a perspective on a divorce, you understand what they want. It's not their fault we don't live together, but they can't decide on that. You'll see; it'll get better.

He smiles apologetically, as if he had just told secrets every divorcing parent will know, in due time.

—I must go, Linda says. They should be home now.

Bo follows her to the door and out onto the porch, wearing a pair of crumbling clogs.

—So when do you want to come? he says. Just so it doesn't coincide with everything else around here—

—Thursday, she says quickly. Thursday and Friday. Then I will stay at home Saturday and Sunday and here Monday, Tuesday, and Wednesday. At home Thursday and Friday. Here Saturday and Sunday. There's that preschool party, right?

He shrugs, and she repeats her schedule, the only thing that still makes her existence bearable. The days with the children. Those who await her. Monday, Tuesday, Wednesday. She'll get off work early, pay them all her time, beloved girls.

Bo nods as if he understands, but Linda realizes he is past the time when you need to keep everything in your head, and when she turns around, he looks at the calendar hanging on the wall.

—That's excellent. Thursday sounds great…I'll be here. I'll turn on the heat, aerate, and clean the house out. You're most welcome. And you're going to the preschool party then? If Stina is at home, I guess we should show up, too, meet the other families. She doesn't see much of it, the everyday life.

He laughs, embarrassed, and Linda has nothing to add—what should she say? Is this when they should share their marital problems, being on the same level? She doesn't want to hear any more, and suddenly he gives her a big hug and holds her a little too long, so that Linda has to twist out of his grip.

—Thanks. Thank you. See you Thursday.

She hurries to the car like Cinderella, but no prince is running after her with a shoe, and everything has already turned into pumpkins. But she has somewhere to stay, even if it's unknown territory. Who cares. It's all about survival.

*

Two streets away from home, the phone rings. Linda slows down, searches for her phone in her handbag, and answers.

—Linda, it's Mom.

Linda could talk to anyone but her right now, but she could make it short and blame her for being late.

—Hey, I don't have much time—

—Tobias called. He said you weren't home. Where are you?

—I took a walk this morning, why? Why does he call you to tell you I'm not at home?

—He had called Håkan also, but Håkan said you weren't at his place either. Where are you going?

Linda pulls over, stops the car, and turns off the engine.

—I'm on my way home, Mom.

—Are you staying now? Have you made a decision concerning your relationship?

Linda has always seen her mother as someone with a clear set of rules, a sense of right and wrong about what you do, say, think, and feel. Nothing in Anita's life has been shades of gray as far back as Linda can remember. Black or white, with no greater possibilities to negotiate the outcome.

It must be about the house. Anita wants to stay until they find someplace else to stay, and they have envisaged that Linda and Tobias will move in as a happy family who keeps the family traditions alive. Though Linda thinks that Anita and Gustav have created this situation, she can, despite what she found out this Sunday morning, feel sorry for them. If only they hadn't interfered.

—Yes, I think we have sorted things out. It's not that complicated.

She says it naturally, and it echoes in a familiar way in her head. Words that mean nothing to her but a lot to her mother. Words that make Anita feel calm and safe, since she has the situation under control.

Linda has said them before.

—Yes, now I'll finish this off, of course. It's not that complicated, only one semester left.

When Anita found out about business school and Linda already was on her way down to Lund, the answer came quickly. Håkan had to speed up his studies in order to take on the responsibilities of the firm. The stroke of bad conscience she hasn't felt in years bubbles up, like a regurgitation. If she doesn't think she should have anything of the firm, it's precisely because of that—Håkan has had to sacrifice a lot. And he has done so without grumbling, at least not against Linda.

—That's great to hear, Anita says. Very good news. It seems as if you have reasoned it out and are all right with everything. You're a sensible person, Linda. And they seem to have had a good time skiing. Was it in Orsa?

—Åre. Everyone goes to Åre. But why did he call you?

—He wanted to pick up a few things if I understood him correctly, and if you both move back home, well, then it was right, and he doesn't have to live here anymore. But he didn't want to bring the girls, even if they are very welcome here, which I told him. They wanted to stay at home and play. So I guess we won't see you either.

Tobias won't stay with them the next few days? And Anita believes he'll be staying at home because they have talked things through? Linda feels sick.

—Yeah, that won't work, not today. We'll see further on. Listen, I need to go. We'll talk another day. Say hi to Dad.

Linda starts the car again and drives into their neighborhood; first right, then left, and then left again. Their house is two hundred meters farther down, the house that used to be their stronghold. Now it's just a small shabby cottage, where the gutter is about to fall off the roof. Tobias hasn't mentioned it, although he usually cares that the house is in order. Linda has a stubborn tummy ache when she walks up the wet and worn stairs. They're all lying. And she can't figure out how these loose ends fit together because she is too tired and upset.

Tobias is standing in the entrance with his hands in his pockets, as if he was waiting for her.

—Your mom called and said you were coming. You said you'd be home.

—I went for a walk.

—Yeah. Why did you take the car? Didn't you walk here, in the neighborhood?

—I went to Djurgården.

—I was hoping you would come and pick us up at the station.

—Oh, she says.

179

Their eyes meet, and she looks defiantly at him until he looks away.

—Did you have a good time, any snow?

—Sure, we had a great time. They can ski alone now, both of them, on the slopes.

She should be proud but doesn't want to give him the appreciation he wants because he, the Dane, taught them to ski.

Fia and Lotta come running from the living room, throwing themselves against her. She sits down and hugs them for a long time. She has to close her eyes and take in the scents of their hair and skin.

—Did you meet someone you knew? she says casually.

—No.

She meets his gaze, but he doesn't move one millimeter.

—Should we have? he says.

—Everyone seems to go to Åre.

The children cling to Linda, but she gets up and says they'll talk about everything later, that they should just say goodbye first.

—Okay, so...I'd better be going, Tobias says. We'll meet on Thursday, girls. I'll pick you up at the preschool as usual.

They let go of Linda and turn to Tobias, who hugs them while they pat him on the cheek as if he were a little dog and he mumbles how much he loves them.

—And you're staying with my parents this week?

—No, I'll...I'll be traveling, he says as he stands up and turns toward the door. But I'll pick the kids up on Thursday. See you then.

They both know he's not traveling anywhere. And Anita is certain he's moved back home, that they've moved in together. Does he think so, too?

—Okay. Then, that's it I suppose. Have a good...trip.

He nods, takes his bag and his portfolio, and is out of the house before she has time to say anything about the photos, Maja, or her mother believing they're back together. All's good; is that what he has told everyone?

*

Linda has missed the kids. And actually, she has missed Tobias, too. It hits her when he slams the door, that she hoped that everything was okay. She had been so close. So close she'd almost decided during these days to let their life go on, together. It's good to forgive, isn't it? Everything isn't black or white, as in Anita's world, but a constant gray scale, where you have to reflect on what you leave—or keep.

The Polaroid pictures burn on the retina—no, they burn almost physically. She can feel the smooth paper and how she wants to let go, but they are etched into her fingerprints, as if someone had put glue on them. When you get it on your fingers, it's as if the skin shrinks and yearns for contact with anything that could cause it to regain its normal shape. She wants everything to be normal. And nothing is anymore.

Why take Polaroid pictures at all? The quality is poor, the light is ugly. He might have received them as a gift.

"Here, a souvenir of a wonderful trip"—were those the photographer's words? That Tobias has kept them makes matters even worse—he has wanted to save a proof. As if he wished to be discovered, just playing hide-and-seek with her. To know that he hasn't even tried to hide from friends or neighbors is disgusting; he has been looking for houses, he has gone on vacation, he has had Maja stay in their house, no, live in their house. What more has he done?

She goes down to the basement and looks at the bags Tobias left in the washroom. They are opened but not sorted. His and the children's laundry is welling out of the bags. The scent of his sweat mixed with the deodorant he has always used, Drakkar Noir, makes her nauseous. Does he think she'll wash all this? She would not touch his clothes, not knowing whom he has laid his

181

body on, if there are traces of someone else. Although she has found nothing before, during the four years he has been seeing Maja, she's still afraid she would find something and that she hasn't reacted because she didn't even imagine there could be anything. Because she's gullible.

She sorts out the kids' clothes, one by one, and puts them in different piles. The big remaining heap she pushes aside with her foot, under the wooden bench, and then she presses the two nylon bags into a closet.

How come the children didn't tell her they met Maja? What if it wasn't her? What if it was someone else, a woman they just sat next to on the train and talked to? Linda regrets she asked, but then she remembers the photos again. It doesn't matter if it were Maja or someone else on the train. But if it wasn't Maja, or if Linda hadn't cared, then she wouldn't have gone to Håkan's…

All these "if not…thens"! Hadn't she been so quick to leave her work Christmas party that night? If she had not, then Maja would've met Karin instead of her. Would it have been different? Would they still be married? Would they have inherited a house, been on the skiing holiday together? How many years would this have continued? She walks toward the stairs, holds on steadily to the rail as she mounts.

The girls sit on the carpet in front of the TV. The contents of the big basket of toys is splashed around them like a battlefield of colorful plastic animals.

—We got these when we went skiing, Lotta says, holding up two pink plastic horses. Because we could ski on our own.

—We got them from Maja, Fia says.

Linda nods.

—I see, she says. That's nice of her. I hope you thanked her properly.

She closes her eyes, and her body shakes as she tries to hold back the tears.

—You're not staying? You told me you would stay?

Tobias looks expectantly at Linda, and she's happy that she already has had time to tell the girls they will continue to see her every few days. And she's especially happy to hear their voices from their bedroom above so she won't disturb them, and won't hear their wishes for her to stay, that she shouldn't leave, that there's room for her, too. Her prepacked bag is waiting by the door, containing all she needs. Tomorrow, she'll see the children again. Tobias seems to not quite grasp the schedule they've decided on, and she has no intention of explaining.

—We can't stay together, Linda says. We'll talk about that, about the things you lied about. But not now.

It's obvious that he doesn't want to understand what she's talking about, and it somehow soothes her, and to her surprise she stays calm. Karin's words echo in her head. "You're not moving back home." No, she isn't.

Tobias clears his throat.

—I told your mom—

—She said so. I just don't get why it's so important to her that we live together, but I can imagine. She would like to stay. But I can't be held responsible for their bad judgment. We have to solve this, somehow. They will eventually understand that we're getting divorced and the house will be sold and you'll get half of the money.

He nods slowly.

—I think she wants you well, he says, putting his sock against a piece of wooden board that sticks up from the floor.

—Could you sand that down, please? Linda says. So that the children won't hurt themselves?

He looks at her in surprise, and she realizes that she has released herself from their relationship for a few seconds, and it's a good feeling.

—Are you staying at Håkan's?

She hesitates. Should she tell him about the handsome man in briefs? And how do you, casually? That there was a half-naked man in the apartment and that she just wanted to leave?

In another time, Tobias would have laughed. Yes, they would have laughed together at the fact that Håkan is maybe hiding in the closet and that he hasn't told anyone, not even them, not even his sister and his brother-in-law, who are probably the least judgmental and who could keep a secret if that's what he wants. Linda is somehow offended that he hasn't told her. That he doesn't trust her. He must have a good reason. He might not trust Tobias, and she can't blame him for that.

—No, he…it doesn't work in the long run. I'm renting a room in an annex to Bo's house. Bo, whose kid is at the preschool, that is.

Tobias coughs.

—Bo? You're kidding, right? Are you moving in with confused, dorky Bo?

—Stop. There's nothing wrong with him. He's weird, but… Anyway, it's better if I'm not that far from here, for the sake of the children. If something should happen.

Tobias continues to laugh to himself.

—Yes, of course…But people might say that you're a couple—

—Stop it. I don't live there; I don't share his bed. It's not as if the entrance is in their house, if that's what you think.

—So how is it?

Linda swallows. She hasn't even seen the rooms, but it must be some kind of extension with a kitchen and toilet and shower and everything one might need.

—It's—simple. Simple, but good. I've got to go now. See you on Sunday, I guess. I'll pick the kids up tomorrow.

—We need to talk about this schedule, how to organize things.
It's—

—Look, we'll fix that some other day. Let's do like this for now.
She doesn't say good-bye to the kids, doesn't want to upset
them. They're with their dad tonight. But only tonight.

*

When she calls at Bo's, the sun has set and the hunger is gnawing.
She hasn't planned for dinner, or for breakfast.

—Are you having dinner? she says when Bo opens the door, still
chewing on something.

—Yes, but don't worry. Here's the key. We'll maybe see each
other next week then? Because this was for a night, right? Great.
It's right there, around the corner, follow the path.

He gives her the key and points out to the right. The garden
path is hardly visible, but she thanks him, and Bo has closed the
door before she turns around.

A lamp lights up automatically as she rounds the house, and
then another when she puts the key in the lock. The brown door
bulges under the metal cover at the bottom, and Linda has to pull
hard to open it. A smell of dust and mildew hits her as in her parents' summer house after the winter.

She stretches her hand along the wall and switches the lights
on. An old bulb hangs askew, spreading a faint yellow light in the
entrance but nowhere else. She closes the door, keeping her shoes
on, thinking she will need a pair of slippers. She opens each door
hesitantly. The first leads to a tiny bathroom: a toilet and a shower
without shower curtain. She leaves the light on. Next, a small
kitchen with two hot plates, a minimal sink, and a coffeemaker
with a yellowed plastic filter holder. A tiny table and two chairs.
She goes straight ahead and looks into what is the bedroom: a
single bed that curves down, a blue-gray blanket on top. Under the
window an old electric heater makes the window blind dance as the
warm air rises. The only door that leads to the left has a high step,

and when Linda switches the light on, she realizes that this must be a part of the original house, as the building seems to hug the smaller construction convulsively. The room is long and narrow with a sofa and a small coffee table, a floor lamp dating from the forties, and a bookcase full of old books. At the other end is a large window facing the garden.

Linda sits on the armrest and closes her eyes. What's she doing? She'll only sleep here for one night, but even a hostel would be cozier. This is like being condemned to prison, but she must tell herself it's a temporary solution, for a few months only, until the divorce is finalized and both houses sold. There's a future. She needs to ask about the rent, but it can't be that expensive given how the rooms look. Had she gotten a place on her own, she would have had to buy furniture she might not need or want later on. This will have to do.

"I think she wants you well," Tobias had said about her mother. What does she want, anyway? She wants to smoothen out the economic differences between Linda and Håkan. If that's the way she wants it, there's no reason to hide. Linda will need the money. Both houses must be sold. Anita only has herself to blame, and now Linda needs to get her to understand. But first, she needs something to eat.

She leaves the lights on and hopes that it will be different when she comes back, that she will feel at home. On the other hand, it's for one night. It should and must work.

Håkan steps into the arrival hall at the Milan airport and is, as usual, hit by the fact that he is so tall compared to everyone he passes. Tall and blond, that's the way he feels every time. Secondly, he's hit by the smell of coffee which always makes him happy because there's nothing he likes more than a real espresso, not too strong and not as bitter as the French do it.

The man at the rental-car counter recognizes him, for the first time. They shake hands. "Signor Adeus, benvenuto!" sounds like "Jingle Bells" in Håkan's ears, and his earlobes turn hot and red. Italy. He loves everything about this country. He even likes working with the Italians; it's better and more straightforward than he had expected. When he gets out on the highway, he leaves the Swedish gloominess behind, and he no longer thinks of anything he needs to get done at home. He'll fix it when he's back; the others can handle the daily business without him. Besides, he's just a phone call away. But he must get Linda on the track or his plan will never work, and this currently occupies more of his thoughts. In fact, it takes up much of his waking hours when he's at home. And yet, he hasn't been able to call her, fearing that she will overreact again. That morning meeting in his apartment wasn't a good start. Ever since, he has wondered how to get the pieces in place, and he believes he's approaching a solution.

They have arranged to meet, but not at the company. It's close to one o'clock, and this is what they usually do when Håkan comes down, to be alone, without everybody checking them out and without starting off in a professional way. That's what they did in the beginning, and it almost derailed the whole relationship—how do you start over when you haven't met for weeks? Should you be personal or professional? Do you shake hands or kiss on the cheek? It took a few months before they found a solution: first, a good lunch, time to tune in to each other again, time to hug and talk about what has happened since the last time and how much they have missed each other. Now everyone at the company knows that their relationship is serious. But when they are at the company, they are still professional, they work together. And they do it well.

He parks the car and sees that the restaurant's outdoor terrace is open. His heart is bursting with spring feelings, with love, with longing. And when he gets out and looks over the green hedge that screens off the parking lot from the terrace, he gazes back and forth. He smiles to himself and raises his hand.

—Amore!

That word. Amore. My love. Not only has he waited since the last time, sometimes he thinks he has waited all his life. And this is what he has waited for, this single person who has lived here forever.

He walks through the restaurant, cheers the waiters, shakes the restaurant owner's hand. Here, he's not unknown; he's one of them, a good friend. To him, it's special to be appreciated as a guest. And the appreciation is mutual; you eat better here than anywhere else. Maybe it's because of the good company since they have always come here together. It's possible that the food doesn't taste as good if you're alone or with some other business acquaintance. But they came here even before they began their relationship, before they became a couple. It's their restaurant, where they have never had to hide but can always be themselves.

The owner directs him out to the terrace. He knows that the Swede wants to sit outdoors, weather permitting. "The Swede," that's what they call him. It's difficult to be named Håkan in Italy, and he always uses his middle name, Alexander. He doesn't know why he got the name Håkan Alexander, but Alessandro is much more viable than Håkan.

Perhaps they shouldn't kiss, but they do. The neighboring table applauds and so does the staff.

—Amore, he says. You are more beautiful than ever.

—You are awaited. I have missed you so much.

He takes Giovanna's hand across the table, looking at her long dark hair, olive skin, and slender arms. She has taken off her sunglasses, and her eyes are a darker brown than he remembers.

—You and Antonio are so different; you look nothing like each other, not like siblings at all.

—He would work well in Sweden, right? Giovanna says. Must be some Viking blood in the family tree. He was very satisfied with the trip, did he tell you? Got a lot of good contacts. He met some newspaper and magazine editors, to show his work, and there were a few families that were interested—did you give him the names?

Håkan nods. He constantly meets people who renovate and purchase new houses and want nothing more than to expose their homes. It's as if all his acquaintances can't let go of the idea of having their homes shown in interior-design magazines. Antonio is a brilliant photographer, even though he wants to devote more of his time to nature photography than architecture and interior design, and Håkan hasn't promoted him in the ordinary sense, only ensured that he got some leads.

—Which means we can soon make an exchange? Håkan says. Antonio moves to Sweden, and I move here?

A smile spreads across her face, and she squeezes his hand tightly.

—Just tell me when, amore. I can't wait.

—Neither can I. I need to talk to my sister. I already asked her once, and I'm convinced she would be great for the firm.

—And when can I meet her? When will I get to meet your family?

Håkan hesitates. To meet Anita and Gustav isn't the best idea. He has never presented any girlfriend to them, and it has always been the right decision. And now, he would like Giovanna to meet Linda first.

—Would you like to come celebrate Midsummer? he says. I'm usually out on the island, at my summer house. It can get a little cold…but if it's at least sunny, it's like magic. Summer nights that never end.

—And what do you celebrate?

—The arrival of summer. That the holidays are near. That school's out. The nights are long and bright. It's an old fertility thing, from when we believed in the Norse gods.

She laughs her dark laugh and wipes away the hair.

—It sounds…exotic.

—The most exotic thing we've got, not counting Lucia. You know, the pictures I showed you last winter, of the girl in white robe and candles in her hair? Antonio may also want to come?

He thinks of Linda, she could come, too, and bring someone, except for the children. Maybe Karin? He hasn't seen her in a while.

—There was this awkward moment, when my sister came over. I don't think she understood—or, I'm quite certain she didn't—who Antonio was, and I didn't have time to explain. She was upset about her husband, and I had to tell her another thing.

Giovanna puts her hand over his and caresses it.

—About me?

He smiles at her.

—No, you are a well-kept secret. But if you come at Midsummer, I promise to present both you and Antonio in the best of ways.

—Promise?

—Promise. With all my heart.

—I would be happy to come. How's your sister doing?

—I…I have no clue. Probably not great. I found some Polaroids of her husband. Photos of him and some other girls, different from the one that visited my sister. She didn't take it too well, but I had to tell her. She was about to surrender and go back to him. We had a small discussion about that.

He pats his thin blond hair.

—But, now, it's not about her. Now, it's about you and me. And I'll stay for a while.

She squints at him and then takes a sip of mineral water, fills up the glass again, and looks over the restaurant guests. The whole terrace is filled, and the waiters are busier than ever.

—Alessandro. Is there a plan? I mean, a real plan? So we can have a life together?

He is glad she asks. In fact, he's happy and excited; there are butterflies in his stomach, and his blood tingles like the mineral water in her glass. Has he ever felt like this before? No, this is different. This is serious—someone who wants to share his everyday life as much as he wants to share her.

—Yes, there's a plan. And I hope it can work out, this fall. What if I move here? If I change my way of working, being in Stockholm a few days a month but most of the time here?

When she nods, his heart is as light as a balloon, and he hopes her heart is the same way, that the strings are tangled into each other over their heads so they can fly away together.

Linda still hasn't come up with any reasonable excuse for why she can't go to the preschool party and neither has Tobias. So here they are, next to each other, in front of the preschool. Tobias pulls his hand through his hair, and Linda stands right behind him so he can enter first. Which he does without hesitation or looking at her, or even holding the door.

Usually, the parents who are divorced show up not with their new fiancés, dates, or spouses but with their exes. One might have thought that the 2010s would be more flexible than that, but the parent cooperative Solstrålen firmly holds onto the idea that the biological parents should appear together, even at an unofficial event, like a preschool party. They could refrain from coming, protest and stay home—nothing would be more natural—but it's as if everyone wants to show they can handle their separate lives and children, that there's nothing complicated about it at all. Linda has always been amazed at how much fun they seem to have. It's polite and friendly, and she has wondered whether it's the preschool's merit or if this is how it is when you separate. That the three couples so far touched had simply grown apart, that no one had been unfaithful, that they are still good friends. In that case, she doesn't belong to the crowd.

Normally, the parties are in connection with the Work Days, a weekend when you clean and scrub; paint; and put up new shelves, hooks, or paintings, according to the staff's wishes. But for the first time, the party has nothing to do with those days. The Board has approved an extra Work Day this fall, but no one wants to miss a chance to party.

—How good to see you two together! Marita shouts.

She is wearing a plaid shirt, tight jeans and cowboy boots, and a big hat.

Linda somehow wants to say that they are still married, but she stops herself.

—This preschool makes all separations better. I mean, the kids are so much better off with parents who aren't fighting, right? Marita says.

—Very much so, Tobias says and hugs her. And we'd rather party!

Inside, the area normally used as the children's dining room is set with long tables, and there are colorful paper hats by each plate. Linda looks down at her black silk dress, the only one of her old dresses that doesn't feature a puffy skirt, but is a little more conservative, more '60s. Rarely has she been so uncomfortable in what she's wearing.

—It's a cowboy theme! We've made chili con carne, but first there's a little Tex-Mex thing in the kitchen. Come on in!

Drinks are being served in the kitchen, where the atmosphere is high, the laughter echoes between the tiles, and there are plastic glasses with lime slices on one of the work benches.

Tobias has already taken a first sip of his drink. Linda sees him shake hands with some of the other fathers who are standing in a corner. The mothers form another cluster; there are five or six of them. Linda gets a glimpse of Bibbi. If Linda could just sneak up by her side, at least the start will be less painful. Linda reaches for a glass and walks toward Bibbi.

They hug, and the surrounding buzz dies as if Linda were mortally ill or contagious. Nevertheless, the crowd opens up and someone sighs.

—How are things? Gabriella asks, who's standing on Bibbi's other side.

—It's okay, Linda says. And here we are together!

The last words she presses out with an apologetic laugh, hoping that someone will laugh with her, but they don't. One mother glances toward Tobias, whose laughter rumbles over the kitchen, not at all as apologetic as Linda's.

—So, are you still staying with you brother? Bibbi says.

—No, that…that won't work in the long run. I rent some rooms. It's fine.

—Yes, I heard, Gabriella says. At Bo's, huh?

—At Bo's? another mother says. Honestly? How does that work? I mean, Stina is pretty jealous, isn't she?

Linda has not even seen Stina, so that she would be jealous comes as news to her, which she also says. There are no secrets in this, and when she thinks of her accommodation, only the stale smell of old summer house comes to mind. It still lingers in her sweaters and her hair when she arrives at work in the morning, but no one says anything about it.

They all turn toward the door where Bo and Stina have appeared, he in a crumpled shirt and a pair of black jeans, she in a simple black dress, semi-high heels, and a beige cashmere cardigan with pearl buttons draped over her shoulders. Her cheeks and neck are red, and she squirms when she sees the group of mothers. Linda discovers that all the others are wearing tight pants; knee-high suede boots in gray, black, and brown; tunics that cover their behinds; and big scarves around their necks, all but Linda and Stina. Their eyes meet, and Linda thinks it should be in some kind of recognition because they are both a bit different, but Stina eyes her from the toes and up before she comes closer. The ring opens up a little and then immediately divides into two. Bibbi, Gabriella, and Linda form a group of their own.

—But jeez…can't she stop staring! Bibbi says. I didn't realize she was jealous, but with that look—

—Oh, that's just because I don't fit in with the crowd. The ugly duckling, you know. My feathers are different.

They laugh since Linda's dress undeniably is different, but Gabriella has already commented on the thick silk and that the handwork is exquisite. Linda can't even understand what she was thinking when she put it on, going to a preschool party. She should get rid of it.

—It looks cool, Bibbi says. And it suits you. What does Tobias say, about you staying at Bo's?

—He doesn't understand why I can't move back home.

—Would you? Gabriella says.

Linda shakes her head and sees herself two weeks ago, in the car, after she had run into the underwear man, and remembers the talk she had with Karin.

—No, no, I can't…There's too much—

She grimaces and waves her hand as if it were a chapter in a book she doesn't want to read.

—We must get together some day, Bibbi says.

—Look, Gabriella says.

Two of the newly arrived mothers join the fathers, who immediately make them a place. And their husbands, two men Linda has never seen before, pull slowly toward Linda, Gabriella, and Bibbi. Linda shakes their hands as they introduce themselves, but she immediately forgets their names. Gabriella and Bibbi start a basic conversation—ten questions of varying personal level—and then a second drink. Linda leans against the cold stone wall and watches Tobias. He has control of all the other men and the two women and seems to enjoy it. Linda can't help marveling at how easily he attracts the attention, how obvious his person is in every social context.

She has always loved to see him fill up an entire room; it had been enough to fall in love with him again. But now, when one of the women throws her hair and turns her face at him as if he were some kind of messiah, she freezes. Bibbi stands next to Linda while Gabriella patiently listens to the two men. They are neither attractive nor interesting, but it doesn't seem to worry Gabriella at all; she politely turns her head to the person speaking and nods.

—He holds court, Bibbi says.

—Have never perceived it like that before, but now I get it.

—Me either. I mean, I have noticed that he was always talking and always in the center of attention, but...

Tobias puts his arm around one of the women and she almost loses her balance. They all laugh. Her voice is higher than everybody else's, and the man who is probably her husband turns around, looking proud, and shouts, "Take it easy with my missus!" and everyone laughs even more.

—Tiring, isn't it? one mother says, who Linda knows separated two years ago and who's here with her ex, but he stands with a third bunch of dads and all are staring at the floor.

—I know how it is, she continues. My ex was the same. Do you remember? It was unbearable.

When Linda looks in Tobias's direction, he has already started talking with another mom, who laughs as much as the first, seeming happy about the attention, probably surprised but proud that someone still sees and appreciates her. The arrow shoots straight into Linda, even though she isn't susceptible to that kind of courtship. She doesn't even notice that the mother who talked to her leaves.

—Is everything okay, in the house? Bo says and looks more awkward than ever.

Linda starts.

Bibbi takes another tequila drink. Linda suspects this is her third.

—Hi Bo, Linda says. Sure. It's fine, great. I'm not there very often, as you might have seen. I work late most of the days when I'm not with the kids.

—Yeah, that's true. And good, too—

Stina glides up next to Bo. Her patchy red neck and face has grown into something that mostly resembles a single rash, and Linda tries not to stare at it.

—Linda, she says. So it's you. See, I don't find it appropriate that you have moved in with us, which is something I just heard. That you live. At our place.

She stares at Bo, who looks down into the glass in his hand. The transparent drink and the lime sway back and forth.

—Maybe you can explain later, Bo, because we haven't discussed this, and I am surprised—she raises her voice—surprised that you didn't have the guts to tell me. Did you plan this, thinking I wouldn't notice, only because this woman isn't there when I'm home? And for how long did you count on it working?

—Could we discuss this when we get home? Bo says.

—This preschool feeds on gossip! Stina says, and her shrill voice kills all other conversations.

The three of them in the middle, Stina, Linda and Bo, are now the center of everyone's interest. Linda takes a step back, but Stina won't let her go that easily.

—And for you, who apparently aren't even divorced but who don't seem to care about your husband bringing home new women, is it a good solution to move in with someone else, with a married man? And that I find it out here, and now!

Linda glances at Bo, but he still focuses on his glass. It looks as if he has fallen asleep.

—I can't understand this sluttishness! Take your stuff and move out, now, do you hear me! Stina screams.

Linda looks around. Along the walls, the parents stare at her, not at Stina, not at Bo. The silence is compact.

—The sluttishness, she hears next to her. Such a fun expression. The sluttishness. Where does that word come from? Tobias says.

—From your wife! Stina roars.

—Nooooo, no way, Tobias says. That would be strange. In our family, the sluttishness is all mine.

197

Everyone laughs with Tobias. Except for Linda. And Stina, who looks back with fury pumping out of her eyes until she realizes she's no longer in focus.

Linda wakes with a start. Her back aches, and when she tries to turn around, she is about to fall out of the bed, but the sleeping bag that covers her like a moist skin stops her. She looks around in the faint morning light seeping through the windows under the ceiling, and it takes a few seconds before she remembers where she is. It's not at Bo's place, and it's not at home either. Right.

"You can stay with us tonight."

Thanks to Tobias's laugh, Stina had calmed down enough to sit down at the dinner next to one of the cheerier fathers who hadn't talked about divorces at all. Linda had been squeezed into a corner, from which she had observed Tobias and one of the women who had held court around him, and by the continuing laughs, she had judged that Tobias had kept at least his dinner companion in a good mood. Linda had had two bottles of beer, skipped the tequila shots, and hardly eaten any of the brown stew called chili con carne. She wondered where she would sleep. She had been thinking about a hotel or about wandering around the suburban streets, waiting for dawn, and then passing by her parents' for breakfast.

It had taken until half past two before Peter wanted to end the evening after talking to Gabriella most of the night. What did they have in common suddenly? Linda had wanted to ask Bibbi, but she had been busy dancing to '80s hits with Mats. When Peter tumbled around in the entrance hall in search of his jacket, Bibbi asked if Linda had somewhere to go. Maybe she realized she wouldn't get Peter home on her own, without him falling in the bushes along the road.

Linda rewinds the scenes from yesterday evening in her head and shudders. Since she was basically sober throughout the evening, her perspective is different from the others, but why do they sit on the kids' small chairs and drink alcohol at the preschool? Wouldn't it be better to party at someone's house? The outcome would be the same, of course. Chaotic.

She picks up her handbag and gets her phone. It's seven o'clock. There's a risk that Bibbi and Peter's three children will soon wake up and burst into the basement, which also serves as TV room and playpen. She crawls out of the sleeping bag only to realize that she has nothing but her party dress to wear. The options she has are either to go home or to go to Bo and Stina's. Plague or cholera.

The dress lies like a dead crow over the couch, and it's the garment she least of all wishes to pull on right now. The thick silk fabric is crisp, and what seemed festive yesterday is more than wrong today. Linda wishes she had been one of the other mothers, with a long tunic and a soft scarf around her neck instead, something she could leave in without feeling ashamed.

She puts on the dress and pulls up the zipper in the back and presses the black panty hose into her purse. In the guest bathroom mirror, her pale face shines, her makeup is passably washed away, and there are dark semicircles of mascara under her eyes; she looks like a panda. Only not at all cute or cuddly.

The stairs creak, although she tries to tread as lightly as possible. Once on the main floor, she hesitates and goes into the kitchen. Should she text Bibbi? That would wake her up, and there's no need talk to her. There's a pen and a notepad by the sink, and Linda writes a short sentence and puts the note on the kitchen table. There's no reason to stay for breakfast, and she knows that Peter wouldn't like it. Her being dressed as a wilted flower? Nope, that would not be acceptable. Better to disappear.

Linda takes her shoes and coat, opens the front door, and steps outside. The area is empty, the sun is rising, but the cold encircles her bare legs. She walks with quick steps toward the grove and remembers how dark it was on New Year's Eve.

—Hi Linda!

Gabriella appears, jogging. She's wearing tight black leggings, a neon-yellow vest over a black jacket, and a neon-yellow cap over her head. Her dark hair is set in a ponytail dangling down her back, and her cheeks are rosy.

—Are you leaving?

Linda nods.

—It was fun yesterday, wasn't it?

—Yes.

There's an awkward silence, while Gabriella is jogging in place.

—You're early, can't have slept for many hours? Linda says.

—As many as you, probably, Gabriella says with a big smile. This is the best way to wake up though. And I almost only had water yesterday, so I am doing great. I might get some rest with the kids in the afternoon instead. Where are you going?

Linda walks in place to keep her bare feet warm in her party shoes.

—I'm, well…home.

—I hope everything will be all right.

—Yes, exactly. Thank you. Have a great weekend then.

—You too! Say hi to your family!

Linda watches Gabriella jog down toward the water and assumes that she exaggerates when she puts in that extra energy the last three hundred meters. She can envisage Gabriella entering their perfect home where Mats has already baked croissants and made frothy milk for their cappuccinos—but they probably don't eat unhealthy stuff, like croissants. A homemade muesli perhaps? Full of fibers, flaxseeds, and antioxidants. It's like a commercial for some new butter that lowers the level of cholesterol or some breakfast cereals where the protagonist moves around in a fluffy white blouse, during which you get a glimpse of a flat stomach. All that Linda doesn't have—a beautiful house, a perfect family, a great body. Happiness? The thought stabs her in the chest.

She turns and hurries the other way, toward the house, while she gets out her phone and taps a message she can only hope she'll get an answer to, but she must write it anyway. It doesn't take more than a minute before the phone vibrates in her coat pocket. Linda reads the text:

"There's a flight in about an hour and a half. You're welcome, of course. I'll book a ticket, will send it by e-mail. Will pick you up at the airport. Hugs, Karin."

It's just after half past nine when Linda, longing for a shower, lands at Sturup. She has only a black nylon bag containing the bare essentials—panties, two T-shirts, a nightgown, socks, toiletries. The sweater and the jeans she's wearing will do for the moment. Karin must have something she could borrow.

There had been no one in the house. The kids slept at her parents', and Tobias should pick them up after lunch, but he wasn't at home. She realized it already at the entrance since neither his shoes nor his jacket were there. The emptiness had been yet another reminder, a slap in the face. Turn the other cheek. She both wants and doesn't want to know where he is—with one of the moms he talked to last night?

Karin walks toward her, twisting herself through the stream of sleepy passengers with open arms, and Linda leans against her with a sudden fatigue, and then those damned tears.

—We'll drive to my place, put on some tea, and have breakfast. And you'll tell me everything. There's plenty of time.

Linda dries her eyes and smiles faintly, a brave smile that contains the knowledge that things should be different, but there's nothing she can do about it. Apologetic.

—I thought it would work, she says while they walk out the doors to the parking lot.

—What happened?

—The guy I rent from, his wife went bananas last night in front of all the parents at the preschool party. She screamed that I had to move, and Bo, her husband, said nothing, just let her call me a slut. As if we had a relationship!

—Do you? Is he your kind of guy?

—Stop it.

Linda tells her how and who he is, and Karin laughs loudly.

—I get it, not your kind of guy at all. Slut. Gets even funnier from that perspective.

—He is kind and everything, and he was cool when we had that preschool flea market and everyone stared at me, but he's a little too caring. And I don't understand what he sees in her, but that's not my problem.

—But you live with them?

—I don't live with them. I rent a house, or an apartment, next to their house. It's ugly, like an old summer cottage invading the real house and so not cozy at all, but I'm barely ever there. There's a bed, that's about it. It's because…I don't know what to do. I've got to get something of my own—

The tears flow, as usual, and she sniffles.

—Did you talk to Håkan?

Linda shakes her head. It gnaws at her, that she hasn't called, hasn't dared to call. There's something in what she saw, although she doesn't care if he likes men or women, that she finds hard to talk about. Or difficult to bring up. How do you start the conversation, without losing his confidence?

—Don't you want to ask? I can do it for you if you want.

Linda looks at Karin, her copper-red hair that shining in the pale morning sun.

—And what would you say? "I heard there was a good-looking guy in underwear at your home—who is he?"

—Oh, I know Håkan. I can talk to him.

Linda knows that Håkan likes Karin the most of all her friends, especially the one from the Culture Club. He has never been interested in her nor Karin in him, much to Linda's disappointment; she would have liked having Karin as her sister-in-law.

They talk about the Culture Club for a while, that perhaps they should meet for the summer—celebrate Midsummer together, for example. And then they both realize that it might only be Linda and Karin who would like the idea, because they're the only ones who are single.

—Can you tell me the background to it all again, Karin says. What happened?

—I told you about the house, right? Linda says. Mom and Dad? They forced me to sign papers for us to become owners, on Christmas Eve?

Karin nods.

—And, then, you hadn't filed for divorce?

—Because I didn't want to say anything. Because I wanted Christmas Eve to be as usual, for the children.

—But why didn't you refuse?

—I tried, but no one listened. And then my mother started nagging about how ungrateful I was, as always. I understand that she wants to pay me back somehow. She thinks that the deal between me and Håkan has been unfair, but I never worked in the firm. I never complained. And there is no conflict between me and Håkan. It's okay, honestly.

—And, now, she wanted to give you and Tobias the house? But then, half of the house belongs to him? Why would she give it to him—to her son-in-law? Do they owe him something? That deal, that you wouldn't get anything with the family firm, it happened before you met Tobias, didn't it?

Linda tries to understand which missing link Karin is looking for. Of course Linda's mother would like to give the house to her. But she's married, and her mother has nothing to do with that. Linda's life doesn't concern her.

—She likes him, I suppose. I don't know. If I'd had a stake in the firm, Tobias would have benefited anyway. I guess she considers us an entity. Håkan doesn't have a family; that's maybe why.

—There's one thing I never understood: weren't you ever angry over that? I mean, it's seriously unfair.

Linda ponders the question. Did she get angry?

—No…We're not the angry kind, our family.

—See, I don't remember you like that from when we met, from the years in Lund. I remember you as a person with quite a lot of emotions. You were angry and happy and sad and mad and content. And all these feelings were you.

Linda swallows. It's partly true, what Karin says. The years in Lund were an enormous freedom from all constraints and must-dos, from the family's expectations. She was away from home, and her parents couldn't force her to come back. They had no power over her as they'd had during her years at business school, when she lived at home.

—That was another part of me. Another life.

—You don't think there's anything left of it? Any anger? You were pretty angry when I called.

—And I still am. Because you guessed it, all the time. Tobias wasn't the person I thought he was.

—It's not your fault, Karin says. I'm not saying I use a sixth sense. It's not like that. But would your mother give him part of the house just because she likes him?

—Can we talk about something else?

Karin wants to tell her something the way she has tried to tell her things many times before, but Linda doesn't want to go there, not yet. They sit next to each other in silence while the sun rises over Österlen and the car travels between faintly green fields and newly cut poplar alleys that are still to come to life. When they turn into the gravel courtyard, tears fall down Linda's cheeks. She shouldn't be here. She should take care of her family.

*

—If I were you, I would go straight ahead. It's about time, Linda.

Karin puts both hands around the large slightly rough teacup she made herself and lifts it to her mouth. She blows on the tea and takes a big swig.

—Make sure you eat something, she says.

There's a wooden cutting board between them on the table, with a large loaf of bread from which she already has cut thick slices. There's cheese, butter, and red jam in a large glass jar. Linda spreads butter on a sandwich and tops it with both cheese and jam. Prohibited in the Adeus family, it's something she learned from Karin and still appreciates but rarely eats. Now it tastes better than ever.

—How do you mean, Linda mumbles between bites.

—When I mediate on this kind of situation, I sometimes force one party to take a step forward. You are stuck, going nowhere. And that's probably partly because of your parents' house being there, between you. Deep down, you don't want to hurt your mother since you put them in an awkward position by throwing them out of the house. Then, of course, Tobias reminds you that it's you who's made the unpleasant decision—he doesn't want a divorce. So in your mother's eyes, he's "the good guy," isn't he? He wants to keep up your marriage, objectively. And, then, your mom thinks that you might as well forgive because it's better for her. Although she—and your dad, perhaps—has put them in this situation.

—But I don't want the house!

—It doesn't matter. You wouldn't want Tobias to get it, sell it, and make lots of money on it?

—I don't care about the money.

It's something she has repeated to herself ever since Anita told her that the firm was Håkan's and Linda replied "okay." She didn't want to work in the printing business, and possibly she didn't understand what "the firm is Håkan's" meant, initially. The width of it. But then, when she moved to Lund, she didn't ponder on the money. She wanted to create her own future and get a fun job, something she found interesting. Anita had said that it wasn't always fun to work, that you'd need to dig in deep sometimes. That if you had a job, you should be happy, and when you had the chance to get one without having to look for it, you should be grateful. Linda didn't want to listen. Had she ever told her mom? Of course she hadn't.

And had she told her she didn't care about the money? She doesn't remember. But she was conscious of the attention Håkan got at all the family gatherings, that he made the company grow and expand its horizons. And she has understood that he has earned good money. It hasn't gone unnoticed that he could buy a large apartment in town and a summer house out on the island. But even if she looks deep inside, there's no envy. Håkan has worked, not had time to raise a family, put the company first. Linda would never have done that. She wasn't interested back then.

—That's something completely different, Linda. You must decide for yourself what you want to do. And you must tell them.

—I have told them.

She'll wait though. The divorce takes six months because of the children, but she won't hesitate. There's no doubt she wants a divorce. And, then, they can sell the houses, and she can get a new place to live. On her own.

—But you must say it out loud, to both of them, to all of them. That this is how you want it.

—I can't spend more time dwelling on this.

Linda takes another sandwich. She's hungry for the first time in several months. The butter forms soft yellow pillows under the slice of cheese. She never takes butter, stopped it when she came to Lund since it was too expensive and because it always got old and rancid before she could finish it.

—Did you tell Tobias that you saw the photos?

She shakes her head. Same thing there. She can't. What's the point? She knows that he has been unfaithful. Does anything change if he knows that she knows? Probably not. He will continue as before. He will find new women. It's as if he's no longer her husband, not when she sees him in the photos. He has turned into someone else, someone she doesn't recognize.

Karin places the teacup on the table with a thud and leans back in the wooden chair with her arms crossed over her chest. It takes a while before Linda realizes that Karin is staring at her.

—Did I ever tell you he tried to catch me? The night you met, when we were out together?

Linda stops in the middle of a bite. The bread tastes sour and sticks to her palate. She won't be able to swallow that piece of dough without choking, and she can't chew it more than she already has. She coughs, and the piece of bread flies out on the table. She looks out the window, divided into eight small squares, all covered by small grains of salt.

—But I married him.

Linda clenches her jaw so tightly that her teeth almost break, and she wishes she had bit her tongue.

—I knew it, Karin says. Stop defending your relationship! Stop!

—But it's all I have! Don't you get it! He's everything!

The words sputter out of her mouth. She's unable to stop them, just as it's impossible to stop the betrayal or the hope that everything was only a bad dream. She presses her hands against her face and her tears, feeling ugly, unworthy, embarrassed.

Karin gets up and walks over to her side of the table. She throws her arms around Linda, hugs and waddles her, and Linda cries, slobbers, and whimpers until there're no sound or tears left. She lets herself be taken care of, and the heaviest emotions slowly subside, but the gnawing feeling in her stomach won't give in.

—We've got plenty of time, Karin says, caressing her hair. But I promise to help you. You'll ride it out. You can do it. I know you, and I know you are much angrier than you show. Let it out, will you?

Linda nods.

—Was he hitting on you? she whispers into Karin's coarse hair.

—I don't understand how you didn't notice. You must have fallen for him the second he walked through the door.

—In the cloakroom, in fact, Linda says.

—As I said, there's plenty of time.

*

The sea fizzes. Linda looks at Karin standing next to her. Their backs are to the wind and their faces toward the steely sea. The white tops of the waves hit the beach as foam, which disappears in the sand before the water is sucked out with a prolonged wheezing sound.

—What would you have done?

—Are we talking present or past? Karin says.

It's late afternoon, and the sun will soon disappear in the waves. Linda's legs burn after the long walk in the sand; she hasn't been working out and she should go to the gym at least once a week, now when she has days without the kids and could go there. But working out has never been her thing. She never needed to in order to maintain her weight or get in shape after the pregnancies. She lost all the pounds she gained, or at least was able to get back in her clothes. She has never owned a scale. Though it would do her good to go to a gym. It's probably what you do when you are single. But she isn't.

—Present.

The night they met Tobias, Karin tried to be a good example of how to handle guys who are not trustworthy. But it was Karin's reaction, not her. Linda can't go on thinking she made a mistake eleven years ago. It's impossible. She and Tobias had a good relationship, they—loved each other. It can't be erased.

—He wasn't my type, that's all. What I would do now? I can't help you...I mean, I can't...I can't give you any advice. Only from a mediation perspective. I've never been in your seat, but I have met others who have.

210

—And?

Karin turns with her back to the wind.

—I should have brought another sweater. Are you cold?

Linda shakes her head. She has borrowed two fleece jackets and a windbreaker, and she is still sweaty after the walk.

—The ones I meet quite often, but not always, have problems with trust, and also with remembering who said what and when. There are long discussions concerning that and if it's true or not. Nowadays, I advise them to use their cell phones to record their talks. If you don't know where to start, it's much easier to begin with what has been said.

—But…isn't that illegal?

—No, not if you are part of the conversation.

—But, why would I record what we're talking about?

Karin turns her head, which gets stuck in her hoodie, and Linda only sees one of her eyes, making her gaze even sharper.

—Because it sounds as if he's not telling the whole truth. Ever. And to put the pieces in this puzzle in place correctly, it's sometimes the only solution available. But you may already know everything, and in that case, you won't need it.

The sand under Linda's feet is soft, and she sinks and wobbles as she pulls her feet out. She squats and touches the soft surface, hoping that it will have been warmed by the sun. It hasn't. The sand is cold, and the finely ground stones are smooth against her palm.

—You should see your parents and Tobias. And that's what you should record, if nothing else.

—It's all about my mom. I'm pretty sure my father has nothing to do with this.

—Okay, you and your mother and Tobias, then. You should meet, right? To explain and unfold. And then you might understand.

211

Karin pulls at her jacket and Linda realizes that she wants to go home. She rises.

—That's what I would have done, in practical terms. I can't give you any emotional advice. I don't want to either, Karin says and puts her arm around Linda.

—And I don't know if I want to have everything explained, Linda says.

She glances over her shoulder at the sea and the sun slowly sinking. The gulls' raucous screams—that's what she would like to record. That, and the sea. But their talks?

Linda has a bad conscience because she called in sick at work, but not because she told Tobias that he had to take the kids an extra day—he should be grateful that she lets him have one of her days, but he said that in the future she will have to plan a little better. She picked up the kids early on Monday, as soon as she had landed. They didn't seem to care at all.

As if Linda ordered her to, her mother asked Linda and Tobias to come over. Bibbi will pick up the kids at preschool. She has Karin's words ringing in her ears as she calls on her parents' house. Tobias is a few steps farther down.

—So glad you could come, Anita says.

Through Linda's eyes, she looks strained. Unnaturally pale and with a tightness over her lips as if she doesn't want to show her teeth. Tobias stands next to Linda in the hall, weighing back and forth in his boots, even though he knows that Anita dislikes it when you wear outdoor shoes indoors because they're dirty. Boots with thick soles make her even more suspicious; there may be small pebbles stuck in those grooves, and in that case, the parquet will get scratches and dents.

Linda takes a deep breath. It's as if it's her initiative, but Anita has taken command; of course she has, since she called, and they are at her house. Nonetheless, Linda has decided that enough is enough, that those photos were the last straw, and no matter how many times Anita tries to play matchmaker, it won't work. But now Linda has to tell her and make her understand that they can only go in one direction—and that Anita has caused it herself.

To keep guilt at bay was one thing, Karin emphasized. It's not about Linda, and she must look at it objectively. When Karin drew it up in front of her, a part of Linda's anxiety disappeared. Anita wanted to be kind, and there's nothing wrong in that. What is weighing Linda down is that she could maybe have changed everything just by protesting on Christmas Eve. Then her parents would still own the house and Tobias would get nothing at all. But—would she have managed? She doubts that Tobias would have let her walk away without signing the papers, although he had already signed them himself. And that's also something Karin emphasized—that in that case he acted in bad faith. He knew the outcome, and more or less, forced her, in order to get his share of the house.

Let them both talk. Try to keep a low profile. Karin has given her some tips to get a better recording. She picks up her cell phone and sees how Anita presses her lips together; being "always available" is nonsense to Anita. Linda knows that it bothers her, but right now Linda doesn't care about her mother's countenance. Her intention isn't to send any text messages, to tweet, or to make status updates. It's much more important than that.

—And it's nice to see you together, Anita says in the tone that means "please put away the phone." Come in.

Linda nods but keeps the phone in her hand.

Anita checks Tobias's boots and hesitates, both in her movement and breathing, but there is no invitation to him to take them off. They follow her into the living room where she slows down in front of the sofas and steers toward the dining table. She sits down on the edge of the table, Linda and Tobias encircling her.

—As I said, I'm happy to see you together.

—Yes, of course, Linda says. It's just that we aren't together at all, Mom. I'm not sure if you understand. We will never be together again. We are getting divorced. And I want you to know that the house, your house, will be sold. Neither I nor Tobias can afford living here.

—What are you two doing? Anita says. You told me you had moved back home, and Tobias sure doesn't stay here anymore. Where do you live? If you're not at home?

Anita looks at Linda, then at Tobias. She smiles. It's a stiff smile, and the corner of her mouth is twitching, as if the smile isn't quite well placed and she must correct it. It's clear that she doesn't understand what Linda just told her.

Linda feels sorry for her mother. Actually, she does. What her mother hoped and wished for—for Linda and Tobias to get back together and forget the past—will never happen. She envisions how they should work things out, how you ought to work it out, but how can she possibly understand that Tobias isn't the man she thinks he is? He's not the man Linda thought he was either.

—This isn't honest, she says, and her voice trembles. You promised me, Tobias…that it was for real this time, that Linda had moved home. You told me so. It's certainly not honest what you have done.

She turns her head violently and looks out onto the garden. Linda suffers with a desire to put an arm around her because this is a failure to Anita, an illusion about marriage she has created, an illusion about her children. Where at least one, the one she had no hope for, had created a family and a reasonably decent life. Linda ignores her mother's view of Håkan, but eventually she'll notice he isn't the man she hoped he was either.

Tobias puts a hand on Anita's shoulder, causing her to start. She looks scared, as if he would beat her.

—Now, it's a little unfair to lay all the blame and burden on me, Tobias says. It was your idea, too. You have to take your responsibility. What I told you was my idea of what had happened.

The dining room is still bright, and between some of the houses below, you can see a thin sliver of water. A "view," in the eyes of a real estate agent.

—Let her be, Linda says.

—No, wait, Tobias says harshly. I don't think…no, I know…

He pauses and smiles back at Anita.

Two statues couldn't have done it better.

—I know it's not about your mom and Gustav wanting to stay in the house. She has promised me some money, if we stay together. I've received the money. You can get half of it if you want to.

Linda stares at him, the silly smile that lies across his lips and seems to roll out over his face until it's completely blurred, only a sardonic flat surface without emotion.

Did she love this man? What has happened? Why is he like this? He doesn't make sense anymore. Her mouth is dry, and her voice becomes strained and shrill.

—Why would you have received money? What are you up to? That's extortion!

Anita's fingers are tangled around each other, but she says nothing. She stares right in front of her, blinking now and then, mechanically, but doesn't meet Tobias's or Linda's gaze.

—Because it's important to her. We are family. For the sake of the children. Why else do you think she hasn't told you?

—Told me what? About the money?

—That she knew about me and Maja!

Linda leans back against the hard dining room chair and pushes it out to increase the distance to Tobias and her mother. The seat back creaks, and she takes a convulsive grip on the seat, pressing her nails into it. The explosion she sees and feels comes from within, from her own brain.

—And now, you assume that it's something I've invented, Tobias says calmly. But you can ask her here and now. I'm sure she has a good explanation, perhaps better than mine.

Linda gasps for breath and doesn't want to look at Anita, but her presence is everywhere. When the words fall into place and she understands what Tobias said, understands it for real, she uses her last force to whisper:

—How long…how long have you known, Mom?

The table trembles a little when her mother puts her hands against it and rises. She walks slowly to the window, the parquet floor creaking under her feet. Linda doesn't dare look at Tobias; she doesn't want to see how he's enjoying the upper hand and how happy he is, now that he can finally tell the truth.

—I can't remember when it was, but you certainly do, Tobias, Anita says in a thin voice. It was a while ago, I guess—

—I realized at once that you knew, Tobias says. I met you and Gustav already the first time. We were at the hotel and spa, for a conference, and Gustav and you were there with some friends, remember? And, Anita, you have a sharp eye. You were incredibly discreet, just looked at me and it was clear as day. You sensed what had happened, didn't you? But you've still kept quiet, all the time. And kept track, I can promise you, Linda. We came across your mom again, at some occasion. But she never told you, did she? So when she started talking about this house, last fall—

—Stop, Linda says. Stop it. I don't want to hear more. I...I can't imagine that you have kept Tobias behind your back, Mom. Mom? Why would you do that? Mom?

Anita looks out onto the garden, still asleep after the winter. If you looked closely, you'd see snowdrops under the apple trees, but Anita's eyes are gazing straight ahead.

The serenity Linda had when she arrived has dissolved and her whole body is tense, every muscle on guard against Tobias's big body on the other side of the table. He has also risen, standing legs apart and arms crossed only two meters away. His gaze wanders between her and Anita, with a faint smile that can be interpreted as "advantage." If he takes a step forward, Linda will hit him and kick him. Even bite. She draws a deep breath and guesses she must try to decide on a new direction. Now. What has become of him? Of her? She has never been afraid of him, but now she is. Her heart is pounding against her rib cage.

—I know more than you can imagine, Linda says. And I don't believe that my mother alone would determine what should happen with the house. In that case, my dad knows, too, and he would never be on anyone else's side but mine. He would never in his whole life let you have a part of the house just to make us stay together. No matter if you have a mistress or not.

Tobias's hands fly out, and he shakes his head, the blond locks dangling on his forehead. He tries that irresistible boyish look, but those days are gone, at least for Linda.

—You'd have to discuss that with your parents. I'm only telling you the truth.

—Great, Linda says.

—It's fantastic to do business with your mom, he says. When she came up with the idea to give us the house, I couldn't say anything but please and thank you. It was more than I could expect. We could move in here and—

—Everything would be all right? And I wouldn't know what you had done?

So he thinks she's that easily fooled. What would he think? It has worked this far.

—And what was my mom's requirements?

—You know that. That we would stay together. Which is what I want, anyway.

—And Maja?

He shakes his head.

—Maja, why do you still talk about her? I told you it's over.

—As much "over" as it is with all the others, I presume, Linda says.

He smiles.

—Because it's not just her, is it? Linda continues. I guess you never told my mother. About the other women? The ones you met on your trips? The trips none of us knew about—but still were, for some reason, immortalized on Polaroid photos and kept as memories, documented. Your other ladies, have you forgotten them?

He doesn't smile anymore, and before he has time to prepare a defense Linda continues:

—No, no, don't tell us you met them at some beach. It sounds a little trite. Considering the detailed—why not call them explicit—pictures. But we could conclude that you fooled both me and my mother. And Maja because she must have considered herself unique.

Tobias puts his big hands in front of his eyes. He sighs, looking up at the ceiling.

—It's not what you think...

Linda doesn't answer.

—I shouldn't...I mean, didn't I throw them away? Damn it, I took a lot of stuff to the dumpster...

And their eyes meet, for the first time in a long while. Linda can no longer hold back the tears. It begins as a tremor in her lower lip, as in a child, and spreads over her face, which starts shaking. Her nostrils flutter, and her throat contracts. She wishes it wasn't so cheap, that their relationship, their marriage, wasn't crumbling in front of them.

—I don't know what happened, he says. I lost control.

The cell phone in Linda's sweaty hand slides back and forth.

—So you admit you cheated on me and hid behind my mother's back? She hoped she could save a marriage, but you thought you could work it out, having two or more mistresses, and that I still wouldn't find out?

—That wasn't my plan, in the beginning—

—No, but what about now? When she, besides keeping your secret, also promised you money? And—a house?

—I imagined it might work out, yes. That it was a security. Not the money—I need it...but the house. You would never sell it. So then we'd stick together anyway.

Linda lets the tears flow down her cheeks, and they gather like beads at her chin and then drop on her blouse. As if her body wants to remind her of the pain over and over again, making it more palpable.

—You're a tough cookie, he says in such a friendly way that Linda gets the feeling he wants to give her a compliment. Tough and persevering. I believe in us, in our relationship. I do.

—But if I were to give up, if I were to tell you I don't care if my parents have to move elsewhere—doesn't part of the shadow fall on you, who convinced my mother that I would never get divorced, never do them any harm?

He shakes his head. He can't solve the equation and shrugs his shoulders, puts his hands in his pockets, and looks like a little boy caught smashing a window. Not his fault. He looks over his shoulder as if there would be anyone else who could take the blame.

—That's your problem. Not mine. I've tried to stick to the agreement. You're the one who won't.

—And what about that money? Wasn't the house enough?

—It was your mother's idea. As a bonus, I guess. So they wouldn't have to move—or why, Anita? And who would refuse cash? We did move back in together.

—When? Linda says.

—A couple of weeks ago. You moved out from Håkan's.

—I didn't move back home!

—That's what you told your mom.

Linda gasps.

—I don't need to tell her every detail, do I? I told her we had worked it out.

Tobias laughs.

—But that little piece of information sufficed. And the money's mine.

—But you lied!

—I said that I wouldn't stay here any longer, at your parents'. And, frankly, wasn't that best for all of us?

—You withheld information, Anita says. You took me for a ride.

He snorts.

—I needed the money, and I won't apologize. We both live at home, just not at the same time.

—Which was the case before our deal, too! You fooled me!

Anita turns, and Linda is afraid she will fall forward, but she wobbles back and forth, holding her arms folded across her body and then releasing her grip to clasp her hands in front.

—We can't solve all of this now, Anita says. I want you to leave. I have to talk to Gustav. He will be home soon.

Linda has never seen her mother in this state of mind. Does she need help? Will she fall apart?

Tobias nods a little, moving toward the door. He takes his jacket hanging over the banister.

—Let's keep in touch, he says.

—See you, Linda says from the opening to the living room. We must get hold of a real estate agent.

She doesn't want to leave with him but doesn't want to stay with her mother either. She stands right between them, not wanting to be part of the conspiracy she doesn't understand, but not wanting to leave her mother like this either.

—Exactly, Tobias says and raises his hand. Bye. Bye, Anita!

Linda goes back into the living room where her mother has sat down in one of the armchairs.

—Sit down, Anita says. I have something to tell you.

—No, Mom, I gather that's enough for today. I must leave. I have to…get out of here.

—But—

Linda shakes her head. She doesn't want to be accused of more things; she wants to be alone with her disappointment, anger, and despair. They planned it, and she has no say. Other people, her family, planned her life.

—Bye, Mom, Linda says, takes her coat, and steps out into the bright spring evening.

Anita watches Linda leave, her fair hair bobbing in the ponytail. She has changed little since she was a child. Her same thin body, the same way she crouches when she is unsure or unhappy—and that's what she is now. Anita knows and understands her, and she wishes she could get a chance to explain, to get Linda to realize she didn't do it to be mean. She finds it difficult to express, but more than anything, she wants Linda to be happy in what she does, in her life. And Anita has concluded that part of her happiness has been due to the relationship with Tobias. Sometimes she has even felt a twinge of jealousy when she has seen them together, that unshakable unity, something obvious and sound. They are close, know each other so well, in every detail. Anita would have liked it that way, too, although she knows that at her and Gustav's age, few care as much for each other as they do. And when she sees a couple who do, it almost upsets her. It's as if older people, yes, she sees herself as older, can't be sincere in their actions. It becomes too cute and silly, not as obvious as it is…or as it was…between Linda and Tobias.

Will she and Gustav be thrown out of the house now? If she remembers correctly, the divorce will take legal force in July. It's perhaps not the best time to sell a house, in the middle of the summer holidays. And the partition of joint property also takes a while. Even if it's done quickly, it would be odd if they would have to leave before early October; they could probably negotiate that. Which would give them about six months to check out the market.

She ought to be sad. But she's more angry that Tobias set her up for $20,000, money she will never get back. She has no proof that what he said wasn't correct. Did he admit that he had lied? No, he blamed it all on Linda, who didn't want to discuss the matter. What a mess. What a tragedy. And amid all this, she wanted to lend a helping hand.

Or—was it a helping hand? Anita thought so. She saw Tobias that first time, but seeing him and that woman again has been a coincidence. She has never since suspected that he wanted to challenge her, to see if she would tell on him. And despite her internal deliberations, she has decided not to interfere in their relationship because she knows what the consequences might be, that not everything is what it seems to be, that not everything turns out as expected, and that sometimes there's nothing to show. You shouldn't draw hasty conclusions, and she didn't, the first time. She observed their interaction and what looked like a hand on his thigh as well as the audacious way he met Anita's gaze. Anyone could have seen what Anita saw—that it had nothing to do with work. And then she couldn't let it happen. She didn't want Linda to get hurt.

She hears the key in the lock, and the door slams.

—Hello?

—Hello. Hi.

Gustav takes off his beige coat, hangs it up, sits down on the stairs to take off his shoes, and comes to meet her.

—Did it go well? she asks.

—Well, as usual.

—Linda and Tobias were here.

—Really? So sad that I didn't see them. What did they want? Were we having them for dinner?

—They will divorce. Which means we will be homeless.

He meets her eyes, raises his arms. She gets up and goes to meet him. They embrace.

—I'm sorry, she says. This wasn't how it was supposed to be. I thought it could work out for them. I don't know what has gone wrong. Or, what's wrong with Tobias. He wasn't himself. Not... nice, at all. This must be hard on them.

—It's all right, Gustav says. I think it's the best thing that could happen. He shouldn't get half of the house, but now it's done.

Nothing to fight about.

—Aren't you sad? It's still your childhood home.

—But it's your house.

She protests. It's not hers, any more than it's his. It was just something his mother was trying to make her believe. Anita knew no better, thought it was a nice and far too valuable gift, and what could she say? That she didn't want it? That it was too much? That it served no purpose?

She would never have expressed herself that way. You didn't back then. It had been terribly embarrassing; she could have sunk into the ground when Anna eyed her.

—I apologize, I mean it, Gustav. Can we buy it back?

—We were moving anyway, weren't we? We decided that a long time ago. So, now, let's look forward instead. If they sell the house, well, then they do. I think we have done what we could. You have done what you could.

Anita leans against him, for the first time in a long while, but now she needs his support, and he gives it to her. How could she have questioned that, all those years ago.

Gustav pats her cheek and lets go of her.

—I'm a little hungry, Sven isn't something of a cook. We had a herring sandwich. I don't think I've ever gotten anything else at his place.

—I think there are meatballs in a bowl in the fridge. Take them. I'm not hungry.

She squeezes his arm. It's not true. She is hungry, but he can have the meatballs.

The chirping birds have woken Linda up two days in a row, but she's still listless and tired; she has never been so tired in her whole life. The meeting at her parents' house had her completely knocked out, and that she gets the kids to preschool and herself to work is a huge feat because now her energy is exhausted. The forthcoming Easter holiday is a blessing; she must get some sleep. Tobias has said he doesn't want to have the children over the holiday. He's busy. But that's not until next week.

She spins around in the office chair, looking down at the desk. Will she need to bring anything for the meeting with her boss? There's nothing to show or discuss. The financial statements are completed, and now there are the quarterly reports and forecasts. She's been working here for such a long time she can more or less do it in her sleep. Perhaps it's just that: she's too tired. They must have noticed that she's not capable of working in this way. If they want to get rid of her, they may do so, because her life can't get much worse.

Her boss's office is big and bright with views of the lake. The sun is beaming through the windows, the water is dark blue, and the city hall's crowns sparkle. In a few months, there will be white sails everywhere, but the winds are still too cold. Only enthusiasts would go sailing on a day like this.

Her boss holds her phone to her ear with her back toward Linda, who knocks on the open door. She gets a nod in response. She enters and sits down in the bright leather chair on the other side of the desk, but her boss points toward the corner where there are two chairs and a small table. Linda knows what that means: informal discussion. Everything that concerns the daily routines is discussed at the desk, as well as performance reviews. If more personal matters are on topic, they are handled in the corner. "Personal matters." That could mean almost anything. Linda yawns and puts a hand to her mouth.

—Great that you could come right away, her boss says, pulls at her skirt, and gets up from the desk to greet her. Would you like something to drink? Coffee?

Linda shakes her head. It's ten o'clock, and she has already had two cups of coffee. If she has another one before lunch, she will only get shaky. Coffee never speeds her up.

—No, you're right. I wasn't thinking, her boss says.

Her white blouse is gaping a little over her breasts, as if they were pumped up, and her blonde hair shines in the sunlight. She is five years younger than Linda and has "ambitions," as they say. Linda's former boss had them, too. They were classmates from business school. This job seems to be a springboard for those interested in finance within the group.

—I'll be brief. And perhaps I'm not the one to discuss this with you, but we'll start here.

She takes a deep breath.

—I'm pregnant.

Linda, who has been waiting for the boss to say they're not happy with her performance, gives a start.

—But, hey, that's great news! Congratulations! When?

—At the end of August.

—Are you feeling okay?

That's what everyone who has children asks. Those who know that the first few months can be awful. Linda was nauseous once during two pregnancies, but she never tells anyone.

—Yes, actually. No problems so far, but now it starts to show.

She pulls her skirt again, and Linda thinks that maybe she's worried about how big she will get because every centimeter feels like a huge belly with the first child. It's impossible to know how that baby will grow—and you.

—It looks neat, you have a perfect baby bump.

Her boss smiles and looks down on her stomach, which doesn't bulge any more than if she'd had one extra serving of pasta for lunch. She clears her throat.

—Yes, but that wasn't what we should talk about. We will need a replacement for a couple of months. I won't take more than six months leave, but there will be summer holidays, too, so let's say closer to seven, until March, after the financial statements next year. It would be pointless to do them when I haven't been in the business for half a year.

—That's probably a wise idea, Linda says, stifling another yawn.

—You don't get enough sleep? I mean, your kids are older, aren't they?

—They are four and six. But, yes, they wake up early. Perhaps more now, with everything going on at home.

Her boss nods. They have talked little about Linda's separation. Her boss got married two years ago and was on a romantic weekend over New Year's to celebrate it. She must already have been pregnant by then, Linda thinks, and she sees how her boss frowns.

—We've discussed this and would like to know if you're willing to take my place while I'm gone. You've been here for a long time, and everyone knows you. Also, you have the experience needed and you, more or less, have the formal background required. We believe that the working experience outweighs the formal.

"The formal background." It's that degree in economics and business administration, the degree that Linda doesn't have because she quit before the last semester. Should she be grateful for their indulgence, that she didn't want to work with this, or are they mocking her? Linda lets the words sink in: "the working experience."

—Wow, she says. It came…a bit unexpected. But, thanks, that sounds exciting.

—We are sure you can handle this. I mean, I have almost finished the performance reviews, and those that remain I will have time to do before summer. And I will be on hand, of course. I won't disappear from the earth's surface just because I have a child.

They laugh together—Linda because the boss doesn't have a clue about what she has in front of her, and the boss because it seems absurd that a baby would need so much attention during its first months that she wouldn't be able to work.

—I have to think about it. It's still somewhat chaotic at home, but the purely practical things should be resolved during summer.

The boss says it will be possible to arrange flexible work hours and that she's sure the others won't mind.

—You could work from home, too. I mean, a lot of paperwork can be managed in the evenings. Because the kids go to bed early, don't they?

Linda sometimes goes to bed shortly after them, especially in the recent weeks. It might be different this fall.

—When do you need an answer?

—As soon as possible. Right after Easter. Will that work for you? I understand if you have a lot to think about, but you're our first choice, and we are confident you can do this without any problems whatsoever. And I'm still at hand as I said; I'm not leaving.

Linda wants to tell her it will be a while before she leaves at all, but she stops herself. They are not of the same generation. Something has happened. These women don't want to be on maternity leave; they think of their careers and the next steps they need to take. That her boss said she's "not leaving" means that she's not actively looking for a new job, right now. But she might as well do so during her parental leave.

They rise simultaneously, the boss pulling her skirt again as they walk toward the door.

—Time for maternity clothes, she giggles. It's not very convenient when they are too tight.

—Rubber band, Linda says. And a loose-fitting blouse on top. Don't buy too many clothes, you will tire. The last few months are…

Her boss's face goes blank and wishes she had said nothing.

—Oh, you'll see, she says, trying to smooth things over. It's great fun to buy those first maternity clothes. You should treat yourself to something.

—Come by when you have decided, the boss says in a louder voice.

—Exactly, Linda says, a little surprised.

—I haven't told the others yet, her boss whispers. About the tummy that is. Will do that when we announce that you'll take over. So I kind of hope you will.

She smiles in confidence and winks at Linda.

Linda smiles back, although her smile is tight and unnatural, and she turns around and walks through the corridor with the same stiff smile, as if she were on screen. When she's back at her desk, her features fall into place again, and she takes a deep breath, lets her shoulders down. Is this how it feels to be promoted? Though she has not been. She has, more or less, been asked to take over her boss's position for a few months, but more on paper than in actual responsibilities.

She brings her coffee cup into the kitchenette. It's as if someone steers her toward the brown liquid from the glass pumpkin, and she's about to spill it all over the threshold when she runs into her boss again.

—Coffee? I thought you didn't want any. Which was good because I don't like coffee right now. Hope it comes back.

Linda looks down at her cup. No, she shouldn't go for coffee. She needs to think. It would be good to talk to Håkan though she doesn't want to. She still has to ask him what's going on, and she would need to get some good advice because he's perhaps the only one who can give that to her.

229

Her whole life is too fast right now. It's as if she were stuck in the spinner and is now being spun around along with everything that is thrown into it—a cheating spouse, a mistress, two children, two houses, a job to do, well-meaning but naïve parents, a brother, her boss, old friends, jealous women, and new and curious acquaintances. Her head spins, and she must lean against the wall.

Håkan's answering machine starts, and Linda sighs with relief. It's Friday night, and she is still at work even though the clock struck nine. Tonight, she has nowhere to go. Karin has insisted she call Håkan, that, of course, he doesn't mind if she stays with him now if he didn't mind it before. His private life doesn't concern her, and if he doesn't want to talk about the handsome man, it probably means this wasn't a long-term relationship. There's nothing and no one to introduce to the family, no one with whom he will build his life. It sounded obvious when Karin said it, but Linda thinks it would be a better solution to stay at a hostel for two nights than with him. After that, she will have about a week to find a more permanent accommodation.

She should be sad. She should be terrified when she has nowhere to go. The easiest thing would be to call Mom and Dad since Tobias doesn't stay there right now. And if that doesn't sound like a great idea, which it doesn't given everything her mom told her, then whipping up enough confidence to talk to her brother shouldn't be a big deal, no matter what men he has staying at his place. Or she could call someone in the Culture Club.

Linda understands that Karin is right, but her hands are still sweaty as she prepares herself to say something snappy on the answering machine, just to get rid of it all. He might call back, if he has anything to say, so she'll tell him she's alive and is doing fine. If he's even wondered, but he obviously hasn't. That's when she hangs up. Only to hear her mobile phone ring.

—Hi, it's Håkan.

Linda gets so perplexed by hearing his voice, so she says nothing at all.

—Are you there? he says.

—Hi, hello. Linda speaking.

—I know. You called my home number, right? I'm on my way to Italy, will soon be boarding. The phone is on call forwarding.

—Well, I didn't want to disturb you—

—No, no, we haven't had time to talk…Are you okay?

Linda sighs. She can't tell him everything, doesn't even know where to start.

—Or did you want anything special? Can I help you? How are you?

—Good, good…

It's so easy to say that word. "Good." And he sounds so happy, she doesn't want to take the joy away; she knows how it feels when leaving for a trip, your head and body filled with positive thoughts. Still she can't stop herself.

—Or, I mean…it's kind of hellish. I don't want to bother you, and I apologize for barging in last time, and I thought I had arranged things with my accommodation, but right now I'm in sort of a trap. And you don't need to say it's okay. I can stay in a hostel. I've already booked, but I wanted to ask—

—No problem. It's okay, you know that. Nothing has changed. I still travel a lot. What happened?

—It's complicated. The guy whose house I rented, his wife suspected us of having an affair and threw me out. And then the Polaroids and Tobias, and so we met with Mom the day before yesterday, and…I can't tell you over the phone.

She hears Håkan's breath, guesses he hasn't listened.

—Why don't we have dinner together? he says. So you can tell me everything? I will be off all week, back on the second day of Easter. How about Tuesday? Would you stay with me? I mean, you can move in right now.

—I have the kids all next week, so then I'll be at home. But I'm probably homeless by Tuesday.

She tries to laugh; the situation is so absurd. She must find her own place to live. Now.

—But can't we meet on Tuesday then, at my place? I'll get us something to eat.

Linda eyes sting. There's so much she wants to talk about, and she's so happy that Håkan says they'll have dinner that she can't thank him without sounding like she wants to cry on his shoulder.

—That would be great, perfect. I'd love to, she says. I can get some wine. But if it's okay, I'll use your guest room tonight—

—But of course. Sure. You've got the key. You can come and go as you wish. It's great that someone stays there. Okay, so I'll see you next Tuesday.

Linda nods at the phone, closes her eyes, tries to sound normal.

—Yes, good. Thank you. And enjoy Italy.

He laughs, the way she wishes she could, too.

—I will.

Linda cleans her desk, putting the papers in piles so she knows where to start on Monday. She should devote the weekend to looking for an apartment. The current situation won't work. She's going crazy playing these games with Tobias, her parents, and Håkan. If only one of them were honest. If someone could tell the truth and nothing but the truth.

—Happy Easter!

—Hi, Mom. And the same to you.

—What are you doing?

—Nothing. What are you doing?

—We're in Falsterbo, and spring is on its way, actually. You ought to have come.

Linda wants to hang up, but she can stop listening instead, just let the words pass without registering them. Another option is to put the phone on the table and let Anita talk into the air—she wouldn't notice.

Fia and Lotta lie on the sofa under a fleece blanket, watching movies. They giggle at some cartoon characters who throw pies at each other. It's nine thirty, but they are all still in their pajamas, and Linda has no plans for the day. They might go to town, to a museum, but she doesn't fancy doing anything, not like before when she would spend the early morning reading what exhibitions were on. That energy doesn't exist anymore, and the few hours they get together during the weekend, Linda prefers to enjoy in the easiest of ways: pajamas, pancakes for lunch, perhaps everybody in bed and reading stories. They might walk to the park in the afternoon.

—I have pondered over one thing, Anita says. You ought to sell the house now.

—What? Why would we do that? You still live there. And the divorce hasn't been completed.

—The house is yours. You can do what you want with it. But this time of year, people want out of their apartments and move somewhere where there's a garden and apple blossoms. I don't mean that someone will move in now. That could be discussed, I presume. Those who'll buy the house will surely have children, either in school or preschool, and they still need a little time—they will want to move in August, after the summer holidays.

Linda wonders if Anita has gone wild. A few weeks ago, Linda had the notion that the house would be inherited, that the whole idea of the paper she had to sign on Christmas was about that. Now her mother suddenly wants to sell it.

—I understand that we must accept our actions and that none of you will be able or willing to keep the house. That's reality, and I'm sure it's better that way. But in that case, get as much money as possible. Don't wait. In the fall, everyone will think of the leaves to rake and the snow to shovel and how much more convenient staying in town is, with restaurants and movie theaters close by. It's either now or in a year.

Linda gets suspicious. Is Anita doing this for Tobias's sake? So he'll get even more money, because she feels sorry for him? He already received $20,000, and he probably wants more. He must have made Anita believe she must persuade Linda.

—There will be more money for Tobias, but you might not care about that?

Anita snorts.

—I don't care about him, Linda. You must understand. All I care about is my children.

—Just about time.

If only she could hang up. If only she could tell her mom that she can't talk. Linda wonders if Håkan will be shocked when she tells him that Anita has known about Tobias's relationship for four years. He will probably wonder what Linda said or did when she found out, and she realizes that she hasn't said or done anything. Why hasn't she?

Because she never did. Because she learned to keep quiet, and it doesn't seem to have any effect anyway. Nothing has changed. She learned that conflicts won't make you win, only lose. And even when she doesn't put on a big scene, as when she moved to Lund, she will be blamed for whatever consequences there are on the family.

—What do you mean? Anita says.

—You should have thought about that a little earlier. Because with this deal, half of the money will go to an idiot who betrayed your daughter for four years!

—I couldn't have known—

—Stop it, Mom. Can't you admit you made a mistake? Can't you just tell me you're sorry that you hurt me? It would mean a lot to me. That someone apologized. But neither you nor Tobias can say you're sorry, only that it wasn't your fault. That's what kids say, Mom.

Anita breathes into the phone, and Linda wonders if it's so she can hear that her mother isn't dead.

—I'm trying to help you, Anita says. It's not that easy. Well, in a way it is. If the house is sold, we won't dwell on this all summer, which would be great. But it's also better for you. You need to get yourself a place to live, for you and the kids. Dad and I will be here in Falsterbo this summer, and if needed we can stay over winter. From Midsummer until August you can use the house in town as you please. Thanks for reminding me.

Reminding her? She must have an incipient dementia. Her mother's delusional thoughts about how to best avoid her being hurt are undeniably interesting. Though when Linda reflects on it, the proposal isn't all that bad. It's even pretty thoughtful, even if conceived by Anita and sprung from an idea that she and Gustav will avoid a prolonged suffering when they need to separate from his childhood home. But it would also make Linda's summer a little easier.

—Will you come here for Midsummer, as usual?

Linda knew there was a catch, that Anita wouldn't offer her something and get nothing in return.

—No, I won't, Linda says. I'm not sure who will have the kids; we must discuss that first. But, anyway, we will stay here. It's too cumbersome to travel for a few days.

—But the kids? The girls have always celebrated Midsummer here, and they enjoy it. Don't let your separation affect them.

Affect them? Linda glances at the girls where they lie on the sofa. They seem to care about nothing but what's happening right now. Here. On the TV. Sure they whine sometimes and want daddy to be home, and she has no idea if they do the same when they are with Tobias, but, otherwise, they have both understood that they meet here, at home, and everything is as usual. They aren't dragged around to different places yet; there are no suitcases in the preschool entrance like there are for some of the other children whose parents are divorced. For now, the children aren't that affected. It's the test period it should be.

—They'll manage, even if they have to miss a year, Linda says. And I can't do the traveling, too. I'm sorry, Mom. There will be other years. I'm sure we'll find some kind of Midsummer celebration around here to visit.

—But if you are alone, wouldn't it be nice to get away?

—No, Mom. I want to be on my own.

—Would Tobias want to come, if he has the kids?

—Can you decide whose side you're on, please?

—I'm thinking of the children!

—But you can stop that. Because we are thinking of them, we who are their parents, and I can guarantee you we won't forget them!

And if Linda hangs up now, how will Anita react? Not at all. Linda should move far away, to find peace. If her job and Tobias weren't stopping her.

—Well, there was another thing, Anita continues as if she hadn't listened to Linda's answer. I would like to see you, because I need to tell you something.

She says it in a tone as if she were about to tell Linda she was pregnant, which, fortunately, is too late.

—When? Linda says, the fatigue weighing on her shoulders.

—Should we meet in town, for dinner?

—I can swing by. On Wednesday, perhaps. Will you be home?

—With the kids? I would like to see you on your own.

—No, they'll be with Tobias. I have had them all week.

—Wednesday night then. We'll drive back from Skåne on Tuesday, when the traffic is less intense. Think of what I said about the house, and talk to Tobias. We need to find a workable solution for everyone. Say hi to the girls. Are you going to do something fun today?

If Anita understood how every word she produces, how everything she suggests, pierces Linda's chest like sharp arrows and how Linda spends hours and days pulling them out and adding them to the collection…

—Yes, we will. We'll do something fun. Bye, Mom. Say hi to Dad from me.

Håkan has set the table in the kitchen. The metal table reflects the candles in the lanterns where the flames are not disturbed by either the fan or Linda walking past. He has found some slightly wrinkled white linen napkins that sag over the large plates. In a gray vase in the window stands a lonely twig of what she believes could be cherry.

—I brought it yesterday, he says when he sees Linda inspect the twig. It reminds me that spring is on its way, moving slowly through Europe, arriving here in due time.

Linda nods and gives him the wine bottles.

—Here. I couldn't choose between red or white, so I brought a bottle of each. The white is chilled; I put it on the balcony at work.

—White will be great. I've made fish soup.

Spring is around the corner, which should make her happy, and summer isn't far away either, which means the holidays are approaching, but Linda doesn't feel a thing.

—They offered me the opportunity to fill in for my boss, who's pregnant, she says flatly and rubs a spot on the window sill with her finger.

Håkan whisks food around in one pan and takes a paper packet out of the refrigerator.

—Sit down, he says. I'm almost done. I'll just cut some bread.

Linda sits down obediently, placing the napkin in her lap.

—So, do you want that job?

Linda puts her elbows on the table and leans her head in her hands.

—I don't know. I don't even understand why they asked me.

—Because you're competent, and you have worked there for more than ten years, and it's not for an extended period of time, I guess?

—She'll be off for six months.

—You see. No reason to turn the department upside down.

—But then she'll be back, and I'll do the same job as before.

—Exactly.

He cuts the fish into cubes, puts them into the casserole, and picks up a can of peeled shrimp. He finds a pair of scissors and cuts some strands from a plant standing in the window.

—Do they survive the winter? Linda says.

—They do. A bit difficult with the basil, which needs more sun, but otherwise they're in great shape.

He unscrews the cork, pours wine into his glass, takes a sip, and fills up Linda's glass.

—Cheers. And welcome back, he says.

—I'm sorry. I don't mean to come barging in like this—

—No, I mean it. Welcome back. I hope you'll find a workable solution for everything.

The wine doesn't have much taste; there's a hint of grass, and she could just as well have had water.

Håkan takes her plate, pours the hot soup, and adds a few prawns on top and one string of thyme. It smells amazing. Linda hasn't been hungry since she had breakfast at Karin's two weeks ago, but now she is. That anyone takes the time to prepare dinner for her warms her more than the soup itself.

—This is what you don't eat in Italy, Håkan says. Not in this way. There's a lot of seafood and, yes, a lot of fish, but rarely like this, in a hot soup, something about the salty taste.

—Do you like Italy? she says.

—A lot, he says, chewing thoughtfully on a piece of bread.

—I must ask another thing, Linda says.

He looks up at her, raising his eyebrows. Linda's heart beats much faster than she wants it to, but now she must ask. She can't cope with the secrecy anymore.

—This guy, not that I care…but it felt so strange…

The words jump uncontrollably from her mouth.

—I don't care about your relationship, if I say so, but if there is one, you may as well tell me, so we can avoid a lot of misunderstandings, she says.

Håkan's eyes are wide-open, but then his face cracks into a big smile, and he starts to roar with laughter.

—Antonio? Yes, he…I admit. He's handsome.

He continues to laugh as a blush spreads over his face, and he wipes his mouth with the linen napkin.

—If I were gay, he'd be a dream. An impossible dream, I should say.

He clears his throat, and this time Linda blushes. She's slightly disappointed because she wouldn't mind, and she rather believed it could be good for Håkan. Now he has nobody and is single, which he has been for an eternity. Doesn't he think so himself?

—I…I didn't mean it like that. But yes, he is handsome.

—I understand what you meant. But that's okay, Linda. You're the first person I would have told had that been the case. He's a photographer, an Italian photographer, and he was here on a visit. I had arranged a few contacts for him, and so he stayed here. I didn't realize you'd be here that day.

Now she's even more ashamed because she not only claimed that he was gay but also didn't stay away, like she had said she would.

—He doesn't look Italian, she says. There must be some Viking blood, or some barbarian.

Håkan brightens.

—That's what Giovanna said, too. That's so funny! Exactly the same.

He clears his throat and takes a sip of wine while his cheeks turn pink for a second time.

—And Giovanna is—

—His sister. His older sister.

The comment that she's his older sister makes Linda smile, as if Håkan wouldn't spend his time with someone younger than this Antonio, who in her memory looked quite young. Håkan puts down the spoon.

—Who is my…girlfriend. Yes, I guess that's what she is, though it sounds corny. She's responsible for the printing business in Italy. The one we invested in.

Linda gets caught with her spoon on the way to her mouth, and the soup drops into the bowl with a plopping sound. She swallows, though has nothing more to swallow than saliva, and opens her mouth but doesn't find the proper words. Their eyes meet for a moment, and Linda lowers the spoon to her bowl again, fishing for a shrimp, and a billion thoughts cross her mind before she finds herself.

—But, that's such great news! Why haven't you told me? Is it new, or—

Håkan shakes his head.

—I have traveled back and forth…But I don't know how to count that. We…we get along well together, and…yes, it's been a while. But I work here, and she works there, and it's somehow easier to meet in Italy since I can also work when I'm visiting. She could work here, too, but it's less convenient.

—But…you said that you would work from there…is that why? Are you moving to Italy?

He nods and says it's a plan they hope will work. That Italy has become his home, too. And that "home is where the heart is."

—So this is where I guess I should ask you again: could you imagine working for the firm instead of taking that job offer? I'm a little nervous. Can't you come out one of these days and get a feel for it?

Linda raises the wineglass and closes one eye to see the world through the pale-yellow liquid. The tea lights seem to hang upside down; it's quite beautiful. Working for the firm? That she has no attachment to, that she has already lost, that she doesn't care about—or does she, deep down?

—I need to give notice this week, she says, taking a sip of wine.

—Then come with me tomorrow morning!

She puts the wineglass down.

—I understand if it's strange, Håkan says. And that's quite natural. But we'll look at some different solutions to make it work. It's not supposed to feel like I'm using you. It's just that I'm not yet comfortable leaving everything in the hands of someone else. I need a person who captures the whole story. Basically, everyone I work with is new to the company; the old staff retired shortly after Dad stopped working, which I guess was good, but—

—When can I see her? Linda says.

Håkan looks bewildered, takes two bites of the sourdough bread, and puts a slice of cheese on the piece he has left.

—We need to talk about the details, he says.

—Sure, but that wasn't what I wondered. There's time for that. But I want to know who she is, your girlfriend. Don't you have a photo of her?

He shakes his head.

—Or, well, I suppose I do, but now it's getting embarrassing.

They laugh because maybe it is, but it's also very funny, and Linda wants to reassure him since she's sincerely happy he has found love.

—Does she speak English? Or only Italian? Do you understand each other?

—Yeah, of course. She speaks lots of languages. But we speak Italian when we are not working with Sweden, and then we speak English.

—And he, Antonio?

—He also speaks English, if that's what you're wondering.

There's a sparkle in his eyes.

—He has the same effect on all women. It's unbelievable.

243

Linda protests.

—I saw him in his underpants!

—Even when he's in proper clothes women turn their heads. I was going to invite them here for Midsummer. In fact, I already have. Could you come, too, to the island?

Midsummer. She has repressed that there will be a summer, a lonely summer with the kids on vacation and a lot of puzzling for her and Tobias. And a divorce, as a stopper to be pulled for the now-cold bathwater to drain and disappear, forever. Midsummer. That's when you should be endlessly happy, and it's obvious that Håkan wants Giovanna to come. There's nothing more magical. If the weather is okay, that is.

—Do you dare to challenge the weather? she says.

It comes out like a snake, even to her own ears.

—Sorry. Midsummer is a fantastic time of the year to visit. I'm not there yet, planning-wise. I don't know if I'll have the kids on that weekend.

—They can come, too. No problem.

Linda has only visited the island once, when the children were very small, because the spot where Håkan has his house is full of cliffs and steep slopes. Now, it shouldn't be a problem; the girls would probably like it.

—Okay. Then I say I will, whatever happens. I look forward to it. And I'm so happy for you.

How different things are, in just a few months. Had they been sitting here less than a year ago, Håkan would perhaps not have said anything about Giovanna, and Linda wouldn't have imagined she was about to divorce. And there's a reversal of roles—he's happy, she's devastated. Was she happy a year ago? How does it feel to be happy? Is that when life just flows? To come home to one's family, cook sausage and macaroni, bathe the children and read them a bedtime story, and then fall into bed after flicking through the TV channels? Is Håkan less happy because he travels to Italy once a month to meet the one he loves?

She's happy for him. And now she's even more pleased that he's not in love with Antonio.

—What happened with Mom and Dad? You must tell me. And with that apartment you rented?

Linda looks up from the soup and drops her spoon, which splashes the pinkish liquid over her and the table. It's as if someone pulls her apart, tearing out her heart and putting it on the table.

—Mom has known all along about their relationship, about Tobias and Maja. And kept him behind her back, kept it hidden.

And then her tears well up in a way they never have before. It's a Niagara Fall and a harrowing whine that leave her body, and Håkan gets all blurry opposite her.

—Oh god, he says. Oh my god.

—I'll come with you to the firm tomorrow, Linda says between tears.

*

Håkan's car is newly washed, and a bunch of guys in their twenties turn around at the sound of the engine when they leave the garage. It smells of new car, of new plastic and new leather, though Linda knows that Håkan has had the car for almost a year.

—This is one of things that would keep you from wanting to work at the firm, I suppose, Håkan says. I mean, it's a bit of a commute. But if you don't leave in the worst morning rush hour—

—I can read on the train. I don't mind it.

When she called work and said she had a doctor's appointment, but would be there after lunch, no one cared. It's an advantage of having worked a long time in the same place.

Linda hasn't been to the firm since she was in business school and worked there during the holiday since her father wanted to show her what awaited her. The idea had been that she would start with accounting since that was the best way to understand the business according to Gustav. This was also what Håkan had done, some years later, but then he had soon devoted more time to looking beyond the Swedish borders. He had studied a semester in Milan and realized that some of the best printing companies in Europe were located there, and when Gustav retired, Håkan had quickly expanded the business. "A stroke of genius," Gustav has repeated with admiration in his voice, but Håkan has never been proud of his doings. They had been necessary, a question of do or die.

The smell is still the same, and the office building hasn't changed with the exception of a new color on the walls and the modern coffee maker in the kitchenette. Moreover, there's a younger crowd that she doesn't recognize at all, but she has heard about a few of them. The ones who worked with her father came to be like an extended family over the years, and when Linda and Håkan were children, they were all invited for Christmas dinner. As kids, they were forced to greet everyone, but soon afterward they disappeared upstairs and peeked down on the grown-ups between the bars in the staircase. Linda can't imagine that Håkan has Christmas parties at his home; she's unsure if he throws any Christmas parties at all. But he probably does. All companies do.

They sit down in a conference room where one side is a photo wallpaper with a backlit lake, which contrasts with the green industry building outside the window.

—Lake Garda, Håkan says. That's where we usually go, over the weekends. When we don't go to Liguria…but that's more during summer.

—Do they have a conference room with a view over Stockholm?

—In fact, they do! You can see the city hall and Riddarholmen, a part of Lake Mälaren—

—You will get homesick, Linda says, knowing Håkan understands her sarcasm.

She would also be prepared to change from Riddarholmen to Lake Garda or Liguria.

—It's produced in Italy. That's where they make the wallpaper. Isn't it good? We do the same here now. But they already had the technology. We had to try it out before we bought a machine. You can select any photo you want, basically.

He takes out two binders and then gets up and says he has forgotten one.

—Coffee?

—Yes, please. With milk.

Håkan disappears out into the corridor, and Linda meets the curious glances from the opposite room. Is this where she will work? Her stomach tingles for it's both a journey back in time and a journey toward the future. As if she navigated around the reefs but forgot to read the map correctly. It will annoy Anita. Not Gustav as much as Anita. Her father isn't a man of conflicts nor someone who, in plain text, would express his disappointment. He can handle it and has done so when times were tough for the firm and the agreements they had weren't held. Linda remembers discussions at home when Gustav explained to Anita how things were, and she remembers how Anita was the one who devoted the most time to finding solutions or making plans to punish the ones involved who hadn't committed to the rules of the game. Gustav moved on.

Håkan pops in with the coffee, shuts the door, and puts the binder on the table in front of him.

—This is my plan: it's important that you get a stake of the company, to be involved. Otherwise, you could work anywhere, I understand that, too. I was thinking you'd get a normal salary, of course, but also shares in the company and an option to buy more shares further on.

Linda clasps her hands. Suddenly, everything is so real. It's a company life, not a job, that lies ahead of her. What she never wanted and what disappeared with Anita's disappointment almost fifteen years ago. This opens the door ajar again, but that's because Håkan is in charge and wants to share lots of information, in order for him to do what he needs to do. She should be grateful, but the sadness settles over her like a gray blanket. Reality has caught up with her. Her palms are sweaty and cold, and the cold spreads over her head, as if she were sitting in a draft.

Then she calms down. This is better, much better, than staying in the accounting department at the publishing house, than acting as deputy head and then going back to something that actually doesn't interest her. That she can help Håkan, who has his heart elsewhere, that's a fresh start for both of them and a way to get on with her life.

—Do you believe I can handle it? she says. I mean, this world is new to me. I can't just come stumbling in, being the boss—

—Calm down. You're exactly the one we're looking for—calm, confident, business-minded. Won't get excited over small things. And I'm not leaving. You will work with me and also with both the finance department and the marketing department. They will be your tutors if you so wish. They will also be offered to purchase warrants. I want to spread the ownership, and Mom and Dad need to release money to buy a new place to stay...so this is a good solution.

—They will lose money on the house, Linda says.

—But they have made a fortune from the firm over the past ten years. Me, too. The only one who hasn't is you. We can't change the past, but had you been a partner in the firm, Tobias would have gotten even more than when the house is sold.

—He shouldn't get anything.

Håkan pulls his shoulders up and raises his hands. It looks Italian, the quick motion and raised eyebrows, while the corners of his mouth fall.

—What?

—You are becoming Italian. How do you say Håkan in Italian?

—You can't, it comes out as "akanne." They call me Alexander.

—Alexander?

—Yes, well, Alessandro.

His cheeks turn pink.

—How sweet. If we'd had a son, he would have been called that. I've always loved that name. Though I can't see you being an Alexander. I guess I should practice, calling you Alessandro.

A dazed fly thuds against the window where the sun warms it the most, and they both watch it climbing, falling, and bouncing back against the window in a new attempt to get out.

—We need to get the windows cleaned, Håkan says and makes a note on his notepad.

—Lots to think of, as a boss, Linda says.

Håkan grins.

—Shall we take a tour, around the office? Or should we finish the financial part first?

Linda nods. The financial part first. To get it over and done with.

—When did you say you would be at work?

—After lunch, but I'll grab something quick on my way back.

Håkan peeks at his watch.

—Okay, shoot.

*

The commuter train slows down at the central station, and Linda puts her half-eaten sandwich in her tote bag.

The gravel, still left after the harsh winter, crackles under her feet as she walks across the bridge and continues on to the Old Town. The buses running past her make the dust swirl, and it's carried away by the strong wind. She lifts her face to the spring sun and realizes she won't need to tie her scarf as tight against her neck anymore. She unbuttons two buttons of her coat and takes off her gloves.

When she walks through the glass doors and cheers the receptionist, it's like walking into a dream she has dreamed before. She knows everything by heart, the smell in the elevator, how the elevator buttons feel against her fingertips, the sound when she steps off on the third floor—there's always someone standing by the photocopier, which buzzes in the corner. She walks the corridor with the yellowish-beige plastic carpet's soft resistance under her boots. Linda hangs her coat on the hanger behind the door and takes a notepad and a pen from the desk. She won't need them, but she doesn't want to show up empty-handed.

—Hello, Linda, her boss says and gets up with her hand outstretched. Sit down.

Linda sits opposite her, with the desk as a barrier.

—Have you considered the offer? her boss says and clasps her hands in front of her on the desk. She leans forward, perhaps in confidence, or maybe she has a sore back.

Linda nods. Her mouth is dry.

—Well, yes. It's, of course, a challenge, and I'm glad you asked me, but I have decided to do something completely different. So I won't take the job, unfortunately. I've come to announce that I will resign.

The boss leans back and grabs the armrests. She blinks, her mouth a thin line. It's impossible to read her emotions.

—What? So you quit? But…what will you do?

Her response, on the other hand, shows a genuine surprise, or dismay. As if there were only one job for Linda, right here at the publishing house.

—I will help my brother in the family business. It's a printing operation. I will be accountable in Sweden, while he moves to Italy.

—Wow. That's a big step.

—I have grown up with the company, so it isn't entirely new, Linda says and wonders if she is convincing and if she manages to convey that this is the most natural thing in the world and that the printing business runs in her blood.

—It puts us in an awkward situation, the boss says. Mostly me, of course, since I'm pregnant, but that has nothing to do with you. I guess that's not what made you want to change jobs. We'll miss you here; your knowledge is indispensable, and you have been the departments center, considering all the years you have worked here. And you would have been more than a substitute, since everyone relies on you.

She puts her hand on her stomach, which Linda still can't see much of, and her attention disappears for a moment. Then she shakes her head and looks as if nothing has happened.

—Well, then we need to talk about completely different things, she says. About your notice and how to resolve this in the best way. One thing at a time. Would you please hand in a written notice that you will resign, and I'll make sure it will be handled in a correct way. When will you leave?

—As soon as possible, says Linda. But I suppose I should stay until the midyear financial statements are done, to finish them off. The way you planned to do with the annual financial statements.

—Seems reasonable to me. Perhaps we can tell the others this afternoon, gather the department? Yes, they need to be informed about my condition, too. Though the overall situation is somewhat different.

—I'm sorry, Linda says.

They rise simultaneously and shake hands, but without congratulating each other. Eleven years vanish in a second. And two of today's three meetings are done.

It's half past six when Linda gets to her parents'. From the subway, there's a ten-minute walk, and she has walked slowly, unable to decide whether it's worth stepping over the threshold to that house again or if she should just cancel. Her mother sounded so sure that the house should be sold, and Linda knows her opening line will be "Have you talked to Tobias?" But she hasn't. She wants to talk to him as little as possible, preferably not at all.

She doesn't want to talk to Anita either, doesn't even want to call her mother anymore after all she has done. She didn't support Linda, and she went behind her back—that's unforgivable. And yet, Linda is on her way to her, to talk about something Anita says is important. It's too late to turn back.

—Hello, Anita says. And welcome. So glad you could come so we can chat. Have you talked to Tobias?

—No, Mom, Linda says patiently. I'll do so later in the week.

—Yes, you know it's important that we get in touch with a real-estate agent now. There are so many holidays in May, you'd have to be aware of that if you want to be seen and get potential buyers. Come in. I made sandwiches. I don't eat much in the evenings, and Dad has his bridge night tonight. Perhaps we can sit in the kitchen?

Linda nods. She hasn't sat in the kitchen for years, and it's a strange feeling to settle on "her" seat, which isn't at all hers anymore because as soon as she and Håkan moved out, her parents changed everything. Consequently, she now sits on her father's seat, and Anita moves his neatly tucked napkin and gives Linda a paper one.

—I can move.

—No no, don't worry. It's perfectly all right. Dad's not here.

She sets a plate of sandwiches on the table, and Linda remembers that they used to be very good. It happened sometimes—

though rarely—that her mother didn't want to cook, and she would instead make these open-faced sandwiches. They never taste the same when Linda makes them herself.

—There's also one with shrimp; take one of those. I guess you're hungrier than I am. Did you eat at work?

Linda nods.

—Would you like a glass of wine? Or tea—it's freshly brewed, in the thermos.

—Tea is fine.

—I'll have a glass of wine.

Anita rises, takes a glass from the cupboard above the sink, and opens the refrigerator. On the first shelf is a bag-in-box, and she pushes the button, as if it were milk in a canteen.

—These are long days for you.

—It evens out. They are shorter when I pick up the kids.

—Are you all right, on one salary?

—Mom, we're not divorced. Everything is as before. But, yes, I will do just fine. I earn more than Tobias.

—But he gets a bonus, doesn't he?

Theoretically, he gets one, and has for the last four years. But every time she asked, he answered he didn't know how much it was or when it would be paid.

—Never saw one.

—Linda, there's something I want you to tell you. Not only am I very sorry for what I've done, but I didn't do it out of malice.

—Can't we stop talking about it? Or I'll leave.

Anita holds up both hands and lowers them slowly.

—The reason, she says, the background and the reason to it all is this...

She clears her throat, and Linda buries her face in her hands. She doesn't want to know how Tobias and Anita planned this for several years. Why can't her mother stop talking about it?

—I was young. And stupid, yes, I was. Young, dumb, and in-experienced. Why your father fell for me is a mystery, but he did. His mother, your grandmother, was a clairvoyant lady. Very deter-mined, not always kind. And used to getting things her way, so to speak. Anyway. She found out about me. And someone else.

—What?

—Let me continue.

Anita raises her hand, sighs, and takes a sip of her wine. She hasn't touched the sandwiches on her plate. Linda puts down her piece of bread with roast beef and remoulade, which reminds her of Tobias and all the times they sat in some basement café in Ny-havn having open-faced sandwiches, real Danish *smørrebrød*, which they both love, and a cold beer. Tobias always had aquavit, a small glass.

—I considered myself smart. And I guess I doubted whether I was in love with Gustav, the same way you can doubt when you are engaged to be married and realize that this person is the one you will live with for the rest of your life. I was out dancing with my girlfriends, without Gustav. This man asked me to dance, and he was extremely charming. Handsome. Very urbane. He had a sports car with an open roof, which was exciting. Gustav had his old Mer-cedes, which was great, but there's this thing about a sports car… Well, there has always been I guess.

She looks dreamily out the window and takes another sip of wine.

Linda sits with her hands in her lap and looks down at the tea-cup in front of her. She's embarrassed to hear her mother talk about her dreams and a relationship she had with a man she still seems to desire. Why didn't she leave? Has she spent all these years longing for him while married to Gustav?

—Yes, it sounds strange, all of it, Anita says. I won't dwell on the facts. They don't concern you. Anyway, he asked me out on a Saturday, at noon, to a garden market. I imagined it being a safe place to meet, but your grandmother happened to be there, too. She saw us. I introduced my friend, but she understood immediately. We had no relationship in that way, me and this man; you could call it a flirtation. And a day later, she confronted me.

Anita empties the wine glass, puts her hands on the table, and leans forward toward Linda.

—She gave me the house, but there was one condition: forget the other man and marry Gustav. It was all she wanted. For me to take care of him. Although I wasn't the one she had dreamed of as a daughter-in-law, she saw her son as someone who would be left over, and I was better than no one at all.

Linda pushes the chair back to avoid having her mom so close. She squints. Is it true what Anita has said, that she had an affair and was persuaded to marry?

—I hadn't planned anything else, which made it even more embarrassing. I had no intentions of being with that other man, no more than to realize that I loved Gustav, because I did. And I didn't understand that half the house would be mine, anyway, when we got married—I didn't know much, then, economically. I assumed she bribed me, and in all the confusion, I accepted, didn't resist. I broke up with the man, never met him again.

She watches Linda helplessly as if she expects Linda to say she did the right thing. But what Anita has told her are things Linda never asked to know and, ideally, never should have been told. Her parents' relationship suddenly has become soiled, and it doesn't seem as obvious as before. What happened to the nuclear family? What happened to honesty? Linda closes her eyes.

—A month later, in the middle of summer, my best friend's mother called and cried. It was almost impossible to hear what she said, and she repeated the same thing over and over again. Dead. Dead. I didn't understand what she meant, and, finally, I asked her angrily who was dead and why she called me. My friend had died in a car accident. The person driving was the man I had met. He also died. That same morning, he had called and asked me to go with him that evening, even though I had told him I was engaged to be married and that I didn't want to see him anymore.

Anita gets up, takes the wine glass, and walks over to the refrigerator where she fills the glass out of the box. She comes back to the table, and Linda sees she's a bit wobbly, but it may not be the wine; it could just as well be the emotions.

—This has, of course, nothing to do with you. Nothing. I'm aware of that. The only thing that concerns you is the way your grandmother handled the whole thing. And I can only assume that I reacted with the same instinct she did when I saw Tobias and his…lady. It was so obvious. Their faces revealed them; it was written in their foreheads what they had done. I am so sorry. I recognized myself in them and assumed it wasn't anything serious, that I could have been wrong. And who was I to confront them? Times are different now from when I was young.

Linda turns her head and looks at the kitchen counter to avoid seeing Anita heave her bad conscience at her. What does she want—forgiveness?

—I have seen them three times, Linda. That's all. The last time was last summer when I went back to town for a doctor's visit while you and the children stayed in Falsterbo. Before that, I saw them one time, a month after I had met them at the conference site. Which means there were three-and-a-half years between the times I saw them. Last summer, I confronted him. I did it for you, Linda, for your life with Tobias. And then I got the idea with the house. That it might make him wake up, the way I did.

She puts her arms around her body, as if she was freezing, and holds onto her upper arms. It's her turn to close her eyes. She sways her head back and forth.

—I want to get rid of the house, Linda. It's not just me who wants to get rid of it; your dad does to. He knows all about what happened. I couldn't lie to him and didn't want to either. But your father has a heart bigger than the world, and he asked me to stay, asked me again to marry him and move in. Your grandmother got a tenancy in the city, which was easy back then, and she was happy as a lark when she moved. Do you remember her apartment? She loved it. She no longer had to take care of this big house where she and Gustav had lived alone since your grandfather died suddenly seven years earlier.

Anita smoothens her hair.

—But enough is enough, she says. The house is full of this and always has been. Your dad and I must put it behind us after all these years. We chose each other, we really did, even though it doesn't sound that way. And I thought I did the right thing, that the house should continue its journey through the generations. But now when I look back, I find it crazy. Who's supposed to get the house?

Anita scoffs.

—So did you marry Dad because of the house? Or to make grandma happy?

Anita flinches.

—Why do you say that? I explained to you I wasn't sure of my feelings. But when I told your father that I regretted what I had done, I knew I loved him. We went to the funeral together.

—What?

—Yes, for my friend, that is.

—And the man's?

—I had nothing to do with that man. It was over.

—Do you know what happened in the car accident?

—They went off-road. They had been to a dance; he'd been drinking. The car flew straight into a tree, and both were dead when the ambulance arrived. They probably died immediately. If I had accepted the invitation, I would have been dead.

—You can't say that. Everything would have been different. You could have left earlier or later—

—But that's the way I think, Anita says harshly, that it could have been me. But I'm still here, I am married to a man I love, and have two children and two grandchildren. And I want them all well. And most of all, I am alive.

Linda takes a sip of cold tea and wonders if her mother will start crying, but when she looks up, Anita is calm. She's not someone who cries, but she isn't someone who tells secrets either.

—So now you know.

—Any other skeletons in the closet? Linda says.

Anita's eyes narrow, she takes a short breath, as if she is preparing to start a new confession. Then her eyelids flicker, as if she has forgotten what she just told or maybe already erased it from her memory.

—No, she says firmly. This is it. And you are brave, Linda, in doing what you do. You have always gone your own way, and I don't know where you got that. Maybe I can learn something from you. If you have that recording of our conversation with Tobias, I would be very grateful. I will sue him. Don't you want another sandwich?

Tobias gets excited when he hears he can get money earlier than expected, and the meeting with the realtor is only a week later. But the idea of selling the house somehow makes Linda nauseous. Not that she doesn't want it to happen, after what her mother told her, she is absolutely convinced that this is the best they can do. But that Tobias is here and that his actions have triggered the sale makes her nauseous. She tries to keep her head clear as the real estate agent walks from room to room with Tobias, Anita, and Linda in tow. They reach the dining room, and Anita shows the agent the door to the terrace and says it's convenient in the summer—you don't have to go out the front door and walk around if you want to dine outdoors. And for kids it's even better, with the staircase from the terrace down to the garden.

—No draft, and you can keep the front door locked. And no need to worry about burglars, she explains.

The real estate agent nods and writes, writes and nods, and inspects doors, asking why there aren't security locks on the windows, which Anita knows nothing about.

Why Tobias is around is unclear, but he presented himself as the owner, which complies with all the papers. Before he explains that he and Linda own the house together and that the house did belong to his in-laws, who still live in the house, and that the situation, therefore, is somewhat complicated, Linda has had time to become sweaty with anger. He's convincing in that natural way, and his ability to take up space and act confidently annoys her. He attracts other people into his world, as if he were a spider and they were all stuck in his sticky web without understanding he will suck all the energy from them.

They go upstairs, and the real estate agent continues to open doors, exclaiming "Oh, wow." Anita and Linda look at each other.

Is the house too old and dated? Too few rooms? Too small rooms? Should they have had the built-in closets removed, or is it better to keep them? Anita mutters when he opens the closets, apologizes for the mess, says she hasn't had time to clear them out, that this is the downside of many years of living in the same place...Linda realizes it will take time to empty the house. And they certainly need to store the furniture and all the other stuff if her parents won't find somewhere else to stay right away.

Tobias is unconcerned. It's as if he doesn't see what Anita, Linda, and the real estate agent see but only the economic value, which he also asks about: "So, what do you think the house is worth? Can you give an estimate?" But the real estate agent just waves his hand and says he must check everything and make a comparison to the price development in the area before he can give an estimate.

In the attic, there are a few boxes marked "Linda" and "Håkan," but Linda has no clue what's in them.

—School books, Anita says. All your old files. Same for Håkan.

But who would save all their old books, notes, and tests?

—The girls might like them. I remember that you enjoyed playing with my old reading and spelling books.

Fia and Lotta don't know that the boxes exist, and today, when Gustav visits Skansen with them, they will probably see enough of what life was like in the old days. It has fascinated generations past and will continue to fascinate, but Linda won't save her old papers for the sake of it. She would be surprised to find any school books at all in those boxes; if she remembers things correctly, they weren't allowed keep them, and everything was collected by the end of the year, unless the books were too used or dated to last another year.

—What if we go downstairs and discuss the price? Tobias says.

The realtor counters that he also wants to inspect the basement and the garden, but Tobias doesn't perceive it as insulting. He struts down the stairs, pointing at a glass window with handblown glass in the staircase, saying it must be quite unusual. Linda is ashamed. It's as if he's trying to talk up the value of a car without having a clue about what it's worth. Is this what he does with his customers, too—sounds so convincing that nobody questions him? Anita is finally down the stairs and looks up at the stained-glass window. When she comes down from the landing, she hisses to Linda:

—I never liked that window. Feels like a church. But these were modern back then, and we never replaced them. Can't imagine that it's an asset to the house!

Linda has never liked that window either, especially not in the winter. The light makes the staircase gloomy and dull, except for a few weeks around midsummer when the reflections are almost pastel colored, which took Linda almost twenty years to experience. They always went to Falsterbo right after school was over, and her dad stayed in town. The first time Linda noticed the beautiful colors was when she was working one summer during her business school years, and she stayed in the house throughout June and July. She's amazed that Anita feels the same way she does, that it's depressing and gloomy. An asset? No way.

When they get out to the garden, Linda notices that no one has yet taken the trouble to cut the grass. There are green patches but also patches that are still flat and beige, and some parts might have died during the winter. Anita walks up to the oldest of the four apple trees that will soon bloom.

—The garden will look its most beautiful in about two to three weeks, she says. That would be a great time for showing the house, don't you think? All pre-summer crisp and idyllic.

—Might want to fix a few things out here, the real estate agent says and points at the flower beds that struggling tulips share with some big dandelions.

—The grass needs to be cut, Linda says. We'll arrange that, won't we, Tobias?

He looks at her as if she has asked him to climb a tree to get the neighbor's cat and turns his head away.

—Yes, well, you don't need to trim the borders with a nail scissors, says the realtor with an embarrassed laughter. But after a long winter, the garden suffers the most. The houses survive if you wish. Otherwise, it's very nice out here. Cozy, lots of privacy. People like that.

Linda thinks of their own house, the patio that everyone sees and that they never use, not even for a cup of coffee. She always sits on the stairs that lead down to the garden to avoid being seen—and to avoid watching the neighbors. It's only when Tobias gets the idea to barbecue that he stands on the wooden deck, well aware that everyone can see him and perhaps admire how he turns the meat or conclude that he's an excellent father who can cook.

—That said, we mostly use the terrace, Anita says. From there you have a view of it all. And the garden, I will gladly hand over to a younger generation. My husband and I are getting old, and the garden is great, as you can see, two thousand square meters and a great deal of fruit trees and berries, which is something I can't take care of anymore. But for a family with children—yes, of course, they will need money to buy the house, too.

She laughs and her cheeks flush. Tobias doesn't flinch. The house is his, and he and Linda are a family. But they would never have been able to afford to buy it.

The real estate agent nods.

—You could do that, too, use the terrace, that is. And it's good that there are several spaces for outdoor living. People are different. Shall we go finish this off? I'm sure there will be a great interest in a house like this. But what if we take the details inside?

Anita leads them back, talking about the house's history, how Gustav's parents had it built, how it has stayed in the family. But there's no guarantee that the next generation will thrive, and you can only hope that the new owners will appreciate the house. Does she even ponder the fact that the house no longer belongs to her? Does she realize that she and Gustav won't get anything in this transaction, and that, on the contrary, they will have to find money to buy an apartment?

It shouldn't concern Linda. She's not the architect of this deal, and yet she seems to be the one doing the worst—Anita's not sad, Tobias doesn't have a bad conscience.

Tobias stops and waits for Linda.

—It would be good if we got it sold now because I need the money, he says. I'm thinking of traveling this summer.

Linda walks past him as if she hadn't heard. That he needs cash is no news; it was the same argument he used for the money he got from Anita.

—I received a letter from your mother, too, a lawsuit? Do you know what that's all about? It's not in relation to the house?

Linda has her phone in her hand, and she picks it up as if she were checking her messages.

—You'd need to ask her. I have no clue.

He grabs her arm and pulls her to him.

—Is it about the house?

—Let go of me. She has said that she wants the money back, which is only fair since you tricked her into giving it to you.

—She can blame herself. And she has no proof I did anything wrong.

—She has proof; she has your own words.

—Like how? Did she record it, or—

—No, but I did.

He pushes her away and takes a few deep breaths, like a sullen bull. His chin protrudes and his jaws move as if he was chewing on something.

—Can't do that, you know. 'Cause half the house is mine.

—That's why we're here, why you're here, right? Can you go in now? It's not about the house. She's not stupid.

—I will be traveling, he says again. So I guess you can take the girls? You want to be with them, don't you?

Linda stops. There are two meters between them, and they feel like twenty kilometers.

—Yes, I do. Don't you?

He doesn't answer.

—When will you leave?

—By midsummer. And I'll be gone my whole summer vacation, anyway. I'll take five weeks.

—And you don't want to see the girls at all?

—I have a few things to do. And I'm exhausted, after this spring.

She thinks of the Midsummer celebration, that she had wondered if Fia and Lotta could stay with him so she could meet with Giovanna and Håkan and Antonio by herself, lead an adult life for a few days. But why? The children are her family. Giovanna and Antonio are Håkan's new family. This is the best solution. Tobias will be far away, and she and the children can create new traditions.

—Yes, I understand, she says. This must have been hard on you.

Tobias doesn't seem to hear the sarcasm. He might not even be listening to her.

—I'll take the children, Linda continues. I'll work things out.

—And it's not about the house—is that what you're saying? It would be bad timing. I soon need to book tickets.

—Where are you going?

—That's a secret, he laughs. That's the way it goes when you want to divorce; then you can't know everything.

He walks in front of her into the house. Linda stops for a while on the steps, perplexed. As if she were curious and wanted to know the details of his holiday plans; Linda couldn't care less, even if he went to Mars. She shakes her head, enters, and closes the door behind her.

At the dining table, the realtor and Anita have already taken their seats, and Tobias is about to sit down. They talk as if Anita owns the house and Linda can understand her; it's just a piece of paper and a lot of good intentions that have reduced her to a supporting actor, a tenant.

—We're discussing the timetable, but if the photographer came here tomorrow, the house could be on the market in two weekends, which would be good, Anita says.

—How long will it take before we get the money? Tobias says.

The real estate agent looks up at him, unsure if it's a joke or if he's serious.

—Well, you'll get it when the deal is done and you hand over the keys to the new owners.

Linda wonders if he doesn't remember how it all happened when they had bought their house.

—And when will you move? Tobias says to Anita.

—The idea was for us to move out in August. If you would help us pack, Linda?

—I won't be able to do that, anyway. And I would need an advance for the summer, if you won't leave until August, Tobias says.

—Excuse me? Anita says. As if I haven't given you enough?

—You don't pay any rent, as far as I'm concerned. And I have other expenses for the summer.

—We pay the mortgages, which are commonly included in the rent. We pay for heating, water, insurances, waste collection. You pay, as far as I know, nothing, and you never did and presumably won't do before the house is sold. Now, if you'd calm down.

In that very moment, Linda likes her mother.

Anita stretches her neck with tightening tendons as she turns with a smile to the realtor.

—The situation is delicate, she says. My husband and I no longer own the house as I said. Linda and Tobias can decide when access to the house will take place. I will not interfere in their decision.

—We'll have that discussion once there's a buyer, the realtor says in a friendly voice. The buyer often has a property he or she needs to get sold, too, so there are generally more transactions to take into account. But the money won't be transferred until the keys are handed over anyway.

Tobias doesn't move.

—But we could always ask them to hurry up, right? To get rid of all this.

Linda's and Anita's eyes meet, and both know that Tobias thinks he's hurt them, when actually they can't wait until the house has been sold so that they all can start their new lives. They shake hands with the realtor, and Anita follows him to the door.

—Did you see the invitation to the graduation at preschool? Linda asks Tobias.

—They didn't give me anything.

—I put it on the refrigerator door. Check it out next time you are home, okay?

—Do I need to come to every graduation? Can't you go there?

—It's not my graduation, Linda says. It's the children's. Lotta's. But you do as you want.

He glares at her.

Linda takes her purse and leaves. Tobias follows on her heels, walking past her on the stairs, and turns halfway toward Linda and Anita.

—You can't win this, he says. Not a chance.

They hear his heavy steps disappear down the street.

—Did you ever think about doing theater? Linda says without turning to her mom. It would suit you.

It takes a while before Anita answers.

—Oh, I had that dream when I was young…

—It's never too late. Or you could always become a director.

266

May passes in a haze. Linda somehow straightens her back, which might be due to the light or the pre-summer heat or perhaps the fact that she understands it's soon time to leave the protective cocoon and unfold her wings. She must survive. The less she sees Tobias, the easier life is. And now that the viewings of the house are done and there seems to be a buyer, she breathes out and starts looking at apartments. These are microscopic steps, but at least she takes them. On her own.

The sun is still high in the sky, shining on the worn ground on the back of the preschool facilities. It's the first days of June. The bushes all have green leaves, and it's almost impossible to see the row of houses on the other side. At this time of the year, they usually show the premises to new parents, and this was the time of the year that Linda and Tobias saw preschool. They adored the playground for the children, lush and cozy. That the area looks like this during only three months a year is something they all try to forget, and today, when there's the official closing of the semester, Linda's thoughts are far from the preschool backyard's qualities. She captures a glimpse of Fia and Lotta next to each other, in the summer dresses she bought them last weekend. One is light blue and the other light yellow, and the rays of sun make the girls' blonde hair shine. Fia holds her sister's hand in a tight grasp; perhaps she understands that Lotta is leaving preschool. Lotta has already been on field trips to school to meet with the new teacher, excited and proud that she is a big girl.

Among the parents, Linda sees Marita standing beside the long table set with flowery paper tablecloths. Linda had been asked if she could make a strawberry cake, but she replied that she couldn't. She knows that she is now at below zero, compared to the other parents, but when Gabriella arrives with two store-bought cakes, she has less of a bad conscience. Marita's face stiffens as she sees the cake boxes from the bakery, and when Gabriella opens one and Marita leans down to look at what's inside, Linda must laugh. She can imagine that the jelly covering the strawberries is too much for Marita's taste and that the cream may be covered with nuts, which is potentially harmful for those with allergies. All families have given their written consent to serving the children cake. Reducing sugar intake is one of the key discussion points at every meeting, and they have banished ice cream and cakes from birthday celebrations at preschool. The only exception has been Lucia and now the graduation, provided that there isn't "too much."

Farther away, Bo stands alone. They haven't seen each other or spoken since the preschool party, and Linda's things were easy to pack. She had put they key in an envelope in the mailbox and pondered awhile over whether she would write something, like "thank you" or "good luck" or "I apologize," but none of the words fit, and all might be interpreted to her detriment, and perhaps also to Bo's, depending on Stina's mood. Linda gets the feeling that the other parents are waiting for an explanation for Stina's behavior a few weeks ago: Is it true? Are they having an affair?

Linda says hi to one mother who passes by, one of those who has now replaced her tunic with an airy summer dress and a pair of low beige suede boots. How do they get those tanned legs this early in the season? Fake tan? She tried it once, when she went to Thailand with the Hamklints, but her tan turned very orange, and after two days it was all flaky; she had tried to scrub away what looked like smears but were merely a vain attempt to look good.

—Hello! It's been a while. How are you doing? Bibbi says.

—Okay. Thanks again for taking the children, before Easter. Bibbi shakes her head.

—And where do you live now? You could have stayed...just so you know. You're always welcome at our place.

Their words and phrases are like that fake suntan lotion: vain attempts, here to bridge the ravine of misunderstandings. Linda doesn't want to reproach Bibbi for anything, especially not that she's married and has a functioning family life. Bibbi, who only wanted to be kind, who saw to it that she had somewhere to sleep, who helped her with the kids. And then she barely even got a thank you! But Linda can't explain, not even to herself.

—Sometimes at home, when Tobias isn't there. Sometimes with my brother, again. It's fine. I will stay at my parents' house from midsummer until early August, at least, though I don't need to. Tobias won't be home. But I must help them get rid of stuff, probably.

—Yes, I saw that their house was for sale? Are they moving?

Everybody checks the house market over the Internet; that's no secret. There's not a single house for sale in the area without everyone knowing how much it lists for and how much it sells for.

—Mmm, eventually. They're looking, but they have their summer house in Falsterbo so they're in no hurry.

—And what about you?

—Should get officially divorced first. But I've been checking out a few apartments. I'd love to find something around here.

Linda smiles, and it only hurts a little, just a small sting, and she's okay with being who she is, now. Soon to be divorced. Bibbi looks around. The other families are slowly joining.

—And who bought your parents' house?

—A couple with older children, eight and ten, I think. Tired of the city life, had a great apartment on Östermalm. It was fast.

—So you will stay here?

There's a barely noticeable tremor in Bibbi's voice, hard to register and difficult to interpret.

—Yes, I hope so. It's the easiest, but everything depends on what Tobias wants. We're not there yet, to be honest. Why?

Bibbi looks around again. She isn't listening at all to what Linda says, and she bites her thumbnail as she says hi to a couple who just arrived. Then she leans against Linda.

—Someone told me that Peter and Gabriella are seeing each other. What should I do? What should I say—do I talk to either of them? Do I talk to Mats about it? Do you think he knows?

Her voice is so low and she talks so fast that Linda has to concentrate on what she hears. When she puts the message into something understandable, it's like an echo through her head, but she can't remember where or when she has heard this before. Gabriella and Peter? An unlikely combination.

—Don't wait, Linda says. I mean, don't wait too long. It's probably better to find out what's going on now, no matter how big or small it is. How do you know it's not only rumors? Talk to him, tell him how you feel.

She puts her arm around Bibbi, who leans her head against Linda's shoulder.

—I have nowhere to go, she mumbles. I can't do what you have done, move in with a sibling.

—You can move in with me, Linda says. But you know what? It might not even be true.

She means what she says. However strangely Bibbi has acted during the last months, she would still help Bibbi should she need it. And rumors—they mean nothing. Gossip.

—It's almost summer, I can't do it right now, but thank you anyway.

Linda grabs her arm, pushing her away.

—Don't do that to yourself, she says. Don't tell yourself that it will get better because you're on holiday. Either something is going on, and then there's the summer to sort things out, or nothing has happened, and you'll have the best summer ever. It's like a plague, thinking about it but doing nothing. You're going on vacation together, right?

—You didn't say anything because of Christmas. We have a lot of things planned with the children—

—And did anything get better because I didn't say anything? You can do the things you have planned anyway. Together or separately.

Bibbi turns to the slope, where the children are now placed in two rows, wearing flower wreaths on their heads. There's a breeze in the treetops and a faint green light covers the playground. The smells of lilac and jasmine linger over them.

—Don't do as I do; do as I say.

Linda tries to sound stern but doesn't succeed very well.

—You're the most rational person I know. I mean it. In a positive way, though. I don't understand how you can be so—cool. And collected.

—I didn't have a choice. But all books don't have the same ending, and I hope yours will be happier so you don't have to be rational. It's effective, I guess, but just as difficult.

They laugh, but stop when Gabriella comes up to them.

—How nice to see you, Gabriella says. Will Tobias be here as well? That's almost the law around here, isn't it?

—I have no idea, Linda says. I hope so. We don't see each other that much.

—Isn't it strange that our oldests won't be here this fall?

—Somewhat, but mostly good, Linda says.

—Yes, Bibbi says. Really good. One down, two to go.

—Oh, I think it's sad, Gabriella says. Mine have loved this preschool. And school's so different. Is Peter here?

—He…can't make it, Bibbi says. He's away.

Gabriella jerks her head, her hair swinging as if on a doll.

—Is he? Oh well. What a shame.

The preschool headmistress claps her hands and presents the summer choir. The children squirm, first in embarrassment when their parents giggle, but those who thrive in the spotlight, including

271

Lotta and Fia, change and look proud. They still hold hands, and when the summer anthem starts, Linda cries. She's tired of crying, tired of all the emotions. Graduation day is a defining moment, almost like a divorce. She hopes that Lotta doesn't see the same comparison and that there's a longing in her heart instead. From Lotta's descriptions after the visits to the school, Linda is certain the change will be good for her. Fia, too, has expressed that she wants to start school because she wants to be where Lotta is. Fall will be different, that much is clear. For all of them.

Through the corner of her eye, she sees Tobias leaning against the wall. It's strange that he hasn't made his usual entrance, but he might understand that the children are at the center of attention today, not him. And then she notices that Peter is standing next to him. But why did Bibbi say he was away? She tries to make contact with Bibbi, but she is engrossed in the songs, her eyes as full of tears as Linda's a moment ago. When the music fades for a moment, Linda walks up to her.

—Why did you say he was away? she whispers. He's right there?

—Just wanted to see her reaction. Heard that they had lunch. She knew. It was pretty obvious.

—Who told you? Are there spies around?

—Bo. I'm not sure why, but he called me one day and said he had seen them and he didn't want to interfere, but it looked like they were more than friends.

Linda remembers. Bo had hinted about it to her, too, already at the preschool flea market.

—Bo? But are you sure he got it right? Linda says.

Should she have mentioned it to Bibbi already in January? Would Bibbi have believed her?

Bibbi shrugs and looks at the kids. The bright voices take up a new song that lifts to the treetops. Linda looks up at the house farther away, where the balcony doors are open and some nimble pensioners have taken place as if they were at the opera. She's happy that her children contribute to the summer mood, that there's sunshine on these early days of summer, and that they'll soon eat strawberry cake.

*

Linda must admit that Gabriella's store-bought cakes were fantastic, which she tells her.

—Oh, how sweet of you. There was no time to bake. And I'm not good at cakes. But Marita wasn't happy. They look better than anything homemade, but that wasn't why I bought them. I don't even like cake.

She looks sad, as if it was something you must like, but Linda says it's probably something you outgrow—when do you have cake, more than at kids' parties?

—If even then, Gabriella says. My kids would rather eat ice cream.

—Mine, too, Linda says. Or possibly a chocolate cake.

They laugh, but Bibbi, who stands diagonally behind Gabriella, gives Linda a nod, indicating that they should leave. Linda wonders if she realizes how she felt when Bibbi and Gabriella were buddies. Gabriella turns around.

—Why did you say that Peter was away, anyway? Gabriella says to Bibbi. He was here just now.

—Well, then perhaps you know more than I do.

—What do you mean?

—That you might be better informed about what he does than I am. People talk about you. That you meet. And I don't like it.

Gabriella's eyes are wide-open, and a faint blush shows on her cheeks.

—No, but, my goodness, how embarrassing, she says. Oh, my god, I'm so sorry. Who's talking? That's awful...It's not at all...I didn't want to say anything. Peter helps me because I want to start a web shop. Selling all kinds of party goods.

—Party goods? What's that?

273

Bibbi looks at Linda, who shrugs. Bibbi probably is on the wrong track.

—Well, we were in the US before Christmas last year, and I saw all these fun decorations and the sales on everything for Halloween…and I…well, I didn't want to tell you, since it might not be doable—

—And what exactly is Peter's role in all this?

—I knew he works with IT solutions, so I asked him if he could help me create a website.

Bibbi collapses like an old party balloon.

—And so you have lunch, out here?

—Yes, because I work from home, and he said it was easy for him to swing by…He promised not to tell you. I guess it was a bad idea.

Bibbi sighs and puts her hands through her hair.

—Sort of.

—I'm sorry. It wasn't…I hadn't imagined that anyone would… It's just a website. He's been really sweet and explained stuff that I have a hard time understanding, though it should be super easy. We haven't met more than that…I don't understand how…

Linda glances at Bibbi. She and Gabriella can sort it out alone. Linda is no longer needed. She turns and walks to the end of the table, where Bo sits on his own. His youngest leaves to go play with the other children.

—Linda! What a pleasure to see you.

—The same. Stina isn't here?

—No, she…has other things to do.

He takes a deep breath. The smile that spreads on his face fades almost immediately.

—Things happen. I apologize. For last time.

Linda nods.

—The most important thing is that it works for you. I don't want to get between you two, but it wasn't great at the party, she says.

Bo scrapes the leftovers from his paper plate, even though there's almost nothing left.

—No, I understand that very well. I can't do much about it. Jealousy is somehow like a…disease. It makes everyone feel bad and constantly on guard. But, no, things aren't going that well. We can talk about that some other time.

—Whenever you want, Linda says.

*

The sun warms her back, and she looks at the group of children playing a little farther away. Peter and Tobias are still by the wall. None of them have said hello to either Linda or Bibbi.

—Dad is here! Fia says. Come on!

She grabs Linda's hand, and Linda rises apologetically. She can't prevent her daughter from assuming they still belong together, as they inevitably do. Lotta comes running down the hill and joins them. She's no longer a small child; her whole body has stretched out during winter.

Tobias is forced to stop the conversation with Peter, who turns around, about to leave.

—You won't even say hello to Bibbi? She didn't think you'd come, Linda says.

She wishes that someone, sometime, had reminded Tobias that she existed and that she also needed to be seen.

—What? No, I had a few things to do, but she knew I'd drop by. We'll meet at home later. It's not like we need to be nailed to each other all the time—

—No, of course not. If we don't see each other before the holidays, have a great summer.

—Yes, you too, Peter says.

—Did you hear us singing, Dad? Fia says.

275

—I did. I was here the whole time. It was great.

—Did you have cake, too? Lotta says. There was one that was really beautiful, with that kind of shiny stuff on top.

—Jelly, Linda says. It was good.

—Though I don't like cake, Lotta says.

There's a silence. The children, standing between them, look up with wondering and hopeful eyes.

—Go play with your buddies, Linda says.

Fia and Lotta run to their friends, perhaps thinking that this moment of family idyll has somehow glued together what was broken.

—Any news about the house? Tobias says.

—I hope we can sign in a week, if I understood the realtor right. Haven't you heard from him?

—Could be.

Tobias pulls out his phone and says he probably has a message he hasn't yet listened to.

—When are you leaving?

—The day before Midsummer Eve. Then I'll get five weeks off. But there is no point in asking where.

—I'm not interested. Will you take the girls until that Thursday, so you get a little extra time together?

—Sure.

She turns around, glancing at Bibbi, Gabriella, and Peter. Bo is nowhere to be seen.

—Is Peter doing business with that good-looking chick?

—Yes.

—Couldn't imagine that. He's such a bore.

—No, there are many boring men you wouldn't think had business going on.

He pretends not to hear.

—Does Bibbi know about it?

—Yes. It's a family-business thing. As in a job. Not too exciting, huh?

—Does she believe that?

He laughs so loudly that some of the other parents turn and smile at them, perhaps with the same hope that has just shown in the children's eyes. The weariness wells over Linda, but she smiles at him, as if to tell the audience that all is well.

—You should tell me the next time you decide to record stuff, by the way. It's illegal, Tobias says.

—Not if you are in the conversation yourself.

—I'm not in a great seat with your mother.

Linda doesn't answer. There's nothing to say. She isn't ashamed anymore that her parents gave them the house, but the $20,000—he should pay them back. And she has nothing to add. What her mother can get out of it is up to her.

—Will you take care of the house this summer?

—I will stay at my parents'; the house must be emptied. Håkan will also be over one or two weekends. I will go get the mail though.

—You could stay at ours.

—I didn't know you'd be gone when I accepted Mom's offer to stay at their house.

—Someone has to mow the lawn.

—Then we should put up a note at the supermarket. I can't be held responsible for everything because you decide to take five weeks of vacation, can I? I'll take care of our other house. By the way, we need to get a realtor over there, too, when you're back.

—I'll keep the house.

He jiggles his car keys in his pocket, trying to look as if he doesn't care.

—Then you can take care of the house yourself.

—It's still ours. We're still married.

Linda gets the urge to stick out her tongue at him.

—Okay, she says grimly. I'll put up a note up at the supermarket. And we'll share the cost. And get that realtor over when you're back; we need to know what the house is worth, and you should pay me for my part.

—Won't you go anywhere this summer?

—No, she says. I won't. I'll change jobs in August. I will work until the second week of July.

—But…where will Lotta and Fia be? Because preschool is closed, isn't it?

—It's only closed in July. Until then, they'll be here and then a week at my parents'.

—With your parents? In Falsterbo?

—Mom has some contact there whose daughter will help out. And there's swim school and other things they can do. Lotta can take tennis classes.

Tobias's nostrils twitch, and he presses his lips together. The rattle of the car keys increases.

—Didn't we agree that they wouldn't take care of the children?

—That was when we, you and I, had vacations together. I've been down there with the children several summers on my own. But perhaps you don't remember that. And if you have other solutions at hand, let me know.

—We should discuss it in the future.

—We should. But you said you would be gone for five weeks and that I would have to take the kids.

—That wasn't what I said.

She closes her eyes.

—It doesn't matter that you don't remember, she says. I recorded it. You can listen to it whenever you want.

Linda stands on the stairs leading up to their house and sees Tobias drive away. He's where the road makes a sharp turn, and she's just about to raise her arm and wave because that's something she would do. Then it strikes her. He's leaving. And when he gets back, they will no longer be married. She collapses on the stairs with all the sadness and the longing, just six months since Maja called on her. Everything falls over her, and she holds her arms around her head to protect herself. It's like an earthquake within, and her head is roaring. What if Maja never had come, if it had been that simple, and the evil hadn't crossed the threshold and poisoned their lives.

The children are already inside. They said goodbye to Tobias as though he were going to work. It's difficult for them to understand how long five weeks is, and that's why neither Linda nor Tobias has told the girls how long he will be gone, only that he's going on holiday. On his own. If he will really be on his own Linda doesn't know and doesn't want to know. The more secrets she learns he has been holding from her, the less interesting she has found him and his entire life.

The garden is deserted. The whole neighborhood seems to be deserted, as if the Midsummer celebrations have already begun, a day early. But most people who are going out into the archipelago or to the summer houses on the countryside leave on Thursday if they can, hoping to avoid the traffic, and this block seems to be one where people have left early. Linda has never reflected on it before; she has always been one of those who left, too. She now realizes that the empty houses meant that Tobias could do whatever he wanted, with Maja or whomever. A deserted neighborhood doesn't talk, and nothing needs to be kept a secret.

The air is warm, almost sticky. It doesn't feel like midsummer; it feels more like August. Linda dreams of the summers when she and Håkan were small. She remembers that they practically lived on the beach, and every meal was dry biscuits and strawberry lemonade. Of course they didn't. Anita always says she would get frustrated because they could never be outside. Yet they returned to town with tanned arms and legs—so there must have been some sunshine.

Their garden is a steady green color, and Linda misses the sheer early summer greenery and the flowering fruit trees. What is left is a lush green, the way nature is when nobody cares about it growing. No one in their area cares that much about the shrubs and trees; they climb, cling, and extend in every direction, and it's between neighbors that one in the spring may agree on cutting a branch or trimming a hedge that looks too overgrown. Over in her parents' neighborhood, the degrees of freedom are nonexistent. There's a certain order, and the bushes need to be trimmed, just like the roses, and the neighbors give each other advice when they aren't simply declaring that the apple trees are obstructing the view. You don't have a garden because it's cozy—you work in and with it. And if you can't do it yourself, you hire someone.

Tobias mowed the lawn, but the children's toys are already scattered over the grass, and he pointed out that they need to be picked up, otherwise the grass won't grow evenly. As if anyone would care if there were traces of hoops, skipping ropes, and balls on a patch of grass you can barely use. Linda goes down the stairs, feels that one stone is loose. "We could put a flower pot there," she thinks—and then forces her mind to stop. It's not her concern. It's up to Tobias.

She quickly recaps what she and the girls need to bring to Stenholmen, to the Midsummer celebrations with Håkan and his Italian guests, his new family. She's nervous. What if Giovanna wears only designer clothes and high heels? Tight and short colorful Italian dresses, maybe wedges. Linda has no idea what kind of girls Håkan falls for—or who falls for him. She remembers that he had a girlfriend when he was studying at the university. They came down to Lund over the carnival and stayed with her. Or they had their bags in her dorm room. She doesn't remember that they actually slept there. She doesn't remember that anyone slept at all, but she could be wrong, or maybe she simply had only been at home when they were not there, and vice versa. The girl Håkan had brought was easygoing and uncomplicated, talkative. But what did she look like? Linda tries to reach back in her memory, but no picture emerges. It's probably not the looks he falls for; it might be that simple. And if Giovanna is easygoing and uncomplicated, then that's the best thing that could happen.

When she reaches the last step and turns around the railing to go out into the garden, she hears a car approaching. The sound is unnatural in the early and peaceful evening, where a minute ago she could only hear the flies and birds singing, and even a lawnmower had been disruptive. Did Tobias forget something? It wouldn't surprise her, but he's more the type who says "I'll buy it there" than someone who turns around to pick up a pair of forgotten swimming trunks or a rain jacket. If there was a ticket or a passport missing, he would have returned, but Linda saw him double-check them both.

There's a black Mercedes slowly approaching, gliding up behind the neighbor's apple tree. Linda's worn shorts and floral sleeveless blouse stand in stark contrast to the polished and refined car when it stops. The engine is turned off, and both front doors of the car open simultaneously. For a second, Linda wonders if those guys from Men in Black will step out, wearing sunglasses and black suits. Her heart beats hard, and she is unsure why. Is it the police? Has she done something criminal? Has something happened? Has Tobias crashed, her parents' house burned down? Will she be accused of any crime? It's like she's in a movie. She should go in and lock the door. Protect the children.

A woman and a man get out of the car. They resemble each other, but that's probably because their hair is almost raven black, and it shines in the same way as the car paint. They look at each other over the car's rear end and then up at Linda, and then their eyes meet again. They nod.

—Hello, the woman says. You may not remember me. Or us.

Linda is certain she has never seen these two people before, and her belly cramps. She puts her hands in shorts pockets, shrugging her shoulders.

—No, sorry, she says, watching first the one and then the other.

There's something familiar about their appearance, but she can't say what.

—It's okay, the man says and raises his hand. It's not that we have met that often.

They laugh, and Linda smiles insecurely. They know something about her that she doesn't remember. She licks her lips.

—I've been looking for you, the woman says. But I couldn't remember the address. And the only one who remembered where you lived was Nikos.

With her hand, she motions toward the man standing next to her. They both take a few steps forward, toward the rusty gate. The woman hesitates as she stretches out her hand. The gate should also be painted, Linda thinks.

Nikos. The name does sound familiar.

—It was before Christmas. I drove you from a Christmas party, or what I thought was a Christmas party anyway. It was the week before Christmas. You took a taxi. I had to stop at the gas station.

The Lotto ticket!

—Yes, yes, yes, I remember! And I owe you money! God, this is so embarrassing! I should have called you or the taxi company. I do apologize—you shouldn't have had to come here! I've had a rough time ever since, personally, but it's…or I'm getting divorced, and it started that evening, so…Come on in. Or, wait, I'll just get my wallet.

Linda runs up the stairs and into the house.

—Who is that? Lotta shouts from the living where the television is on and a cartoon has caught Fia's attention. Is it someone we know?

She is about to rise, but Linda says it's an acquaintance and that she could stay inside. They will soon have dinner, she tells her.

She comes out on the stairs again. The man and the woman are still there. They have made their way through the gate, and Linda flicks nervously through her wallet. The coupon says it cost ten bucks.

—Here, here's your money, look, and the Lotto ticket. Isn't that great? It says it cost ten dollars, could that be correct? Here's fifteen. For all the trouble you've had.

The dollar bills are already sweaty in her hand when she gives them the woman who looks bewildered.

—Yes, oh well, great, she says and takes the money. My name is Elena, by the way.

She puts the notes in her pocket and extends her hand.

—And this is Nikos, who drove you home.

Nikos also extends his hand, which is large and warm and dry, not humid like Linda's. He smiles with his whole face and his eyes, too. Linda looks down at her dark-red toenails, embarrassed.

—Cool, she says. That you remembered.

—I've been here a few times, but at first there was no one at home. Then there was this woman who didn't look like you and, last time, a man who was quite aggressive and told me to leave.

—My husband, Linda says. Soon, my ex. I only stay here a few days a week. It takes a while to find a place to live and the kids—

—I was certain you had moved, he says. That's what I told Elena, too, but she wanted to give it one last try.

—I am so sorry. I remembered straight away that I hadn't paid, as soon as you drove off, Linda says.

Her face is probably scarlet red by now; her cheeks are hot and she's sweating. Luckily, her blouse is sleeveless and airy.

—That's not why we came, Elena says. I don't know if you remember, but I also bought a ticket. And then, we couldn't tell whose ticket was whose, and I said we would share if either of us won. I don't know if you did…

She nods at the ticket that Linda holds in her hand. Linda looks down at the ticket.

—But I did, Elena says.

—Did you check the Lotto ticket? I didn't. It was supposed to be a Christmas present, but I changed my mind. It was chaotic—

—Yes, I did check it, Elena says impatiently. I won. We won.

Linda raises her head, not daring to look at either Elena or Nikos. Instead, her eyes fly between the neighbor's tree and the rusty gate, as if there were a table tennis match going on behind Elena's and Nikos's backs.

—Sorry, Linda says. What did you say?

—I won. We won. We won the lottery. It was 1.6 million dollars.

She holds out her phone and shows Linda a picture of herself and a diploma. The dollar amount Linda sees there is almost blinding: $1,600,000.

—Oh, Linda says. Congratulations.

—No, but I mean…we will share the money!

Linda's head spins. She stands with her empty wallet in one hand and the Lotto ticket she had never taken the trouble to check in the other. She doesn't see or hear anything, but for a short time, she has time to think that this can't be true.

—Are you serious? But…it can't be! It's…It's not true, is it?

Then it strikes her that it isn't the least bit fair. It's not her ticket; it belongs to the taxi driver, and had the opposite occurred, had it been Linda's coupon, none of them would have won anything at all since Linda had forgotten about it.

They both look at her, laughing, because it took her so long to understand and perhaps because her face oscillates between surprise and something that mostly looks like despair.

—You'll get half of it, Elena says.

Linda shakes her head.

—I can't, she says. It's your money.

—But this is what we agreed on. And I don't want you to be without it. Please. Please. I've been looking for you for five months. Don't say you don't want your money!

Linda must laugh since it's the sweetest wish she has ever heard. That someone wants to give her money, because they, two otherwise strangers to each other, agreed on something on a December night half a year ago.

—Really…I don't know what to say. Thanks. I mean, it's…surreal.

—I know, Elena says. It took a while for me to grasp, too.

—But…what have you done since? Because you already got the money, right? Are you still a taxi driver?

—I took a break, Elena admits. I took a two-week vacation, back in March. But, you know, I kind of like my job…I haven't figured out what else I should do, so, for now, I don't mind. It might change.

She looks at Nikos as if he could be the solution, which he might be.

—But for right now, I want you to get your share, Elena says. It wouldn't be fair otherwise. You see, I have never bought a Lotto ticket before, and I would never have bought this one if it wasn't for you. And I will never do it again. I meant what I said—that if we won, we would share. Only I never thought it would happen.

Linda couldn't agree more on the last one. It's too good to be true, and she still has a hard time believing Elena. It might be a scam or a setup from Tobias's side, although Elena seems to be honest in what she says.

—Will you come in for a moment? Linda says. It's complicated, you see, this thing about money. But there might be a way to solve it.

Elena and Nikos look at each other and then follow Linda up the stairs. She won't believe it's true until she sees the money in her bank account. But until then, she will dream of all the things she could do if she had $800,000.

There are three bags in the entrance, one with just sheets, towels, and swimsuits; a backpack with Linda's and Fia's clothes; and a small bag that Lotta packed.

—I'll carry it myself, Mom. You can when you are as big as I am now.

Linda is about to explain that she doesn't even need to carry it since the bag has wheels, but she is sure that Lotta will manage anyway.

—Yes, you can, I know.

Fia has her backpack on her back. It's just big enough for her plush animal, a game, some pens, and a coloring book.

Håkan has told them not to bring any food, that he will arrange everything because it's easier that way. Though Linda knows that most of all he wants it to be perfect, as you would when you are about to show something to someone you love. To invite Giovanna and Antonio to Stenholmen is among the most perfect things he could do when Midsummer is like it is today and like the weather forecast says it will be over the weekend. Linda guesses Håkan has gone to Östermalmshallen to find the best food he can. At the same time, he's not one to make a lot of fuss. It will be subtle but good, and he has promised that there will be things that Lotta and Fia can eat as well, assuming they don't like herring.

The door is open, so she will hear when the taxi comes. In the neighbor's trees, a few birds chirp, and the grass is still wet with dew. Linda sees the children's fleece jackets and tucks them inside the bag with the bathing suits.

Linda looks at the clock; they are ten minutes early. The phone rings in the kitchen. She wonders if she should avoid answering it. Those who want to reach her will call on her cell phone, but it's already too late, for Lotta has answered the call and comes walking toward her, telephone in hand.

—It's Grandma, Lotta says.

Linda sighs.

—Happy Midsummer, Anita says. How clever of Lotta to take the phone and say her name.

—Yes. Happy Midsummer to you, too.

She waits, assuming her mother wants something, perhaps regarding the house or the children's trip next week.

—Are you still at home?

—We're going out to Stenholmen.

—All of you?

—The children and I, yes.

—What about Tobias?

Linda wonders if her mother is becoming senile. How many times can she repeat that they are divorcing, that they soon, in about a week or two, will be divorced? She remembers that she forgot to take out the garbage bag and puts the phone against her shoulder while she ties the bag.

—What are you doing?

—Throwing out the garbage, why?

—While we're talking?

—We leave in five minutes. Was there anything in particular you wanted? I have a few things to do before the taxi arrives.

It isn't true because everything is done. She tossed the last things from the fridge, what Tobias hadn't taken: a half-rotten cucumber, two soft carrots, a dried piece of cheese. What was left, they had for breakfast. But her mother's call doesn't seem to lead anywhere, and Linda has nothing to say.

—Will there be a big party, at Håkan's?

—No idea, Linda says.

—But probably, if he invited you.

As if Linda's company wouldn't be sufficient, or as if she had been invited because there would be enough people for Linda to not be noticed.

—Yes, maybe, she says.

—I wanted to check that you have the keys to our house and the alarm code. And that you'll water the flowers when you come back. Are you staying all weekend?

—Yes, Linda says. I have the keys, I know the code, and I will take care of the flowers.

—And then you'll start clearing out your stuff?

They have now talked about this four times, and although it isn't something that Linda wants to do, she will do it.

—As we said, yes. Håkan will also come. But we can talk about all this next weekend when I bring the girls.

—Yes, you're right. It will be a long journey for you. Why don't you fly?

—I'll do so when I pick them up.

Which is a strategy to not be persuaded to stay a few extra days, since Linda told her that her vacation starts at that time.

—Oh, so that was your plan? I wanted to hear if you'd stay.

Linda explains that she has two houses to clean, two gardens to care for, and two children to occupy.

—The children could stay; it's sad for them to be in town all summer.

—They will handle it.

Her conscience, her bad conscience, presses against her temples. It's perhaps not the most enjoyable summer for any of them, but this is how it is. Hopefully, there will be many summers to come that everyone will enjoy. And Linda has promised herself that she'll go somewhere with the kids at fall break; this summer they will browse the Internet and determine where they'll be going. All inclusive, children's clubs, and big pools. Somewhere warm, that's all she knows. Warm and luxurious. She remembers the meeting last night and has to pinch herself because she's still not sure it's true. But why would Elena lie? Why would she invent that she's been spending months looking for Linda, only to share the lottery win? It's too incredible to be true—but also too incredible to be made up.

—Well, then, enjoy Midsummer. Say hi to Håkan. I'll try to call him, too, but if I don't catch him, please tell him I called. I don't want to disturb him.

—He's off work, Mom. It's Midsummer.

—Yes, I know. But he has a lot going on. He mentioned that he might move to Italy. Have you heard anything about it? Dad and I were a little worried. Who will take care of the firm?

—I'm sure he has considered all that, don't you think? And I'm sure he will tell you before he leaves.

—Yes, because if he leaves, in the fall, then Dad and I could stay in his apartment. So it's not empty. And it would actually suit me quite well since I found a theater class I want to take and it's in town.

—Great. But you'd need to talk to him, Mom. I have nothing to do with that.

—But you could mention it, when you see him.

She hears a car arriving and sees it behind the trees.

—The taxi is here, Mom. Say hi to Dad.

—I will. Don't forget your life jackets! And keep the girls away from the cliffs!

Linda puts the phone down, calls out for the children, and puts the bags on the porch. She makes sure she has her purse and thinks quickly through what she has packed: mosquito spray, toothbrushes, nightgowns, swimwear, fleece jackets, jeans. She should have everything.

—Can I help you?

It's Nikos, stretching out his hand to Lotta, who's dragging her bag down the stairs.

—No, thanks. I can do it myself. But my mom may need help.

He looks up at Linda.

—Can I help you?

—Gladly.

She gets warm and happy inside when she sees him again since he has offered to drive them down to the boat and also pick them up on Sunday so they wouldn't need to bring the car seats. She locks the door and follows him, down the stairs, with Fia's hand in hers.

*

—See you Sunday, then. I'll wait here, at half past five. Is that OK?

Nikos takes Lotta's bag and sets it beside her.

—Great, thanks a lot, Linda says.

There's this strange calmness around him. He doesn't seem the least bit stressed out. There's not the usual taxi-driver jargon; he hasn't told her all of his life or what he thinks of politicians in general, the government in particular, or the nightlife of Stockholm. On the few occasions that Linda takes a taxi, she has a feeling it's the same experiences that go around. Maybe it's what taxi customers want to talk about, that the driver is only doing his or her job. Either it's quiet, because the customer wants it, or they talk. About wind, weather, politics, and work. It occurs to her that this is what she talks about to her colleagues as well, although their talks are shorter than those when she occasionally takes a taxi.

They have discussed apartment prices in Stockholm and where she could go on holiday this fall. After Linda explained that she needs to take care of her parents' house and the garden, they fell into talking about apple varieties and if maybe the black and red currants would be ready to pick before the new owners arrive, in which case Nikos would be interested in helping out.

—Happy Midsummer, she adds before he gets back into the car.

He stands up again, smiling over the car roof.

—And to you, too, he says. Sounds wonderful with the archipelago on a weekend like this.

Linda nods and takes Fia's hand. Lotta walks in front of them, her bag jumping over the cobblestones. The quay is full of people, but they have plenty of time and can sit down on a bench. This is clearly a move-out-to-the-country-house weekend but also a we-are-going-to-a-Midsummer-party ditto, since there are not only suitcases, pulling carts, and paper bags filled with food but also cans of beer and boxes of wine that will be brought out to the islands. In the air, there's both the intensity of Midsummer and the stressed-out family conflict, but Linda has a smile on her lips. All she needs to do is to take the boat out to an island; everything else is already arranged for. Rarely has she been so calm in the midst of all the chaos.

The archipelago boats honk, and people press against the walkway. There's pushing and yelling when a paper bag breaks or a child loses grip of a parent's hand. But the sun is warm, the gulls are squawking, and the sea laps against the dock; it's as if the archipelago made its way into town.

—Della magia.

She hears the words, which she understands without knowing a word of Italian, and reacts immediately because the children have already thrown themselves against Håkan, who first lifts Lotta and then Fia up in the air.

—I thought you were already out there?

—We were. Though we went into town for a moment yesterday; I didn't want Giovanna to miss out on Stockholm on a night in June. It will be something to remember when you come here in December.

—Giovanna…this is my sister, he says in Italian.

—Linda…Giovanna.

—Nothing more than Giovanna? Giovanna says.

—There is no need for more. She knows that you are my love.

The glance they exchange says it all. Linda notices it but doesn't mind.

—Mom called. She told me to say hi. And she wondered if she and Dad can stay in your apartment this fall. I'd better tell you before I forget it. I apologize, Giovanna.

—Oh, never mind. I've heard a lot about your mother. They all have their quirks.

Linda exhales, both because she doesn't need to defend their mother or explain more of the situation and also because Giovanna's English is so good they will be able to talk to each other.

—Would they stay in my apartment? Why?

—Because you will be in Italy.

—Oh, well. I might have other plans for it. I'll talk to her later.

Their boat arrives, and Håkan takes Fia on his shoulders. Lotta pulls her bag sullenly, but Linda won't intervene. It was she who wanted to bring the bag.

—So you got your own bag? Håkan says.

Lotta nods.

—Well, you'll be gone for a whole weekend, so there's a lot to bring.

Lotta nods again, and Giovanna whispers something in Håkan's ear.

—Giovanna wants to say that she finds your bag gorgeous.

Lotta's face lights up, and she smiles sheepishly but nods to Giovanna.

—Shouldn't your brother be here, too? Linda says and remembers how she saw him in his underwear a few months earlier.

Just the thought of it makes her blush, but she tries to look cool.

—His plane should be here now, so he'll arrive with a later boat.

Linda can't decide whether she's relieved or more nervous. Now, she must first try to talk to Giovanna, which might be easy when Håkan is around, but how should she behave when Antonio comes? As if they had never met? She can't tell him that she thought he and Håkan were a couple.

—What's your impression of Stockholm? Linda asks as they cross the boardwalk. Is it your first time here?

—It's fantastic, Giovanna exclaims. Fantastic in every way. We have the photo wall at the office, of course, but I've never been here. Alessandro has kept it secret for me…Excuse me—Akanne.

Linda has to laugh. It sounds insane when she says Akanne instead of Håkan. What were her parents thinking when they gave him that name, a name that couldn't even have been popular in the seventies?

—You can call him Alessandro. It's much better. Surely that's what you must call him?

—And he himself, when we meet.

—Well, then.

—I heard…

Giovanna pauses, bites her lip.

—I want to say I'm sorry for your sake and for your children. Alessandro has told me you are about to separate.

Linda swallows. It's better that she knows; otherwise, she would ask where Tobias was and why he didn't want to come. It's better, but what felt good this morning is suddenly a heavy burden. If only life could be normal again. If she could avoid the fluctuations between relief and despair, faith and sorrow. The roller coaster of emotions, as if Tobias had died, not cheated on her. With all these women.

—It's okay. Sometimes. And sometimes, it's a little harder.

—I understand. I ended a long relationship several years ago. We had no kids, so it didn't matter, but I know what it's like. Partially.

The way that Giovanna says it makes Linda relax. She hasn't asked for anyone who hasn't been through a breakup to understand what it feels like, but there are few who have even dared to talk about it in this way.

They sit down around a table. The children get to sit by the window. Linda knows that they will want to go out on deck and that they will all need to move over, but before everyone gets on board, it's easier if they sit down. They'll still be on the boat for two hours, before they can take Håkan's motorboat the last leg.

When the boat pulls out, Linda takes a deep breath. It's as if it isn't until now that she feels free. As if it's she who's pulling out from the quay, not the boat. She's the one to cut the moorings. Håkan looks at her as if he is thinking the same thing. He bends over and picks up three champagne glasses and two plastic cups. Then a bottle of Pommac and half a bottle of champagne.

—Antonio should be here, too, as we start our celebrations. But we can't wait. We will simply continue later on, he says.

—But we can wait. It's Midsummer throughout the day, Linda says. And tomorrow, too.

—No, it's not Midsummer we should celebrate, he says, and puts his hand over Giovanna's. We're engaged. We're getting married.

*

Linda is alone on the jetty. It smells as it should, of tar, and she searches in her memory for the words to a song about someone painting the jetty with tar. It's a smell of summer. The girls stand barefoot in the water some distance away. They haven't asked for their swimsuits yet, and are both busy picking rocks and digging in the sand, which is still new to their feet after a whole winter in boots and Wellingtons. The flies are buzzing, and there's a rattle in the reeds when small gusts head for the island. Linda wonders if there's any fish and if she should tell Lotta and Fia to go get the rods that Håkan has said are in the shed. It can wait. Maybe when he's back. Linda knows nothing about fishing; she has never tried. It surprises her that Håkan has fishing rods, for she has never heard him talk about it either. Perhaps it's something you do if you have a beachfront house on an island in the archipelago.

The girls have had a late snack while they're waiting for Antonio to arrive so they can set the Midsummer table. Linda should go prepare everything. She promised Håkan she'd have it ready by the time he is back. Giovanna has gone to her room, doubtless as confused as Linda. They had a good time on the boat. Linda can't say anything but that she seems kind—how do you know if you like each other if you almost don't have a choice? She wonders if that same thought ever passed Håkan's mind, with Tobias. He kind of just existed and was Linda's boyfriend and then fiancé and then husband, and there was little room for protests. In the Adeus family, protesting might take place by ignoring other people or a certain behavior, but Håkan has never done so. He has persisted, talked to Tobias, but they never socialized. Will Linda and Giovanna get further?

Linda suddenly feels sorry for Giovanna and Antonio, who won't have a clue why herring, Janzon's temptation, meatballs, and crisp bread must be eaten on this very day. It seems very Spartan and almost stupid to serve this to foreigners, especially to someone from a country where good food is key. But Håkan has said it can't get any more Swedish than this, and if you haven't celebrated Midsummer in Sweden, you can't understand why it's so special. But when Linda thinks of the soused herring, she can't understand the necessity of it either.

She calls to Lotta and Fia; they can play on the wooden deck by the house instead. She doesn't want them near the water unattended. They walk the long, steep stairs, and Linda follows behind, afraid that they will fall, but the higher up they go, the more she relaxes; they can do it. They have neither poor balance nor vertigo, and they think it's fun. Once they are up by the house, Linda looks out over the water to see if Håkan is coming back, but she can't see his boat. Which means she has time to get everything ready.

—Alessandro said I shouldn't do anything, but I could at least set the table, Giovanna says coming out on the deck. I fell asleep on the couch. The weather and the temperature are perfect.

—And unusual, Linda says. It's almost never this warm at Midsummer. We are blessed.

—Alessandro says that quite often, that we're blessed with good weather. I have never thought of it like that before. It's weather.

—But for us, having so little sun in the winter, it's extremely important. The weather is part of the experience, and since we can't take anything for granted, it becomes a sore point for us. This kind of Midsummer is rare, and for us it's pure magic. I must prepare the potatoes, or Alessandro will go crazy. And the eggs. Please feel free to set the table—I don't know where he keeps the tablecloths, but there are glasses and plates in the kitchen.

—I know, Giovanna says.

When the potatoes and eggs are on the stove, Linda opens the refrigerator. Pickled herring, soused herring, chives, butter, sour cream, various cheeses, of which at least two are Italian, she notes. Crisp bread and thin bread. Shrimp salad. Janzon's temptation, which she puts in the oven. Meatballs and small sausages. She checks that there is beer and aquavit. She's a little excited to celebrate Midsummer with people who mean a lot to Håkan and with him, after many years with only Anita and Gustav.

The mobile phone vibrates in her pocket, and she takes it out.

An image showing Tobias and—a mast? A boat beneath him? It looks as if he clings to a sail high in the air. He's out sailing?

"Ship ahoy! Happy Midsummer! Say hi to the girls!" the message says.

The wave of sadness swamps her, all the memories of how Tobias has called on Midsummer morning and said he's sorry, that he doesn't have time to come. When was the last time they celebrated together? Before Fia was born, in the summer when Linda was pregnant? She tries to repress it and remember it at the same time—it's like trying to sit on a volcano. And the same thought she had on New Year's Eve pops up: has she ever had a fun Midsummer celebration? After too much beer, too many glasses of aquavit, nightly swims and hours in the sauna, all hopes of summer loving have been buried before even existing.

Giovanna puts a hand on her shoulder.

Does she understand? Probably. Although she can't comprehend the dimension of "Midsummer," Linda's red-rimmed eyes hide no secrets. She wonders how Tobias got the idea of sailing.

She wipes her nose with a dish towel and watches Giovanna, who moves gracefully, like a cat, while she sets the table. That the curly blond Antonio would be her brother is almost impossible to imagine. She clears her throat. She can't walk around being depressed. It's a fun and happy day, not only because it's Midsummer.

—Had you decided to get engaged, or did Alessandro surprise you?

—I knew nothing.

Giovanna smiles, tucks away a strand of hair.

—He is very romantic, your brother. And caring. The way in which he also invited Antonio, it means a lot to me. Our father is no longer alive. He died a year ago, and my mother can't travel, but he had already asked her for permission. And an Italian mother can be nothing but happy when a prospective son-in-law like Alessandro requests her daughter's hand. I'm more surprised that my mother didn't say anything, to be honest.

Her cheeks are the pink color only someone in love can have, and her eyes are warm. Linda must have looked like that, too, at one time, but she can't remember what it's like. How was her and Tobias's engagement? He had surprised her. They were in Copenhagen, at Tivoli. They had celebrated with open sandwiches, beer, and aquavit before they went back home and told Anne.

She pours cold water on the eggs, checks the potatoes. They are almost done. She should perhaps have waited a little longer because the butter is supposed to melt on them, but Håkan said that the boat would come in half an hour ago, and it doesn't take that long to get out to the island. They set out the plates of food on the table, and the girls come running, each with a bushy bouquet of summer flowers.

—Just what was missing, she says as she gives them each a glass of water for the bouquets. No Midsummer table setting is complete without flowers.

—There should be seven, Lotta says, counting the varieties.

—What's she saying? Giovanna says.

—Superstition says that you should have seven kinds of flowers to put under your pillow. You should pick them before going to bed and not talk to anyone, and then you'll dream about the man you should marry.

—I hope I'll dream about him anyway.

—Me too.

Linda would like to add "but for the rest of us..." but stops herself. The bitterness. If it could simply fly away. And she isn't bitter because of Giovanna and Håkan since it's amazing, almost incomprehensible, that they have met each other. That they got engaged. What are the odds?

She takes the potatoes off the stove, pours the water, puts a sheet of paper towel over the pot, and closes it with the lid. Why aren't they here?

Then she sees them coming over the cliffs. First Håkan. He looks relaxed, and she rarely sees him this way. Does Giovanna? Have they had times when they were on vacation, when Håkan wears shorts and a linen shirt as they sit at a cafe on some forgotten tourist spot and drink cool wine? It would suit him perfectly.

Then Antonio, with a straw hat over his blond hair, slim black shorts, and an unbuttoned white shirt, as if picked out of a fashion magazine, and Linda must, just like last time, look down to the ground, still blushing without knowing why. Because he's—

good-looking? Young and good-looking. There's some kind of glow around him. He has an aura, she thinks. It's ridiculous. He's a young, handsome guy, but he has something else, too—that unconscious charisma. When he looks up, she notices he has the same dark eyes as Giovanna and the same intense gaze. He waves at his sister, who goes to meet him and kisses him on both cheeks. They say something to each other in Italian, laughing along with Håkan. Linda wishes she, too, could understand what they said so she wouldn't have to stand with this silly smile on her face and wait for a translation that doesn't come. They have something in common. It's painful to see that her brother also belongs in that other constellation, in which she herself has no place. She has to create it, work her way into it, deserve to be included the way you deserve to be included in a secret sect.

Families are remarkable energy associations, not always with a single solid core, like an atom, yet full of tensions and attractions, although this one seems simple and powerful. She thinks of her own family, of Anita and Gustav, and on what has kept them together through the years. They have not kept it together because of the children. They overcame what happened, Gustav grateful that she was there, Anita grateful that she could come back, because she was still alive. Energy, but in a different way.

Linda sees a shadow by the stairs and looks around for the girls. They haven't run off, have they? She takes a step forward but discovers that both are standing next to her. Lotta is the first to react, when she has stopped staring at the blond man and Giovanna; she has been standing perfectly still and looks as if she was trying to understand the Italian gibberish. Now she throws herself forward, out over the wooden deck and the grass and then the rocks, with her arms stretched out.

—Karin! she cries. Karin!

—Little flea, Karin cries back and opens her arms. I can't believe we are celebrating Midsummer together!

300

Linda can't hold back the tears. The stupid tears. But she can see Håkan's satisfied look before everything becomes blurred, and she wipes her eyes with her palms. He thinks of everything, her brother. It could be a perfect Midsummer, if she stops thinking of Tobias and instead enjoys the company here.

—Don't look so sad, Antonio says and stretches out his hand to her. You must be Linda. And your friend is the sweetest. So is your brother, but I already know him.

—I know, Linda responds. Welcome, by the way.

—Mandatory bath before a late lunch! Håkan shouts, while Karin and Linda hug each other, both watching Antonio taking off his shirt. Linda closes her eyes.

—You get it, huh? she says into Karin's red hair.

—Let's get changed, Karin says. Can't miss this one.

At that moment, they are twenty-three again, and Linda's panic vanishes in their giggles.

—Girls, we're going swimming. Are you coming along? she cries, enjoying the thump of Lotta's and Fia's bare feet against the wooden deck.

Midsummer can begin.

*

Karin has left the shop over Midsummer, which is almost incomprehensible, and Linda can't stop thinking about how unreal it is that they are sitting here next to each other on the terrace. She remembers a Midsummer, a fun Midsummer they had together, the year they met. They were in a big group that stayed in Skåne over the summer. Linda had gotten a summer job at a museum in Malmö and didn't feel at all welcome home, although her mother had invited her to Falsterbo. Karin was taking various summer classes in Skåne, but at Midsummer they were in someone's summer house outside Helsingborg, and the weather was like it is now: magical. All other Midsummers must have been rainy, or uninteresting, since they are all one single blurry memory.

Since then, they haven't celebrated any important holidays together. Though Linda has been in Falsterbo with the kids, only a few kilometers from where Karin lives, they haven't met. Or rather, Karin hasn't wanted to see Tobias, who always said that he would be there but never came. And when he didn't, it was too late to change the plans.

Karin has helped Lotta and Fia make wreaths for their hair, but also ensured that Giovanna, Linda, and she herself has one. Antonio, who has been crawling around in the grass photographing them all afternoon, has also begged for one, which has ended in both he and Håkan now carrying flowers on their heads. They look like poets in their airy linen shirts, as if they did nothing but set out in the archipelago and wrote poems, and were particularly creative after a couple of glasses of aquavit.

—Do you remember what it was like when we were little? Linda asks Håkan. Did we go dancing around the pole, in Falsterbo?

—Probably. Though those neighbors also did something, the ones with the huge garden? Weren't we there with Mom and Dad, at big parties where the whole neighborhood was invited? I remember a long table, with all the children sitting together and then running off, playing hide-and-seek or something.

—Do you celebrate in the same way all over Sweden? Giovanna says.

—More or less, Karin says. But Dalarna, one region around the middle of Sweden, would say they have the strongest traditions. They have kind of decided that they are the most Swedish. But the Midsummer pole, herring, potatoes, and strawberries, that's probably the same everywhere.

—It's interesting, Antonio says. What do we have, in Italy that would gather everyone? Nothing, I think. Each village has its own little party, for something they produce or eat right there.

—You are a young nation, Karin says. At least much younger than Sweden. Our regions have stuck together longer. It doesn't make you less Italian, but this doesn't make me more Swedish either. And it's strange: I perceive Italians as much more distinctive characters than Swedes.

—How? Antonio says.

Karin looks thoughtful, but Linda knows she's thinking of when they took the train down to Rome, and she starts laughing.

—Are you going to tell them about our Interrail trip? she says in Swedish, and Antonio looks bewildered.

Karin laughs, too. Now they can't hold it any longer; they are laughing so hard that their tears are falling.

—It's impolite, Håkan says. What's so funny?

Linda wipes her tears, and so does Karin. In unison, they tell stories about their two weeks in Italy one summer long ago, about a picnic on a farm and offers of excursions on vespas. How they watched the sunrise and sunset over the Roman Forum in the company of many intrusive Italians. How they both wondered if the other would fall for the southern temperament and how they were afraid to ask each other.

Håkan admits that he has never heard these stories and that he had no clue what happened. Antonio tries in every way to deny that Italians are the way Karin and Linda describe them, and Giovanna can, at the end, only say she understands the attraction between the Swedish woman and the Italian man.

—The contrast. North and South. The blonde and the dark. The strangely closed off blonde, during much of the year, against the dark, almost always open and readily available in Italy. I think that's where it is. You should try to catch it on camera, Antonio, Giovanna says.

—I have already spent two days working on it, Antonio says. There's a big difference, just in a few months, since I was here last time.

—Linda thought we were a couple when she saw you the first time, Håkan says.

Linda looks down at the table and glances at Karin. She feels stupid, but how was she to know?

—I couldn't know…, she says. And it's not too often that I meet a handsome man in underwear. I was mortified. I'm embarrassed just thinking of it.

Karin saves her.

—Which means we have taken advantage of the moment during the afternoon—with you walking around in your swimming trunks—to work on the embarrassment. And now it's much better.

The laughter echoes across the table, and Linda is eternally grateful to Karin; the last thing she wants is to make it sound as if she were interested in him, which isn't at all the case. He is both fun to be with and her future in-law.

—Yes, but isn't that why we are such a good match, Italian men and Swedish girls? Deep down, you like to watch us, and we only have eyes for you. It's simple. Why make it so complicated? Antonio says.

—It isn't complicated at all, Karin says. But it might take a few years for us to understand. We are quite innocent when young.

Karin's right. They were very innocent on that Interrail experience. Anything could have happened. They had no idea how exposed they were. They had been laughing at the invitations, as if they also had been innocent, which they, of course, weren't. Life will never be like that again.

The discussions are many and last forever. They have strawberries and meringue, coffee. The sun is still high in the sky, and the Italian guests, who are used to lunches that last until dinner, don't seem to realize that it's near half past eight. Lotta and Fia have been wandering between the table and the living room, eating, playing, even had them all dancing around a somewhat odd-looking Midsummer pole.

—I'll see to it that the girls get to bed, and then maybe we can start the barbecue, Linda says as she rises from her chair.

—Do you want us to stick around? Håkan says. Or we can go down to the boathouse for a while, so that things will be quieter for you.

—It's okay. I'll be with you in a moment, Linda says.

They take out the plates and cups. Håkan follows her into the kitchen and gets a bottle of champagne and five glasses. Linda watches their four silhouettes as they walk over the cliffs. They seem to belong together in some strange way, even though all differ from each other, and it strikes her that Antonio is much taller than she first thought. The glistering in Karin's red mop of hair is the last thing she sees before they disappear down the stairs.

The girls sit on the sofa, with sleepy eyes. Midsummer is the longest day of the year in many ways, and she lifts Fia, sniffing her sun-warmed skin.

—Are we staying in here? Lotta says.

—No, we sleep in the guesthouse, where we put our things. Karin does, too. But we will come a little later. We're very close if you need us. Come, now, get into your pajamas and brush your teeth, and I'll read you a story.

There are no protests, Midsummer is yet to be a special day for them, and she is happy for that. In due time, they will have their own memories and programmed must-dos, but right now it's an evening like any other when you can be just as tired as you are and fall asleep without feeling that you are missing out on anything, and with a stomach full of sausages and meatballs.

*

It takes longer than Linda expected to get the girls to go to sleep. She was convinced that they were exhausted, but instead they had a thousand questions about Håkan and the Italian guests, about when and how Håkan will marry and if they will get to be at the wedding, about what Linda thinks Giovanna will wear, about if she will learn Swedish and if they will have children. She has promised to get the answers tomorrow, and since she is pretty curious herself, her steps are light as she runs over the cliffs and hurries down the stairs when the children are asleep.

The boathouse has large windows overlooking the bay. You can sit in there if it's too cool to be outside, but it isn't tonight. The four are sitting on the jetty, and the water is almost an unnatural blue behind them. On the other side of the bay, a Swedish flag waves by a small red cottage on a green grove of trees; it's like a commercial for washing powder.

Håkan pours champagne in the empty glass, telling her to come and sit next to him. Then he raises his glass, and the others turn silent.

—Thank you all for coming. You are all very important people in my life, for various reasons. I hope you will continue to be so. I would like to raise a toast to my future wife, my sister, my future brother-in-law, and Karin. Thank you for being here. And Happy Midsummer!

Linda toasts and takes a sip of the cold champagne. She clears her throat.

—Sorry if it took some time. The girls have a billion questions and have asked to receive answers to them by tomorrow morning, and I think that the questions are so interesting that we should start them off at once. The first one, to Giovanna: will you learn Swedish? Thus, they would like to talk to you.

Giovanna giggles in embarrassment.

—In this case I will have to learn your language. That's good to know, a great motivation. So far I can say "tack so micket."

—I haven't thought of that, Håkan says. But we'll have to start practicing.

—Question number two: when are you getting married and where?

Håkan and Giovanna look at each other.

—I…well, that, we haven't decided. But, in Italy? Håkan asks.

—I would like to do so, Giovanna says. In spring?

306

—Why not?

—Question three: what kind of dress will you wear?

—Uh…long? White?

—Lovely. That is what they wanted to hear.

—Can they be flower girls, maybe, your girls? Do you think they would like to? Or, what do you think, Alessandro?

Håkan nods. It's clear he hasn't yet considered the details, but he plays the game.

—You can ask them tomorrow. I don't think they will decline the offer…if you show them a picture of what it is.

—Oh, that's adorable. Two blonde flower girls! Fantastic! Everyone will think they're your children, Antonio!

—Anyone who doesn't know me at your wedding. Like, no one? The rest will probably know Linda? Antonio says.

—And the last question, so far, from Lotta and Fia: will we have cousins?

It becomes quiet, and Håkan and Giovanna smile at each other in a way lovers do, with all the warmth and all the feelings that only they understand.

—Well, we'd hope so, Håkan says.

Giovanna nods, gazing out over the water.

—It wasn't supposed to be embarrassing, Linda says. I took the questions the children had, so that you are prepared for breakfast. A Midsummer day morning can be tough on its own.

They toast again, thank her for the questions, and hope that the answers were satisfactory.

—Everything we had ever wanted to know, Karin says. And more. Very informative.

When the champagne bottle is empty, Håkan rises and says he'll light the grill but that they can stay by the water if they wish. Giovanna and Antonio offer to help him, and despite Håkan's protests, the three leave for the house.

On the jetty, Linda and Karin are left on their own. Karin squeezes the last drops of champagne from the bottle. It's more than they thought. They toast to each other, into the air, and out over the water.

—I'm so happy that Håkan invited you, Linda says. Have you known this for a long time?

—Surely not any longer than you. He called, asked if I had something to do for Midsummer. And I thought it was such a long time since you and I met other than for "necessities," and the shop can wait for two days. It's not that all sales are made during Midsummer. And I was touched. Because he said I meant a lot to you, and because he always liked me as a friend. And he wanted me to meet his girlfriend.

Linda must admit that it surprised her as well—they have met occasionally, Håkan and Karin, and have always gotten along well and always somehow found each other at the children's baptisms and birthdays and at Linda's wedding. They sat next to each other when Linda and Tobias got married. Linda insisted that Håkan should have the nicest girl by his side.

—But, Karin says suddenly, this Antonio.

—Yes, Linda says.

They look out over the water.

—Am I embarrassing? Karin says.

—I wouldn't call any of you embarrassing.

—Is he very young?

—I don't know. Who cares?

It's as if an express train rushes through Linda's mind and her senses are sharpened. All shades and all smiles become evident, every step and every breath becomes clear to her. She hasn't bothered about the game for so many years since she imagined she was in a spot that she didn't need to question. She closes her eyes.

—I don't...I mean if you—, Karin says.

—No, no, Linda says. No, not at all. Absolutely not.

Linda sees the pictures on her eyelids, of herself and Tobias, of when the children were born, her parents, Maja. But they no longer burn with tears, at least not tonight. Here and now it's different, and it's different in a good way.

When she opens her eyes, the summer night is even more luminous than before.

—Can you keep a secret?

Karin doesn't respond.

—Yesterday, a taxi driver came by and said that I had won eight hundred thousand dollars.

Karin coughs.

—On that Lotto ticket I bought for Tobias before Christmas, remember?

—Holy shit, Karin says. Didn't you give it to him?

Linda shakes her head, and Karin begins to laugh. She laughs so that it echoes across the bay, and when Linda looks at her, she can't help laughing herself.

—And even if I had, it wasn't the winning ticket. It was the other one, bought at the same time as mine. We said we would share if we won. Promise me you'll never tell anyone! Linda says between tears and laughter. Promise!

—You are so worth that money! Karin screams. So incredibly worth it!

She puts her arm around Linda and shakes her head, wipes her tears with her index finger.

—I understand that it isn't the most important thing…But it's good to know. I won't tell anyone.

Through the corner of her eye, Linda sees the blond man coming down the stairs, a fresh bottle of champagne in hand. He walks over and sits down next to Karin, who puts her hair to one side and reaches for her glass. Linda wonders if she should leave, but up by the house, Håkan and Giovanna surely also want to have a moment for themselves.

Karin signals she should stay, and Antonio doesn't protest.

This is the way it should be. Honest and obvious. Something she hasn't understood until now, something that required a detour and so many years to realize. She forces the lurking tears to leave, and the anxiety and the longing too. She's calm, right here in the Midsummer night. She's calm.

Everything can change for the better. From now on.

They get two days together on the island, two days of summer sun and heat, a magical Midsummer weekend.

—You mustn't think that it's always like this at this time of the year, Linda, Håkan, and Karin repeat, explaining how many cold and rainy Midsummers they've had, to build a correct image for the Italian guests and make them understand how extremely grateful they should be. But Giovanna and Antonio just laugh and say that they focus too much on the weather—it's the atmosphere and the light that makes it all special. When the summer night sets over the archipelago on Midsummer's Day, they all must admit that it's as if everything is alive.

*

After a long Sunday breakfast, it's time for Linda and the girls to go back home.

—I didn't get a flight ticket back until tomorrow, Karin says. I thought that maybe you, too, could stay?

—There are no boats that fit my schedule tomorrow morning, and even so, I must get the children to preschool, and it takes forever to go back and forth into town. And I have piles of work, so I can't lose any time.

—I can go with you now, if you want me to.

Linda smiles.

—No, that'd be super stupid, she says. It's far better that you stay.

Karin's cheeks are pink. She hugs Linda, who disappears in her red frizz of hair.

It's a funny bunch of three who stand on the jetty when Håkan leaves with Linda and the kids—a curly blond, a bright red, and a raven—so different, but still they match. They raise their arms

311

and wave, and the last thing Linda sees is Antonio putting an arm around Karin's waist.

*

In town, Nikos is waiting with the child seats already installed in the back. Linda buckles up the girls and, without thinking, gets in the front seat.

—Oh, I would sit between the children, of course—

Nikos stops her.

—Is everything okay back there? he asks.

Lotta and Fia nod.

—This car is nice, Fia says. And clean.

—You should wash ours, Lotta says.

—We can do it when we are at Grandma and Grandpa's, Linda says.

—Shall I drive you directly there? Nikos says. Or to what address do you want to go?

—We have to go home first, and unpack our stuff. It's a bit complicated…there is a lot to sort out, in two houses, and I can't say I look forward to it. And I just want to find something of my own. How was your Midsummer?

They have equally as interesting discussions now as they did on the way into town the other day, and Linda thinks that she wouldn't mind if there were problems with the car now. When they drive up to the house, she falls silent. Everything has an end.

Nikos helps the children with the seat belts and takes out the luggage and the child seats while the children run up to the house. Linda follows, while Nikos brings the remaining bags. She unlocks the door, asks Nikos to put everything in the hallway, and walks him back down the stairs to the car.

They nod at each other, the way you do when you wish you knew each other better and when a hug is too much and a handshake too little.

—Thanks for the help, Linda says. How much do I owe you?

—Nothing, of course. Tell me if you need help, if you have stuff to move, or so... Just call. It would be great to see you again.

Linda raises her hand to stop him and take a deep breath.

—I'm sorry, I didn't mean—, Nikos says, looking down at the ground.

—No, but...Here's the thing...

She closes her eyes, biting her lip as if she would start crying, but she doesn't. Instead, she thinks it's silly, all of this. That she doesn't have time. Really doesn't have time. She opens her eyes again.

—Here's the deal: this week, I have the kids. But next weekend I'll drive them down to my parents' summerhouse in the south of Sweden. Then I'll be alone in the city for a week. If you want to, perhaps we could get together. Swing by, and check out the garden—I'll be at my parents' house.

He nods. A cautious smile spreads over his face.

—I will, he says. Just give me the address. I don't have time to drive around for another six months looking for you.

ABOUT THE AUTHOR

Elisabeth Oweson has worked as a public-relations writer, as a conference producer, and with marketing in the Swedish food industry.

She was born and raised in Sweden, but since 2004 she has lived with her family in the French-speaking part of Switzerland.

Open Your Eyes is her first novel.

For more information and updates, visit
www.elisabethoweson.com
and www.facebook.com/elisabethoweson/

www.ingramcontent.com/pod-product-compliance
Lightning Source LLC
Chambersburg PA
CBHW022137170626
46807CB00005B/1970